# Wreck the Halls

# Wreck the Halls

## A NOVEL

# TESSA BAILEY

AVON

*An Imprint of HarperCollinsPublishers*

HarperCollins books may be purchased for educational, business, or sales promotional use. For information, please email the Special Markets Department at SPsales@harpercollins.com.

FIRST EDITION

Designed by Diahann Sturge

Christmas lights © Angelinna / Shutterstock

Library of Congress Cataloging-in-Publication Data has been applied for.

ISBN 978-0-06-334134-0 (paperback)
ISBN 978-0-06-330829-9 (library hardcover)

23 24 25 26 CPI 9 8 7 6 5 4 3 2 1

# *Acknowledgments*

Some of my favorite recent advice came by way of *The Bear* (an incredible television show on Hulu). *Let it rip.* The idea for this story seemed easy on paper, but when I started writing it, I realized I was holding more than just the outcome of a romance in my hands, but the friendship of two iconic women, in the form of Octavia and Trina, Beat's and Melody's mothers. They deserved words and weight, too. Because when you're bold enough to take big chances, when you *let it rip*, the result might just echo across decades.

I hope Beat and Melody's love story (and the friendship story between Octavia and Trina) stay with you at least that long. I know they will for me.

Thank you to my Mac and Pat. Thank you to my team at Avon Books and HarperCollins, stateside and abroad, including (but not limited to) my talented editor, Nicole Fischer, my publicity team, D. J. DeSmyter, Danielle Bartlett, Mary Interdonati, Alice Tibbetts, Shannon McCain, Madelyn Blaney, and Liate Stehlik at Morrow Group.

Last but never least, thank you to the readers. Each of you is glorious.

All my love,
Tessa

# Wreck the Halls

# Prologue

2009

*T*he second Beat Dawkins entered the television studio, it stopped raining outside.

Sunshine tumbled in through the open door, wreathing him in a halo of glory, pedestrians retracting their umbrellas and tipping their hats in gratitude.

Across the room, Melody witnessed Beat's arrival the way an astronomer might observe a once-in-a-millennium asteroid streaking across the sky. Her hormones activated, testing the forgiveness of her powder-fresh-scented Lady Speed Stick. She'd only gotten braces two days earlier. Now those metal wires felt like train tracks in her mouth. Especially while watching Beat breeze with such effortless grace into the downtown studio where they would be shooting interviews for the documentary.

At age sixteen, Melody was in the middle of an awkward phase—to put it mildly. Sweat was an uncontrollable entity. She didn't know how to smile anymore without looking like a constipated gargoyle. Her milk chocolate mane had been carefully styled for this afternoon, but her hair couldn't be tricked into forgetting about the humidity currently plaguing New York, and now it was frizzing to really *accentuate* the rubber bands connecting her incisors.

Then there was Beat.

Utterly, effortlessly gorgeous.

His chestnut-colored hair was damp from the rain, his light blue eyes sparkling with mirth. Someone handed him a towel as soon as he crossed the threshold and he took it without looking, rubbing it over his locks and leaving them wild, standing on end, amusing everyone in the room. A woman in a headset ran a lint brush down the arm of his indigo suit and he gave her a grateful, winning smile, visibly flustering her.

How could she herself and this boy possibly be the same age?

Not only that, but they'd also been named by their mothers as perfect complements to each other. Beat and Melody. They were the offspring of America's most legendary female rock duo, Steel Birds. Since the band had already broken up by the time Beat and Melody were born, their names were bestowed quite by accident, without the members consulting each other. Decidedly *not* the happiest of coincidences. Not to mention, children of legends with significant names were supposed to be interesting. Remarkable.

Obviously, Beat was the only one who was meeting expectations.

Unless you counted the fact that she'd chosen teal rubber bands.

Which had seemed a lot more daring in the sterility of the orthodontist's office.

"Melody," someone called to her right. The simple act of having her name shouted across the busy room caused Melody to be *bathed in fire*, but okay. Now the backs of her knees were sweating—and oh God, *Beat was looking at her.*

Time froze.

They'd never actually met before.

Every article about their mothers and the highly publicized band breakup in 1993 mentioned Beat and Melody in the same breath, but they were locking eyes for the very first time IRL. She needed to think of something interesting to say.

*I was going to go with clear rubber bands, but teal felt more punk rock.*

Sure. Maybe she could cap that statement off with some finger guns and really drive home the fact that he'd gotten all the cool rock royalty genes. Oh God, her feet were sweating now. Her sandals were going to squeak when she walked.

"Melody!" called the voice again.

She tore her attention off the godlike vision that was Beat Dawkins to find the producer waving her into one of the cordoned-off interview suites. Just inside the door was a camera, a giant boom mic, a director's chair. The interview about her mother's career hadn't even started yet and she already knew the questions she would be answering. Maybe she could just pop in very quickly, recite her usual responses, and save everyone some time?

*No, I can't sing like my mother.*

*We don't talk about the band breakup.*

*Yes, my mother is currently a nudist and yes, I've seen her naked a startling number of times.*

*Of course, it would be amazing for fans if Steel Birds reunited.*

*No, it will never happen. Not in a million, trillion years. Sorry.*

"We're ready for you," sang the producer, tapping her wrist.

Melody nodded, flushing hotter at the suggestion she was holding things up. "Coming."

She snuck one final glance at Beat and walked in the direction of her interview room. That was it, she guessed. She'd probably never see him in person again—

"Wait!"

One word from Beat and the humming studio quieted, ground to a halt.

The prince had spoken.

Melody stopped with one foot poised in the air, turning her head slowly. *Please let him be talking to me*, otherwise the fact that she'd stopped at his command would be a pitiful mistake. Also, *please let him be talking to someone else*. The train tracks in her mouth were approximately four hundred pounds per inch, and the teal dress she'd worn—oh God—to match her rubber bands didn't fit right in the boob region. Other girls her age managed to look normal. *Good*, even.

What was it TMZ had said about her?

Melody Gallard: always a before picture, never an after.

Beat *was* talking to her, however.

Not only that, but he was also jogging over in this athletic, effortless way, the way a celebrity might approach the mound at a baseball game to throw out the ceremonial first pitch, the crowd cheering him on. His hair had arranged itself back to a perfect coif, no evidence of the rain that she could see, his mouth in a bemused half smile.

Beat slowed to a stop in front of her, rubbing at the back of his neck and glancing around at their rapt audience, as if he'd acted without thinking and was now bashful about it. And the fact that he could be shy or self-conscious with charisma pouring out of his eyeballs was astounding. Who *was* this creature? How could they possibly share a connection?

"Hey," he breathed, coming in closer than Melody expected, that one move making them coconspirators. He wasn't overly tall, maybe five eleven, but her eyes were level with his chin. His sculpted, clean-shaven chin. Wow, he smelled so good. Like a freshly laundered blanket with some fireplace smoke clinging to it.

Maybe she should switch from powder fresh Speed Stick to something a little more mature. Like ocean surf. "Hey, Mel. Can I call you that?"

No one had ever shortened her name before. Not her mother, classmates, or any of the nannies she'd had over the years. A nickname was something that should be attained over time, after a long acquaintance with someone, but Beat calling her Mel somehow seemed totally normal. Their names were counterparts, after all. They'd been named as a pair, whether it had been intentional or not.

"Sure," she whispered, trying not to stare at his throat. Or inhale him. "You can call me Mel."

Was this her first crush? Was it supposed to happen this fast? She usually found members of a different sex sort of . . . uninspiring. They didn't make her pulse race, the way this one did. *Say something else before you bore him to death.*

"You stopped the rain," she blurted.

His eyebrows shot up. "What?"

*I'm dissolving. I'm being absorbed by the floor.* "When you walked in, the rain just . . . stopped." She snapped her fingers. "Like you'd turned it off with a switch."

When Melody was positive that he would cringe and make an excuse to walk away, Beat smiled instead. That lopsided one that made her feel funny *everywhere.* "I should have thought of switching it off before walking two blocks in a downpour." He laughed and exhaled at the same time, studying her face. "It's . . . crazy, right? Finally meeting?"

"Yeah." The word burst out of Melody and quite unexpectedly, her chest started to swell. "It's definitely crazy."

He nodded slowly, never taking his eyes off her face.

She'd heard of people like him.

People who could make you feel like you were the only one in the room. The world. She'd believed in the existence of such uni-corns, she just never in her wildest dreams expected to be given the undivided attention of one. It was like bathing in the brightest of sunlight.

"If things had been different with our mothers, we probably would have grown up together," he said, blue eyes twinkling. "We might even be best friends."

"Oh," she said with a knowing look. "I don't think so."

His amusement only spread. "No?"

"I don't mean that to be offensive," Melody rushed to say. "I just . . . I tend to keep to myself, and you seem more . . ."

"Extroverted." He shrugged a single shoulder. "Yeah. I am." He waved a hand to indicate the room, the crew who were still cap-tivated by the first—maybe only—meeting of Beat Dawkins and Melody Gallard. "You might think I'd be into this. Talking, being on camera." He lowered his voice to a whisper. "But it's always the same questions. Can you sing, too? Does your mother ever talk about the breakup?"

"Will there ever be a reunion?" Melody chimed in.

"Nope," they said at the same exact time—and laughed.

Beat turned serious. "Look, I hope this isn't out of line, but I notice the way the tabloids treat you. Online and off. It's . . . different from how they treat me." Fire scaled the sides of her neck and gripped her ears. Of course he'd seen the cringe-inducing critiques of Melody. They were usually included in articles that profiled him, as well. The most recent one had whittled her entire existence down to the line, *In the case of Trina Gallard's daughter, the apple didn't just fall far from the tree, it's more of a lemon.* "I always wonder if it bothers you. Or if you're able to blow that bullshit off."

"Oh, I mean . . ." She laughed, too loudly, waved a hand on a floppy fist. "It's fine. People expect those gossip sites to be snarky. They're just doing their job."

He said nothing. Just watched her with a little wrinkle between his brows.

"I'm lying," she whisper-blurted. "It bothers me."

His perfect head tilted ever so slightly to one side. "Okay." He nodded, as if he'd made an important decision about something. "Okay."

"Okay, what?"

"Nothing." His gaze ran a lap around her face. "You're not a lemon, by the way. Not even close." He squinted, but not enough to fully hide the twinkle. "More of a peach."

She swallowed the dreamy sigh that tried to escape. "Maybe so. Peaches do have pretty thin skin."

"Yeah, but they have a tough center."

Something grew and grew inside of Melody. Something she'd never felt before. A kinship, a bond, a connection. She couldn't come up with a word for it. Only knew that it seemed almost cosmic or preordained. And in that moment, for the first time in her life, she was angry with her mother for her part in breaking up the band. She could have known this boy sooner? Felt . . . *understood* sooner?

Someone in a headset approached Beat and tapped his shoulder. "We'd like to get the interview started, if you're ready?"

Unbelievably, he was still looking at Melody. "Yeah, sure."

Did he sound disappointed?

"I better go, too," Melody said, holding out her hand for a shake.

Beat studied her hand for several seconds, then gave her a narrow-eyed look—as if to say, *don't be silly*—and pulled her into the hug of a lifetime. The hug. Of a lifetime. In a millisecond, she was warm in the most pleasant, sweat-free way. All the way down to the soles of her feet. Light-headedness swept in. She'd not only been granted the honor of smelling this boy's perfect neck, he was encouraging her with a palm to the back of her head. He squeezed her close, before brushing his hand down the back of her hair. Just once. But it was the most beautiful sign of affection she'd ever been offered, and it wrote itself messily all over her heart.

"Hey." He pulled back with a serious expression, taking Melody by the shoulders. "Listen to me, Mel. You live here in New York, I live in LA. I don't know when I'll see you again, but . . . I guess it just feels important, like I need to tell you . . ." He frowned over his own discomposure, which she assumed was rarer than a solar eclipse. "What happened between our mothers has nothing to do with us. Okay? Nothing. If you ever need anything, or maybe you've been asked the same question forty million times and can't take it anymore, just remember that I understand." He shook his head. "We've got this big thing in common, you and me. We have a . . ."

"Bond?" she said breathlessly.

"*Yeah.*"

She could have wept all over him.

"We *do*," he continued, kissing her on the forehead hard and pulling Melody back into the second hug of a lifetime. "I'll find a way to get you my number, Peach. If you ever need anything, call me, okay?"

"Okay," she whispered, heart and hormones in a frenzy. He'd given her a *nickname*. She wrapped her arms around him and held tight, giving herself a full five seconds, before forcing herself to release Beat and step back. "Same for you." She struggled to keep her breathing at a normal pace. "Call me if you ever need someone who understands." The next part wouldn't stay tucked inside of her. "We can pretend we've been best friends all along."

To her relief, that lopsided smile was back. "It wouldn't be so hard, Mel."

A bell rang somewhere on the set, breaking the spell. Everyone flurried into motion around them. Beat was swept in one direction, Melody in the other. But her pulse didn't stop pounding for hours after their encounter.

True to his word, Beat found a way to provide her with his number, through an assistant at the end of her interview. She could never find the courage to use it, though. Not even on her most difficult days. And he never called her, either.

That was the beginning and the end of her fairy-tale association with Beat Dawkins.

Or so she thought.

# Chapter One

December 1
Present Day

*B*eat stood shivering on the sidewalk outside of his thirtieth birthday party.

At least, he assumed a party was waiting for him inside the restaurant. His friends had been acting mysterious for weeks. If he could only move his legs, he would walk inside and act surprised. He'd hug each of them in turn, like they deserved. Make them explain every step of the planning process and praise them for being so crafty. He'd be the ultimate friend.

And the ultimate fraud.

When the phone started vibrating again in his hand, his stomach gave an unholy churn, so intense he had to concentrate hard on breathing through it. A couple passed him on the sidewalk, shooting him some curious side-eye. He smiled at them in reassurance, but it felt weak, and they only walked faster. He looked down at his phone, already knowing an unknown caller would be displayed on the screen. Same as last time. And the time before.

Over a year and a half had passed since the last time his blackmailer had contacted him. He'd given the man the largest sum of money yet to go away and assumed the harassment was over. Beat was just beginning to feel normal again. Until the message he'd received tonight on the way to his own birthday party.

*I'm feeling talkative, Beat. Like I need to get some things off my chest.*

It was the same pattern as last time. The blackmailer contacted him out of the blue, no warning, and then immediately became persistent. His demands came on like a blitz, a symphony beginning in the middle of its crescendo. They left no room for negotiation, either. Or reasoning. It was a matter of giving this man what he wanted or having a secret exposed that could rock the very foundation of his family's world.

No big deal.

He took a deep breath, paced a short distance in the opposite direction of the restaurant. Then he hit call and lifted the phone to his ear.

His blackmailer answered on the first ring.

"Hello again, Beat."

A red-hot iron dropped in Beat's stomach.

Did the man's voice sound more on edge than previous years? Almost agitated?

"We agreed this was over," Beat said, his grip tight around the phone. "I was never supposed to hear from you again."

A raspy sigh filled the line. "The thing about the truth is, it never really goes away."

With those ominous words echoing in his ear, a sort of surreal calmness settled over Beat. It was one of those moments where he looked around and wondered what in the hell had led him to this time and place. Was he even standing here at all? Or was he trapped in an endless dream? Suddenly the familiar sights of Greenwich Street, only a few blocks from his office, looked like a movie set. Christmas lights in the shapes of bells and Santa heads and holly leaves hung from streetlights, and an early December cold snap turned his breath to frostbitten mist in front of his face.

He was in Tribeca, close enough to the Financial District to see coworkers sharing sneaky cigarettes on the sidewalk after too much to drink, still dressed in their office attire at eight P.M. A rogue elf traipsed down the street, yelling into his phone. A cab drove by slowly, wheels traveling over wet sludge from the brief afternoon snowfall, "Have a Holly Jolly Christmas" drifting out through the window.

"Beat." The voice in his ear brought him back to reality. "I'm going to need double the amount as last time."

Nausea lifted all the way to his throat, making his head feel light. "I can't do that. I don't personally have that kind of liquid cash and I will not touch the foundation money. This needs to be *over*."

"Like I said—"

"The truth never goes away. I heard you."

Silence was heavy on the line. "I'm not sure I appreciate the way you're speaking to me, Beat. I have a story to tell. If you're not going to pay me to keep it to myself, I'll get what I need from *20/20* or *People* magazine. They'd love every salacious word."

And his parents would be ruined.

The truth would devastate his father.

His mother's sterling reputation would be blown to smithereens.

The public perception of Octavia Dawkins would nose-dive, and thirty years of the charitable work she'd done would mean nothing. There would only be the story.

There would only be the damning truth.

"Don't do that." Beat massaged the throbbing sensation between his eyes. "My parents don't deserve it."

"Oh, yeah? Well, I didn't deserve to be thrown out of the band, either." The man snorted. "Don't talk about shit you don't know, kid. You weren't there. Are you going to help me out or should I start making calls? You know, I've had this reality show producer contact me twice. Maybe she would be a good place to start."

The night air turned sharper in his lungs. "What producer? What's her name?"

Was it the same woman who'd been emailing and calling Beat for the last six months? Offering him an obscene sum of money to participate in a reality show about reuniting Steel Birds? He hadn't bothered returning any of the correspondence because he'd gotten so many similar offers over the years. The public demand for a reunion hadn't waned one iota since the nineties and now, thanks to one of the band's hits going viral decades after its release, the demand was suddenly more relevant than ever.

"Danielle something," said his blackmailer. "It doesn't matter. She's only one of my options."

"Right."

How much had she offered Beat? He didn't remember the exact amount. Only that she'd dangled a lot of money. Possibly seven figures.

"How do we make this stop once and for all?" Beat asked, feeling and sounding like a broken record. "How can I guarantee this is the last time?"

"You'll have to take my word for it."

Beat was already shaking his head. "I need something in writing."

"Not happening. It's my word or nothing. How long do you need to pull the money together?"

Goddammit. This was real. This was happening. *Again.*

The last year and a half had been nothing but a reprieve. Deep down, he'd known that, right? "I need some time. Until February, at least."

"You have until Christmas."

The jagged edge of panic slid into his chest. "That's less than a month away."

A humorless laugh crackled down the line. "If you can make your selfish cow of a mother look like a saint to the public, you can get me eight hundred thousand by the twenty-fifth."

"No, I can't," Beat said through his teeth. "It's impossible—"

"Do it or I talk."

The line went dead.

Beat stared down at the silent device for several seconds, trying to pull himself together. Text messages from his friends were piling up on the screen, asking him where he was. Why he was late for dinner. He should have been used to pretending everything was normal by now. He'd been doing it for five years, since the first time the blackmailer made contact. Smile. Listen intently. Be grateful. Be grateful at all times for what he had.

How much longer could he pull this off?

A couple of minutes later, he walked into a pitch-black party room.

The lights came on and a sea of smiling faces appeared, shouting, "*Surprise!*"

And even though his skin was as cold as ice beneath his suit, he staggered back with a dazed grin, laughing the way everyone would expect. Accepting hugs, backslaps, handshakes, and kisses on the cheeks.

*Nothing is wrong.*

*I have it all under control.*

Beat struggled through the inundation of stress and attempted to appreciate the good around him. The room full of people who had gathered in his honor. He owed them that after all the effort they'd clearly put in. One of the benefits of being born in December was Christmas-themed birthdays, and his friends had laid it on thick. White twinkling lights were wrapped around fresh garland and hanging from the rafters of the restaurant's banquet room. Poinsettias sprung from glowing vases. The scent of cinnamon and pine was heavy in the air and a fireplace roared in the far corner of the space. His friends, colleagues, and a smattering of cousins wore Santa hats.

As far as themes went, Christmas was the clear winner, and he couldn't complain. As far back as he could remember, it had been his favorite holiday. The time of year when he could sit still and wear pajamas all day and let his head clear. His family always kept it about the three of them, no outsiders, so he didn't have to be *on*. He could just be.

One of Beat's college buddies from NYU wrestled him into a playful headlock and he endured it, knowing the guy meant well. God, they all did. His friends weren't aware of the kind of strain he was under. If they did, they would probably try to help. But he couldn't allow that. Couldn't allow a single person to know the delicate reason why he was being blackmailed.

Or who was behind it.

Beat noticed everyone around him was laughing and he joined in, pretending he'd heard the joke, but his brain was working through furious rounds of math. Presenting and discarding solutions. Eight hundred thousand dollars. Double what he'd paid this man last time. Where would he come up with it? And what about next time? Would they venture into the millions?

"You didn't think we'd let your thirtieth pass without an obnoxious celebration, did you?" Vance said, elbowing him in the ribs. "You know us better than that."

"You're damn right I do." A glass of champagne appeared in Beat's hand. "What time is the clown arriving to make balloon animals?"

The group erupted into a disbelieving roar. "How the hell—"

"You ruined the surprise!"

"Like you said"—Beat saluted them, smiling until they all dropped the indignation and grinned back—"I know you."

*They don't know you, though. Do they?*

His smile faltered slightly, but he covered it up with a gulp of champagne, setting the empty glass down on the closest table, noting the peppermints strewn among the confetti. The paper pieces were in the shape of little B's. Pictures of Beat dotted the refreshment table in plastic holders. One of him jumping off a cliff in Costa Rica. Another one of him graduating in a cap and gown from business school. Yet another photo depicted him onstage introducing his mother, world-famous Octavia Dawkins, at a charity dinner he'd organized recently for her foundation. He was smiling in every single picture.

It was like looking at a stranger. He didn't even know that guy.

When he jumped off that cliff in Central America, he'd been in the middle of procuring funds to pay off the blackmailer the first time. Back when he could manage the sum. Fifty thousand here or there. Sure, it meant a little shuffling of his assets, but nothing he couldn't handle in the name of keeping his parents' names from being dragged through the mud.

He couldn't manage this much of a payoff alone. The foundation had more than enough money in its coffers, but it would be a cold day in hell before he stole from the charity he'd built with his mother. Not happening. That cash went to worthy causes. Well-deserved scholarships for performing arts students who couldn't afford the costs associated with training, education, and living expenses. That money did not go to blackmail.

So where would he get the funds?

Maybe a quick call to his accountant would calm his nerves. He'd invested in a few start-ups last year. Maybe he could pull those investments now? There had to be something.

*There isn't,* whispered a voice in the back of his head.

Feeling even more chilled than before, Beat forced a casual expression onto his face. "Excuse me for a few minutes, I just need to make a phone call."

"To whom?" Vance asked. "Everyone you know is in this room."

That was not true.

His parents weren't here.

But that was not who his mind immediately landed on—and it was ridiculous that he should still be thinking about Melody Gallard fourteen years after meeting her *one time.* He could still recall that afternoon so vividly, though. Her smile, the way she whisper-talked, as if she wasn't all that used to talking at all. The way she couldn't seem to look him in the eye, then all of a sudden she couldn't seem to look anywhere else. Neither had he.

And he'd hugged thousands of people in his life, but she was the only one he could still feel in his arms. They were meant to be friends. Unfortunately, he'd never called. She'd never used his number, either. Now it was too late. Still, when Vance said *Everyone you know is in this room,* Beat thought of her right away.

It *felt* like he knew Melody—and she wasn't here.

She might know him the best out of everyone if he'd kept in touch.

"Maybe he needs to call a woman," someone sang from the other side of the group. "We know how Beat likes to keep his relationships private."

"When I find a woman who can survive my friends, I'll bring her around."

"Oh, come on."

"We'd be on our best behavior."

Beat raised a skeptical brow. "You don't have a best behavior."

Someone picked up a handful of B confetti and threw it at him. He flicked a piece off his shoulder without missing a beat, satisfied that he'd once again diverted their interest in his love life. He kept that private for good reason. "One phone call and I'll be back. Don't start the balloon animals without me. I'm going to see if the artist can create me a sense of privacy." He gave them all a grin to let them know he was joking. "It means a lot that you organized this party for me. Thank you. It's . . . everything a guy could hope for."

That sappy moment earned him a chorus of boos and several more tosses of confetti until he had to duck and cover his way out of the room. But as soon as he was outside, his smile slid away. Back on the sidewalk like before, he stood for a full minute looking down at the phone in his hand. He could call his accountant. It would be a waste, though. After five years of having the blackmailer on his back like a parasite, he'd wrung himself dry. There simply wasn't eight hundred thousand dollars to spare.

*You know, I've had this reality show producer contact me twice. Maybe she would be a good place to start.*

His blackmailer's words came back to him. Danielle something. She'd contacted Beat, too. Had a popular network behind her, if Beat recalled correctly. His assistant usually dealt with inquiries pertaining to Steel Birds, but he'd forwarded this particular request to Beat because of the size of the offer and the producer's clout.

Instead of calling his accountant, he searched his inbox for the name Danielle—and he found the email after a little scrolling.

Dear Mr. Dawkins,

Allow me to introduce myself. I'm your ticket to becoming a household name.

Since Steel Birds broke up in ninety-three, the public has been desperate for a reunion of the women who not only cowrote some of the world's most beloved ballads, but inspired a movement. Empowered little girls to get out there, find a microphone, and express their discontent, no matter who it pissed off. I was one of those little girls.

You're a busy man, so let me be brief. I want to give the public the reunion we've been dreaming about since ninety-three. There are no better catalysts than the children of these legendary women to make this happen. It is my profound wish for you, Mr. Dawkins, and Melody Gallard to join forces to bring your parents back together.

The Applause Network is prepared to offer each of you a million dollars.

Sincerely,
Danielle Doolin

Beat dropped the phone to his thigh. Had he seriously only skimmed an email that passionate? He hadn't even made it to the middle the first time he'd seen the correspondence. That much was obvious, because he would have remembered the part about Melody. Every time someone mentioned her, he got a firm sock to the gut.

He was getting one now.

Beat had zero desire to be a household name. Never had, never would. He liked working behind the scenes at his mother's foundation. Giving the occasional speech or social media interview was necessary. Ever since "Rattle the Cage" had gone viral, the requests had been coming in by the mother lode, but remaining out of the limelight was preferable to him.

However.

A million dollars would solve his problem.

He needed to solve it. *Fast.*

And if—and it was a *huge* if—Beat agreed to the reality show, he'd need to talk to Melody first. They might have grown up in the same weird celebrity offspring limelight, but they'd gotten vastly different treatment from the press. He'd been praised as some kind of golden boy, while every single one of Melody's physical attributes had been dissected through paparazzi lenses—all when she was still a *minor*. He'd watched it from afar, horrified.

So much so that the first and only time they'd met, he'd been rocked by protectiveness so deep, he still felt it to this very day.

Was there any way to avoid bringing her back into the spotlight if he attempted to reunite Steel Birds? Or would she be dragged into the story, simply because of her connection to the band?

God, he didn't know. But there was no way in hell Beat would agree to anything unless Melody was okay with him stirring up this hornet's nest. He'd have to meet with her. In person. See her face and be positive she didn't have reservations.

Beat's pulse kicked into a gallop.

Fourteen years had passed and he'd thought of her . . . a weird amount. Wondering what she was doing, if she'd seen whatever latest television special was playing about their mothers, if she was happy. That last one plagued him the most. Was Melody happy? Was he?

Would everything be different if he'd just called her?

Beat pulled up the contact number for his accountant, but never hit call. Instead, he reopened the email from Danielle Doolin and tapped the cell number in her email signature, with no idea the kind of magic he was setting into motion.

# Chapter Two

December 8

Melody stood at the top of the bocce ball court, the red wooden ball in hand.

This throw would determine whether her team won or lost.

How? How had the onus of demise or victory landed on her birdlike shoulders? Who'd overseen the lineup tonight? She was their weakest player. They usually buried her somewhere in the middle. Her heartbeat boomed so loudly, she could barely hear the *Elf* soundtrack pumping through the bar speakers, Zooey Deschanel's usually angelic voice hitting her ears more like a witch's cackle.

Her team stood at the sides of the lane, hands clasped together like it was the final point at Wimbledon or something, instead of the bocce ball league. This was low stakes, right? Her boss and best friend, Savelina, had *assured* her this was low stakes. Otherwise, Melody wouldn't have joined the team and put their success at high risk. She'd be at home watching some holiday baking championship on the Food Network in an adult onesie where she belonged.

"You can do it, Mel," Savelina shouted, followed by several

cheers and whistles from her coworkers at the bookstore. She hadn't known them well in the beginning of the season, considering she worked in the basement restoring young adult books and almost never looked up from her task. But thanks to this semi-torturous bocce league, she'd gotten to know them a lot better. She *liked* them.

*Oh, please God, grant me enough skill not to let them down.*

Ha. If she didn't screw this up, it would be a miracle.

"Do you need a time-out?" asked her boss.

"What made you think that?" Melody shouted. "The fact that I'm frozen in fear?"

The sprinkle of laughter boosted her confidence a little, but not by much. And then she made the mistake of glancing backward over her shoulder and finding the entire Park Slope bar watching the final throw with bated breath. It was the equivalent of looking down at the ground while walking on a tightrope. Not that she'd ever experienced such a thing. The craziest risk she'd taken lately was hoop earrings. *Hoops!*

Now she was breathing so hard, her glasses were fogging up.

Was everyone looking at her butt?

They had to be. She looked at everyone's butts, even when she tried not to. What would make this crowd any different? Did they think her floor-length pleated skirt was a weird choice for bocce? Because it totally was.

"Mel!" Savelina gestured to the bocce lane with her pint of beer. "We're going to run out of time. Just get the ball as close to the jack as possible. Piece of cake."

Easy for Savelina to say. She owned a bookstore and dressed like a stoned bohemian artist. She could pull off gladiator sandals and had a favorite brand of oolong tea. Of course she thought bocce was simple.

The crowd started cheering behind Melody in encouragement,

which was honestly very nice. Brooklynites got a bad rap, but they were actually quite friendly as long as they were being offered drink specials and strangers regularly complimented their dogs.

"Okay! Okay, I'm going to do it."

Melody took a deep breath and rolled the red wooden ball across the hard-packed sand. It came to a stop at the farthest position possible from the jack. It wasn't even remotely close.

Their opponents cheered and clinked pint glasses, the home team bar heaving a collective sigh of disappointment. They probably thought an underdog-to-hero story was unfolding right in front of their eyes, but no. Not with Melody in the starring role.

Savelina approached with a sympathetic expression on her face, squeezing Mel's shoulder with an elegant hand. "We'll win the next one."

"We haven't won a game all season."

"Victory isn't always the point," her boss suggested. "It's trying in the first place."

"Thanks, Mom."

Savelina's tight brown curls shook with laughter. "Two weeks from now, we have the final game of the season, and I have a good feeling about it. We're going to head into Christmas fresh from a win and you're going to be a part of it."

Mel didn't hide her skepticism.

"Let me clarify," Savelina said. "You *must* be a part of it. We only have enough players if you show up. You're not taking off early to visit family or anything, are you?"

As a rare book restoration expert, Mel's work schedule was loose. She could take a project home with her, if needed, and her presence in the store largely depended on whether or not there was even a book that currently required tender loving care. "Uh, no." Mel forced a smile onto her face, even though a little dent formed in her heart. "No, I don't have any plans. My mother is . . .

you know. She's doing her thing. I'm doing mine. But I'll see her in February on my birthday," she rushed to add.

"That's right. She always comes to New York for your birthday."

"Right."

Mel did the tight smile/nodding thing she always did when the conversation turned to her mother. Even the most well-intentioned people couldn't help but be openly curious about Trina Gallard. She was an international icon, after all. Savelina was more conscientious than most when it came to giving Mel privacy, but the thirst for knowledge about the rock star inevitably bled through. Mel understood. She did.

She just didn't know enough about her mother to give anyone what they wanted.

That was the sad truth. Trina love-bombed her daughter once a year and once a year only. Like a one-night sold-out show at the Garden that left her with a hangover and really expensive merch she never wore again.

Melody could see Savelina was losing the battle with the need to ask deeper questions about Trina, probably because it was the end of the night and she'd had six beers. So Mel grabbed her kelly green peacoat from where it hung on the closest stool, tugged it on around her shoulders, and looked for a way to excuse herself. "I'm going to settle my tab at the bar." She leaned in and planted a quick kiss on Savelina's expertly highlighted brown cheek. "I'll see you during the week?"

"Yeah!" Savelina said too quickly, hiding her obvious disappointment. "See you soon."

Briefly, Mel battled the urge to give her friend something, anything. Even Trina's favorite brand of cereal—Lucky Charms—but the information faltered on her tongue. It always did. Speaking with any kind of authority on her mother felt false when most days, it seemed as though she barely knew the woman.

"Okay." Mel nodded, turned, and wove through some Friday night revelers toward the bar, apologizing to a few customers who'd witnessed her anticlimactic underdog story. Before she could reach the bar, she made sure Savelina wasn't watching, then veered toward the exit instead—because she didn't really have a bar tab to settle. Customers who recognized her as Trina Gallard's daughter had been sending her drinks all night. She'd had so many Shirley Temples she was going to be peeing grenadine for a week.

Cold winter air chilled her cheeks as soon as she stepped out onto the sidewalk.

The cheerful holiday music and energetic conversations grew muffled behind her as soon as the door snicked shut. Why did it always feel so good to leave somewhere?

Guilt poked holes in her gut. Didn't she *want* to have friends? Who didn't?

And why did she feel alone whether she was with people or not?

She turned around and looked back through the frosty glass, surveying the bargoers, the merry revelers, the quiet ones huddled in darkened nooks. So many kinds of people and they all seemed to have one thing in common. They enjoyed company. None of them appeared to be holding their breath until they could leave. They didn't seem to be pretending to be comfortable when in reality, they were stressing about every word out of their mouth and how they looked, whether or not people *liked* them. And if they did, was it because they were a celebrity's daughter, rather than because of their actual personality? Because of who Melody was?

Melody turned from the lively scene with a lump in her throat and started to walk up the incline of Union Street toward her apartment. Before she made it two steps, however, a woman shifted into the light several feet ahead of her. Melody stopped in her tracks. The stranger was so striking, her smile so confident, it was impossible to move forward without acknowledging her. She had dark blond hair that fell in perfect waves onto the shoulders of a very expensive looking overcoat. One that had tiny gold chains in weird places that served no function, just for the sake of fashion. Simply put, she was radiant and she didn't belong outside of a casual neighborhood bar.

"Miss Gallard?"

The woman knew her name? Had she been lying in wait for her? Not totally surprising, but it had been a long while since she'd encountered this kind of brazenness from a reporter.

"Excuse me," Melody said, hustling past her. "I'm not answering any questions about my mother—"

"I'm Danielle Doolin. You might recall some emails I sent you earlier this year? I'm a producer with the Applause Network."

Melody kept walking. "I get a lot of emails."

"Yes, I'm sure you do," said Danielle, falling into step beside her. Keeping pace, even though she was wearing three-inch heels, her footwear a stark contrast to Melody's flat ankle boots. "The public has a vested interest in you and your family."

"You realize I was never really given a choice about that."

"I do. During my brief phone call with Beat Dawkins, he expressed the same."

Melody's feet basically stopped working. The air inside of her lungs evaporated and she had no choice but to slow to a stop in the middle of the sidewalk. Beat Dawkins. She heard that name in her sleep, which was utterly ridiculous. The fact that she should still be fascinated by the man when they hadn't been in the same room in fourteen years made her cringe . . . but that was the *only* thing about Beat that made her cringe. The rest of her reactions to him could best be described as breathless, dreamlike, whimsical, and . . . sexual.

In her entire thirty-year existence, she'd never experienced attraction like she had to Beat Dawkins at age sixteen when she spent a mere five minutes in his presence. Since then, her hormones could only be defined as lazy. Floating on a pool raft with a mai tai, rather than competing in a triathlon. She had the yoga pants of hormones. They were fine, they definitely *counted* as hormones, but they weren't worthy of a runway strut. Her lack of romantic aspirations was yet another reason she felt unmotivated to go out and make human connections. To be in big, social crowds where someone might show interest in her.

It was going to take something special to make her set down the mai tai and get off this raft—and so far, no one had been especially . . . rousing. A fourteen-year-old memory, though? Oh mama. It had the power to make her temperature peak. At one time it had, anyway. The recollection of her one and only encounter with Beat was growing grainy around the edges. Fading, much to her distress.

"Well." Danielle regarded Melody with open interest. "His name certainly got your attention, didn't it?"

Melody tried not to stumble over her words and failed, thanks to her tongue turning as useless as her feet. "I'm sorry, y-you'll have to refresh my memory. The emails you sent me were about . . . ?"

"Reuniting Steel Birds."

A laugh tumbled out of Melody, stirring the air with white vapor. "Wait. Beat took a phone call about *this?*" Baffled, she shook her head. "As far as I know, both of us have always maintained that a reunion is impossible. Like, on par with an Elvis comeback tour."

Danielle lifted an elegant shoulder and let it drop. "Stranger things have happened. Even Pink Floyd set aside their differences for Live 8 in 2005, and no one believed it was doable. A lot of time has passed since Steel Birds broke up. Hearts soften. Age gives a different perspective. Maybe Beat believes a reunion wouldn't be such an impossible feat after all."

It was humiliating how hard her heart was pounding in her chest. "Did . . . did he say that?"

Danielle blew air into one cheek. "He didn't *not* say it. But the fact that he contacted me about the reunion speaks for itself, right?"

Odd that Melody should feel a tad betrayed that he'd changed his position without consulting her. Why would he do that? He didn't owe her anything. Not a phone call. Nothing. "Wow." Melody cleared her throat. "You've caught me off guard."

"I apologize for that. You're very difficult to get in contact with. I had to dig quite a bit to find out where you worked. Then I saw a picture of your bocce team on the bookstore's Instagram. Thank goodness for location tags." Danielle gestured with a brisk, gloved hand to the general area. "I assure you, I wouldn't have ventured into Brooklyn in twenty-degree weather unless I had a potentially viable project on the table. One that, if done correctly, could be a cultural phenomenon. And it *would* be done correctly, because I would be overseeing production personally."

What was it like to be so confident? "I'm afraid to ask what this project entails."

"That's why I'm not going to tell you until we're in my nice, warm office with espresso and a selection of beignets in front of us."

Melody's stomach growled reluctantly. "Beignets, huh?"

"They piqued Beat's interest, as well."

"They did?" Melody's breathless tone hit her ears, cluing her in to what was happening. The tactic that was being employed. "You keep bringing him up on purpose."

Danielle studied her face closely. "He seems to be my biggest selling point. Even more than the money the network is willing to pay, I'm guessing," she murmured. "If I hadn't mentioned his name, you never would have stopped walking. Surprising, since the two of you haven't maintained any sort of contact. According to him."

"No, I know," Melody rushed to blurt, heat clinging to her face and the sides of her neck. "We don't even know each other."

And that was the God's honest truth.

Fourteen years had passed.

However. Beat was a good person. He'd proven that to her—and he couldn't have changed so drastically. The kind of character it took to do what he'd done . . .

About a month after they'd met in that humid television studio, she'd passed through the gates of her Manhattan private school, expecting to walk to class alone, as usual. But she'd been surrounded by buzzing girls that morning. Had she seen Beat Dawkins on TMZ?

Considering she avoided that program like the plague, she'd shaken her head. They'd cagily informed her that Beat had mentioned her during a paparazzi ambush and she might want to watch the footage. Getting through first period without exploding was nearly impossible, but she'd made it. Then she'd rushed to the bathroom and pulled up the clip on her phone. There was Beat, holding a grocery bag, a Dodgers ball cap pulled down low on his forehead, being pursued by a cameraman.

Normally, he was the type to stop and suffer through their silly questions with a golden grin. But this time, he didn't. He halted abruptly on the sidewalk and, to this day, she could still remember what came out of his mouth, word for word.

*I'm done talking. You won't get another word out of me. Not until you—and all the similar outlets—stop exploiting girls for clicks. Especially my friend Melody Gallard. You praise me for nothing and disparage her no matter how hard she tries. You can fuck right off. Like I said, I'm done talking.*

That day, Melody hadn't come out of the bathroom until third period, she'd been so frozen in shock and gratitude. Just to be seen. Just to have someone speak up on her behalf. That clip had been shared all over social media. For weeks. It had started a conversation about how teenage girls were being portrayed by celebrity news outlets.

Of course, their treatment of her didn't change overnight. But it slowly shifted. It lightened in degrees. Bad headlines started getting called out. Shamed.

And shockingly, her experience with the press got better.

Melody was so lost in the memory, it took her a moment to notice the smile flirting with the corners of Danielle's glossy mouth. "He's coming to my office on Monday morning for a meeting. I've come all the way here to invite you, as well." She paused, seemed to consider her next words carefully. "Beat won't agree to the reunion project unless *you* are comfortable with it moving forward. He made your approval a condition."

Melody hated the way her soul left her body at Danielle's words. It was pathetic in so many ways.

Beat Dawkins was eons and galaxies out of her league. Not only was he blindingly gorgeous, but he had *presence*. He commanded rooms full of people to give speeches for his mother's foundation. She'd seen the pictures, the occasional Instagram reel. His grid was brimming with nonstop adventures. Equally glamorous friends were pouring out of his ears. He was loved and lusted after and . . . perfect.

Beat Dawkins was perfectly perfect.

And he'd taken her into consideration.

He'd thought of her.

This whole Steel Birds reunion idea would never fly—the feelings of betrayal between their mothers ran deeper than the Atlantic Ocean—but the fact that Beat had said her name out loud to this woman basically ensured another fourteen years of infatuation. *Sad, sad girl.*

"You mentioned money," Melody said offhandedly, mostly so it wouldn't seem her entire interest was Beat-related. "How much? Just out of curiosity."

"I'll tell you at the meeting." She smiled slyly. "It's a lot, Melody. Perhaps even by the standards of a famous rock star's daughter."

A lot of money. Even to her.

Despite her trepidation, Melody couldn't help but wonder . . . was it enough cash to make her financially independent? She'd been born into comfort. A nice town house, wonderful nannies, any material item she wanted, which had mainly turned out to be books and acne medication. Her mother's love and attention remained out of reach, however. Always had—and it was beginning to feel as though it always would.

Melody's brownstone apartment was paid in full. She had an annual allowance. Lately, though, accepting her mother's generosity didn't feel right. Or good. Not when they lacked the healthy mother-daughter relationship she would gladly take instead.

Could this be her chance to stand on her own two feet?

No. Facilitating a reunion? There had to be an easier way.

"At least take the meeting," Danielle said, smiling like the cat who'd caught the canary.

The woman had her and she knew it.

To be in the same room with Beat Dawkins again . . .

She wasn't strong enough to pass up the chance.

Melody shifted in her boots and tried not to sound too eager. "What time?"

# Chapter Three

December 11

As Melody Gallard walked into the office, Beat was reminded why he'd never called. The feeling that swept through him was so fierce, he launched to his feet at the sight of her without thinking, hastily buttoning his suit jacket. Wow. He'd always wondered if his memory was playing tricks on him, but no. That same urge to protect her that he'd experienced at sixteen was still alive and kicking inside of him at thirty.

Beat swallowed hard and mentally shook himself, stealing a few seconds to look at her, this girl who had grown up in roughly the same conditions as him. She'd been hounded, asked questions, lived with outrageous expectations on her shoulders. Unlike Beat, she'd been scorned for not being what the press considered perfect. During *puberty*. He could still remember the time a photo of Melody dealing with an acne outbreak had gotten shared six thousand times on Twitter. Brutally unfair.

If the press only knew about *his* nocturnal activities. He should be thanking his lucky stars that the blackmailer didn't know, either, or he'd never get out from under his thumb.

Funny how the weight placed on his shoulders by the threat

to his family seemed so light at the moment. In the same way it happened fourteen years earlier, something clicked into place as soon as Beat and Melody were breathing the same air. It was almost alarming, this invisible net that cast itself around them, dragging them into their own world that no one else would understand.

The woman was beautiful as hell. Had been fourteen years ago and still was, in a softer, more polished way. But she hid that beauty well. Underneath a wool skirt, huge-ass sweater, and thick-rimmed glasses. If he undressed her, if he tugged her long, golden-brown hair out of that bun, she would be the kind of hot that men noticed a hundred yards away.

He found himself grateful for the loose-fitting clothes. *Why?*

It wasn't as if Beat could or would be taking them off her. No, he had certain . . . tastes that ensured he kept his sex life private. He catered to them with willing parties behind closed doors, then he got the hell back to reality. The two aspects of his life never intersected. In deference to his mother's fame, he'd been raised to be fiercely private, and his life experiences along the way had only hammered home how important it was to trust himself—and himself only.

Bottom line, Melody's clothes and how they looked on her body were exactly none of his business. He'd brought her here today to formally ask her if he could open a giant can of worms. While he didn't yet have the full details of the project, the possibility that a reality show could affect Melody negatively bothered Beat enough that he hadn't slept last night. Somewhere around three A.M., he'd given up and gone to the gym.

Even now, he had the urge to carry her back to the elevator, apologize profusely, and send her on her way. Back to Brooklyn where she lived a normal life, as far outside of the spotlight as was possible, given their last names.

Instead, Beat could indirectly drag her into something she definitely wanted to avoid. Attention. Because no matter how many angles from which he viewed the situation, he couldn't figure out a way for Applause and Danielle to accomplish the reunion without Melody's name coming up at some point.

It just wasn't possible.

"Mel," he said gruffly, his smile feeling heavy.

"Hey," she responded, her voice barely above a whisper.

And he hadn't planned on hugging her, but as soon as that single, husky word was out of her mouth, he couldn't stop himself from crossing the office and wrapping his arms around her. His eyelids drooped involuntarily, because she fit against him as well as he remembered. Like she was meant to be there all along. A star-crossed best friend.

Melody dropped her giant purse onto the floor and hugged him back—and that made him feel more important than any press coverage or birthday party in his honor. It was instantaneous. Honest. How had he missed her like this when their acquaintance had been so brief? It made no sense, but there it was. His reaction to her at sixteen hadn't made a lot of sense, either. It just was.

"Thanks for coming," he said into her hair. She smelled of gingerbread and wind.

"You're welcome." Her amused reply was muffled by his shoulder. "*Someone* has to try and talk you out of this."

His smile turned lighter. He squeezed her. Just a little more.

"Miss Gallard," said Danielle gently from behind her desk. "I'm so glad you could make it. I hope the subway commute wasn't too much of a hassle on a Monday morning."

"Um . . . it was fine, all mystery substances considered." Slowly, Beat and Melody disconnected from each other, and she seemed to realize for the first time that she'd dropped her purse, the skin of her cheeks pinkening slightly as she stooped down to retrieve it. "It wouldn't be a New York commute without at least one unidentified substance congealing on the seat beside me."

Danielle laughed, gesturing to the side-by-side chairs facing her desk. "Very true. Please. Have a seat."

Beat held out Melody's chair and did his best not to inhale her scent as she sat. He forced himself to park his ass a good foot away from her, as well. To give himself time to come down from their hug and prevent the strange impulse to continue touching her in some way.

When they were both seated, they went right on looking at each other for several moments, like they were the only two people in the room and Beat started to wonder if seeing her again was an even worse idea than he'd originally thought. Why did he have to like her so much? What was it about her that made him feel normal almost instantaneously?

He forced himself to break their stare. It took him effort to focus on Danielle, but once he did, he couldn't miss the producer's keen speculation. And she was pleased as punch over whatever she'd witnessed. Why? Did she think his distant-but-potent relationship with Melody would be an entertaining angle for the show? Because Melody wasn't going to be involved. Not directly. No way would he let that happen, especially since he had an ulterior motive.

To make enough money to pay off his blackmailer.

"Okay. First of all, wow. I did it. I got you two in a room together and that's a victory in itself," Danielle started, clapping her hands. "But I digress. You both have busy lives and I won't waste your time. In fact, we *have* no time. Applause wants to reunite Steel Birds and bring the public along for the ride. If we're going to move on this, it needs to be fast." She gestured at Beat. "During our phone conversation, Beat made it clear that he is volunteering as tribute. He will be the only one participating in the project." She transferred her focus to Melody. "However, because of your proximity to the band, Melody, he won't do it without your consent." She folded her hands together on the desk. "Unfortunately, due to the time crunch, if you're going to give your approval, it needs to be today."

Beat's pulse started to thrum faster. "We're going to need more details first."

Danielle nodded. "Essentially, we need to strike while the iron is hot," the producer continued, splitting her focus between them. "'Rattle the Cage' is number one again on Billboard. *Thirty years postrelease.* The hashtag #BringBackSteelBirds has been trending on and off for weeks on various social media platforms. A new generation is demanding a reunion of this band that wasn't even around when they were born. I've never seen anything like it. If there was ever a time to consider bringing Octavia and Trina back together, it's now, when there is a shit ton of money on the table and enough demand for a possible tour."

Silence fell heavily in the room. Beat's heart pounded in his ears.

"I was promised beignets," Melody said.

He laughed. It shot out of him like cannon fire, unexpected and . . . real. When was the last time he'd laughed for real? And not because it was expected?

Melody grinned over at him. "Well, I was."

"So you were," Danielle said, visibly amused. She picked up her phone and punched a button, speaking briefly to the assistant on the other end, before hanging up. "Forgive me."

"I'll think about it," Melody teased while crossing her ankles, Beat doing his honest best to ignore the way her calves flexed. How palm-sized they were. *Quit looking, man.* "So . . . you are asking Beat to meet with our mothers on camera to try and convince them to reunite? You want to film the process on the off chance it works out? That's all?"

Danielle tilted her head. "If it were that simple, it wouldn't make for good television."

"Gulp," Melody said.

Beat got trapped between the urge to laugh again and the need to end the meeting, because the more information Danielle revealed, the more intrusive the whole idea sounded.

Could he simply walk away from this chance to pocket a million dollars, though? If he didn't come up with the blackmail money, his parents would become internet fodder. Laughingstocks. If he had a way to prevent that outcome, he should do everything in his power. Shouldn't he? They'd given him a life of privilege, everything handed to him. This was the fucking least he could do. "Mel." He turned in his chair to face her, once again tamping down the urge to hold her hand. "Did you read the email from Danielle?"

She shook her head, looking between them. "I'm pretty sure I deleted it."

Beat hummed. "Applause offered each of us seven figures to do this."

"Seven?" she choked out. "As in, a million?"

"Yes. A million exactly."

"Not to interrupt," Danielle chimed in with a cough. "But the million is contingent on the reunion *actually* taking place."

Beat had seen that coming. In fact, he'd instructed his accountant to start formulating a secondary option, in the very likely event that he couldn't make the reunion happen. A loan appeared to be his only choice besides winning the million dollars—but God, borrowing that much money from the bank was not his preference. It made him nauseous. Looking at Melody helped settle that roiling sensation, though, so he kept his attention locked on her. "I would never bring you into this on purpose. I'd ask them to do everything possible to maintain your privacy, but if the show is successful, there's a good chance you'd get the blowback attention."

"The plan is to reunite them on Christmas Eve." Danielle jerked a thumb over her shoulder. "Right here in Rockefeller Center during the annual holiday show."

Melody wasn't moving.

"Mel?" Panicked by her sudden, frozen silence, Beat cupped a hand around her shoulder and squeezed. "Are you okay?"

"Yes. I'm just . . . so soon? *This* Christmas Eve? As in, two weeks from today? And if the reunion happens, Beat makes a million dollars."

"That's right," Danielle confirmed quietly, her eyes narrowed on Mel in a way that made Beat want to pull Mel into his lap. "For clarity's sake, if the band reunites, Applause will own the rights to the reunion footage and easily recoup the cost of Beat's prize. Otherwise, they won't. Mere participation in the project will earn him a decent payday, but without their appearance at the Christmas Eve show, it's nowhere in the neighborhood of seven digits. More like five."

"No pressure," Mel muttered.

Beat's mouth arranged itself in a lopsided smile.

After a long stretch of silence, Danielle leaned forward. "Like I said, we have to act while they're hot. We could wait until next year when they don't have a viral hit and public fascination has waned." Now she zeroed in on Beat—and he got the sudden sense that Danielle had buried the lede. "*Or* we can pull the trigger on a new form of entertainment I've been dying to play with. A reality show in real time. Unedited, unfiltered. Streaming live from the network's social media accounts, twelve to fifteen hours a day. We would also dedicate several hour-long slots throughout our conventional television programming to *The Parents' Trap*. That's what I'm *tentatively* calling it." She paused to smile. "My goal would be to broadcast this journey into every household worldwide. Live."

Beat's stomach was in the vicinity of his loafers. He should have known better. How many times had he agreed to participate in some behind-the-music special about his mother only to have the producers dive straight into his off-limits topics, like his parents' marriage or details about the 1993 Concert Incident? The goal would always be entertainment value, no matter the cost. Did he really think this was going to be easy? And now he'd brought Melody into it, too? "This is the first time you've mentioned the show being a live stream," Beat said, keeping his voice even. "I assumed any footage would be in editing for months afterward, the final product to be approved by approximately sixteen lawyers."

Danielle didn't bat an eyelash. "I wanted to wait until you were in my office to give you the full scope of the project."

"Why?" Beat stood without waiting for an answer, hastily buttoning his suit jacket. "I'm sorry about this, Mel. Let's go. I wouldn't put you through something like this."

"I know," Mel said automatically, before shaking herself. "I mean . . . it's a *lot* to take in."

"Too much," Beat agreed.

Danielle remained serene. "If I could just—"

"Beat," Melody said, standing, looking at him as if through fresh eyes. "Could we speak somewhere privately?"

*Being alone with you isn't a good idea.* Why was that his first thought?

Something about this woman magnetized and fascinated him, but surely he could refrain from asking her out long enough to have *one* conversation. "Yes. Of course."

"There is a cafeteria on the fourth floor. They have coffee. I'll have my assistant prepare the table." Danielle smiled. "I'll wait here until you're ready to talk again."

Beat gestured for Melody to precede him. "*If* we decide to talk again."

The cheerful-looking receptionist chose that moment to enter the office with a tray of beignets, which Melody intercepted before the girl could set it down on the desk. She held it out to a bemused Danielle so the producer could snag a few, then carried the rest of the baked goods out of the office while Beat followed in her wake. And it didn't make any sense, but as they rode downward in the elevator chewing on beignets and staring at each other, he wondered if he'd been missing Melody his entire life.

# Chapter Four

Melody sat down across from Beat at a small, square table that was positioned up against a window overlooking Tenth Avenue. When they arrived at the employees-only lounge, an assistant had been waiting to hand Beat two paper cups of coffee and guide them to their seats. Beat placed Melody's drink in front of her, turning the cup until the little drinking spout on the plastic lid was closest to her. It was an unconscious move that made Melody's pulse sprint like a child chasing down an ice cream truck.

Asking Beat to speak privately had taken all her courage.

The meeting had been ending. The premise of *The Parents' Trap* was preposterous. Invasive. Ridiculous. Obviously Beat had been caught off guard by the nitty-gritty details and had no intention of entertaining the idea any further.

Curiosity continued to weigh heavily in her gut, though. And Melody found she couldn't get back on the train to Brooklyn without satisfying it.

Needing a moment to gather up another supply of courage, Melody sipped her coffee, watching Beat watch *her*. A gust of wind blew through her stomach and disorganized everything at the way he regarded her mouth closely, sitting very still while she brought the cup to her lips, as if he wanted to make sure he'd positioned the cup perfectly to meet them. When it did, because of course he'd judged it correctly, a muscle slid high in his throat and never seemed to come down.

He could still make a person feel like they were the only one in the room. It was his superpower, wasn't it? It drew people to him. It wouldn't hurt to remember that.

It also wouldn't hurt to ignore the way his sculpted lips suctioned the spout of his coffee cup lid. Or the sheen of moisture he licked away when he set the drink back down. But it took her a moment to find her voice because it was lost somewhere among the pandemonium of her hormones, which hadn't been this noisy since the last time they'd been together. That wasn't to say Melody hadn't been with men sexually. She'd experienced pleasure with men. But the bond, the trust she needed to feel truly fulfilled, it never materialized. She was only ever one solitary figure copulating with another solitary figure. There was never a sense of partnership or belonging. What would touching Beat be like? Being touched *by* him?

*You're never going to find out.*

He almost definitely had a girlfriend. She was shocked he didn't have a gold band on his finger, this wildly handsome, successful thirty-year-old who happened to be kind. *Kind!* Who was kind anymore? Such an outdated and underrated quality—and Beat Dawkins had it.

"Mel," he said now, shrugging off his jacket and twisting to hang it on the back of his chair, a tidy region of obliques shifting beneath his white dress shirt. "I'm so embarrassed that I brought you all the way out here for nothing." Nothing? She would have driven to the opposite coast just for the coffee date. "Please believe me, I wasn't aware of the twist."

"No, of course you weren't."

Her confidence relaxed his shoulders, but the strain around his eyes, the tension she'd noticed immediately upon walking into the meeting, remained. He wasn't a carefree sixteen-year-old anymore.

"I hope you didn't have to take a day off work . . . ?" Beat prompted.

"No. I have a project at home that I'm working on, but I'll make up for lost time tonight."

"What kind of project? I read in an article a while back that you work in rare books." A frown marred his forehead. "I just realized that most of what I know about you comes from articles."

"Same." *Or your Instagram captions.* Which were usually just a location and date. No pithy one-liners or inspirational quotes, as if she needed more reasons to like him. "I'm restoring a Judy Blume book—*Superfudge.* An original printing from 1980. It's weathered a few spills and the binding is weak, but it's a beautiful specimen." She couldn't keep a dreamy sigh from escaping. "I've sort of made young adult literature my specialty."

"Why?"

She shrugged. "I lived inside of those books growing up. I want to take care of them, the way they took care of me."

His expression remained thoughtful, maybe even a little troubled until he coughed into a fist, seeming to mold his mouth into a smile. "Do you work with a magnifying glass attached to your head?"

"I work mostly from home. Sometimes that's *all* I wear."

Beat choked on his sip of coffee, and flames climbed Melody's cheeks.

*Does this window open so I can leap through it?* "Another drawback of working from home is a glaring lack of social skills."

He laughed, one of his hands traveling across the table to squeeze her wrist. "You just caught me off guard." A moment passed. Then very, very briefly, his thumb slipped beneath the cuff of her blouse and swept smoothly over her pulse, lingering for a heavy second before he abruptly pulled away.

Beat cleared his throat hard, shifting in his chair.

Melody couldn't move at all. That itty-bitty touch had turned her thighs to jelly. If she tried to cross her legs, she would slowly topple sideways like an underbaked cake.

Did Beat touch everyone like that? Was it a perk of his undivided attention?

"Um." *Don't be awkward.* She hunted for something to say. "I'm not *totally* without a social calendar. I'm on a bocce team."

He leaned forward, amused. "Are you?"

"Yes. We are the opposite of undefeated. We're defeated. But being on the team forces me to take off the magnifying glass hat and talk to actual people, instead of books." She dried her sweating palms on the tweed material of her skirt, hoping he couldn't see. "Actually, that's where I met Danielle. She was lying in wait for me outside of the bar after a match."

His smile faded. "I'm sorry. About all this." He started to pick up his coffee, but hesitated. "Are the bocce games at night?"

"Yes."

"Do you walk home alone? At night?"

"Yes. I do. It's perfectly safe." She paused to think. "I do have coworkers who live in the same direction. I could probably wait and walk home with them. But I just want to . . ."

"What?"

"Get out," she murmured. "I just have to get out of there. Get away. You know?"

She expected him to be confused by her admission or change the subject. But she should have known not to underestimate him, because he only looked . . . relieved. "Yeah, I do know, Mel. Toward the end of the night, everyone's filters are off and people start asking uncomfortable questions. Or they ask me if I'll FaceTime my mother."

"Or they take selfies without asking," she breathed.

"Endless selfies." His expression turned thoughtful. "Even my friends that I've known for years—and I love them. I do. But this feeling never goes away of . . . wondering if they're just in it for the clout. I keep my guard up."

She got the sense he was underselling that last statement. Was Beat very guarded now? He hadn't come across that way at sixteen, but a lot of time had passed.

"Yeah. It's exhausting," she said, finally.

They looked at each other across the table. For the first time in a long time, Melody was devoid of the tension that came from being out in public. Just being outdoors. This was safe. She was with someone who navigated the same waters. Mostly. Hers had been a little more treacherous. At least, she thought so. Who knew what his experience was like?

No one knew but Beat.

"So, just to be clear . . ." He looked down at his coffee cup, then back up at her, his gaze a touch sharper than before. "No boyfriend to walk you home, Melody?"

His use of her full name made her toes dig into the soles of her boots. "No."

He swallowed.

*Stop reading into every little movement he makes.*

"What about you?" She did her best to sound bright, casual. "No girlfriend or—"

"No."

How? That was what she wanted to ask. Instead, she crossed one leg over the other and dug her fingertips into her kneecap. Just to redirect some of the pressure in her chest. In her stomach. The overall effect of being around this man. "Our last match of the season is just over a week away," she said, trying to keep her breathing steady. "I would invite you to come watch, but . . . for one, I would rather you didn't witness my sheer lack of athletic ability. And two, the both of us together in public . . ."

"Yeah." He sighed. "It would cause a stir."

"A big one. Us doing anything together would get a lot of attention and . . . I kind of thought we were on the same page about not wanting so much attention. Which is why I wanted to speak to you alone." She watched his face carefully. Closely. "Why did you want us to take this meeting in the first place, Beat?"

His chin jerked up a notch. When he might have spoken, his jaw only clenched down.

"There must be a reason. We could fill an ocean with the requests we've gotten for reality shows and reunion attempts and interviews. Why this one? Why did you entertain it?"

"I'd rather not get specific, Mel."

That was it. He didn't continue.

And despite her odd sense of kinship for him, this was where she needed to let the subject drop. Her imagination might be telling her something different, but in reality, they weren't friends. They weren't close. Another fourteen years might pass before they even crossed paths again, so she definitely didn't have the right to press him for an answer.

But she couldn't seem to stop herself. Maybe it was the sense that he was struggling and doing his best to hide it. Or maybe she had inherited some of her mother's stubbornness. For whatever reason, Melody took a deep breath and pushed a tad harder.

"There's only one reason to do this . . . and it's money."

He closed his eyes.

Bull's-eye.

"Okay." Sympathy tunneled right through her chest. "You don't have to tell me the finer details—"

"It's not that I don't want to, Mel. I *can't*." He shook his head. "And it doesn't matter anyway, because there is no way in hell that I'm going to attempt to reunite Steel Birds on a live stream, where I can't control"—he seemed to bring himself even again with a slow breath—"how it affects *you*. I won't do that."

Melody's entire body throbbed like one giant heartbeat. "I'm . . . *I'm* the reason you won't do this. What's holding you back is . . . *me*?"

Beat's chest rose and fell, his hold tightening around his coffee cup.

No. No, she couldn't be his reason for turning down the chance at a million dollars. It had to be about the media attention, the lack of privacy. Right?

Regardless of his reasons for saying no to Danielle, if he'd come this far, he must really need the money. Badly. Could she let herself be one of the reasons he turned it down?

She might not know this man well, but she knew him enough to be positive that he hadn't made the decision to take this meeting, to consider this offer, lightly.

Was Beat Dawkins in trouble financially? *How?*

It wasn't her place to ask.

She couldn't simply turn her back and walk away, either. Not on this man.

"What if you said yes? Just . . . hypothetically."

He was already shaking his head. "Mel. No way."

"Hear me out." Visions of cameras chasing them, snapping photographs, calling out uncomfortable questions about her developing body, made Mel squirm in her seat. Still, she didn't let it deter her. "Let's say you agreed to do the show. Agreed to reunite our mothers while the world watches . . ." She let out a breath. "You'd never pull off a reunion."

He started to say something, but she cut him off first.

"Not without me, at least."

Beat did a double take. "Excuse me?"

"Even with me tagging along, the chances of a reunion are less than one percent. But if we were giving it a real, honest-to-God shot . . ." Here she was, considering an idea she'd long thought was impossible, *absurd*, so she couldn't help but laugh. "My mother wouldn't even let a Dawkins through the front door of her house. Which, by the way, is a commune of no-account called the Free Loving Adventure Club, according to her most recent update. In the by-God *wilderness*. Imagine trying to reason with a rebellious rocker turned nudist turned possible cult leader who shuns civilization. On a *live* stream. I mean, you seriously need backup."

Beat's hand shot across the table and grasped her wrist, cutting off her amusement. "Melody. I'm not putting you back in front of a camera. You know how shitty they treated you."

"You made it bearable. You . . . knowing you were out there on my side made it bearable." She'd waited years to tell him that and it was like releasing a boulder from her chest. "What you said that day changed things. Or it got the ball rolling. And anyway, I'm megahot now," she deadpanned. "It's different."

He didn't seem to grasp the joke, his forehead only wrinkling in confusion. "I'm sorry I brought you here. It was a bad idea. I'll get the money . . ." He trailed off with a curse, slowly releasing his hold on her wrist. "I'll get it another way."

"Wait. I'm not done." This time, she closed her fingers around *his* wrist and pressed down tight—and something unexpected flared in his light blue eyes. Was it . . . was that *lust*? Not attraction or interest. Lust. A flaming hot flare of it shooting across the sky of his face.

Whatever it was, the effect was so potent, Mel needed a moment to catch her breath.

"Um . . ."

Unsure where the impulse came from, she dug her nails into his wrist ever so slightly.

Beat expelled a harsh exhale.

The unexpected quickening in her belly made her let go of his wrist like it was on fire.

He closed his hand around the spot, twisted, and dropped both hands into his lap, his breathing a little shallower than before. Or was she imagining that?

"What were you going to say?" he prompted after several heavy moments.

Melody did her best to focus. "My mother. I was going to tell you . . ." Her throat started to tighten up, making her voice sound slightly unnatural. "Growing up, she was always traveling. A free spirit to the bone. Now, I see her even less. Only once a year. She comes to New York on my birthday and takes me to her favorite old thrift shop on St. Mark's Place and the venues on Bleeker where she got her start. She decries how the rich have ruined New York City, we have dinner at a bar that's too loud for conversation—and then she's gone. It's a whirlwind and I barely get in a word edgewise with her, but . . ."

She blinked back the moisture that tried to coat her vision.

Beat didn't appear to be breathing.

"I always think, this is the time I'm going to impress her. Or she's going to finally be interested in my life. She's finally going to see me. And every year, I'm wrong." This was the first time Melody had ever said these words out loud and they sunk in her stomach like great big stones. One year, in her early twenties, she'd even taken guitar lessons to try and impress Trina, but when her mother actually arrived, Melody didn't even tell her about the bi-weekly classes she'd been taking. She was too afraid to find out that even learning to play "Rattle the Cage" on her acoustic Gibson was underwhelming. "She goes back to her nudist colonies or her adventurous friends and I just . . . wait for next year."

"Mel . . ."

"Sorry, just let me get this out." She waited for him to nod. "I've been working on myself for a long time. Independently. I've been going to therapy. Lately, I've started venturing outside of my comfort zone and I think it's time. Finally time to stop the visits in February. They just make me feel terrible. Inadequate." She took in a breath and released it slowly. "I have nothing to lose here, Beat. My relationship with Trina either needs to change or . . . be paused for a while. Moneywise, too. In which case, a million dollars would go a long way to achieving some independence. Finally." Thinking about that made Melody feel a little light-headed. She'd been living with Trina's wealth for so long. "Maybe *The Parents' Trap* is the only way to shake up my relationship with Trina enough to elicit a change. And if it doesn't work, at least I've done something new and scary. I've pushed myself. I tried."

Something brushed her kneecap beneath the table and when she realized it was his fingertips, she almost swallowed her tongue. "You shouldn't have to pull a stunt to make her see you."

"It's easy to say that when fate gave you the elegant philanthropist mother." Melody shrugged and attempted a smile, tamping down the urge to fan herself. "Fate gave me the wild child. She requires explosions."

He remained still. "Do you really want to do this or are you inventing a reason to say yes?"

Melody appreciated him asking, because whoa, this *was* moving very quickly. When she woke up this morning, she did not expect to be agreeing to a live reality show before lunchtime. But truthfully, she'd been stuck lately. Stuck between this world of solitude she'd built after years of being raked over the coals by the press and the need for something more.

There was *more* out there for her.

If not a solid, healthy relationship with her mother, then a better sense of who she was *supposed* to be, instead of a side character who had been shoved into a claustrophobic box by the media. And underneath it all, there was Beat. A chance to spend time with Beat. He'd become a fairy-tale figure in her head, but he was a real human being.

"Do you need me to do this show with you, Beat?" murmured Melody.

Beat shook his head. "I don't want to put that kind of pressure on you, Peach."

*Thwack* went her heart. The nickname he'd given her at age sixteen came seemingly out of nowhere, yet it felt like he'd called her that a thousand times. Maybe because she'd replayed those gruff consonants so often over the years.

"Do you need me?" she asked again.

He didn't answer right away. "There isn't a single other person in the world I would ask."

A ripcord released and pleasure flooded in from all directions. "Then, okay," Melody said. When Beat only continued to look at her in an unreadable way, she picked up the last beignet, ripped it in half, and handed him one side. "I don't usually share food. Don't get used to this."

His lips jumped. "Noted." He tossed the confection into his mouth and chewed, the world spinning behind his eyes. "One more thing, before we go put Danielle out of her misery." That gaze captured hers and held. "If the cameras and the attention—

any of it—become too much, you have to tell me, Mel. I'll shut it down so fast, they won't know what hit them."

Her mouth turned drier than a saltine cracker. "I'll tell you."

"Good." He exhaled roughly. "I can't believe we're doing this."

"Me either." An involuntary smile played around the edges of her mouth. "Can you imagine if we actually pulled it off, though? Brought Steel Birds back together for a reunion show? The world would lose their collective minds."

"It's never going to happen."

"Never," she agreed.

Still. When Beat stood up, grinned, and offered Melody his hand, nothing felt impossible.

# Chapter Five

**W**hen they returned to Danielle's office, they were already being filmed.

With Melody walking at his side, Beat's first instinct was to swat the lens away and hustle her out of there, but Jesus, this is what they were signing up for. Life under the microscope, even for just a brief period of time. Just under two weeks remained between now and Christmas Eve, when this supposed Steel Birds reunion would take place. If he and Melody were going to deliver their best effort, they needed to start immediately.

But God, he already didn't like this.

Melody knew. She knew he needed the money, even if she didn't know *why*. But Beat knew the blackmailer wasn't going to be his only problem over the next thirteen days.

Beat rarely spent that much time with anyone outside of his immediate family. He kept things surface level. Casual. Spending long lengths of time one-on-one with someone meant getting personal. It was why he vacationed in large groups of coupled-up friends. Why he always snuck out of the party earlier than everyone else. To avoid those booze-soaked moments where a longtime buddy was expected to open up.

He'd learned the hard way that if he allowed himself to be vulnerable, people didn't always like what they saw.

Everything had been handed to Beat. Not only was he born into wealth and tangential fame, but people naturally took a shine to him. He'd assumed it was normal, the way everyone seemed to be smiling at him everywhere he went. Paparazzi would compliment his clothes. If he didn't have a chance to study for an exam at the private Hollywood school he'd attended, the date simply got switched. His mother and father never stopped telling him he was special, that he made them proud.

But life wasn't like that for everyone.

At age thirteen, Beat had been sent to summer camp for two months, at the behest of his father. Rudy Dawkins had grown up in rural Pennsylvania and believed a break from the LA smog would do his son good. Being in nature, breathing fresh air, crafting things with his hands. Sounded interesting. How hard could it be?

Over the course of that summer, living in cabins with boys who *didn't* have famous parents, Beat had been smacked in the face with the knowledge that he led a ridiculously charmed life.

Money and his mother's notoriety had essentially handed Beat anything he needed on a silver platter, right down to his six-hundred-dollar sneakers. *These* kids made their own breakfast. No teachers gave them special treatment. They wore knockoffs and shared bedrooms with siblings. Their parents had sent them to summer camp because they worked and needed childcare, not on some nostalgic whim.

At first, camp went great. He got along amazingly well with his fellow campers, just like he got along with virtually everyone else. They'd talked about girls by the campfire, traded embarrassing stories, swapped dreams for the future.

But once they'd realized who Beat was, they'd slowly started to resent him, feeling as though he'd misrepresented himself. Pretended to be just another kid roughing it, when in reality, he'd be returning to a life of luxury they'd never experience for themselves. He'd spent over a month cleaning the cabin and mustering up his best jokes to win them back over.

For once in his life, however, charm—and his name—held no sway.

It was shortly thereafter that he'd started *enjoying* when things were difficult for him.

By the time he'd met Melody at sixteen, he'd gone through puberty, and this emotionally charged transformation, at the exact same time, leaving him in a place that still confused him sometimes, even though he enjoyed it. Quite a lot.

A place where he liked to be denied.

Loved when things weren't so *easy* for him.

The flashing red light of the camera distracted Beat from his thoughts and on reflex, he put his arm around Melody's shoulders, tugged her up against his side, and ushered her into the office, trying and failing not to glare at the cameraman who patiently shifted to keep them in his sights. "You were so confident we would *both* agree to this?" Beat asked Danielle.

"If the best-case scenario happened, I simply wanted to have the footage."

"This isn't live?"

"No." Danielle's smile stretched across her face. "Not yet." Her gaze ticked between Beat's and Melody's faces. "But like I said, we need to move quickly to make this happen by Christmas Eve. My vision is a sudden social phenomenon that will captivate even the most casual consumer of pop culture. None of the usual advertising for eight months until everyone is bored with the concept by the time it's out of postproduction." She planted both hands on her desk and leaned forward. "All we need is Joseph and his camera, platforms, bandwidth, and a plan. If the answer is yes, we will film some testimonials for promo on Wednesday and go live at the end of this week."

"Our answer depends on a few important details," Beat said.

"It does?" Melody whispered up at him from the corner of her mouth.

He squeezed her. "Yes."

Beat really needed to remove his arm from Melody's person, especially now that they were being filmed, but he couldn't seem to make his body cooperate. And he really needed to stop thinking about the way her fingernails had briefly dug into his wrist back in the cafeteria. Damn, the memory made him hang heavier inside of his briefs.

*Stop right there.*

They were going to be spending a lot of time together over the course of the next thirteen days and he could not, *would* not, lay a fucking finger on Melody. She claimed she was participating in this sideshow to separate her finances from her mother's, but . . . he had strong suspicions that Melody was also doing this for him, too. Which meant he needed to be grateful and protect her at all costs. In other words, keep his hands to himself.

Personal life and sex life. Never the twain shall meet.

Now was not the time to start breaking his own rule.

"What important details?" Danielle asked, clapping once. "Let's knock this out."

The cameraman chuckled.

Danielle shot the man a pointed look.

Was there a little . . . tension in the room between Danielle and Joseph? It appeared so, but Beat didn't have time to focus on it now. "First off, I want security for Melody. A lot of it."

Melody poked Beat in the side. "What about you?"

"Don't worry about me." She tried to protest, but he spoke over her, though he gave her a quick shoulder squeeze to apologize. "Filming stops at night. We're going to need downtime."

Danielle nodded. "Like I said, we'll be shooting you twelve to fourteen hours a day."

"Great."

"And I think I speak for both of us when I say, make sure you book a backup act for Christmas Eve, because if our mothers agree to share a stage again, we will have witnessed a divine miracle."

"There are four other acts to carry the show, if the reunion doesn't happen. Not that they'll live up to Steel Birds, but the show must go on."

"Good, because seriously, Beat is right about us performing a miracle. They haven't seen one like this since the Bible," Melody said, backing up Beat. "Growing up, my mother had a Steel Birds accolades room and Octavia's face had been slashed to ribbons in every picture. A veritable museum of hatred."

"My mother took ten years of primal scream therapy after the Concert Incident. In the house. We had a scream *closet*. I have actually never said Trina's name out loud, because it was forbidden in our home." He pointed at his mouth. "That was it. First time I've ever said it."

Melody tilted her head at him. "How did it feel?"

"Like . . . relief. I always assumed it would set off a plague of locusts or cause mountains to collapse."

"Quick. Someone check on Machu Pichu," Melody said, pointing to the desk phone.

"This is going to be gold," Danielle breathed, shoving the cameraman's shoulder. "You keep filming. We can use the footage as promo. You two—keep talking. There has been so much speculation about the Steel Birds breakup, but since none of the finer details were ever made public, those details are largely guesswork."

Beat looked down at Melody. She met his eyes, searched them.

How deep were they willing to let people in?

"Thirty years have passed since it happened," Danielle said, speaking with her hands. "Thirty. Years. The public's adoration for this band knows no bounds and they—*we*—have never been given a satisfactory explanation. Granted, we might not be owed one. But it would be a shame to leave it a mystery forever. Was a love triangle the culprit? Some other kind of betrayal?" Slowly, Danielle came around the desk, the cameraman stepping out of her way without looking. "You never asked to carry around the burden of this knowledge, but you've been pestered about it your whole lives. Day in and day out for three decades. You have the power to release yourselves from that."

Him? *Burdened?* Try the opposite. Blackmailer notwithstanding, Beat had everything he could ever want. Friends who cared about him, a thriving career, comfort, opportunities. However, he couldn't discount Danielle's words entirely, because he had more than just himself to consider. He and Melody *had* been placed in a position to be questioned since birth about why the band broke up. And while he could take it, could handle the constant badgering for the rest of his life, he wouldn't have minded ending it for Melody, right then and there.

The thought of making life even a fraction more enjoyable for her made him feel a hell of a lot lighter. But more than likely, the live stream could have the opposite effect and create an entirely new thirst for details. Oh, and his mother would probably stab him, so there was that.

"That's not our story to tell," Beat said finally, looking at Melody and winking where the camera couldn't see. "But we have others."

So easily did she read his meaning. Stories. They could get through this without revealing too many truths while still keeping things interesting, couldn't they? It might even be fun. "Oh yeah," Melody said, winking back. "Stories you won't believe."

"Cut!" Danielle squeaked. "Get it to the team," she whispered to Joseph. "We're going to get this up on all network socials immediately with a drop-in about the live stream starting Friday. That was our hook—and it was more like a harpoon."

The cameraman lowered the piece of equipment from his shoulder and Beat and Melody got a look at the guy's Gerard Butler look-alike face for the first time. Joseph gave Danielle a once-over, a succinct nod—and then he threw a fond grin at Melody.

Melody smiled back.

"One more condition," Beat said, without thinking. "I want a different cameraman."

Joseph laughed on his way out the door.

Danielle watched him go with a cross between hostility and reluctant interest. "Don't worry, he's professional to a fault. The best in the business if you disregard his cynical ogre vibe. He gets the work done and goes home, wherever that may be."

Beat suspected Danielle might have an idea where Joseph lived, but he'd be keeping that theory to himself. Or so he thought. Melody subtly elbowed him in the ribs and gave him a tiny eyebrow waggle, to let him know she'd picked up on the romantic tension, too. How did they seem to be on the same page so easily?

What if the next thirteen days weren't such a hassle after all?

What if he . . . enjoyed them because he was with Melody?

*Just don't enjoy them too much.*

"So . . ." Melody started, blushing. Probably because he was staring at her like he was trying to count her eyelashes. Did she know how pretty she was? "What's next?"

Danielle let the silence stretch until Beat managed to stop *actually* counting Melody's eyelashes, the producer not quite managing to hide her amusement. "Go home and get some rest. Meet back here on Wednesday morning for your promotional confessionals. I'd planned to do them separately, but I've changed my mind. We're going to do a joint interview. You're incredible together." Danielle didn't break for air while Beat and Melody traded a fleeting, but heavy, look. "Due to simple geography, Beat, I think we should approach your mother about the reunion first."

"Fuck."

Melody giggled.

The producer picked up her phone and tapped a few times on the screen. "According to Octavia's social media, she has a gala Friday evening to benefit her foundation."

"Yeah," Beat confirmed with a sigh. "I should know. I'm the one who organized it."

"That's where we'll strike." Danielle smiled, waved her hands innocently. "Or get the show on the road. However you'd like to term it."

"Tempt death," Beat suggested. "Inflict betrayal."

"Wreck the halls?" This from Melody. "Too bad my mother isn't a nudist anymore. There would have been nowhere to hide weaponry."

A cough snuck out of him, then expanded into a full-on belly laugh. How was he *laughing* right now? He'd just agreed to his—and Melody's—privacy being invaded straight through Christmas Eve.

"I wish I hadn't sent the camera away," Danielle mused.

"Why?" asked Melody quietly, wetting her lips.

And Beat watched it happen, because he couldn't get his attention off her mouth.

Danielle hummed, her gaze ping-ponging between Beat and Melody. "No reason." She tapped a finger to her mouth. "Wreck the halls. Is that what you said, Melody? Forget *The Parents' Trap.* I think we have our new name."

"I'll accept all future royalties in beignets," Melody said, seeming a little flummoxed over her offhand idea being deemed network-worthy. "Uh. There is one little problem with Friday's plans."

What was it? He'd fix it for her right now.

"I don't have anything to wear to a gala."

Danielle picked up her office phone and hit a button, her eyes twinkling with something that made Beat's stomach churn. Mischief. Anticipation. Plans. "Oh, I think I can help with that."

# Chapter Six

December 13

Melody arrived in Manhattan too early Wednesday morning. She stood to the side of the subway exit, debating her options. Kill time by going into Duane Reade and buying eyeshadow palettes she would never wear, sit in a coffee shop and people watch . . . or text Beat. He lived in Midtown, right? Maybe he wanted to get coffee?

*Again?*

Boring!

She had this fantastic vision of them dashing through the city and committing spontaneous pranks, like Paul and Holly in *Breakfast at Tiffany's*, but Melody was less Holly Golightly and more Holly Gohomeandstaythere.

Although maybe that wasn't entirely true anymore. After all, she had signed on for a reality show with no idea what lay ahead. She'd taken the steps to stop depending on Trina for monetary support—even if the million dollars was contingent on a pipe dream. The decision was something and something was more than nothing.

Riding high on her burst of positivity, Melody took out her phone and texted Beat.

> **MELODY:** I'm early. Tell me where to get the best coffee.

Wow. She even impressed *herself* with that text message. It informed Beat she was in the city and looking for something to do, without asking him to commit to an activity.

*Not too shabby, Gallard.*

> **BEAT:** I'm at the gym. Come here? They have coffee.

> **MELODY:** Sounds like a trap.

> **BEAT:** Would I do that to you?

> **MELODY:** Someone might have stolen your phone. I could be speaking to a guy named Lance who wants to sell me a gym membership.

> **BEAT:** HAHA. It's me, Peach. I'm dropping a pin.

> **MELODY:** OK. I'm coming, but I'm dubious.

Her phone dinged, adding a layer of warm shivers to the ones he'd set loose by calling her Peach. It was there in her phone forever now. She could look at it whenever she chose. Melody tapped the directions button, relieved to find she was only an avenue and one block south of Beat's gym. Seven minutes later, she pushed cautiously through the revolving door with an expression that dared any Lances to try and sell her a Pilates package.

Not today, Satan.

But as predicted, a smiling jock in a purple polo shirt was already approaching her, straight off the finish line of an Ironman competition. Those weren't even real calf muscles. They were veiny boulders shoved into skin-tone nylons. "Welcome to Core. Are you a member?"

*Run while you can.*

"Sorry, I have the wrong address—"

"Mel!" Amid the distant metal clanging and high-energy notes of an "All I Want for Christmas" remix, she heard Beat calling her name and turned.

There he was.

Running toward her through the reception area. In black athletic shorts and no shirt.

Sweating. Sweating all over the place.

Oh my God, she was looking at his nipples. *Stop. Don't look down, either.* She had to stop herself from looking at those high cuts of muscle above his hips. Or the rivulet of perspiration dripping off the meatiest part of his left pec. Or that little peek of happy trail. *Too late.* She saw everything. She'd perused him like the specials menu.

Thankfully, he didn't seem to notice. Or was he pretending not to?

"Hey, man." Effortlessly, Beat high-fived Boulder Calves and grabbed her wrist. "She's with me. Can I bring her in while I finish up?"

"Sure." The guy took a respectful step backward, out of her orbit. "No worries, Beat."

"Thanks."

Beat winked at Melody, guiding her through reception and into a small café that looked more like a nightclub. It was dark, except for the pulsing red Christmas lights surrounding the order window. "Hi," Beat said to the girl behind the counter, giving her a warm grin—and the phone slipped right out of her hands, followed by a stuttered apology. Beat only smiled wider. "Did I dream this or do you guys make coffee? It's not all smoothies and bee pollen and protein bars back there, is it?"

"We have coffee," she said throatily. "No one ever orders it, but we make it anyway."

"Oh. You're amazing." His whole body flexed with the power of his relieved exhale, the smile crinkles around his eyes deepening. "What's your name?"

"Jessica," she breathed.

"Jessica." He nodded. "Could I please get a large one for my girl, Melody?"

"S-sure." Jessica attempted to hit the right buttons on the register, but she kept having to start over, the color deepening on her cheeks with every failed attempt. "How do you want it?" She winced. "The coffee, I mean."

"Milk only," Melody said, giving the girl a look of pure understanding. "No bee pollen, please. Nothing healthy whatsoever, in fact."

Beat laughed, bringing Melody's hand to his mouth and brushing a kiss over the back of it, just a casual kicking of the hornet's nest that was her libido—where Beat was concerned, at least. He had two women completely flustered simply by existing. By being friendly and complimentary and hunky—and most importantly, genuine.

Someone *should* film this. Danielle was a genius.

Jessica slid the paper cup of coffee across the counter. "Do you have an account?"

"Yes." His eyes actually twinkled. "Dawkins."

"I already knew that. I don't know why I asked."

Beat picked up the coffee with a laugh and handed it to Mel, throwing his arm around her shoulders. "Thank you for saving the day, Jessica."

"Any time."

They left the café area, traveled down a hallway toward the source of the music and entered a gymnasium full of equipment. There were a few nods to Christmas—boughs and holly strategically nestled into corners, but for the most part, this place was all business. And in her kelly green coat and boots, Mel was not dressed appropriately. "How is it?" Beat asked.

"Intimidating. A little smelly."

"I meant the coffee, Peach."

"Oh." She peeled back the tab and took a sip, swallowed. "It's good! Made with lust."

He tilted his head. "Huh?"

She studied him closely. "You just put poor Jessica through a second round of puberty. You don't realize that?"

"What? No." He shot a skeptical look in the direction they came. "I was just being nice. I'm like that with everyone."

"I know. You were that way with me when I was sixteen."

Frown lines appeared on his forehead. "No. That was different. Not every encounter stays with me for years to come. Like ours." He seemed to realize he'd revealed too much and self-consciously swiped a hand through his damp hair, opening his mouth and closing it again.

"Well," Melody said, unable to feel the coffee cup in her hands. It could have been burning the skin from her palm and it wouldn't have registered. "RIP Jessica."

Beat chuckled, took her wrist again, and led her toward the back of the gigantic workout space. "Come on. I'm forcing myself to do twenty box jumps before I quit for the day."

"Sounds hellish."

"That's because it is."

"Why do you do it?"

His thumb brushed over the tiny veins in her wrist. "A little torture can be fun."

Melody wished she could see his face when he said those words, because his tone of voice was kind of . . . funny? Or was she imagining it? "Can't you just doomscroll like everyone else?" His laugh made her pulse skip. "The only torture I occasionally endure are jeans."

"Until today." Beat clapped and rubbed his hands together vigorously. "You're going to box jump with me, right?"

"Oh my God, I've been bamboozled. It's you. *You're* Lance."

"Only kidding." He turned in a circle, searching the immediate area. Melody didn't realize what he was looking for until he was pulling a leather bench in their direction. "Place for you to sit. I won't take long." He hung his head a second. "I just realized how weird it is that I've dragged you in here to watch me box jump. I swear it wasn't my intention to make you my audience, I just thought it would be a good chance to plot our strategy for the confessional."

She took a seat on the bench and crossed her legs, her skin flaming when he openly watched the move, the fingers of his right hand flexing at his side. "Strategy. Yes."

Now she sounded like Jessica.

"Obviously, we don't want to embarrass Octavia and Trina," he said, after a moment. "We can give their fans some intrigue without any big reveals."

"Cagey, but friendly. Engagingly evasive."

"That's exactly it." His expression was one of mock surprise. "Have you done this before?"

"Only about a million times."

"Sounds like torture," he quipped.

"Maybe I'll follow your lead and see if I can make torture fun."

His smile remained in place, but his eyes changed. Darkened. If he wasn't shirtless, she never would have noticed the way his stomach hollowed, ever so slightly, but he *was* sans shirt. And she happened to be sitting eye level with that slow contraction of his abdomen, the thick slide of muscle that coincided with his deep inhale. *Everything* inside of her turned jumpy. It was like someone plugged her into a charged outlet and shot every single one of her nerve endings into a chaotic dance. The whole scene must have been showing on her face, if her hot cheeks were any indication. *Distract him. Distract yourself.*

"Maybe I *will* try box jumping?"

That blurted pronouncement sent his dark eyebrows sky-high. "Really?"

Melody shot up from the bench, set down her coffee, and started to unfasten the buttons of her coat. "Is there a miniature one?"

"No."

"Oh."

"But you can do it," he said encouragingly. "I'll spot you."

"Spot me? I'm right here."

God, he had such a dreamy smile. "I mean, I'll help you if something happens, Peach."

"Something probably will," she warned.

"Nope," he said, shaking his head adamantly. "You've got this. You're going to nail it, Mel, just not in those boots."

"Barefoot is better?"

"Better than boots."

Grumbling a little, she reached down to unzip the sides of her leather ankle boots, trying and failing not to stare at his happy trail while she was down there, but it was so very sexy and unattended. Not landscaped, but not abundant. A tease. An amuse-bouche of hair. "Are you okay down there?"

"Not as okay as you are down there."

"What was that?"

"I think I better jump on the box now."

"Right." He circled around behind Melody, putting both hands on her hips and guiding her to the spot in front of the box. From up close, it looked a lot larger than it had from five feet away. In fact, it looked insurmountable.

"I think I might have overestimated myself."

"That's the fear talking."

Melody groaned. "Are you sure you're not Lance dressed in a Beat suit?"

His grip tightened on her hips and pinwheeling sparks lit up in front of her eyes, her toes curling into the cushioned gym floor. Were those his thumbs pressing into the small of her back, massaging gently? Or were those the hands of God? "It's all in your legs," Beat said, his breath warm against her ear, the right side of her neck.

That wasn't very reassuring since her legs were currently made of pudding. "Okay."

Another firm molding of her hips, then they slipped upward to do the same to her waist and God, she wished more than anything she was wearing one of those cool crop tops, so she could feel his hands directly on her skin. "I'm going to catch you if you don't make it. But you *are* going to make it."

"What if I fall forward, instead of backward?"

"You won't, but I'd catch you, either way."

"You're assuming I have so much faith in someone I haven't seen in fourteen years?"

A few seconds slipped by. "The faith is there, though, a little. Isn't it? Kind of like how I knew you would show up for the meeting. Show up for . . . me."

Melody closed her eyes, grateful he couldn't see her face. "Yeah." She swallowed. "Okay, Lance. Count me down."

"Three, two . . ."

She dug down for every ounce of power and strength in her body—and it turned out, she didn't have very much. Not physically, anyway. She jumped as high as she could, but her toes missed the ledge of the box by a couple of inches and she went flailing backward, landing with her back against Beat's chest, her feet dangling off the ground.

"I didn't make it on my first try, either," he offered.

"Yes, you did," she said on an unsteady exhale.

"Fine, I did. But my form sucked."

"No, it didn't."

He settled her down on the ground, his fingertips immediately attacking her ribs—tickling her so unexpectedly that she spun around on a squeal. "Jesus, Mel," he growled through his teeth. "Would you just accept my comfort?"

"Fine. *Fine!*" She was laughing. At the gym! "I'll get it next time. Your turn."

With a final squeeze of her side, Beat went to complete his box jumps while Melody plopped herself down on the bench and watched him move like an effortlessly graceful animal, all smooth skin and muscle pops and flashes of that reassuring grin. She'd always believed in her heart of hearts that being around Beat would make her feel normal. More comfortable in her own skin, like she'd been that day at age sixteen.

But as she left the gym heading to the Applause offices with Beat at her side, the reality of that seemed too good to be true.

# Chapter Seven

*L*et's start with the Concert Incident of 1993."

Melody sighed fondly. "Ah, I remember it like it was yesterday."

Beat bit the inside of his lip to quell a smile and found a more comfortable position in his director's chair. They sat side by side in a dark, airless room in the depths of the Applause offices, recording their "confessionals," although *they* weren't doing any confessing themselves. This was about their mothers' past.

Based on the uneasy look Melody sent him, talking about those long-held secrets in front of the cameras felt as unnatural to her as it did to Beat.

Damn, she looked pretty today.

A skirt, a *snug* skirt, the waistband of which hugged the bottom of her rib cage. Black tights tucked into scuffed ankle boots with a moon-shaped buckle. She'd walked into his gym wearing this coat—a bright green color that made her hazel eyes look bottomless. Her bangs were all blown around from the winter wind, cheeks red. He'd had to restrain himself from begging them not to put any makeup on her for filming. Why ruin something that was already beautiful to begin with? Still, whatever they'd put on her lips made them almost . . . plumper?

*Stop staring at her mouth.*

*Stop thinking about how her hips felt in your hands at the gym and concentrate.*

Shit. She was signaling him for help with a rapid series of blinks.

"The Concert Incident." He coughed into his fist and sat up straighter. "Right. That is how people commonly refer to the final show. It took place in Glendale, Arizona."

"Both of your mothers were pregnant at the time, correct?" asked the interviewer, a young man named Darren, a content manager for the Applause social media channels. "Trina was pregnant with Melody. Octavia with Beat."

"That's right," Melody said. "Octavia was a little further along. Beat is older."

"You're going to hold two measly months over my head?" Beat asked.

"Is your hearing aid turned all the way up, dear?" She patted his forearm. "I want to make sure you can hear all the questions clearly."

"What?"

Melody's laugh filtered into the studio and Beat's flipping stomach wasn't the only one who responded to it. Danielle and Joseph smiled behind the camera. Even the lighting technician flashed a grin. "Okay, the Incident." Melody tugged her skirt down to cover her knee and the rasping sound of wool on nylon made Beat's mouth go dry. "The angst had been building up to that point. I think everyone would agree that Trina and Octavia are extremely different personalities to begin with. My mother, Trina—"

"Lyricist. Bass. Backing vocals," contributed Darren.

"That's right. She is more of a . . . restless, volatile soul, while Octavia . . ."

"Is more reserved. Most of the time," said Beat. "Being the lead singer, she had sort of a poise about her, but when the song called for it, she could roar with the best of them."

"That's putting it mildly," the interviewer said. "Octavia Dawkins has been referred to as one of the greatest rock vocalists of our time. You must be very proud."

"I am," Beat answered honestly.

"And you?" Darren raised an eyebrow at Melody. "'Rattle the Cage' has long been known as the anthem of the nineties and it was written by your mother, Trina. That must fill you with tremendous pride."

Melody opened her mouth but didn't speak right away. "It does," she said, eventually.

Darren shifted in his seat, obviously scenting some intrigue. "And is that pride more for the music or would you say you're a proud daughter?"

Her fingers curled on the arm of the chair. "Well . . ."

"Back to the Incident," Beat slid in firmly, wishing his chair was closer to Melody's. Wondering if he could somehow make that happen without being obvious. "The previous tour had only ended months prior. Stress was high. There had been some . . . typical backstage drama. Things that occur behind the scenes with a band in a fast, flashy environment."

"Leading to the big breakup," Darren said, leaning forward. "Fans have been speculating about the cause for years and the leading rumor has always been a love triangle. Could you shed any light on this decades-old mystery, Mr. Dawkins?"

Could he? Yes. *Would* he? Absolutely not. And it wasn't merely a matter of keeping his mother's past private. There would be repercussions if he outed the third player in the love triangle.

Also known as the one who broke up the band.

His blackmailer—and biological father.

Melody must have picked up his inner conflict, because she cleared her throat and said, "That's the thing. If, in fact, there was a love triangle, which we are neither confirming nor denying . . ."

She angled her head and winked at him from behind the curtain of her hair. "According to the fans, any number of fellas could have been the culprit."

Beat's chest swelled with gratitude. She was giving him an avenue of escape—and reminding him of their agreed-upon strategy. Friendly but evasive. "Axl Rose, obviously, is the big one," he said.

"Yup," Melody agreed without hesitation.

Darren's jaw dropped. "*Axl Rose?*"

"Keanu," Beat sent back to Melody. "That theory is a contender."

"*Reeves?*"

"That's my favorite one." Melody sighed. "I just like knowing I could be connected to John Wick in some small way. Even if it's just that my mom smashed him in ninety-two. But you're forgetting about the strongest possibility."

"Am I?"

"Mr. Belding."

Beat snapped his fingers. "Right. He was *always* backstage."

"They couldn't keep him out! Belding was a secret freak." She spoke to the camera out of the side of her mouth. "Seriously. Watch the earlier episodes. The signs were there."

Darren was starting to catch on to their subterfuge. "You're telling me the principal from *Saved by the Bell* might have been the catalyst that broke up the band."

Melody shrugged, her right toe digging into the ankle of her left foot. Was that a tell? Something she did when she lied? "Your guess is as good as ours," she said, finally.

The interviewer sniffed, splitting a skeptical look between them. "All right, back to the topic at hand. During the tour *before* the final tour, a love triangle ensued. We don't know who they fought over, we just know it was *someone*."

Melody was nodding along. "Like I said, my money is on Belding."

Unamused, Darren checked his notes. "During that final tour, Steel Birds had a new drummer. The old drummer, Fletcher Carr, had been ousted. Did that have anything to do with the feuding?"

Beat could feel Melody looking at him askance. "If so, I have no knowledge of it."

"Me either," said Melody slowly, her eyes still warming his cheek.

"Very well," continued Darren. "Then we have a six-month break for Steel Birds, followed by one month in the studio, recording their final album, *Catatonic Blonde* . . ."

"At which time, my mother had met my father, Rudy."

"And Trina had met . . ."

"A roadie named Corrigan." Melody smiled, obviously comfortable reciting information that had long been released to the press by Trina herself. "He lives in Detroit with his family now. We met once and I liked him, but we don't have a lot of contact. It's a Christmas and birthday card kind of relationship."

Darren shifted. "How do you feel about that?"

"Confused about how DNA works, mostly. Roadies have good technical skills and I can't even install software."

Beat's fondness for Melody swelled up so huge inside of him in that moment, he wondered if everyone could tell. Could see it. How hard he had to work to contain the bombardment of feeling inside of his chest. Again, he wondered how different life might have been if she'd been in it all along. Even in short bursts. They'd only spent a matter of hours together at this point and already her impact was making itself known. He was lighter and more at home in his skin when Melody was around. He had purpose. A coconspirator. A friend.

A friend he wanted to make out with.

A friend he wanted to tease and torture him—

"So when Steel Birds went back on the road for the final tour, both our mothers were pregnant," Beat blurted, needing to keep them—but mainly himself—on track.

Darren took the cue, picking up where Beat left off. "Their relationship must have been somewhat harmonious for them to release an album and plan more shows."

"Correct." Melody snuck a look at him. "They were good for a while."

"Until the tour," Beat added.

"Culminating in the Incident."

"Yes," they answered together.

Darren put the pedal to the metal. "Melody, has your mother ever confirmed to you that she was the one who put the live scorpion in Octavia's acoustic guitar?"

"She hasn't verbally confirmed, but . . ." Melody itched her eyebrow. "I mean, can we all agree she probably did put the creature in the guitar? Who are we kidding? That's totally her style. She wrote a song on the final album called 'Scorpion Bite.'"

"Some say it was a warning," Darren pointed out. "Or a foretelling of things to come."

"I'm not sure she's organized enough to be that diabolical," Melody mused. "I think they just happened to be in Arizona."

"Everyone knows that's where you get the freshest scorpions," Beat tacked on.

She gave him a grateful smile. His pulse moved faster.

"And Mr. Dawkins," Darren said, transferring his attention. "Has your mother ever claimed responsibility for the lighting and sound issues? Midway through the first song, the spotlight on Trina failed and never came back on. Her microphone was faulty throughout the show, right up until the scorpion was discovered and Octavia slammed her guitar down on the amplifier. Causing the fire and the ensuing panic."

"My mother wasn't responsible for the lighting and sound. That's not her job."

"No, but she might have influenced whoever *did* hold that job."

Beat conceded that with a nod. "She's denied it and I believe her."

"Sure, be loyal to your mother," Melody teased. "Make me look bad."

"There isn't a single thing that could make you look bad," Beat said, without thinking. In fact, it took him a full ten seconds to realize he was openly staring at Melody. And everyone was openly observing him in the dead quiet of the office.

"B-bold claim," Melody stuttered, finally breaking the silence. "Considering you've seen me in braces." She visibly gathered herself, once again pulling that skirt over her knee—rasp—and Beat's blood ran unwisely south. What sound would those nylons make if she wrapped her legs around his hips? "Bottom line, the Incident was thirty years ago and no one will ever know what truly happened behind the scenes. We're just glad no one was hurt."

"Yes. Thank God for that," Darren agreed, steepling his fingers. "Although the public's sympathies have largely gone to Octavia, while Trina—the quintessential bad girl, if you will—seems to be the scapegoat for the breakup. Do you feel that's unfair?"

"I don't know," Melody said, honestly. "We don't . . . it's not something we've gotten into. The breakup isn't her favorite topic of conversation."

"I see," Daren murmured. "Now, for the question on everyone's minds. Will you be *able* to reunite these women? Do you two have the power to bring these forces crashing back together in one of the most anticipated shows of all time?"

Beat looked at Melody.

She smiled back wistfully.

They stayed that way for several drawn-out seconds, letting the hope build. Then they both faced the camera. "No," they said at the same time. "Absolutely not."

"But we're going to damn well try," Beat added.

"For Belding," Melody breathed.

They clasped hands, raising them high above the gap between their chairs. "For Belding."

*And for blackmail*, Beat thought, forcing his smile to remain in place.

## Chapter Eight

December 15

*W*as she in the middle of a makeover montage?

Since arriving back at the Applause Network offices bright and early Friday morning, Melody had been trapped in a whirlwind of grooming tools, hair products, self-tanning paraphernalia, and sequins. So many sequins. Initially, she'd been asked by the various aestheticians and hair gurus about her typical routines, but when she couldn't provide them with anything resembling a satisfactory answer, they stopped talking and quite simply began tearing strips of hair off every inch of her body, shaping her bangs, buffing and polishing her nails and never once offering her any more beignets.

Of course, Beat was nowhere to be seen. *He* didn't need to undergo a transformation to be camera ready—he'd been born that way. All he had to do to prepare for tonight's gala was don a suit and spritz on a little cologne and he'd have everyone's panties around their ankles. Probably even hers.

Fine. Definitely hers.

Come to think of it, she was kind of grateful to the woman currently lecturing her about the importance of wearing the correct bra size. At least it was distracting Melody from the butterflies in her stomach that had been circling madly since Wednesday's confessional taping.

*There isn't a single thing that could make you look bad.*

Beat had said those words to her. Meant them.

And then there was the fact that she'd be dropping in unexpectedly on her mother. Did she have an undiscovered sadistic streak? Because the simple act of imagining the shock on Trina's face was enough to make Melody breathless. Not once in her life had she managed to render Trina speechless. Or any form of surprised, really.

During those February visits, Melody usually spent most of the time nodding along to Trina's stories and rants. What if signing on to this reunion show and putting herself out in front of the world made her mother see her differently? Maybe Trina would recognize something of herself in Melody and want to explore their commonalities? It was a lot, maybe too much, to hope for. But their relationship couldn't remain status quo.

Whatever happened over the next nine days . . . *something* was happening. Either she was kicking the beehive of their mother-daughter relationship, hoping to change it. Or she was finally taking steps toward cutting the purse strings.

Right now, in this moment, *anything* happening felt like enough. She'd swung the bat instead of hoping to get walked to first base. She was participating in her own life, instead of trying to blend into the wallpaper.

"You are only filling out half this bra, my friend." A woman named Lola with swooping eyebrows and black lip liner was dangling Melody's most basic of beige bras in front of her face. "Typically, women wear bras that are too small and put themselves in a whole double boob situation, but not you. This thing reaches all the way up to your freaking collarbone. It might as well be a turtleneck."

"It's comfortable."

"Comfortable!" The woman's nostrils flared to the size of quarters. "Who said wearing a bra is supposed to be comfortable?"

"Maybe someone *should* have said that?"

Melody was whisked out of the chair and pulled across the carpeted wardrobe space to stand in front of a full-length mirror. Lola unbelted the silk robe Melody was wearing and pushed it dramatically to the ground.

"Hey!" Melody squeaked, wrapped her arms around her chest.

Lola shooed them away. "Look! Look at those cute little boobies. Let's give them a proper home."

"My God. They're breasts, not rescue pets."

"Aren't they, though?"

"I see you've met Lola," Danielle drawled from the entrance. "She'll be packing you a wardrobe for the next nine days to make sure you look your best." She held up a hand to someone in the hallway behind her. "No filming. She's getting dressed." Danielle made a wrap it up gesture to Lola. "Can you . . . ?"

"Working on it, boss. She's not the easiest client." Melody sputtered while watching Lola rummage through a plastic crate full of undergarments until she finally selected a bra, holding it up like it was baby Simba. "This will work with the gown I have in mind."

Before Melody could say a word, Lola had circled around behind her and hooked the bra into place, twisted it around her waist, and jerked it up to cover her boobs. Lola wiggled it higher and then Melody was looking at herself in the mirror in nothing but a strapless bra and thong underwear.

Instinct screamed at Melody to cover herself. No one had seen her in this state of undress in *quite* a while. Even the times she'd been intimate with a man, she'd wrestled with going completely naked, struggling with those leftover body insecurities she'd developed as a teen. Hard not to develop a few of those suckers when tabloids were zooming in on her thigh dimples and circling them in bright yellow, right?

Instead of lunging for the silk robe, though, she forced herself to stand still and wait for Lola to carry over the sepia-colored gown. The whole situation seemed run-of-the-mill to the other two women in the room. Maybe it was. Melody has seen behind-the-scenes footage of her mother doing costume changes during concerts while forty crew members stood by. Was this a miniature version of what Trina felt in those moments? Self-conscious and exposed?

No. Definitely not.

Trina would request less clothing. She'd throw her arms up over her head and dance.

"Don't forget the mic," Danielle said briskly.

"Forget the wire and battery pack that ruins the perfect lines of my dress? Never." Ignoring Danielle's snort, Lola attached a small black box to the rear waistband of Melody's thong, circling around with a wire and clipping a tiny microphone to the cup of her strapless bra. "They don't want me telling you this," Lola whispered, "but if you need to turn off the mic, like maybe you want some privacy in the bathroom, there is a button on the top of the pack. Just reach back and squeeze the box through the dress—you'll feel it."

"Thank you," Melody said, but the stylist was already halfway across the room.

"Incoming," Lola sang a moment later, holding the gown over Melody's head and letting it tumble down her body in a shimmering wave. "Oh, this color is incredible on you."

"First nice thing you've said to me all day."

"That's how you know I really mean it."

Laughing under her breath, Melody shifted her body around. "Actually, it's pretty comfortable—"

"Stop using the 'C' word in my presence."

"Lola hates the 'C' word," Danielle interjected, while looking down at her phone.

"It is, though—"

Lola drew the back of the gown together and zipped it up. In an instant, the bodice went from loose to skintight. "Oh no."

"Oh yes." Lola grabbed Melody by the shoulders. "Look at yourself. *Look*."

Danielle came up beside her, no longer distracted by her phone. "Wow." She inspected her, head to toe. "Melody, you were beautiful before. You didn't *need* a makeover. No one does—"

Lola snorted.

"But damn." Danielle's reflection winked at Melody in the mirror. "A little extra effort looks good on you."

"Thanks," Melody murmured, because that single word was all she could muster.

This was far from the first time she'd worn a dress. Growing up, she'd attended countless honors ceremonies, awards shows, and festive parties at the penthouses of music producers. In fact, those events were the main reason Trina landed briefly in New York, before taking off again, leaving Melody with a rotating staff of nannies. The longer Steel Birds remained broken up, the more those events thinned out. Since turning eighteen and living on her own, it never occurred to her to make more than a cursory effort with her appearance, because when she'd done so in the past, it was usually met with criticism from the press. Or she'd open *People* magazine and see cringeworthy pictures of herself wide-eyed and shiny-faced coming or going from a restaurant. Was it any wonder she'd selected clothing that kept her the most well hidden?

This woman in the mirror, though . . . she was a far cry from the teenager who couldn't seem to find a single piece of flattering clothing. The dress hugged her breasts and hips, accentuated her waist. Her skin was clear of the acne that had plagued her growing up. The hairdresser had trimmed her hair and left it falling softly around her neck, not a frizzy flyaway wisp to be seen. Who *was* this person?

"Oh." Lola couldn't hide her smug expression. "She's speechless. This is satisfying."

Danielle high-fived her. "You did good."

A quick sniff. "Yes, I did."

The phone buzzed in the producer's hand and she checked the screen. "Beat is en route." She took a few steps backward and craned her neck to address someone in the hallway. "He's already mic'd?"

"Yes, the PA met us downstairs and wired him for sound," came the deep-voiced, muffled reply. "Bases are covered, Dani."

"Great." Danielle looked momentarily thrown by the shortening of her name, but she beamed a smile at Lola. "Would you mind giving us a moment?"

"My work is done!" Lola sang on her way out the door. "I'm getting a drink."

"Thank you," Melody called after her, still observing herself in the mirror and feeling a little stunned. For the first time in her life, she could actually see the tiniest resemblance to Trina. "We're going straight to the gala when Beat gets here?" she asked Danielle.

"Yes. We're already broadcasting live, if you can believe it. Beat gave a confessional on the drive over. This is a good opportunity to bank one for you, too."

"Confessional. Right." Melody turned from the mirror to face Danielle. "You're going to be asking me the questions this time?"

"Yes. Are you comfortable with Joseph entering the room?"

Melody nodded. "Sure."

"Great." Danielle leaned into the hallway and waved the cameraman forward. "Let's do this standing so we don't wrinkle your gown."

The camera's red light winked at Melody, her face staring back from the lens.

Live. This was *live*.

"H-how many people are watching this?"

"Right now? It's in the low thousands, but we've only just started. It's going to grow."

Melody absorbed that. Low thousands. Okay, she could deal with that. Odds were, she'd never meet these faceless viewers in real life. She was nothing more than internet noise among louder internet noise that would eventually swallow her whole. They'd watch for a few minutes from their desks in Milwaukee or Bakersfield, then move on to something and someone more interesting, like a baby giraffe being born at the Bronx Zoo. No big deal.

This was *no big deal*.

Melody focused on Danielle and did her best to pretend the camera was invisible. "I'm ready when you are."

Danielle shifted side to side and lifted her chin, giving Melody the impression that she was delivering her own mental pep talk. "We've been running your confessional with Beat for the last forty-eight hours and there is significantly more interest now. Our main request on the message boards has been for information about you."

"About . . . *me*? The questions are normally about Steel Birds or Trina," she muttered, smoothing the front of her dress unnecessarily. "I'm . . . well. I live in Brooklyn and I work in book restoration. Try not to die from excitement. I'm basically a shut-in, but once a week I play in a bocce league. I use the term 'play' loosely. It's more like throwing the ball with my eyes closed and praying I don't knock anyone unconscious. Um. I date myself. Is that . . . should I talk about that?"

Danielle nodded vigorously.

"Okay. I take myself on dates once a week. Sometimes thrifting, if there are no good movies playing and I'm feeling adventurous. But always to a *new* restaurant. It's kind of a game where I never go to the same place twice. Has our viewer count dropped into the hundreds yet?"

The producer checked her phone but didn't answer Melody's question directly. "You have a partner in crime on this mission to reunite Steel Birds. Do you and Beat have a game plan?"

Hot sand filtered down from the top of Melody's head to the soles of her feet, the pulse fluttering in the smalls of her wrists. At the mention of his name. Pathetic. "Yes." *Speak up. You sound breathless.* "We're going to gently approach our mothers about a reunion and probably have ourselves written out of their wills."

The cameraman's chest rumbled with mirth.

"How well do you know Beat?" Danielle asked, after a brief glance at Joseph.

"Not well. Not well at all." Danielle didn't ask a follow-up question and the silence stretched out so long that Melody felt compelled to fill it. "I-I mean, I *feel* like I know him. That doesn't mean anything, does it? A lot of people probably feel like they know Beat, because he's so personable. When he looks at you, everything just kind of fades away and . . ."

Danielle gave her a signal to keep going.

Going where, though? Melody hadn't intended to say any of this out loud.

Not in her lifetime.

But the red light was blinking. People were watching, waiting for her to continue. "Yeah, everything just kind of fades away when he's around, I guess. He's kind and thoughtful and you've seen him. He's . . . beautiful." Her palms were beginning to sweat, head feeling light. "Is it possible to take a quick bathroom break—"

Beat rounded the corner into the room.

Joseph's camera remained pointed at Melody—and she wished it wasn't, because it captured the exact moment she saw Beat in a tuxedo for the first time. Somehow, the sight was superior even to sweaty shorts and a bare torso. Her brain sort of blubbered around for a few seconds, then slid out of her ear in a soupy substance. Had the tuxedo been constructed around his every muscle?

*Yes, dum-dum. That's called tailoring.*

Briefly, she flashed back to the first afternoon they met, when he'd blown in out of the rain and charged the atmosphere with electricity. He still had that ability in spades, especially in that custom tuxedo, but it was subtler now. Like his spectacular energy had been depleted by his surroundings. Perhaps by whatever had caused him to need this show.

He *needed* this show.

It was even more obvious today, thanks to the dark circles under his eyes.

Okay. She would tap-dance in front of the camera, if necessary.

*Mel*, he mouthed. Then, out loud, "Mel?"

"I'm sorry. Do you see this dress?" She pursed her lips. "I only respond to my name if it's pronounced with a French accent now."

His blue eyes dropped to her toes and slowly raked upward. That ribbon of something potent, something she couldn't name, took a staycation before he managed to hide it. Wow. Was it possible he found her attractive? Today, she could sort of believe it, thanks to the makeover, but that didn't explain the other times she'd caught him staring.

In the interest of making good television, she threw her arms out wide and dove straight into some unpracticed jazz hands—as if to say *ta-da!*—but Beat must have misinterpreted the action as her asking for a hug, because he took two lunging steps in her direction and locked her in a tight embrace. "Oh," she breathed, her arms turning to thousand-pound weights and hanging there, her heart firing up into her mouth. "Hi."

"Hey, Peach." He dipped his head, his nose brushing the side of Melody's neck and *oh God*, she could actually feel her pupils dilating. A tidal wave of blood traveled south, heating along the way and her pulse skip, skip, skipped before settling into a sprint. "You still smell like gingerbread. At least they didn't fuck with that."

"I love a seasonal scent," she responded dully, her eyelids drooping involuntarily.

Beat's laugh sounded almost pained as he stepped back, his attention lingering and sharpening on her breasts, before he dragged a hand down his face and turned away.

"Um." Melody tucked some of her freshly glossed hair behind her ear. "How did your mother react to the whole live stream thing?"

He sighed. "She'd already heard about *Wreck the Halls*, thanks to her manager—and she was definitely surprised I'd signed on. We tend to be very private, so live streaming isn't exactly my style. But if my mother loves one thing, it's the spotlight. She agreed to sign the release form and appear on camera tonight." He performed an absent adjustment of his bow tie. "The calls for a reunion have been increasing for months and she's going to use the opportunity to shut the idea down once and for all."

Danielle slumped. "Excellent."

"You can't say we didn't warn you," Beat said. "I've asked the venue manager to have guests sign a release form when they arrive, so we're clear to film inside the party, but we'll have to find an opportune moment for a quiet meeting between Octavia, Melody, and myself."

"During which we attempt to convince her of the impossible," Melody tacked on.

"Correct." A furrow appeared on Beat's brow. "Is there no way the meeting between Octavia and Melody can be private? No camera? My mother is a very patient and generous person, but she tends to quietly cut people off at the knees when she's backed into a corner. I don't want her to feel like she's being ambushed, and I don't want to subject Mel to a verbal sucker punch."

Danielle made a weak sound. "Those are the moments we really want to see."

Beat closed his eyes and nodded once, holding his hand out for Melody to take. "Time to face the music, I guess."

Mel threaded her fingers through Beat's. Did she imagine the way his breathing pattern changed. "Are we done shooting the confessional?" she asked Danielle, her voice embarrassingly husky. "Or were there more questions?"

"We're good for now. Let's head out."

Beat and Melody left the room hand in hand, walking side by side down the brightly lit hallway, her gait feeling slightly unnatural in the elevated shoes. Beat asked, "So what did you confess?"

*Nothing.*

*But I'm pretty sure I made it obvious to the world that I've had a lifelong crush on you.*

Hopefully nobody had been watching by that point.

"Oh, you know . . ." *Waxing poetic about you.* "Basic stuff. Name, age. Can you sing like your mother—the usual flimflam." She glanced over at his profile, noting the furrow between his brows. "What about you? Did you tell them your deepest, darkest secrets?"

Something like alarm flared in his features. "No. I managed to hold back." He opened his mouth and closed it. "They're focusing on our personal lives more than I expected. I thought it would be a lot of questions about Octavia and Trina, but they asked me what a day in my life is like. How I felt about turning thirty. How my friends feel about my 'peripheral fame.'" He rolled a shoulder. "It was unexpected."

"I'll try not to be offended they didn't ask if I had any friends. They were more interested in my self-dating habits."

"Your what?"

"Self-dates. Once a week, I wine and dine myself and I really enjoy it. Except when the hostess sits me two inches from a couple on a real date and I make them uncomfortable, because it seems like I'm listening. Which I am."

Beat hit the button for the elevator and the doors flew open, already waiting for the prince to require its use. They stepped in with Joseph and remained in silence for ten full seconds, before Beat asked gruffly, "Do you ever go on dates with other people?"

"Mmm. I have." His fingers jolted around hers. Did he have a fear of elevators? She'd talk him through it. "I even had a four-month relationship once. But my mother was coming to town for my birthday, and I started to see my boyfriend through her eyes, wondering what she would think when she arrived. That's when I realized it wasn't working. We weren't compatible and I just needed to step back and look to see it. Or admit it, I guess." Beat still looked tense, so Melody sucked in a deep breath and kept going. "Have you been in many relationships?"

"No." He gave her a tight smile that never reached his eyes. "None."

"*None?*" She could even sense Joseph's bafflement from the other side of the elevator. If Beat was a workaholic bachelor type with a personality defect, she could see him remaining relationship free, simply hooking up when the mood struck him. But Beat was sensitive, a good listener, gorgeous. If he crossed paths with a woman worth her salt, which he must have done hundreds of times, he would consider her, not disregard her. How was this possible? "But you have so many boyfriendly qualities."

His laughter was brief. "I like being single, Mel."

The elevator doors opened and Melody faced forward quickly. Did she secretly, deep down enjoy knowing that Beat had never been in a serious relationship?

Maybe. Just a little. But not enough to keep her from wondering—and worrying—what might have prevented it.

# Chapter Nine

*T*hey walked out of the building hand in hand and Beat squinted into the fading winter sunlight. Bells jingled somewhere in the distance. The lights strung between lampposts on the avenue were flickering on for the evening, casting the sidewalk in a muted glow. Cinnamon and sugar hung in the air, courtesy of the bakery across the street. There was something about holding Melody's hand while surrounded with Christmas nostalgia that forced Beat to slow his step, experience it a little longer.

Or maybe he was just stalling.

An SUV idled at the curb, waiting to take them to the gala, where they would pose the possibility of a reunion to his mother. On camera. In all likelihood, the show could be done before it started. What would he do about the money then?

Melody squeezed his hand and smiled at him, like she knew his thoughts had taken a troubling turn. Christ, she looked beautiful. Soft and sexy, like a classic movie star who'd stepped straight off the screen. That gown hugged her in places he was doing his best not to notice, but obliviousness would be extra impossible tonight. At least, for the moment, she was wearing a coat to cover the pale swells of her tits. The neat curve of waist into hips where he wanted to plant his hands and *mold* her. Examine her. *Feel* her.

His growing attraction to Melody was the exact last thing Beat needed right now on top of everything else. They were on camera; their every move was being documented. His blackmailer wouldn't stop leaving messages. His mother might disown him by the time the night was over—and all he could think about was using his teeth to rip down the front of Melody's dress.

"It's going to be fine." She inflated one of her cheeks with air and slowly let it out, so endearing his throat tightened up. "What kind of food is going to be at this party?"

"I have no idea," he said softly.

"I thought you said you organized this gala."

He tugged her in the direction of the SUV, Joseph walking backward in front of Beat and Melody to keep them in the camera's sights. "I'm more of the big-picture guy."

"You tell people the vision and they make it happen."

"Correct."

She laughed. "I'm sure it's slightly more complicated than that. I've followed the progress of Octavia's Ovations over the years. It's incredible—the way the foundation finds talented kids without a lot of resources, plucks them out like diamonds in the rough and installs them in Juilliard or some other amazing performing arts school. One of the Ovations kids performed the national anthem at the Super Bowl last year, right? I mean, they never fail to blow everyone away. Whoever is selecting those kids must have sharp intuition."

Beat helped Melody into the middle seat of the SUV, scrutinizing her face as she passed, trying to determine what she knew. But he didn't have to study her too closely, because she wasn't hiding anything. It was all right there on her face. "You're . . . aware it's me that does the selections?"

"Yes. Therefore, you're forgiven for not knowing if there will be shrimp cocktail."

"Oh, there's always shrimp cocktail. That falls under the category of big picture stuff."

"You're obviously a visionary. What about dessert?"

He settled into the seat beside her. "A wide selection."

She gasped. "That's my favorite dessert."

Beat's laughter boomed through the SUV and Melody smiled, a pleased flush coloring her cheeks. Even though it was a terrible idea, he wanted to study that blush closer, so he scooted over, reached up, and grabbed her seat belt, greedily inhaling her gingerbread scent while he dragged the nylon strap across her body and engaged it with a click. Then he made the mistake of looking at her mouth and the zipper of his tuxedo pants turned restrictive. *Jesus.*

There was a camera recording his every move and still he couldn't quite stop weighing the pros and cons of kissing her—

"Hey!" Someone shouted into the SUV through the door, which hadn't been closed yet. Beat turned slightly to find a woman he didn't recognize waving her phone around. "Holy shit. I'm watching your Instagram live right now."

A pair of young men stopped in their tracks behind her on the sidewalk, their mouths dropping open. "Oh my God," shouted one of them, jogging toward the car, his friend close behind. "Can we get on camera?"

Stranger number one used her body to block the men from entering the car. "Where is the gala? Are you really going to reunite the band? Are you two a couple? Seems like it!"

The two men were growing impatient and began elbowing their way into the SUV around the woman. A squabble ensued and Beat took their distraction as an opportunity to reach for the handle, swing the door closed, and slap the lock down. It wasn't until the sound of the argument cut off and the SUV roared away from the curb that he realized his pulse was drilling like a jackhammer in his temples.

When he managed to find his voice, he turned toward Danielle where she sat in the rear row. "What happened to the security you were supposed to hire?" A finger poked Beat in the ribs and he realized he'd squashed Melody into the corner, using his body as a shield. With a muttered apology, he eased away. Slightly. "What if Melody had been sitting closest to the door?"

For once, Danielle looked caught off guard. Dumbstruck, even. "I . . . the security team is meeting us at the gala. I didn't think we would require them this quickly."

"I wouldn't have thought so, either," Melody murmured.

They looked at the camera simultaneously.

Beat cleared his throat. "How many people are watching now?"

"Do you really want to know?" Danielle asked after a few seconds of tapping on her phone.

"No," Melody said, quickly.

Beat thought of how easily Melody could have been yanked out of the car. Or asked something a lot more mortifying than their relationship status. "Hire more security."

Danielle let out a breath and lifted her phone to her ear. "Good idea."

Not five seconds later, everyone traveling in the SUV—him, Melody, Danielle, Joseph, a lighting technician, and the driver—seemed to get a text. Then another and another, turning the interior of the SUV into an echo chamber of electronic chimes.

Beat was almost afraid to look, but he did so anyway, watching messages from his friends populate the screen, one by one. Of course, they were texting him with questions. He'd told them nothing about the live stream and they'd obviously missed any promo. In other words, they were finding out in real time on social media.

He started to pull everyone into a group chat, so he would only have to explain the situation once. A blanket message to keep things impersonal and vague, as was his modus operandi. But before Beat could tap out an explanation and get the thread started, a video clip from his buddy Vance popped up, accompanied with a text that read: someone has it bad. Beat tapped the play icon, quickly hitting pause when he saw it was a clip of Melody. Clearly, the footage was taken recently, because she was wearing the same gown.

*Don't watch it.* Some intuition told Beat it was a bad idea. But when Melody turned around in the seat to speak with Danielle, Beat couldn't talk himself out of tapping play again and holding the speaker of his phone closely to his ear.

"How well do you know Beat?" came Danielle's voice.

"Not well. Not well at all," responded Melody. Beat held his breath. "I-I mean, I *feel* like I know him. That doesn't mean anything, does it? A lot of people probably feel like they know Beat, because he's so personable. When he looks at you, everything just kind of fades away and . . . yeah, everything just kind of fades away when he's around, I guess. He's kind and thoughtful and you've seen him. He's . . . beautiful."

Those words might have been enough to tell him Melody was harboring a crush on him, but her tone of voice sealed the deal. She may as well have been a devout Catholic speaking about the Second Coming. And his behavior was doing nothing to dissuade the crush, either. Case in point, their hands were still locked together on the seat between them. Two seconds after this footage was recorded, he'd barged into the room and hugged her, because he'd been utterly compelled to . . . touch her in some way. *Any* way.

Safe to say they were both nursing a crush.  ·

Might as well acknowledge the facts.

Unfortunately, Melody didn't know his sexual interests were . . . slightly complicated. He came part and parcel with that complication, and he'd decided early in his life, before he even reached adulthood, that he would handle his particular needs privately and keep his social life separate. That included Melody. Most of *all* Melody.

*Stop leading her on, then.*

Knowing what he had to do—and doing it—were two very different things. Touching Mel came naturally in a way it never had with anyone else. It felt necessary, like he was making up for lost time. They might have grown up separately, thanks to the Steel Birds breakup, but their mothers' past kept them tethered, along with something intangible. When they were together, his senses heightened, and his two-dimensional world expanded into three. Like it was supposed to be.

As soon as Beat let go of Melody's hand, the tip of a blade dug into his chest and twisted. Immediately, he wanted to thread their fingers back together, but he forced himself to keep both hands on his phone, instead, tapping out a message to his friends without really processing any of what he was saying.

Minutes later, when they reached the venue, he was relieved to see a security team of half a dozen men waiting for them just beyond the valet line. But when he climbed out of the SUV and automatically turned to help Melody from the vehicle, one of the guards performed that duty instead and his stomach shrunk in on itself. Briefly, their gazes met over the guard's shoulder and she quickly looked away, which told Beat she'd felt him withdraw on the ride over.

Of course she had.

And it was for the best, even if his stupid heart was in his mouth.

Realizing the camera was trained on his face, Beat let security sweep him and Melody toward the entrance, forcing himself to prepare for what was to come.

Nothing major. Just a little thing called Armageddon.

# Chapter Ten

*M*elody hadn't been to an event like this in a long time.

And she'd been more than happy to be left off the guest lists.

Celebrity-held charity galas were over-the-top displays of extravagance—and as soon as they pulled up to the benefit, it was obvious that this one would be no different. Lines of limousines paraded slowly along the curb, passengers alighting to an eruption of camera flashes. Garlands, heavy with blue lights and sparkly crystal icicles, were hung from the entrance of the building, fake snow fluttering down from an unseen source overhead. A frowning, long-haired musician in a tuxedo played a sexy version of "Silent Night" at the edge of the carpet.

"The theme can never be pajama party, can it?" she said, wryly, hoping to make Beat laugh.

The side of his mouth jumped subtly, but he continued to look down at his phone.

Melody wondered if it would make for great television if she hoisted up her dress and hauled ass down the avenue. Ratings spike, anyone? She'd be a meme by dessert.

It took serious restraint not to follow through on that impulse. This whole evening was scary enough, but the sudden lack of warmth coming from Beat made it terrifying.

*Relax. He's probably just nervous, too.*

After all, they were preparing to propose a reunion to his mother with, apparently, a lot of people watching. He wasn't obligated to hold her hand and rain down his golden energy on her every second of the day. Sometimes he probably turned that sunshine-level wattage off completely. What was he like in those moments?

Her chest ached with the need to know.

When a muscle leapt in Beat's cheek, Melody realized she was staring at him and quickly looked ahead. They were the sole SUV in line and . . . they'd been noticed. At first, she assumed her mind was playing tricks on her, but no. Additional camerapeople were sprinting toward the red-carpet line, along with pedestrians, phones glowing in their hands. A group of very large men in black jackets and headsets stood at the curb, waiting on their arrival. And then it was Beat and Melody's turn to step out of their vehicle and everything happened so fast, she could only put one foot in front of the other and keep moving.

Someone took her hand and helped her out of the SUV. Not Beat. This hand was thicker and all business. "It's best if we get inside quickly, ma'am."

"Just Melody is fine."

"Melody," the gruff voice said, not warming in the slightest. "Let's move."

Flashes blinded her, but she could see just enough to catch Beat's tight expression. His eyes were trained on the security guard's hand where it now gripped her elbow to hustle her forward. One of the cameramen called his name and he seemed to snap himself out of the daze, at least halfway, striding down the red carpet in front of her while frequently glancing back over his shoulder at Melody.

"Smile, Melody!" someone barked at her. "Smile over here!"

Where? She couldn't *see* anything. Too many flashes going

off. "Silent Night" was hitting its crescendo in a wild stampede of notes. Unfortunately, the combination of temporary blindness and attempting to keep her eyes open for pictures proved a hazard. A piece of artificial snow landed snack in the middle of her right eyeball and she flinched, stumbling to a stop. "The snow. It . . . it got me." She clapped a palm over her eye, waving Beat forward with her opposite hand. "Save yourself."

"Melody. Over here!"

"Sure, ignore my pain." She squinted at the row of paps. "I have a two-part question. One, does artificial snow melt? And two, would I look dashing in an eye patch?"

She was surprised to hear them laugh.

In fact . . . were they laughing *with* her? Growing up, the laughter was directed *at* her.

Maybe the fact that she couldn't see their faces was helping. But the snowflake in her eye was thankfully beginning to melt, restoring her vision, and the brief pause of flashbulbs brought the veritable sea of faces into view.

She almost tossed her cookies.

"Melody!" someone screamed, just as the security guards shuffled her forward again. "Are you single?" Two brass doors swung open, two trumpets heralded her arrival, and then she was inside, the cacophony of outdoors sounds cutting off.

"Yes," she said. "Brutally."

A low chuckle behind Melody reminded her that Joseph was hot on her trail.

She'd escaped the physical crowd, but an *online* crowd was still observing her every word and movement. She really needed to stop forgetting that.

Inside the lobby of the lavish hotel now, Melody couldn't help but marvel at her surroundings. Whoever oversaw the task of decorating tonight had kept the blue Christmas theme, the entire space lit by a glowing azure ceiling of lights. LED snowflakes danced on the walls and across the faces of guests. A string quartet played in the center of the room, greeting everyone with a refined rendition of "Silver Bells." Waiters in top hats passed through the space with trays of cranberry-colored champagne, bowing to those who took one.

Beat materialized in front of her, his gaze running over her from head to toe. Why did his hands appear to be fists in his pockets? "Are you okay?"

"Yes. Are you?"

"Yes, of course." A blinding smile spread across his face, but never quite reached his eyes. "Although in all the excitement, I forgot that tonight was a masquerade." He held up a slim, black velvet mask in between his middle and forefinger. "Good thing we offer spares at the door."

Melody watched as the other guests in the lobby started donning their masks, obviously having waited until they'd been photographed to put them on.

"Ah yes, the classic holiday masquerade theme." Melody took the mask he offered and slipped it over her head, arranging it in place across her eyes. "The season wouldn't be complete without one."

"If only there was a mask to keep me from being disinherited."

Melody laughed. "On a scale of one to ten, how ready are you for this?"

One of his cheeks inflated with air while he considered the question. "Three point five," he answered, cheek deflating.

"That's higher than I expected."

"I just shotgunned two glasses of cranberry champagne," he explained, indicating one of the waiters nearby. "And then I turned around and you weren't behind me anymore."

"There was a drive-by snowing outside and I was the unfortunate victim. I hope your survivor's guilt doesn't keep you awake at night."

That dazzling quality of his smile was beginning to spread back into his soulful eyes and she cheered it on with every bone in her body. Was she responsible for the shift? It . . . seemed so? Apart from bocce games and the occasional work interaction, Melody kept to herself. In the past, nothing she did in public was right. Every movement, every outfit, every word out of her mouth had apparently been cringe-inducing. Was it possible that was no longer the case?

Beat started to say something to her, but a man approached, also in a top hat. "Can I take your coat, miss?"

"Oh, sure."

She popped out the buttons and shrugged off the garment, giving a cursory, downward glance to be certain her boobs were still strapped in correctly, then handed over the coat to the attendant with a murmured thank-you.

She caught the tail end of Beat looking at her breasts, before he cleared his throat hard and averted his gaze. Just not quick enough to quell the chain reaction that started at the top of her head, earlobes throbbing, mouth turning dry, before moving downward to her belly where a hot, liquid pool began churning in a circular current.

This was not the time or the place to be turned on.

Tell that to her Beat-specific hormones, though. They rose most dramatically to one occasion and he was standing in front of her in a tuxedo and now, a very rakish mask had been added to the mix. *He'd checked out her boobs.* Her libido was just expected to remain calm?

"H-how are we going to play this?"

Beat must have noticed the breathless quality of her voice, because he looked back at her sharply, that warmth fleeing from his eyes once again. Like it had in the SUV. Why?

"We'll have to improvise to get Octavia alone and it won't be easy. Everyone wants to speak to her at these things. It'll have to be sometime after the wish ceremony."

"What is a wish ceremony and how do I get one?"

A grin briefly parted his lips. "We hold this party every year and the wishes have become something of a ritual," he explained. "There is a big table inside, beneath the fifteen-foot Christmas tree, and it's loaded with wish cards. It's tradition for everyone in attendance to write out a wish and hang it on the tree. I choose one halfway through the evening and Octavia makes it come true. Of course, I'm under strict instruction to pick one that begs my mother to entertain us with a song." His lips twitched with fondness. "Then she says no and claims she's had too much champagne, everyone begs harder and finally, finally, she gets up and sings the song she's probably been practicing since August."

"You don't seem annoyed by this at all."

"No." He lifted a shoulder and seemed to search for the right words. "Everyone has a vice they need to satisfy, right? Hers is vanity. A need to be in the spotlight. And it's harmless. It's not hurting anybody. On the contrary. Everyone enjoys it."

"God. I wish I understood my mother like you understand yours," Melody said, resisting the constant need to step closer to Beat. Even the simple brush of her elbow against his tuxedo jacket would have sufficed. Was he avoiding eye contact with her? It seemed like it; something felt off, but what could it be? "What's *your* vice, Beat?"

Well, that was one way to make eye contact.

His attention shot to hers like a bullet, tension bracketing his mouth.

The golden pallor of his skin lost its glow, leaving an ashen complexion behind.

"I . . . what?" He reached for another glass of champagne off a passing tray. "Clearly, it's drinking." But he made no move to sip the drink, merely staring into its fizzy depths. "My vice is not telling anyone about my vice. I guess that falls under the category of pride."

Melody wasn't expecting that answer. "Why don't you tell anyone? How bad can it be?"

"It's not bad. It's just private." His attention briefly fell to her lips. "What about you, Mel? What's your vice?"

"Refusing to call my super to fix anything in my apartment because I want to be his favorite. I think that's a cross between sloth and greed."

He shook his head. "It's neither. It's . . . Melody."

"I'm not a vice."

"You could be." Had his voice gotten deeper? "Easily." Melody sincerely hoped he couldn't see the pulse racing at the bottom of her neck, because she could definitely feel it thrumming dramatically. "They're probably getting ready to open the doors to the ballroom," Beat said, clearing his throat. "Should we—"

"Mel, can I grab you for a second?" Danielle said, coming up beside her.

By now, the lobby was full enough of guests waiting for the gala to begin that Danielle had no choice but to stand close. The producer sent a semianxious smile in Beat's direction, leading Melody in an awkward sidestep through a few of the partygoers until they were standing approximately ten feet from Beat—who watched them curiously, still not drinking the champagne in his hand.

"What is it?" Melody asked Danielle.

"Turn your mic off." With a swallow, Danielle looked down at her phone, thumb blurring as she scrolled. Melody stared for a moment, then reached back to do as instructed, compressing the tiny box between her thumb and index finger. "I just want to be honest with you, the broadcast is seeing a steep incline of viewers. It's impossible to predict what will catch their interest, what they will latch onto . . ."

Melody's stomach started to gurgle. "What have they latched onto?"

Danielle blew out a stiff breath. "We're trending under the hashtag #MelodyIsABeatSimp." She threw a concerned glance at Melody, went back to scrolling. "That's only one of them, mind you! There are also, #DriveBySnowing and #EyepatchQueen."

"Seriously? Based on something I said ten *minutes* ago?"

"This is moving at the speed of light. I cannot stress that enough."

"I can't . . . wow." Melody was winded. She didn't really care about how quickly the internet could turn something into an inside joke but was desperately trying to focus on the phenomenon of it all, because otherwise she would have to acknowledge . . . #MelodyIsABeatSimp. Oh no. Oh God. "So . . . the main draw is . . ."

"At this very moment? Your obvious crush on Beat," Danielle finished, finally locking her phone. "There is a clip of you circulating from the dressing room. You're talking about him and . . . it's obvious there is something there." Melody started to turn around to look at Beat through fresh eyes, now that she'd been dealt the blow of this humiliating information, but Danielle stopped her with a hand on her arm. "I'm telling you this off camera, because I truly don't think you're aware of how you look at him. Or speak about him. And while my job is to grab views, I like you. I'm giving you a heads-up, in case you want to . . . temper yourself."

"Thank you," Melody managed, her voice just above a whisper.

It was no longer a mystery why Beat had put up a wall between them. He had been looking at his phone on the ride to the gala, occasionally pressing the speaker to his ear. He'd clearly seen and heard her gushing about him, like a lovesick schoolgirl.

He didn't feel the same. Obviously. *Obviously.*

Why would he? Not only was he leaps and bounds out of her league, but he also hadn't spent the last fourteen years pining over a romanticized version of her. She was the anomaly here, just like she'd always been.

Danielle stepped closer, settling a hand on her arm. "Mel—"

"Thanks for letting me know," Melody interrupted, stepping back and bumping into something. "Oh! I'm sorry."

The blond man she'd collided with did a half turn. "It's—" His gaze widened slightly beneath his mask. "It's fine. Tight quarters in here, isn't it?"

"Yes."

"Mic back on, Mel," Danielle called.

"Right." Melody did as she was told, even though her fingers were numb. Was her face visibly boiling? Felt like it. Felt like she'd dipped it in a bowl of melted candle wax. She told herself not to look over at Beat, but she couldn't help it. Eyebrows drawn, he stared at her over the heads of the milling crowd, as if to ask what Danielle had wanted. What was she going to tell him? Ugh, didn't he already *know?*

"They've opened the doors," said the blond man, offering her his arm. "May I escort you in? My date has gotten lost in the wilds of the women's bathroom." He winked at her. "*Platonic* date."

Melody really didn't want to link arms with this man. Not after he'd winked and emphasized the word "platonic." Yuck. But she was also a balloon broken free of its bunch in that moment, and she needed something on which to tie her string. Moreover, she wanted to let Beat off the hook. He was probably dreading having to escort her in himself and she didn't want to make him do that. Nor did she want to spawn any more hashtags with her embarrassing display of affection for someone she'd met for approximately six minutes as a teenager.

"Sure," she said quickly, hooking her arm through the stranger's.

Up ahead, the entrance to the ballroom beckoned, the graceful swell of more stringed instruments reaching out from within. Once again, she tried to avoid making eye contact with Beat, but he was standing in their path and despite the crowd surging around him, he remained still, watching her approach on the man's arm. Vaguely, she was aware of the camera that was fastened on the proceedings and wondered what the actual hell she'd been thinking saying yes to a live streamed reality show in the first place. Half a day into the process and she'd already exposed herself. Reverted straight back into an awkward teenager.

They drew even with Beat, and Melody craned her neck, as if admiring the shimmering garland framing the ballroom entrance. Just keep walking. Just keep walking—

"Mel," Beat said, his laugh humorless, his focus far too intent on her face, which had to be the color of a plum tomato. "You ditching me or what?"

Before she could answer, the blond man stuck out his left hand to Beat. "Beat Dawkins. I thought that was you. How have you been, buddy?"

Mel watched in fascination as Beat straightened his shoulders and executed the handshake, his mouth arranging itself into a winning smile. "Can't complain, Rick. How about you? How is that drive coming along?"

"Mastered it, thanks to my golf pro." He shook his finger at Beat. "I'll get you back out on the green one of these days. Come to the club as my guest."

"You mean, your victim? Not if I can help it."

Rick threw back his head and laughed, briefly removing his attention from Beat. In that tiny sliver of time, Beat's smile dropped like a boulder into a pond. He flicked a glance down at Melody's arm, still entwined with Rick's, then at her face.

Finally, his smile engaged itself again.

"Listen, Rick, thanks for finding my date for me." He extended a hand toward Melody. "Do you need some help finding yours . . . ?"

Oh. Rick was *shook*. He lurched slightly, opened his mouth and closed it.

Apparently, they'd stepped outside the circle of social niceties.

Was interrupting a man midescort simply not done?

Mel really didn't care about the unspoken rules; she was more intent on saving a scrap of self-respect. Beat shouldn't have to suffer through her unwanted adoration. "Beat, it's fine. I'm not your date."

"Since when, Mel? We came here together." He shot a narrow look over her shoulder. "What did Danielle need to tell you?"

"Nothing important."

He studied her. "I think you're fibbing."

"Why?"

"Your right foot is digging into your left ankle."

"I'm . . ." Melody looked down, seeing that she did, indeed, have all her weight balanced on her left foot, her right toe smashing into her opposite ankle. "I had no idea I did this when I lie."

"*Aha.* I knew it." Under his breath, she thought he said, "I'm fucked."

But she couldn't be sure.

Melody placed both feet firmly on the ground, growing increasingly desperate for that scrap of pride. If she couldn't come by it through avoidance, she could at least tell the truth. "Fine. She let me know that . . . the internet has decided I have an . . . affinity for you. A crush, for lack of a better term. They have focused in on it, what with their hashtags and things. She wanted to let me know that . . ."

Beat had rocked back on his heels. "Let you know what?"

She glanced anxiously at the camera, its red light flashing, and dropped her voice to a pained whisper. "That I was being obvious about it."

*Oh, good Lord.*

She'd done that. She'd just admitted her crush to her crush. Out loud.

For the whole internet to see.

Surprisingly, Melody didn't immediately want to find a dark corner to wrap herself in the fetal position and shame-spiral until the sun came up. The admission was almost . . . freeing. Like she'd been running with a parachute strapped to her back, but someone—no, she herself—had finally reached back and snipped the strings.

"Uhhh," Rick said. "I think I see my date."

*Rick* was still there?

Yes. Not only that, she had his arm in a death grip.

Loosen. *Loosen.*

"Sorry," Melody murmured, setting the blond golfer loose.

Beat still hadn't moved, his jaw bunched as he looked down at her. Eyes unreadable.

She forced herself not to look away, but the fetal position was becoming more inviting.

"I'll just see you in there—"

"We should talk," Beat interrupted.

"We really don't have to talk about it. The . . ."

"Your crush on me."

She gulped. "Yes."

"We *do* need to talk about it." He wet his lips. "You . . . it's complicated, Mel."

"I super don't want the 'it's complicated' talk."

"This isn't the typical 'it's complicated' talk. We're not typical."

"You mean, *I'm* not," she blurted.

His eyebrows slashed together. "*What?*"

The camera was two feet away. They both seemed to realize it at the same moment, her brain engaging just in time to snap her mouth shut, Beat visibly shaking himself. "Come on. We have some time before my mother makes her grand entrance." He gave Joseph a pointed look. "No cameras allowed on the dance floor."

Before Melody knew what was happening, Beat took her hand and pulled her through the entrance into the ballroom—and she couldn't help but marvel at her surroundings for a second. The room had been transformed into a veritable winter palace, cast in silver and gold hues, several large sculptures in the shapes of snowflakes hanging from the ceiling, lights twinkling, champagne glasses clinking. The tables were garnished with lush holly wreaths and hurricane candleholders that flickered and glowed. Tasteful, elegant perfection.

Her mother would have hated it.

It took Melody several beats to realize she was being pulled into the center of the dance floor—where no one else was dancing. Like, zero.

"Oh. No. I don't think so. I don't need all these witnesses when I accidentally kill you. The coroner will determine you died from a freak accident. 'The high heel went straight through the sole of his foot, John. Death by stiletto.'"

Beat sent her an amused glance over his shoulder. "Who is John?"

"The coroner's plucky assistant."

"Obviously." Beat turned on a dime and trapped her with an arm around her waist, his public smile tilting his lips beneath the black velvet mask. "We need to talk off camera. This is the best way to do it, okay? Do you know how to turn off your mic?"

"Do you think Danielle wants us to turn them off right now?"

"I don't care."

"Right." She reached back and pressed the button on the battery pack for the third time in under ten minutes. "It's off."

"Mine too." He shook her a little, his attention straying to her breasts, before returning to her face resolutely, though . . . were his eyes slightly glazed? "Loosen up, Melody. I've got you."

"Oh. Full name. He means business." The raw kick of his cologne invaded her nose. She gave into the urge to memorize it. The masculine notes of charcoal and sage and black licorice. Darker than she would have imagined for Beat. "You're making a big deal out of nothing. I swear, I'm not suffering from some delusion that you're going to be my boyfriend. It's just a holdover from my youth, I guess you could say?"

No. She was selling the whole thing short.

*You've come this far, why not let the whole truth out?*

And it wasn't merely that being honest released the pressure she'd been housing in her chest for a decade and a half, but she trusted Beat. Trusting Beat was like a built-in mechanism she couldn't remember being installed. For some reason, that faith in him had always been there. Maybe she'd been born with it.

"Okay, here's the truth. I don't date very often. Lately, not at all. You understand what it's like to grow up with a famous parent, you never know if someone is in it for you. Or if they just want a good story. 'I dated Trina Gallard's daughter.' You know?" They were moving, but not really. Swaying to the swelling of strings, without bothering to turn in a circle. Beat was staring at her mouth, as if concentrating hard on the words that were coming out—and she couldn't have imagined a better reaction to what she was saying.

Listening. He was listening. "When I met you a million years ago, I was right in the middle of a hard time. I was just this awkward presence bumbling around, being nothing like my badass mother. I was a disappointment. But you treated me like . . . a person. A real person who was going through the same thing as you. Or have I overblown the whole thing in my head?"

"No," he said, voice rusted. "You haven't."

Relief grew like branches in her veins, straight into her fingertips where they rested on his broad shoulders. "Thank you."

"Jesus, Mel. You have nothing to thank me for."

"Okay." They were being careful to keep their bodies a centimeter apart, but her nipples were slowly drawing into tight points, as if attempting to reach out and brush his chest. His firm hands gripped her waist, thumbs resting on the points of her hips. She had to bite her tongue to keep from requesting that he dig them in. Just once. Just so she could know what it felt like. But that wouldn't be right. "Beat, my attraction to you isn't your responsibility."

When he made a frustrated sound and leaned down to speak against her ear, Mel could only hold her breath, the room pausing around her. "I'm grateful for the way you feel about me, Mel. It's a beautiful thing. But . . . ah . . ." He seemed to search for the right words. "Now it's my turn to point out how we were raised. To keep things quiet. Private. I was taught that trusting people, even friends, could ultimately hurt my family, so I've probably taken my privacy too far. My romantic life . . . my *sex* life, I should say . . ." He exhaled hard. "It's something I keep separate from everything. Everyone."

Melody's world shrunk down into that moment, like she'd gone from his big, noisy ballroom to huddling under a blanket fort with him in the dark. What exactly did he mean? *How* did he keep his romantic life separate? "Beat—"

Trumpets.

So many trumpets blared at once.

They went off in every corner of the ballroom, making it impossible to talk. To hear.

Beat's lips twisted wryly, mouthing a single word.

*Octavia.*

Mel quarter turned just in time to watch her mother's former bandmate enter the ballroom to thunderous applause.

On a throne.

Being carried by four large men dressed as swans.

# Chapter Eleven

*B*eat's fucking heart was pumping in his throat.

He'd come so close to telling Melody everything. What would have been her reaction? He found himself craving it, even as he stuffed the information back down into its box, sealing the lid shut with a blowtorch. Every eye in the ballroom was on the spectacle taking place in front of them, but he couldn't tear his gaze from Melody to save the world.

*Beat, my attraction to you isn't your responsibility.*

Christ, his body disagreed. Vehemently.

His fingertips had no purpose because they hadn't traced that collarbone. Or the soft swell of her tits. He wanted to drag a hand up her throat, bury it in her hair, and beg her . . .

To withhold pleasure from him.

Until he was fucking shaking.

He wanted to take her into a dark corner and kiss her mouth while she stroked the front of his trousers, but never let him come. It would feel *incredible.* That wouldn't be happening, though. He'd been keeping his interests behind closed doors since he turned sixteen.

What would happen *if* he told her, though? *I enjoy being brought to the brink of pleasure and left there.* That he refused to let himself be completely vulnerable with anyone—at least at the end of the act? What would she say? What if she trusted him enough to go there with him?

God, she might.

But two things were holding him back. One, he was keeping the blackmail a secret from her. Touching Melody without full honesty between them . . . bothered him. A lot. And two, he wasn't sure he'd be able to hold a goddamn thing back from Melody in bed. She wouldn't just be another partner. There could . . . no, there *would* be something deeper and more meaningful here than his usual hookup. He wasn't even sure he knew *how* to let go with someone like that. Completely. Start to finish. Could he even go there considering the secret he was keeping from her?

Until he figured it out, he needed to keep Melody at a proper distance.

A feat that was growing harder by the second.

And they would be spending *a lot* more time together.

Beat dragged a hand down his face, lifting it to return a wave from his mother. Despite the golden mask she was wearing, he didn't miss the way Octavia tilted her head, pinning Melody with an analyzing look. Like she was searching for a resemblance to Trina. Or maybe Octavia was simply stunned to see Melody's back pressed to his chest, Beat's hands on her waist. He forcibly stepped back now, suffering through Melody's resulting shiver.

They weren't on a date. He needed to stop acting like they were.

Feeling like they were.

Beat's dates were usually private and had more of a transactional nature.

Finally, the trumpets died down and his mother was helped from her throne by one of the human swans. She noticed the camera hovering at the edge of the dance floor and gave an exaggerated eye roll, before smiling conspiratorially at her rapt audience. "Let the party commence," she purred, eliciting whistles and applause from the crowd. Someone handed her a glass of champagne in a special golden goblet and off she went, working the crowd like a fairy granting audiences to commoners.

The ballroom eased back into motion, crowds gathering around high-top tables, other couples making their way out onto the dance floor. Now that Octavia had made her entrance, the lights were gradually dimming and the classical music was being replaced with a sexier beat to inspire dancing. Even early in the evening, guests were happy to oblige.

Melody turned, blinking up at him. "Wow. Your mother really just rolled up into this joint like Cleopatra."

Beat chuckled, a sense of camaraderie he rarely allowed himself to experience making his ribs expand.

Shit. He liked Melody. A lot. And he could tell she wanted to dig into the conversation they'd been having before his mother arrived. It was right there in the slight pinch of her brow. But he wasn't surprised that she could read his reticence to return there. They had a way of communicating without words.

They shifted at the same time. Regrouped.

"Where is your father?" she asked.

"He waits until the fanfare dies down and then he slips in through the side door, holding a brandy snifter and wearing the ugliest Christmas sweater he can find."

"You're joking. Does your mother hate it?"

"On the contrary. She loves it."

Melody gasped. "Why?"

Beat shrugged. "He lets her shine."

Whoa. His voice came very close to catching on that last word. It wasn't unusual for him to talk about the love he had for his parents. But their happiness wasn't usually hanging in the balance. Or resting on his shoulders, as it were, along with the truth that could destroy them as a family.

As if on cue, his phone started vibrating in his pocket. Of course, it could be his friends watching the live stream and wanting to pepper him with questions, which would only be natural. Intuition told Beat his blackmailer was calling, though. He always seemed to find the most inopportune moments to take a swing at him—and this would definitely be one of them—the gala benefiting the charity he and his parents put so much work and love into.

"Hey, Beat!" called a familiar voice as they passed on the dance floor.

He tore his eyes off Melody and waved at Ursula Paige, an up-and-coming opera singer and one of their past scholarship recipients. "Ursula." He nodded, quickly shaking hands with the performer's date. "Happy Holidays. Nice to see you both."

"I would say it's nice to see you, too, but . . ." Ursula pulled out her phone and shook it around a little. "I've *been* seeing you. All over the damn place."

"Right." Beat breathed a laugh, settled a hand on Melody's back. "Then I guess you've met my . . ." His what? The sentence trailed off into silence, three sets of ears waiting for him to finish. His friend? His costar? His . . . what? "My Melody," he said, trying to laugh off the blunder.

No one said anything for long, torturous seconds. Melody looked down at her dress.

Beat stared at an escaped strand of hair by her cheek, wondering if he should tuck it behind her ear for her.

Ursula elbowed her date hard in the ribs. "No offense, but we're going to stop talking to you now, so we can keep watching you."

"What are: phrases that sum up 2023," Melody mumbled,

answering in *Jeopardy!* format. And tucking that strand of hair back on her own. *Damn.*

Ursula and her date laughed, high-fiving Melody. "Oh my God, Melody. The internet is so right to be in love with you. You're *hilarious.*"

Melody's nose wrinkled. "The internet what?"

The pair only laughed harder.

Beat and Melody exchanged a lost expression, but there was an odd gurgle in Beat's stomach. Was the internet falling in love with Melody? Of course it was. And he didn't have any right to feel the sharp prickle of possessiveness, but there it was. He liked the world having access to her even less than he'd been expecting, which wasn't fair. He didn't have any claim on Melody, despite what every fiber of his being seemed intent on telling him.

"Don't worry, Beat. There are already several campaigns underway on your behalf." Ursula thumbed through her phone. "One to make you the next James Bond and another to elect you as president of this puss—" She snapped her mouth shut. "Sorry, I should have read that one all the way through before saying it out loud."

Melody snorted. "I'm so glad you didn't."

Beat felt the urge to smile. Even as the phone continued to buzz relentlessly in his pocket. "Would I secure your vote as the next president of pussy?" he asked Melody.

"Your name is Beat." She gave an exaggerated wink. "You're a *natural fit.*"

A laugh cracked in his throat. "Your mind is a dumpster. I had no idea."

Melody pointed at Ursula. "She's obviously a bad influence."

"Okay, sorry, we are *so* going on a double date," Ursula decided. "When this reality show is over, obviously."

"Oh, we're not . . ." Melody started, making a rapid gesture between them.

*Help her out.* Why didn't he want to? "We're . . ." What? "Friends."

That word tasted like expired pastrami in his mouth.

"Right," Melody agreed, her smile serene. "Friends."

The expired pastrami turned to dust.

"Uh-huh." Ursula's dude spoke for the first time, his demeanor clearly skeptical. "We'll see you soon for that double date."

When the couple walked away, Beat and Melody snuck each other sidelong glances.

After a few tense seconds, she laughed. "Can you imagine if the relationship our mothers manifested by giving us these names *actually* came to fruition? They would need to be sedated."

Beat said, "That's one way to guarantee a reunion—a wedding."

She laughed. Because he was so clearly joking.

Was this bow tie extra tight, or what?

A waiter stopped in front of them and Beat plucked a glass off the silver tray, handing it to Melody, since he was still holding a full glass of now piss-warm champagne. As soon as the waiter departed again, she held up her flute. "I just want you to know that I'm glad we're friends." He followed the progress of her blush, all the way to the tips of her ears. "I'm content with friendship. Okay? I hope . . . all this crush stuff won't make things weird. Is there a chance that maybe you could forget you ever found out?"

He thought about it. He really did.

Whether or not he could put on blinders and pretend Melody wasn't attracted to him . . . well, he decided that if a man could forget that this woman felt *anything* for him, that man would be a waste of a human being. Still, he didn't want her to be embarrassed around him. He wanted her to be comfortable.

"What crush?" he said, resisting the urge to rub at his windpipe.

Melody blinked several times, attempted a smile, then gave up and ducked her head. Shit. Had he been too flippant?

"Mr. Dawkins!" A frazzled young man in a headset skidded to a stop between Beat and Melody. "I'm Lee. Assistant to the party planner. I've been looking everywhere for you."

"Here I am, Lee," he murmured, still watching Melody closely. "What's up?"

"Your mother has decided to do the wish ceremony early this year."

Beat reared back slightly. "When did she do that?"

"Eight minutes and thirty seconds ago," panted Lee. "Would you come with me? We have lighting and audio on standby."

"Sure." Over Lee's shoulder, he mouthed *Be right back* at Melody.

Melody saluted him. "You've got a very brief window before I track down the shrimp."

He pointed at her. "As long as you wait for me to eat dessert."

"I'll prawn-der it."

How was it possible to be having fun in this moment? The phone in his pocket still buzzed periodically, reminding Beat he was being blackmailed, he was minutes from formally requesting a Steel Birds reunion *on camera*, and he was still worried he'd been too dismissive of Melody's feelings for him. Yet here he stood, chuckling over shrimp puns.

"Mr. Dawkins, we really need to move."

Still, he hesitated. "Right."

Suddenly, his hand moved of its own accord, reaching for Melody's. Before Beat could analyze his own decision-making, they were following Lee, hand in hand. All because Beat didn't want to spend a few minutes away from her. Wow. "You're taking me down with you? I thought we were friends!"

"You wanted a wish ceremony, right? Here's your chance." He squeezed her hand. "Don't worry, I'll do the talking."

"That was never in question. When I'm getting ready to take my turn on bocce nights, my nervous system just assumes I'm addressing the entire nation. Have you ever heard knees knocking? Mine actually tap out 'pathetic' in Morse code. And I don't even *know* Morse code."

A familiar, deep chuckle sounded behind them and they simultaneously realized they were being trailed through the crowd by Joseph, their conversation recorded. "Do you two mind putting your mics back on? Danielle is screaming in my ear."

"Sorry." Melody winced, reaching back to press the button.

Beat did the same.

A fifteen-foot Douglas fir towered beside a wide, sweeping staircase. Along with the gentle glow of gold and perfectly spaced ornaments, little white notecards decorated the fragrant branches. As Beat led Melody up the stairs, he scanned the cards and stumbled upon one requesting that Octavia sing them a song almost immediately, snatching it up between his middle and index finger. "Got one."

"Holy Hannah, you're really bringing me up here in front of everyone."

A tremor moved through her fingers. *Distract her.*

"I'm coming to one of your bocce games, Mel," Beat said in a lower voice.

"You most certainly are not."

"What are the team colors? For body paint reasons."

She shook against him with laughter. "Pink."

Beat winced. "That's fucking unfortunate, but okay."

"Nope. You won't do it."

His lips spread into a smile. "You are dead wrong."

Midway up the staircase, they turned and faced the crowd, side by side, Lee pressing a microphone into Beat's hand and reminding him to wait for the spotlight.

"*Spotlight?*" Melody squeaked.

"Fair warning, Peach," Beat said, clearing debris from his throat.

God, he loved calling her Peach. The way it made her blush, exactly like the fruit in question, was addicting. "When the spotlight comes on, it's a little startling. It's just . . . *pop*."

"Pop. Got it." She lifted her chin. "I'm ready."

The room went black.

A laserlike beam burst onto them from across the ballroom, hitting them like a sucker punch—and it propelled Mel straight backward, her ass landing on a higher step.

"*Mel*."

"Wow," she whispered. "You undersold that a little."

Beat dropped the microphone, sending a squeal of feedback through the room while helping Mel to her feet. "Are you okay?" He turned her slightly to observe the impact point, not really stopping to think about how the *impact point* was her *rear end*. "Does it hurt?"

"My butt? No, it's just startled." She squeezed her eyes closed. "I mean, *I* was just startled. Not my butt."

Laughter rang through the ballroom.

Apparently, the handheld mic was picking up every word out of their mouths, to say nothing of the smaller ones strapped to their bodies.

"I think I'll just hide back here for a while."

Melody sidestepped behind him, earning another laugh from their audience. Beat looked out over the sea of faces, but it took him a moment to summon the words that normally came to him easily. Had he been selfish to bring Melody up here? Sure, she'd agreed to appear on a live television show in front of an unknown number of people, but maybe being able to *see* a crowd in front of her was too much? He struggled against the need to turn around and reassure himself she was all right, but wouldn't he merely be drawing *more* attention to her?

Beat bent down as quickly as possible to pick up the dropped mic, swallowed, and forced a smile onto his face. The one everybody was accustomed to seeing on him. "Good evening, friends, and happy holidays. On behalf of the Ovations family, myself and my parents, Octavia and Rudy Dawkins, we thank you for being here tonight and your generosity toward the scholarship fund."

To everyone in this room, to everyone watching the live stream, he was the furthest thing from a mess. But secretly, that's what he was, right? A mess. He used to be capable of getting through these public appearances without that fact screaming in his ear, but the performance was getting harder—

Melody laid a hand on his back. *There you go. Easy.*

No one knew about the half dozen threatening voice mails on his phone.

No one knew how he liked to be punished for everything in life coming so easy. For never being told no or deprived of anything.

Air filled his lungs and he forced his smile wider.

"In keeping with tradition, Octavia will be granting one of your wishes this evening. I can't imagine what it will be . . ."

A knowing ripple of amusement went through the guests.

On cue, the crowd parted, and his mother made her way toward the staircase, a second spotlight encapsulating her in a hazy glow—and if he wasn't mistaken, the lighting was a lot more flattering than the one glaring down on him and Melody. He couldn't help but laugh at that.

Octavia's expression wasn't as indulgent as usual, however.

It was curiosity laced with dread—and Melody, who was now in a full body press against his back, her hand twisted in the tail of his tuxedo jacket, was the focus. His mother craned her neck to get a look at Melody, her brow quirking higher. She looked at Beat as if to say, *Excuse me, are you sleeping with the enemy?*

If only.

With a deep breath, Beat raised the mic. "This year's wish is for—"

"A Steel Birds reunion," someone shouted in the crowd.

Applause and whistles ripped across the ballroom like wildfire. And then the chanting started.

# Chapter Twelve

Re-u-nite! Re-u-nite!"

Still in her hiding spot behind Beat, Melody's mouth dropped open. It appeared the crowd was doing their job for them? The public's investment in a reunion had been increasing for months now. Was it possible the live stream had spurred that interest even further? *Already?*

Melody peeked around the side of Beat's shoulder to gauge Octavia's reaction to the chanting guests and was once again struck by the vast differences between Beat's mother and Trina. Trina would already be kicking over tables or storming the stage, while Octavia's expression was a mask of absolute calm, her hands folded neatly at her waist.

Melody had once watched a cable television documentary about Steel Birds titled *A Flight of Fancy*. In one of the interview segments, the former band manager claimed that Octavia Dawkins couldn't be rattled. *Nothing* caught the lead singer off guard. A rotisserie chicken had once been tossed onstage and she'd ripped off a leg midair and chomped into it, without missing a lyric, which had to be the most badass thing Melody had ever heard. *She* definitely would have been knocked unconscious by a flying chicken. No question.

Man, Melody envied that kind of cool.

The kind on display now.

Octavia was a golden goddess in a Grecian-style gown, trimmed in crimson lace, her dark hair in a twist atop her head. She *pulsed* with presence, surrounded by a rapt, now eerily silent audience, and there wasn't so much as a tick behind her eye. "Beat, darling, please read the *correct* wish," she finally called.

The chants returned and only swelled in volume then, swallowing up whatever Beat said into the microphone. Octavia tossed an indulgent laugh at the enthusiastic crowd, one that said, *Ha-ha, very funny, but there is not a chance in hell.* And then she began to ascend the staircase like a queen preparing to address the population. The hand Beat was using to hold the microphone dropped to his side, and he sighed, obviously waiting for his mother to put an end to their mission before it even got off the ground.

His resignation kicked something into gear within Melody.

She couldn't just *hide* back here. Octavia was going to take the mic, disregard the idea of a reunion, and their first—maybe only?—attempt at making it happen was going to be wasted. Perhaps Beat wasn't ready to confide in Melody *why* exactly he needed the million dollars so badly, but the point was, he did. She'd agreed to this live stream to help him—*and* help herself. She wanted independence? Remaining in the background wasn't an option.

Before Octavia could reach them in the center of the staircase, Melody stepped out from behind Beat and removed her mask. Based on the room's reaction, half of them already knew her identity—thanks to *Wreck the Halls*—and the other half were only more confused.

Octavia paused midstep and slowly removed her own mask. "It stands to reason that the first time I lay eyes on you, you're crashing my party. Like mother like daughter, I suppose."

*Now* the other half of the ballroom was up to speed, gasps abounding.

"Hi. Hello, Mrs. Dawkins. This isn't how I pictured us meeting. I mean, I never expected us to meet, really, but definitely not at a party where you've been carried in by a bank of swans. That's what you call them when they're in a group. A bank. Unless they're in the water, in which case, it's a bevy."

Her cheeks warmed and she glanced up to find Beat watching her with a bemused smile. "This has been swan talk with Melody Gallard," he said.

Her chest loosened. Not quite enough to laugh, not with every eye in the joint trained on her, but something inside of her relaxed. "Um." With an effort, she stopped staring into Beat's sparkling blue eyes and shifted her focus to Octavia once more. "Like I said, it's so nice to meet you. I'm a big fan, like everyone else. Could we . . ."

*Talk privately.* That's what she was going to say. But . . .

*Oh no.*

A terrible idea occurred to her. Or perhaps, a glorious one.

Saying it out loud was probably going to be a huge mistake.

But it was one of those moments where the impossible seemed possible. This idea was the one chance to save humanity in the *Avengers: End Game*, as predicted by Doctor Strange. It might be their only hope of actually making this reunion happen and for some reason, maybe because she was currently looking a legendary rock star in the eye, Melody suddenly wanted very much to make the Steel Birds reunion a reality. She wanted to have this success with Beat. She wanted it for everyone on the planet. Maybe she'd been laughing at the idea for so long she'd never stopped to consider how *happy* it would make billions of people.

And wow, the fact that they had the responsibility in their hands was a rush of power.

Since when did she enjoy rushes of power?

*Just say it.* Before this little squiggle of time passed them by.

"I'm here because my mother, Trina Gallard, wants to reunite the band."

She sensed Beat's jaw dropping.

Octavia jolted.

Had Melody just rattled the unshakable lead singer?

"Rotisserie chickens have nothing on me," she murmured.

Beat made a choked sound. "I never know what's going to come out of your mouth."

"Me either."

"I'm sorry," Octavia said, coming closer. "Did you say that Trina wants to *reunite*?"

Camera phone flashes were going off at the speed of light. Melody thought of her mother, holed up in her New Hampshire hippie compound, shunning the outside world, including television and the internet. She no longer had a manager or an agent to relay news to her. The chances were extremely high that Trina knew nothing about *Wreck the Halls* and wouldn't see this moment unfolding. Thank goodness.

"Yes, that is what I said."

"What have you done?" Beat whispered to her out of the side of his mouth.

"This is improv," she whispered back. "At least, I think it's improv. I was too afraid to take the classes. Or ask for a refund."

His sides started to shake.

Octavia regarded their interaction like a scientist peering through a microscope. "How much time have you two been spending together exactly?" She sounded fascinated, speaking almost to herself. "I'll admit, I've always wondered if you two would . . . click."

Beat cleared his throat. "Maybe we could continue this conversation privately?"

"No need." Octavia's laugh carried across the stone silent ballroom. "There isn't enough Botox in New York to erase the kind of wrinkles Trina's presence would give me." She waved an elegant hand at Melody. "No offense, darling."

"None taken. She could overwrinkle a shar-pei."

A guffaw burst out of Octavia. "Oh God, you just had to be adorable, didn't you? I'm going to hate telling you no."

"So don't," Beat said. "Hear us out."

Applause and whistles broke out around the ballroom. When the sound continued to escalate, Beat pulled Melody into his side and partially blocked her from view, ignoring the cameraman's signal to bring her back into the shot. Melody was so caught off guard by the protective gesture that she almost missed Octavia's interested head tilt.

"Oh dear . . ." muttered the former rock princess, sauntering back down the stairs and indicating a doorway into the adjoining coatroom. "Fine. I suppose I will hear you out, before I decline. But only because it's Christmas."

"That's the spirit," Melody said, starting to follow Octavia. But she was brought up short by Beat circling an arm around her shoulder, keeping her glued to his side.

He leaned down, brushing his lips against her forehead in what seemed like an unconscious gesture. "Wait for the security team, okay?"

"We were just down there. It was fine."

"You had your mask on. And Melody, I don't think you realize you're charming the pants off everybody."

"*Me?*"

"Yes," he said, exasperated, his gaze busy scanning the crowd. "You haven't been in the public eye for a while, so maybe you don't remember how it is. Sometimes people feel like they already know you, so they act . . . overfamiliar. Just stay close to me, okay?"

Melody thought maybe Beat was being a little paranoid but agreeing to stay close didn't cost her anything. In fact, being near him was a huge reassurance in the midst of this unusual situation, so she nodded. "Sure."

The security team arrived at the bottom of the stairs and they formed sort of a pathway for Beat and Melody that allowed them to follow Octavia out of the noisy gala, into a coatroom that was large enough to qualify as a studio apartment in Manhattan. The red-jacketed attendant stared wide-eyed at the sudden intrusion of the guest of honor—and it wasn't lost on Melody that the coat check employee was watching the live stream on her phone. Melody could literally see herself on the screen and closed her gaping mouth as a result.

The attendant bolted from the room, leaving Octavia, Beat, Mel, Joseph, and Danielle, who managed to sneak in just before the security team closed the door.

"Well," Octavia began, turning on a heel and sending everyone a smile that Melody could only define as pleasantly murderous. "My annual, *famous* holiday charity bash has been hijacked. I hope you're all happy."

Beat started to speak, but Danielle launched in quickly, holding up a finger with her clipboard hand. "I don't mind taking point on this."

"And just who the fuck are you?" Octavia asked, without dimming her smile.

"Wow," Melody breathed.

Beat squeezed her hand.

"Executive producer of *Wreck the Halls*, among other shows on Applause Network. Danielle Doolin." She seemed to weigh the pros and cons of attempting to shake Octavia's hand and visibly decided against it. "It's a true pleasure to meet you."

Octavia blinked. "I'm sorry I can't say the same."

"That's fair enough."

"The badassery of the women in this room is unparalleled," Melody whispered to Beat. "I bet neither of them have ever been knocked down by a spotlight."

"That's not true, dear," Octavia said, her gaze cutting away from Danielle to land on Melody. "At the first stadium show for Steel Birds—Dallas, I believe—I was so startled by the spotlight that I tripped backward and nearly concussed myself on the drums. Those motherfuckers pack a punch." She tilted her head, her eyes tracing Beat's arm where it wrapped around Melody's waist like the harness on a roller coaster. "Son, why are you trying to squeeze the girl to death?"

Two seconds ticked by. "I don't know."

"I see." Octavia blew out a breath. "Oh Lord. Let's get on with this."

Beat cleared his throat. "As we spoke about earlier, the goal of the show is—"

The door of the coatroom flew open and in walked a man smoking a cigar in a an abominable snowman sweater with glowing LED eyes and Louis Vuitton slippers. Rudy, Beat's father. "Oh, I see, this is where the party is." He sauntered over to Octavia's side, observing everyone through mirthful blue eyes. "Why does everyone look like Santa Claus just crossed the rainbow bridge?"

"Allow me to bring you up to speed, my love." Octavia sighed, tapping her cheek and waiting for the robed man to lean over and kiss the spot noisily. "Our son is filming a reality show with Trina's daughter—wave at the camera—" He saluted it, instead, cigar ash fluttering downward. "They are on a crusade to reunite Steel Birds."

"On Christmas Eve," Danielle added. "Onstage at Rockefeller Center."

Instead of being shocked by that explanation, Rudy merely

looked impressed. "*Really*, son. How industrious of you. Where do you find the time?"

Melody watched fondness soften the lines around Beat's mouth. "Hello, Dad."

"Looking forward to the spring when we can get back out on the green. A *reality* show? Really?" He puffed his cigar. "Shame your mother would rather swim in shark-infested waters than get back onstage with Trina." He directed his next question at Melody. "How is the mistress of mayhem doing these days?"

"Still mayheming and mistressing, as far as I know," Melody answered. "I see her every February, so it has been a while."

Octavia pounced on that. "But you said she *requested* the re-union."

"Over the phone. Zoom, actually. We Zoom," Melody blurted. She knew she was doing that thing people did when they lie—adding too many details—and she couldn't help it. "She had a lovely cat eye going on last time we spoke. Yes. It was two and a half days ago when she said, 'You're right, Mel. It's time. It's time to get the band back together. It's time to shred once more.' And she cried. Right there on Zoom."

No one said anything.

Melody elbowed Beat subtly in the ribs.

"Right there on Zoom," he corroborated. "She wept. Openly."

Octavia narrowed her eyes. "That doesn't sound like Trina."

"She has changed a lot over the years. Matured like a fine wine." Now that was the biggest lie Melody had told tonight. If anything, Trina had regressed since the days of yore. "Mrs. Dawkins—"

"Oh, you might as well call me Octavia, dear." She crossed her arms delicately. "It's only fair since my son is trying his best to stuff you into his pocket."

Heat bloomed in Melody's cheeks. Beat wasn't trying to stuff her into his pocket. That was an exaggeration. Though he'd hauled her so close that only one of her feet was fully balanced on the ground. Was he simply nervous about the whole ordeal?

"Are they dating?" Beat's father asked, followed by a hearty laugh that filled the coat check closet. "Wouldn't that be a kick in the ass?"

"We're not," Melody said as quickly as possible. Mainly, because she didn't want to hear a vehement denial from Beat. She wiggled and ducked until she'd extricated herself from his hold, noticing that Beat only looked perplexed over the way he'd been hanging on to her in the first place. "We're not dating, but we are on a mutual mission."

Speaking in front of such an intimidating group made her feel as though she could break out in a million hives at any second, but Melody forged ahead. After all, she'd been the one to spout the lie about Trina requesting the reunion. She'd steered the adventure in a whole new direction, she couldn't very well let go of the wheel now, could she?

"There are thousands of people watching, Octavia," Melody started.

"Millions," Danielle corrected in a whisper.

"Millions." Melody breathed through a wave of dizziness. "They've waited—*we've* waited—thirty years for a Steel Birds reunion. Sure, there are recordings, songs that can be downloaded. But there is nothing like hearing your favorite songs live. You and Trina have the power to make it happen. To give fans that moment they've been dreaming about since ninety-three."

Beat settled a hand on the small of Melody's back. "You miss it sometimes. Don't you, Mom? The crowd belting 'Rattle the Cage' at the top of their lungs. Feeling it. You miss that long, drawn-out break before the key change. That final, blood-pumping solo."

"The rotisserie chickens," Melody murmured, pressing a hand to her heart.

"Never forget," Beat deadpanned.

A tiny, bemused laugh bubbled out of Octavia's mouth. "You know . . . when Trina and I were pregnant with you two, Stevie Nicks blessed our bellies backstage at a Rock and Roll Hall of Fame induction ceremony. Sly and Family Stone was being instated, right? Yes. And Stevie, she recited an old proverb and waved a bundle of burning sage, which she was literally carrying in the pocket of her dress, and she said the two of you would always be . . . was it protected or connected? I can't recall." She lifted a shoulder and let it drop. "Steel Birds broke up six days later. I've always wondered if she cursed us, instead."

"We could call her and find out," Danielle suggested, discreetly steering Joseph's elbow. "On camera."

Octavia scoffed. "Stevie Nicks doesn't have a *phone*."

"Wow," Melody whispered.

"Look." Octavia waved her hands. "It's almost time for my champagne toast and I *am* going to sing 'Santa motherfucking Baby' tonight, whether or not anyone wished for it . . ." She sent a sniff in Beat's direction. "Let's wrap this up. If you two manage to bring Trina to New York, I will perform *one song* with her onstage. But there will be no communication between us beforehand or afterward. This isn't going to be some big, emotional reunion where we lament the three decades we've lost being enemies and plan an international tour. If that's the ultimate goal here, you will all be sorely disappointed."

"Understood, Mom," Beat said with a nod. "One night. One song. No chitchat."

"Send it to my manager in writing, please," Octavia added, sailing for the door with a cigar-puffing Rudy in tow. "Son, I love you dearly, despite this total nonsense." She stopped midway through the exit to the ballroom where guests were already beginning to cheer over her reentry to the gala. "And Melody . . ."

"Yes?"

"Next time the spotlight lands on you, sucker-punch it back."

# Chapter Thirteen

*F*or the last hour, a lead weight had been sitting in Beat's gut.

It was a cross between dread and urgency.

Something about the way everyone at the bottom of the staircase had looked at Melody troubled him. They got it. They saw what he did. And part of Beat really enjoyed the fact that people seemed to be recognizing Melody's uniqueness. Celebrating those special quirks that made her so . . . Mel. Because it was about damn time.

The dread kicked in when he realized all her earnest, vulnerable charm was being broadcast in real time to *millions of people,* apparently. So, when it came time to leave the gala, the protective instinct that had been rising inside of him all night started to hum. Louder and louder, until he could barely hear the security team's instructions over the noise.

Beat stooped down to catch the view from the front of the venue—and his stomach dropped through the floor. The crowd waiting outside stretched down the block.

He couldn't even see the end of it.

The live stream had only been going for a matter of hours and somehow viewers had already found the time to make signs.

Vaguely, he registered his name on a handful of them, but he was far more concerned with the ones that mentioned Melody.

PEACHES ARE MY FAVORITE FRUIT

COME PLAY WITH MY BOCCE BALLS, MEL

MELODY, WILL YOU MARRY ME?

Several people were also wearing . . . eye patches?

Melody seemed to be oblivious to the pandemonium outside, casually allowing security to guide her to the exit. "Hold up," Beat growled, shouldering his way past them and blocking the exit. "Don't you think a back door is a better idea?"

"He's right." Joseph approached with Danielle and momentarily lowered the camera. He coughed once. "I don't want you outside in that, either, Danielle."

The producer looked nonplussed, but quickly recovered. "I . . . very well." She waved at the security team. "Would you mind consulting with the building manager to find a more discreet way for us to leave?"

"On it," said one of the men, striding past while already speaking into a headset.

Danielle looked down at her clipboard where her phone was resting. "I expected a healthy viewership, but I didn't expect this kind of . . . intense reaction." She shook her head. "The numbers we're seeing are shattering records. We're at—"

"Is there any way we could *not* be informed of the viewer count?" Mel interrupted with a wince. "I'm sorry, I just don't want to know."

"Understood," Danielle answered. "Beat?"

"I want to know." He needed to know what they were going into at all times, so he could make sure Melody was protected. "Just inform me privately, I guess."

"Will do." A beat passed while Danielle darkened the screen of her phone. Did she appear to be working up the nerve to ask something? "Just to keep everyone up to speed, we have a flight out tomorrow morning to New Hampshire. We don't have exact coordinates as to where Trina's compound is located, but we have a general idea." She squared her shoulders. "It's tonight I'm more concerned about."

Melody frowned. "Tonight?"

As if on cue, the crowd outside started chanting her name.

Melody looked utterly and adorably confused. For some reason, Beat's heart started to flop around in his chest like a trapped, injured bird. "She can't go home," he murmured, beating Danielle to the punch. "We're going to be followed, right?"

"Right." Danielle opened her mouth and closed it. "I didn't expect this to get so out of hand so fast, Melody. But yes, I don't think it's a good idea for you to go back to Brooklyn tonight. You're in that ground floor apartment facing the street. It's too exposed. Lola packed you a bag of essentials and I have one of my assistants looking into a hotel reservation as we speak, but it's tricky, because we need permission to film—"

"Why doesn't she just stay with me?" As soon as Beat offered the suggestion, some of the tension in his chest started to loosen. "I have a spare room. I'm on the twenty-second floor of a doorman building. She'll be safe with me."

"I'll stay in a hotel," Melody said quickly. "But thank you for the offer."

Caught off guard, Beat tried to read her features and for once, he couldn't figure out what she was thinking. "Why?"

She flicked a glance at the camera, her color deepening.

Beat turned, blocking the camera's view of Melody. The noise coming from outside gave him no choice but to pull her close and speak against her ear, saving their voices from being picked up on the microphones and causing an eruption of cheers *and* boos on the street. "Why won't you come stay at my place?"

"Just let me stay in a hotel."

"Tell me why."

She hesitated. "The crush thing. I don't . . . it'll be weird. For you."

It took him a full five seconds to piece her explanation together. She thought her coming to stay at his apartment would make things awkward for him. And yeah, Beat had to admit there was a good chance Melody was right. Not only because she was nursing an infatuation with him, but because it ran both ways. If something physical happened between them, he'd have to share the parts of himself that he normally kept private. Strictly.

Still. "No. We won't let it be weird." He tugged her closer by her elbows and tried not to moan out loud when her tits met his chest. "Please don't make me worry about you."

She started to protest again, but the security team surrounded them before she got the chance. "We're ready. The SUV is waiting around the block, so it doesn't draw attention. It's going to pull up at the last second, so be ready to hustle into the back seat."

Melody nodded, transferring her attention from the security guard to Danielle. "Is this going to be forever?"

"I don't know. I have nothing to compare this to."

They all started cutting through the lobby toward the west side of the building, Beat keeping a hand on the base of Melody's spine. When they reached the side door and the sound of tires screeched, followed by a cacophony of shouts, Beat's heart lurched straight into his throat. The door opened and flashbulbs blinded him, but he squinted through the barrage of light and put himself between Melody and the fans rushing toward the SUV from the front of the building, obviously having figured out the plan. Thankfully, the door was opened and waiting, allowing Beat to lift Melody and all but throw her into the vehicle, launching himself in quickly behind her.

"She's staying at my place!" Beat shouted over the noise to Danielle in the front passenger seat. He barely caught the producer's nod before the SUV was peeling away from the curb onto the avenue. Escaping from the crowd did nothing to slow the pace of his pulse, however, and he found himself already picking apart the security plan for tomorrow. "It won't be like this at Melody's mother's house, right?" Beat shot a quick glance over his shoulder at the camera, which of course, was still capturing their every mood. "No one knows where it is."

"Correct," Danielle said, communicating directions to the driver. "It should be low-key."

Nothing about this experience was going to be low-key, Beat suspected. But before they faced the possibility of another mob scene . . . he needed to get through tonight. He'd meant it when he told Melody they wouldn't let staying together be weird, but his attraction to her was increasing in volume with every passing moment. Not typical for Beat. Not at all.

He'd felt more than his share of sexual attraction throughout his life, sure, but it was normally toward the female form, in general. The promise of sustained, heightened pleasure was what drew him in. There was never a specific individual in mind.

But every hour he spent with Melody changed that a little more.

Now, with the chaos of the night behind him, he could no longer keep the thoughts at bay. Melody in his bed, edging him to the point of agony, his muscles straining, teeth drawing blood from his bottom lip, sweat pouring down his chest.

If he wasn't planning on revealing his mutual crush on her—and doing something about it—then his protective attitude was likely leading her on. Giving her false expectations? That was unconscionable. He couldn't seem to stop himself from guarding her, though, especially in this fraught situation. Protecting Melody Gallard was instinctive. Always had been.

How the hell did he turn it off?

"That's me up ahead," he told Melody, realizing their fingers were linked and resting on her crossed legs. Jesus, his hands were moving without a single command from his brain. Touching her was like breathing. "On the corner."

She peered through the windshield. "Your doorman has a top hat."

"That's Reeves. He's not going to be thrilled about the camera. Does anyone have a chocolate bar on them, by chance?"

"There's one in my camera bag. Several, actually."

"You've still got that sweet tooth, huh?" Danielle asked, looking at Joseph in the rearview mirror. "One more way in which we're incompatible, I suppose."

"Agree to disagree," was all Joseph said back, his tone suspiciously lower.

Melody perked up while Beat rooted around in the camera bag and pulled out a Baby Ruth. *That'll do.* "How did you say you two met?" Melody asked.

"We didn't say," Danielle replied breezily, as the SUV pulled up along the curb. "And anyway, it's ancient history. Shall we get inside before another crowd forms?"

"Yes." Beat waited for a member of the security team to alight, before stepping out onto the sidewalk and turning to help Melody—and froze. She hadn't buttoned her coat upon leaving the gala and when she leaned forward to take his hand, the sides gaped, giving him an up-close-and-personal look at her tits where they struggled to stay secured inside her neckline. God help him, his dick turned to concrete at the sight, his bow tie becoming a noose.

A horn blared on the avenue while passing the SUV and Melody started, her foot catching on the lip of the door frame, and she pitched forward out of the vehicle. Beat's thoughts were fuzzy, thanks to every ounce of blood in his head going south, but when she flailed, his panic galvanized him and he opened his arms just in time to catch her.

And oh God, her warmth, her shape and weight. Gravity gave all of it to him at once and the sensation was so incredible, sparks sizzled at the edges of his vision. Her breasts were full against his chest, her knees grazing the sides of his hips. Their laps smacked together and pressed, held, and he knew she could feel his hard-on, because her breath caught in his ear, the sound only making him stiffer.

*Set her down.*

How long was he going to stand there holding her?

Beat attempted a swallow and it got caught in his throat, but he disguised the resulting choked sound with a cough and reluctantly settled Melody onto her feet. Two big spots of color were spreading on her cheeks, her eyes landing on everything but him.

Oh yeah, she'd definitely felt it.

Another car passed with a series of staccato beeps and they simultaneously started speed walking to the building entrance. Reeves stepped out onto the sidewalk and doffed his hat, using it to ward off the approaching group. "Now, see here, you fine folks. Building management must sign off on any filming or things of that nature—" Beat handed Reeves the candy bar. "Oh, a Baby Ruth! Why, I haven't sunk my teeth into one of these in an age. Now let's see if I remember the ingredients. Peanuts, caramel . . . *nougat.*" The doorman broke off when he realized the whole crew had stepped into the elevator at the rear of the lobby. "Pardon me, Mr. Dawkins—"

"Could you guys stay with Reeves and bring him up to speed?" Danielle called to the security team where they lingered behind in the lobby.

"Yes, ma'am," one of them shouted back.

"Mr. Dawkins," Reeves tried again.

Briefly, Beat leaned out of the elevator and winked. "You never saw us, Reeves."

The doorman sighed, regarding the candy bar in his hand. "You've tricked me again with chocolate. You've had my number since you came for visits as a teenager."

Before the elevator door could close, Joseph reached into his camera bag without a break in filming. He extricated a yellow package and lobbed it through the opening where Reeves caught it midair. "Oh, a Butterfinger! I haven't had one of these in—"

The steel doors of the elevator snicked shut.

Everyone exhaled at once.

"What did he mean you've had his number since you were a teenager?" Melody asked.

"This used to be my parents' place. One of them, since they liked to split time between LA and New York. Whenever I was in town, I used to bribe him with chocolate not to squeal on me when I broke curfew."

Melody's lips twitched. "He won't get in trouble?"

"Not a chance. He's been manning the door so long, a bunch of the residents chipped in a few years back and bought him a partial stake in the building. Unless he fires himself, he's not going anywhere."

Melody's shoulders relaxed. "Good." Her fingers shifted in his grip and he couldn't even remember when he'd started holding her hand. "So . . . when does the filming stop for the day?"

"We'll get a final shot of you entering the apartment, then we'll call it a night," Danielle said briskly, handing Melody a leather bag, presumably packed by the network stylist. "We'll be back at nine A.M. to pick you up for the flight." She held up six fingers to them, mouthing the word *six* A.M. off camera, obviously to mislead the viewers. "Sound good?"

Beat wanted to argue about the final shot of them going into the apartment together. It was a move that would be purposely suggestive. Viewers had linked them romantically since the first second of filming and this would only increase speculation. But if he took issue with the final shot, he might give Melody another reason to find a hotel for the night. And he wanted her going back out into the cold to combat overzealous fans about as much as he wanted his wisdom teeth pulled without Novocain. Bearing that in mind, he kept the argument in check and a few moments later, he closed his apartment door behind Melody.

And they were alone.

Well and truly alone for the first time in their lives.

"The quiet has never been more noticeable," she said, closing her eyes.

Her voice sounded incredible inside his walls. "Long day."

"The longest."

*Make it better for her.* After all, he was the one who'd dragged her into *Wreck the Halls* in the first place. With a lurch in his midsection, he took the overnight bag out of her hands. "Come on, I'll show you the guest room. Do you want coffee, tea, or alcohol?"

"Tea. Actually, alcohol. Definitely alcohol."

Beat tipped his chin at the hallway leading to side-by-side bedrooms. She toed off her high heels and followed him, their footfalls soft on the living room carpet. Without turning, he could sense her looking around at his furniture, his artwork, the view of the East River. Was his place what she'd expected? Better? Worse? He'd had a lot of friends here over the years, but never a lone woman. Something about Melody being the first felt alarmingly right.

He reached the guest bedroom and flipped on the light, smoothing down the dimmer to lessen the brightness, and set her bag just inside the door. The skin of his left shoulder prickled when she stepped up beside him, his obliques contracting. "It's perfect," she said, sliding past him, obviously being careful not to let them touch. "Thank you."

A hum was all he could manage until his muscles loosened. "I'll meet you in the kitchen for that drink."

"Okay."

He closed the door behind him, staring at it for a moment. The sound of her dress zipper coming down was like a stroke of finger-tips across his lap. His mounting attraction to Melody had already been difficult to manage, but now that the camera was gone, there was a sense of freedom he hadn't been expecting.

*Ignore it.*

Jesus, he had to ignore it.

They had a long way to go before Christmas Eve and he was already stumbling.

With an irritated headshake, Beat strode to the kitchen while removing his bow tie and tuxedo jacket. He unbuttoned the cuffs of his dress shirt and rolled the sleeves up to his elbows, pulling down two glasses from the cupboard and setting a bottle of triple malt scotch beside them. He'd just about gotten his shit together when Melody walked out of her bedroom in a long, oversized T-shirt that really, truly shouldn't have been so fucking sexy. But when she stopped in front of his floor-to-ceiling window, her silhouette against the glowing city lights made one thing painfully obvious.

She'd taken off her bra.

Beat poured himself a double.

"Is this how your parents decorated the apartment, or did you change it?"

"I changed it," he said into his glass, before taking a long sip. "My mother's style is . . ."

"Palace chic? Lots of whites and creams and golds? Swan-headed fixtures."

The scotch burned his throat when he laughed. "You nailed it."

Melody stooped forward slightly to peruse a collection of framed photographs on a table in the living room, causing the rear hem of the T-shirt to ride up, exposing her to midthigh. Beat swallowed thickly, begging the scotch to kick in and numb his reaction to her. Unfortunately, the sting of the alcohol only seemed to make it sharper.

"You know, I didn't expect to be starstruck by Octavia tonight, but I was. She really lived up to her legend status. Stars are two-dimensional beings and some of them, in my experience, remain that way when you meet them in real life. But not your mother; she was brighter and more captivating than I expected. I can only say that about two other celebrities."

Beat's drink paused on its way to his mouth. "Who?"

She gave him a twinkling smile over her shoulder. "Springsteen and Tina Turner."

"Wow. Good ones. Mine is McCartney."

"You just had to one-up me with a Beatle." She shook her head at him playfully while tapping one of the picture frames. "Who are the kids in this picture?"

The scotch took a wrong turn and settled uncomfortably in his stomach. "That was taken at summer camp. Those are my cabinmates."

She straightened on a gasp and padded barefoot to the kitchen, mouthing a *thank you* when he nudged her glass of scotch in front of her. "You went to summer camp?"

He nodded once. "When I was thirteen, my father thought it would be good for me to get out of LA. Get some dirt under my fingernails and eat terrible food for a month."

Melody sipped her drink experimentally. "Was it?"

When the prompt went right over his head, Beat realized how

hard he was staring at the sheen of alcohol on her mouth. "Was what?"

"Were bad food and dirty fingernails good for you?"

"Sure were." He forced a broad grin. The one he used with his friends. Everyone, really. "If I'm ever stranded in the woods, I'll have a fire blazing within minutes. Two hours, tops."

Why was she looking at him funny? Did she . . . actually see through his phony front?

"Was it really a good experience, Beat?" she asked, quieter this time.

"At first, it was, yeah." God, his voice sounded hollow now. Unfamiliar. "Then the other guys slowly realized who I was. I think maybe they overheard some of the counselors talking. And then . . ." He tried to laugh, but it emerged flat. "Well, then . . ."

Melody's hand fell away from her glass. "Oh, Beat," she whispered. "They hated you."

There was no comparison for the rush of gratitude he felt in that moment. He'd never experienced anything quite like it in his life. Not since the first time they met, at least. This woman sitting on the other side of his breakfast bar was the only person he knew who understood the weird shame that came along with being the offspring of a world-famous icon. It took every drop of his willpower not to reach across the marble countertop and drag her over the damn thing into his arms. "Yeah," he said. "The first week was fine. Great, actually. Until my mother sent a care package containing smoked oysters, an engraved pepper mill, and Pellegrino. She meant well. She really did. But after the counselors revealed who the package was from, the cat was out of the bag. They started asking me questions about my life in LA and I had no choice but to be honest. At first, they seemed interested. They wanted every detail. But those details only served to make them resent me. There were still three weeks to go and . . ." He shrugged. "I went back every summer until I was sixteen, hoping it would be different. But it was the same every time. Let's just say I slept out in the cold a lot."

"What did they do? Lock you out?"

Locked him out. Sabotaged his campsite. Put dirt in his food. Every time, he sucked it up, too embarrassed to explain the situation to his parents. "Mel, it was good for me."

Her nose wrinkled. "It . . . what?"

"Yeah." He drained his scotch. "Everything came too easy. I didn't even have to ask for new clothes or shoes or my own *boat*, Mel—they just appeared. Vacations, friends, even the press was so easy on me, compared to you. God, I hated that." He closed his eyes briefly, until the memories of some of the meaner headlines faded again. "When I returned from camp, after weeks of having my food stolen and my survival skills ridiculed—and rightly so, I couldn't light a fire for shit—everything went back to normal, but I . . . couldn't stand the excessive comfort anymore. I just couldn't stomach it."

Melody watched him, not moving. "And now?"

"I still can't." *Don't say the rest.* He needed to keep his mouth shut, but stemming the flow of his words was next to impossible when the one person who'd lived through a parallel existence was sitting right across from him, looking into his eyes like she could see clear through them into his thoughts. "But I have a way to manage it," he said, voice like gravel.

His chest should have loosened with that confession, right? But it only grew oddly taut, like he'd swallowed a chicken bone. Melody seemed to sense the gravity of what he was saying, because she didn't seem to be breathing. "How?"

"Mel."

"*How?*"

He was already shaking his head. "Let's get some sleep, all

right?" Forcing a smile, he checked the time on the stove. "We only have six hours before that camera is back in our faces. And it sounds like we're going to need some rest before we face Trina."

"There isn't enough rest in the world," she said, absently, still scrutinizing his face. And he wanted to lay her down somewhere, press their heads together, and let her look, because no one would ever see him more accurately in his life. But that would invite more between them. More than he could afford or offer.

"Night, Mel."

After a moment's hesitation, she slid off the stool and crossed the living room, looking back at him once before disappearing into her bedroom. Her glass of scotch sat unfinished in front of him, but he could see the faint outline of her lips where she'd sipped. Without thinking, he picked up the glass and closed his mouth around the exact spot hers had been, gulping the clear liquid greedily, feeling a corresponding tug in his groin. He let the need bleed in . . .

And knew he was only about to make it worse.

## Chapter Fourteen

**M**elody had been sitting on the edge of the guest room bed for twenty minutes, staring at the wall. Beat was right, they needed all the rest they could garner, because, to put it mildly, tomorrow was going to be a challenge and a half. But she couldn't seem to make herself lie down and close her eyes. Not with Beat's words lingering in her head.

*But I have a way to manage it.*

Pushing him once for a more detailed response had been overstepping. Hadn't it? When they were alone, though, like they'd been in the kitchen, nothing felt off-limits. It was like they could finally let down their guards and just . . . be. A sort of magic she didn't have with anyone else. But he'd stopped short of sharing his secret with her—and now she couldn't stop picking up theories and discarding them. Not out of sheer curiosity, although there was *some* of that.

But more because she could sense the answer was a huge part of him that he held back.

Melody didn't have a claim on all Beat's secrets and intricacies, obviously. She only wanted him to know that he *could* lay them on her. That she would understand. That he didn't have to shoulder something difficult alone.

A muffled sound reached her through the wall. It was brief and could have been a plane passing in the distance, perhaps lowering its equipment to land at JFK or LaGuardia. She knew that sound well. So why was her pulse galloping in the wake of it?

She'd almost convinced herself that she'd imagined Beat having what felt like an erection when she stumbled coming out of the SUV. That hard ridge against her thigh was his phone, right? But in general, people didn't carry their phone front and center. Nor were phones so large. There was also the matter of him hissing a breath when she pressed against it . . . and maybe she *hadn't* imagined his arousal?

What if it hadn't been for her, though?

It was totally possible that Beat's erection was basic anticipation of blowing off the day's natural steam? Did men get hard thinking about masturbating? Was he masturbating right now?

Melody shuddered through an exhale and squeezed her legs together. Exhilaration trickled down to her toes, her head falling back. Heat bloomed between her thighs and an invisible feather tickled the inside of her belly. She tried to separate the sensations from Beat and just enjoy them for what they were, but without his image, the memory of his touch, his lingering energy, the need began to subside.

"No," she breathed, the need starting to rekindle when a gruff sound slid beneath the door. It would be a violation of privacy to go inspect that sound, but she found herself balanced on the balls of her feet nonetheless, her ears hunting the air for another one of those deep burrs of sound. When another one finally came, her skin grew so sensitive that the mere act of breathing was nearly unbearable.

She would just go out into the hallway. Maybe she could hear him better there and when would she get this chance again? To be near this human being who attracted her so intensely? To memorize his scent and sound?

Sucking in a deep breath and holding it, Melody eased open the guest room door and stepped out into the dark hallway. The apartment was silent, dead silent, for long moments. Then she heard an unsteady gasp from the other side of Beat's bedroom door and her knees almost buckled. She pressed the flat of her palm to the wall for support and took one tiny step closer. Thirty seconds. She would give herself thirty seconds.

The creak of a bedspring tightened something in her core so brutally, her toes curled into the carpet runner, her free hand lifting to twist in the front of her nightshirt—

Beat's bedroom door opened.

He stood there shirtless in the lamplight, his chest rising and falling in great heaves, sweat dotting his brow and upper lip. A thick curve shaped the front of his sweatpants, pulling the material away from his body in a way that was . . . sexual and private and *not* for her eyes. But she couldn't stop looking at him to save the world, because he was the most beautiful person on the planet, his eyes cloaked in shadows, hair finger fumbled, body carved with muscle.

"You made a sound," he rasped.

She shook her head. "No, I didn't."

"You did."

"Maybe it was a plane getting ready to land . . ."

Her words trailed off into hard breathing, because he emerged from the room, coming toward her in a prowling, purposeful way and she was so overcome by being his destination that she started to shake. She was *shaking*, head to toe, when he flattened her between his strapping body and the wall. "Mel."

"Hold on," was all she could think to say. "I just . . . y-you have to stop touching me."

Immediately, he pressed his palms to the wall beside her head and shifted so they were no longer touching. But his nearness set off eruptions in her nerve endings anyway. Not a phone. That was *definitely* not a phone. There weren't even pockets in those sweat-pants. "Because you *want* me to stop?"

"No, because I'm going to embarrass myself," she said on an ex-hale.

"No. I love the way you're fucked-up over me." He crowded in tighter again and dropped his mouth to her ear, his lips grazing her lobe in a way that made her see stars. "Mel, I like things a little fucked-up."

This was it.

They were on the precipice of sharing his secret. It was so much at once. Having every line of his body corresponding to hers, that rough, intimate press, and his trust within reach. Melody's heart hammered wildly, not sure if she could stand any more without collapsing under the weight of having so many pieces of him at the same time. Still . . . "Tell me."

"I'd rather talk about what you like." She felt, rather than saw, his brows knit together. "It sort of feels like I'm the only one who should know."

A single word gusted out of her. "*Oh.*"

"Give me back permission to touch you, Peach," he begged into her neck.

"Touch me," she whispered.

"Good girl." Very slowly, he suctioned the skin below her ear. Hard. *Harder.* Making her gasp, body liquefying between him and the wall. "I'm waiting to hear what you like."

*This. This all day.* But he was looking for more. "I don't think I know what I like yet," she said in a rush. "I'm always too afraid to let my guard down. It just . . . maybe I'm imagining it, but I'm always worried they're just taking notes so they can tell their friends."

Beat lifted his head, studying her closely. There was total and complete understanding in his eyes. So powerful that a sense of belonging, a feeling of security crowded into her throat. "I get that, Mel. That's why I . . ." He paused, gave a quick shake of his head. "God, I want to kiss you more than I've ever wanted anything in my fucking life."

"Then maybe you should," she sobbed.

A grating sound rumbled in his throat.

He kissed her, then. Fully.

Beat kissed Melody.

Joy roared through her at the speed of light. Oxygen rushed in her bloodstream and her lungs became gluttonous for air. Beat's lips slanting over the top of hers, his tongue begging hers to dance, was like having her life force doubled. Tripled. For once . . . she was comfortable in her own body. There were pulses in amazing places and her limbs felt the opposite of stiff. They were energized and languorous at the same time. Glorying in the hard angles of him where they moved and swelled against her curves with urgency.

"Jesus Christ, Mel. Your mouth." He growled against it. "Of all the privileges I never feel like I've earned, you're going to be the ultimate one, aren't you?"

"You deserve everything," she whispered.

"No." He fisted the hem of her shirt, dragging it up to her throat, lust bracketing his mouth at the sight of her bare breasts, her panties. "But I'm going to rub and suck that gingerbread smell off you, anyway, aren't I? Until you soak that tight thong they made you wear."

*Oh my God.* The fact that he had a whole secondary vocabulary for these private moments was such delicious knowledge. "Yes," she whispered. "Please."

"I'm the one saying please." He hooked an arm around the small of Melody's back, drawing her high onto her tiptoes. The position curved her spine, the hard tips of her breasts lifting closer, closer to his mouth. Just before he could take her nipple into his mouth, he let out a shuddering breath. "Don't let me come, Mel."

"Okay," she managed, a little confused. Maybe . . . because they hadn't talked about birth control yet? But her thoughts scattered and she couldn't focus on anything except for the hot, panting breaths against her nipple. The incredible tide of pleasure that rose when his tongue lightly grazed her right nipple, then again, more firmly this time, long savoring licks until his lips closed around the bud and sucked, a groan issuing from his throat.

An acute gathering started beneath her belly button. So fast. Too fast?

Her thighs jerked together to stem the tide of pleasure, but his hips blocked them from closing and she whimpered, worried, excited, disbelieving. Was she going to have an orgasm from having her nipples sucked? No, no. No, surely not.

He watched her with glittering eyes while trailing his tongue from one puckered peak to the other, his tongue batting the sensitive bud, then taking it into his mouth with a hard punch of his hips, a surge of need seeming to travel through his frame. Her back flattened to the wall once more and her toes hovered above the ground, the hard surface anchoring her while his left hand twisted in the side of her thong. She could sense a struggle taking place in him, as if he wanted to tear off the undergarment. The suction of his mouth ceased briefly, his stiffness so insistent now that she couldn't help moving against it. Riding up and back on the tented seam of his sweatpants, moaning when he moaned, that gathering in her belly pulling tighter.

*Oh God.*

Oh no. Not yet.

"Is that how you want to get off? Grinding through our clothes?" He angled his hips for her, looking down, biting his lip and grunting over what he saw. The up and back drag of her sex, the probable wetness of the silky material. The way she couldn't seem to help it, her hips and thighs flexing with the effort to writhe on top of his thickness. *Faster, faster.* "Or, Christ . . . do you want me to get a condom?"

How did he make that word sound so sensual? "D-do you always use them?"

"Yeah." He exhaled roughly, forehead rolling side to side on hers, lower body moving, moving. "Although God knows I wouldn't want to with you."

"Me either. I'm okay to go without if you are, but . . . maybe not yet . . ."

"Yeah, Mel. More than okay. But we do what you want, when you're ready. So don't stop what you're doing, baby. You're so fucking beautiful. Don't stop. We can keep it hard like this as long as you want."

She cried out, palmed her breasts. She'd never done that before. Her breasts had never been this connected to the core of her, but they were now. The fiery tingle in her nipples was turning as unbearable as the one between her legs and all she could do was pinch them to lessen the pain, the strain, but that only made matters worse. More urgent.

She was so close. And the power of letting go with another person was almost shockingly intense, but letting go with Beat, specifically? A singular sort of happiness rose within her like a giant bubble, preparing to burst.

And then he tugged the elastic of her panties away from her mound, seeing her bare sex for the first time and gritting his teeth, chest shuddering. "Goddamn, Peach. Are you on the pill, just in case? Pulling out of that pussy is going to be torture."

"Yes," Melody gasped—and promptly lost her head.

The fact that Beat looked up the second she peaked only made the climax sharper, more concentrated. She whimpered, the sound breaking into a long, wailing moan while surge after surge of unimaginable pleasure ripped through her body, rattling her spine against the wall, the utter euphoria making her teeth clench painfully. The perfection of the orgasm stole her breath, and she couldn't control her actions. Not for long, shuddering moments, as her breath sawed in and out. And not only hers.

Beat was still looking her in the eye, his expression one of . . . surprise? Dread? Awe?

She couldn't think clearly enough to tell. Only knew she wanted him to leave the planet, too. She wanted—needed—him with her on the journey.

"I want you to come, too," she whispered, panting. "Please."

Conflict and regret seemed to weigh him down. With a whispered apology, suddenly Beat was lowering her to the ground with his own shaking hands, backing away from her with a perspiring, heaving chest. "I'm sorry, Mel. *Fuck.*"

Her orgasm-muddled mind struggled to play catch-up, but his words carried back to her from only moments before. *Don't let me come.*

When he'd made that request, she'd been too overwhelmed by him to examine it.

Now, with him moving farther and farther away, she couldn't help but feel like she'd been deprived of something. Rejected. Her stomach dropped to her knees, hands moving quickly to cover herself back up with the shirt. A jagged hiccup rose in her throat and she quickly swallowed it, lunging for the guest room door, loss and a lack of closure making her feel light. Too light. Untethered.

As soon as she closed the door, she heard his footsteps carrying him to the spot outside of the guest room. "Mel. Let me in."

"No." She worked to modulate her voice. "It's okay."

Something full, like his forehead, bumped the door.

"Everything is fine. I'm just ready for bed."

"Everything isn't fine, Mel."

"It is. I promise."

A few seconds ticked by. "I'm sorry I couldn't . . . that I don't know how to share that with you. If I could be with anyone when it happens, it would be you."

Melody's throat was too tight to respond. Feeling painfully exposed, she climbed into bed and wrapped herself in the covers, burying her face in the pillow. What had just happened? Had her orgasm turned him off? Had she been too eager? Had she come across as desperate? That last one made her cringe into the pillow.

A few seconds later, Beat's heavy footsteps carried him back to his bedroom, the door shutting with a note of frustration, leaving them separated by more than one kind of wall.

# Chapter Fifteen

*December 16*

**B**eat paced in front of his apartment door. 5:50 A.M. and Melody still hadn't come out of the guest room. He could hear her moving around in there. What was her plan? Walk out at six on the dot so they would be on camera and not have to talk about what happened last night?

He'd approached the door once already with the intention of knocking, so they could have a face-to-face discussion without the glowing red light blinking two feet away and Danielle's pen scratching on her clipboard. But what the hell could he say to make the situation better? He needed to figure it out, because they had eight more days in close quarters—and he really should be less grateful and turned on thinking about that. Hours spent together in the back of a dark SUV. And later tonight, more chances to be alone.

More chances to fuck up this friendship he was valuing more by the minute.

A quiet cough on the other side of Melody's door made his pulse skip, followed by the sound of her uncapping lipstick, if he wasn't mistaken. God, then he couldn't think of anything but her mouth. Kissing Melody was like a welcome home party in a place he'd never be lucky enough to call his home. It was trespassing. He'd had no right teasing open those lips so wide or sweeping his tongue that deep. Getting his hips good and notched between her thighs, so she could push down and pulse and get him so goddamn horny he'd nearly lost his grip on control.

That had never happened. Not once.

Beat always finished alone. The pleasure was measured and drawn out for maximum suffering, but he never stayed for the end. That was done on his own time. Being vulnerable like that with someone? No. He didn't trust anyone enough. But . . . he'd never faced anyone like Melody. That darkening of her cheekbones and the stutter of her breath, the uncontrollable trembling. The trust she seemed to have in him. Their bond that was so tangible, it almost didn't make sense. He'd felt the signs of her release straight through his pants and she'd almost ended him, then and there.

He'd hurt her feelings by backing off, withholding himself, which was the absolute last thing he would ever do intentionally. Why did he have to be so magnetized to someone he had the ability to hurt?

They needed to talk now.

This standoff was no good.

If he had to go the entire day without knowing where they stood, he was going to do something ill-advised, like give into frustration and hash it out in front of a worldwide audience.

Beat squared his shoulders and started to cross the apartment toward the guest room. Before he could take a single step, though, a knock sounded on the door.

He raked a hand through his hair. "Of course, you're early—" He broke off when he opened the door. Because instead of finding Danielle and Joseph, his blackmailer was leaning against the door-jamb. Ice formed an immediate layer on Beat's skin, his heart sling-shotting up into his throat. Apart from shock, he had one thought and one thought only.

Keep him away from Melody.

"What are you doing here?" Beat asked, pushing him out into the hallway and closing the door behind him. "How did you get up here?"

"How else? Candy bars. Thanks to the live stream, the secret is out."

"We agreed you would never come here."

The man's smug smile didn't slip one iota. "You haven't been answering your phone," he drawled. "How else am I supposed to reach you?"

"I've been busy."

"Oh, I've heard. Everyone has. Your little project is all anyone can talk about."

"Did you come here to congratulate me?" Beat asked. "After all, I wouldn't be doing the show if it wasn't for you."

"Bullshit, Beat. I know the amount of cash Ovations rakes in every year in donations. It's a matter of public record. You didn't need to participate in some reality show to pay me."

"I don't use the foundation money to shut you up. I use my own." Beat leaned in and got in the drummer's face. "The Ovations money goes toward scholarships for talented people. Not opportunists *disguising* themselves as artists."

That smile turned brittle. "I'd tread carefully if I were you."

"You're not me. We're nothing alike, thank God."

"Personality-wise? Maybe." He stroked his chin. "Genetically? That's another story."

All at once, Beat felt like he'd been box jumping for an hour straight.

Melody was in the apartment and he wanted this slimeball a

million miles away from her. Away from his family. Unfortunately, he wasn't done with Fletcher Carr yet. He might never be, if he wanted to keep the secret of his paternity right here. Between the two of them. Where it couldn't hurt anyone or drag his mother's name through the mud.

"Real heartwarming scene last night, the whole family gathered for your mother's annual ego trip. Your"—he performed air quotes—"father still has the wool pulled over his eyes when it comes to your mother. If only he knew."

"Get out," Beat clipped. "Get out of the building and don't come here again. Whether I have to secure a loan or we make this gig happen, I'll have the money by Christmas, as agreed upon. There is no reason for you to keep contacting me."

"Isn't there?" The blackmailer stepped into Beat's space and his skin shrunk in around his bones. "One of these days, you're going to think about getting brave, maybe letting the truth come out. I think these little visits from me remind you exactly how little you want people to know that I'm your real father. Not the man everyone thinks it is. Not the man who thinks your mother was faithful from the day they met."

A ring tightened around his jugular. "I said, get out."

Beat's blackmailer sauntered backward with a skin-crawling laugh. "Have fun with Trina—that crazy bitch." He spun toward the staircase and threw open the door. "I'll be watching with a bowl of popcorn."

The blanket of silence after the stairwell door snicked shut was deafening. Instinct begged Beat to go back inside the apartment, knock on the guest room door, and tell Melody everything. The relief of having her on his side would be incredible. He could almost feel the burden toppling off his shoulders. But it would land right on top of hers—and he couldn't do that. Not after he'd already brought *Wreck the Halls* to her doorstep. Not after last night, when he'd hurt her by backing off at the last second. Melody was a rare, perfect bright spot in his life and if he piled too much of his shit on top of her, he'd dull that luminous glow.

No, he'd keep his mouth shut and handle Fletcher on his own, thank you very much. This was *his* problem pertaining to *his* family. She didn't need this on her plate.

Beat was in the middle of a deep breath when the elevator doors slid open. Danielle and Joseph stepped off midargument. The camera was down by Joseph's side, Danielle backing off the elevator with hands planted on her hips. And she continued to back up until her back met the wall of the hallway, the cameraman towering over her, looking very much like he was thinking about kissing the producer.

At least, until they simultaneously noticed Beat standing there.

"Beat!" Flustered, Danielle smoothed her hair and sidestepped her way free of the trap Joseph was creating with his body. "Good morning. What are you doing out here?"

"I was just speaking with one of my neighbors," he said, briskly, already turning the knob to let himself back into the apartment. "I'll let Mel know you're here."

Beat drew to a halt when he found Melody standing in the foyer, overnight bag in hand.

"Consider me informed," she breathed, looking at his chin. Not his eyes.

Sweet hell, she looked hot. She wore a white T-shirt tucked into a pair of high-waisted jeans, and the curve of those hips belonged in a man's hands. His. He'd squeezed them at the gym and again last night. His palms recalled the shape now, flexing at his sides. What would it feel like to grip them from the back? Or dig his thumbs into them while he used his tongue between her thighs? Because he had a lot of regrets from last night, but very, very close to the top of the list was not getting on his knees in the hallway.

If last night was the only chance he'd ever get to touch Melody, he could have at least lived his life knowing what one of her orgasms tasted like.

"Are we okay to start filming?" Danielle asked, hesitantly.

"No," Beat said.

"Yes," Melody chimed in at the same time.

"We should talk," he said, shaking his head at her.

"We can talk on the plane, right?"

Danielle laughed nervously. "Everything okay with you two?"

"No," Beat growled.

Melody widened her eyes at him. "Yes."

"Melody."

She set down her overnight bag and slipped past him to take her coat off the rack, shrugging it on. When she couldn't seem to locate one of the armholes, Beat stepped up behind her without thinking and helped, her gingerbread scent making him feel lightheaded. "Thanks," she murmured, walking away to retrieve her bag once again.

Everyone was silent, Joseph obviously not sure if he should start recording, trading a surreptitious glance with Danielle.

"You're all staring at me." Melody laughed.

*Who would ever want to look anywhere else when she's in the room?*

"You seem uneasy," Danielle pointed out, instead.

Melody expelled a breath. "Of course I am. I'm going to see my mother. At her *compound*. She has no idea that we're coming, as far as we know. And I have no clue what I'm going to find when we get there. Compound could be code for cult. They could be praying to a statue of Chester Cheeto when we arrive." She paused. "It's not even February."

Danielle's phone rang. She didn't answer it right away, the ring going off three times in the quiet apartment before she apologized and tapped the screen. "Hello?" She listened. "Okay, thank you.

We'll be there shortly." She hung up, her gaze darting between Beat and Melody. "Our private charter came through. I didn't think it was wise to fly commercial after last night, but it took some sweet-talking to get the network to approve it." She pocketed her phone. "Unfortunately, we need to move. A lot of rich people are traveling at this time of year and our pilot is on a tight schedule."

Vaguely, Beat registered what Danielle was saying, but mainly he replayed Melody's words. How she'd said them, her anxiety and apprehension clear. Yeah, they were far from done with the Trina conversation. Today was going to be hard enough for her without him forcing her to talk about their encounter last night, however. They'd get there. But right now, all he wanted to do was relax her nerves.

He was dying to walk straight to Melody and wrap her in his arms, but holding her without resolving last night first would be too much, right? Still, he had to do *something* to ease her worries. After shouldering his duffel, he closed the distance between them and picked up her bag. Then he took her hand and twined their fingers together, squeezing.

Looking into her troubled eyes, he quickly replayed their conversation from last night.

"Do you need to see my Springsteen impression, Peach?"

At the very least, he'd distracted her. "Um. What?"

He raised an eyebrow.

She blinked. "I mean, who could turn an offer like that down?"

Maintaining a serious expression, Beat cleared his throat. He was a god-awful singer, but the growling was hereditary and that's all he needed for a proper Bruce imitation. Lowering his forehead until it was an inch from hers, he drawled the opening lines to "Born to Run."

Slowly, her entire face brightened.

Her jaw dropped, the twinkle returning to her eyes, along with the little dimple on her right cheek. Even as he stumbled over the lyrics, he'd never felt more like a hero in his life. Eventually the impact of her delight became too great and he was forced to trail off. With a cough to ease the pressure in his throat, he added, "Your mother isn't in a Chester Cheeto cult."

Melody's lips twitched. "You can't guarantee that."

"Oh, I'm pretty sure I can."

She let out a breath. "When I'm around her, I'm sixteen again. You know? That awkward girl you met a million years ago who thought choosing teal rubber bands for her braces was living life on the edge."

"That awkward girl was the best."

She gave him a grateful half smile. "That's easy to say when you weren't her."

"I was awkward, too. But I'd already gotten really good at hiding it."

She studied him with a slight indent between her brows, as if trying to read into the revealing statement. "For the record, my orthodontist implied clear rubber bands were a boring choice. I'm pretty sure he was a sadist."

*She's so wonderful, my stomach is going to fall out.* "I'm telling you, Mel. You looked great in teal."

"My sixteen-year-old self is smiling down on us. With wax stuck between her teeth." She bit her lip. "That was a solid Springsteen. A boss Boss, if you will."

"I will." It took an effort not to promise her the moon. "Any time you need it."

"Mics on. We have to go, kids," Danielle said, answering another call and speaking to someone on the other end while walking out of the apartment. She held the door for them and waited as they hooked their battery packs to the smalls of their backs, feeding the mics through their shirts and pressing the almighty button that would pick up their voices more clearly for the home audience. When Beat turned around, he saw that Joseph had been filming and wondered how much he—and everyone watching—had overheard. Did it even matter anymore? Hiding things from the camera only reminded him how privately he normally lived. Letting everyone close, but never close enough. Never revealing anything too deep or important.

With Melody's hand tucked into his, Beat wondered for the first time if maybe he could learn to be a little more trusting. And what could be waiting for him on the other side.

# Chapter Sixteen

On the flight to New Hampshire, Melody tried desperately to focus on her TED talk about insect brains being the key to great artificial intelligence, but every time five minutes lapsed, she realized she'd retained nothing.

Obviously she had the furthest thing from an insect brain.

Striving for casual, Melody turned in her wide, leather seat and glanced toward the rear of the plane to where Beat was thumbing through a neat bundle of paperwork, his brow in a furrow. He licked his index and middle fingers to turn the page, and a huge, industrial-sized crank turned below her belly button.

It seemed that every time she blinked, she would remember those long fingers tugging the band of her panties forward to look at her.

*Goddamn, Peach. Are you on the pill just in case? Pulling out of that pussy is going to be torture.*

In the heat of the moment, those words had made her hot. Brought her to the brink. In the light of day—or bad airplane cabin lighting, as it were—they only made her wonder. Made her think. *Physically removing* himself from her seemed to be a . . . theme? Or a need?

As if he'd heard her thoughts out loud, Beat's attention snapped up and gripped her with enough intensity to power the airplane.

"Psst." Danielle elbowed her in the ribs. "You're staring."

"Right." Wetting her suddenly dry lips, Melody whipped back to a forward-facing position, keeping her eyes closed until her pulse slowed down. "I don't suppose I could persuade you to distract me with the truth about you and Joseph, our trusty cameraman?"

"Distract you from what?"

"Air travel makes me anxious."

"If you're going to demand the truth out of me, you have to return the favor."

"I guess I owe you one," Melody grumbled. "For letting me know I was mooning over Beat on camera."

"Whatever you tell me stays between us." The producer crossed her legs and shifted to face Melody more fully. "The two of you are interesting enough in front of the lens. I don't even have to stir the pot behind the scenes."

"Is that standard practice on a reality show?"

Danielle considered spilling, then visibly changed her mind. "You'll have to read about it in my memoir one day."

Melody used a finger to click the air. "Preorder." Danielle smiled, but remained silent, giving Melody an encouraging nod. "We kissed last night," she whispered. "Made out, really."

"Shock of the century."

Just say it. Rip it off like a Band-Aid. "He sort of . . . walked away."

Danielle did a double take. "I actually didn't see that one coming. Elaborate?"

"No." Melody shook her head adamantly. "Your turn."

The producer definitely wanted to dive deeper into Melody's explanation, slumping comically. "Joseph and I came up through the ranks together at a twenty-four-hour news network. We ran in the same circles, crossed paths, and always had that . . . flirty nemesis thing going on. Then around eight years ago, we were on a field assignment, covering a storm, and we were forced to spend the night in the news van. I'll let you fill in the blanks."

"Sounds like he filled in the blanks."

Danielle snorted. "Anyway, he's got this whole 'I'm in charge' bullshit going on and . . ." She picked up the magazine she'd been reading and absently started to fan herself. "It's the opposite of what I want. *Outside* of bed, anyway. In bed . . ."

Melody examined that statement. "Were you surprised to find out you enjoyed being with someone like that in bed?"

"Surprised doesn't even begin to cover it." The producer threw an irritable glance over her shoulder. "And the bastard *constantly* reminds me I enjoyed it."

"That accounts for the tension, I guess," Melody murmured, replaying the conversation in her head. Danielle and Joseph had clear preferences in bed. Melody had never been comfortable enough to explore her own . . . but maybe Beat had? What if he had certain interests and she hadn't discovered them yet? He'd certainly dropped some hints last night. Maybe the problem hadn't been her eagerness . . . and instead, he just needed a little more time to share what turned him on?

*Don't let me come.*

Melody realized her heart was racing and unbuckled her seat belt with fidgety hands, needing desperately to move—and unfortunately, there was only one place to hide on a plane. On the way to the bathroom, she passed a dozing Joseph who was napping at the rear, his camera off and buckled into the seat beside him, like a small child. Melody used the restroom quickly, washed her hands, splashed some cold water on her face and then started to return to her seat when the plane hit a patch of turbulence—

She stumbled sideways in the aisle, reaching for purchase.

"*Mel*," Beat said sharply, catching her wrist.

Before she knew what was happening, he'd changed her flailing trajectory and pulled her down into his lap. She winced at the crunch of paperwork beneath her butt. "Oh God. I'm sorry. I hope that wasn't important."

A muscle jumped in his cheek. Did he just glance at her mouth? "It's only paper." Melody nodded, started to get back up, but the plane jolted again, rocking her on his lap toward his chest and prompting him to take a sharp inhale. "*Mmmm*."

Hunger swooped down inside of her. Deep. "I should go back to my seat."

The plane disagreed by traveling over several bumpy air pockets. Beat's hand tightened on the seat's armrest with each one. "You'll get hurt. Stay here until it stops."

There *was* some truth to his words. She wasn't coordinated on her best day. Trying to make it back to her seat while the plane was going over turbulence could easily end in a concussion. But pretending the position wasn't coaxing something to life inside both of them was growing more and more impossible. If the sheaf of papers wasn't trapped between them, she suspected Beat would be hard beneath her butt. The hand he'd been using to clutch the armrest slid onto her knee, his thumb digging into the sensitive inside. It inched higher after a particularly rough bump of turbulence. Squeezed.

The seam of her jeans became too tight. But she would get through this unscathed. They would. They just needed a distraction.

"Tell me about the paperwork I just butt crushed?"

"Yeah," he rasped, closing his eyes. "It's, uh . . . applications. From scholarship hopefuls. We'll announce our January recipient on New Year's Day." He appeared to be trying to focus on the subject she'd broached. "It's always a hard choice, but picking from this group is almost impossible. There isn't a single one of them that doesn't deserve it."

"What kind of criteria do you look for?"

Something sparked in his eyes. Excitement. A passion for his job that made her chest carve itself open for him even wider. "Obviously, academics are paramount, but that's just the tip of the iceberg for these kids. They're all at the top of their class. So we have to go beyond that. Look at their club participation, recommendation letters. Once we have about a dozen standouts, that's when we watch their recorded audition files."

Melody felt her own excitement building. "How do you inform the winner?"

A corner of his mouth lifted. "We usually contact their parents or guardian, arrange a Zoom call. Octavia appears on the screen and tells them college is paid for. It's . . ." He trailed off, nodding. "It's something."

"And you make it happen."

"They make it happen. I just do the research."

A bigger picture began clicking into place. "Did your mother create the scholarship program, Beat? Or was it you?"

"I don't know." He stared off over her shoulder a moment, eyes narrowing slightly. "It has been so long, I can't remember."

That was the truth. He honestly didn't recall. "I'm betting on you."

"Why?" They did nothing but communicate through a long, silent look. "You think I do this to balance out the wealth I've been born into," he said slowly.

"I think maybe that's part of it. The rest is just being a good person who wants to help."

"I don't know about that. It's like . . . I can't believe all this talent is out there and so much of it will go undiscovered. They have all the aptitude and none of the advantages. Meanwhile, I'm the op-posite. None of the talent, all of the—"

"No. You have to stop that."

He laughed without humor. "It's not that easy."

"Oh. Believe me, I know. We have these tremendous, unrealistic expectations on us, because of who our mothers are." She thought back to her many hours of therapy, the conclusions they'd drawn over and over. Ones she'd only started believing recently. "But, Beat, we get to be people. We get to *just* be people."

This time, when his gaze fastened on her mouth, there was no pretending she'd imagined it. "Privately, maybe, we get to just be people." He leaned in. Or maybe she did. "Around everyone else, though . . . friends, colleagues, the press, it's always been about keeping relationships superficial, distracting people from look-ing at anything too deep. Too personal." She heard him swallow. "Maybe I take that a step too far, you know?"

Their foreheads met, eyes searching.

No. She wasn't imagining the weight of importance between them. This conversation.

She wasn't imagining it at all.

"It's really hard to be around you," she said without thinking. "It's also really easy to be around you. Does that make any sense?"

"I've never understood you more."

"I wish I could say the same." He looked a little wounded by that, but she didn't take it back. "You say you keep relationships superficial. That you take it a step too far. Tell me what you mean."

His chest lifted and fell. He opened his mouth to speak twice, before finally proceeding. "Like I told you, when I was younger, it got too hard for me to accept . . . being indulged all the fucking time. I wasn't doing anything to earn comfort. Relief. That guilt started to creep in everywhere. I needed an outlet. And when I was sixteen, I asked a girl I was seeing to keep me right on the edge.

Tease and torture me, but not let me finish. She did it, but she didn't want to see me again after that. Neither did the next girl." His shoulder rolled back jerkily. "I learned not to share this part of myself with people I care about. I learned to keep it private and somewhere along the line, it stopped being about guilt and more about enjoyment. But most importantly, not having to confide in anyone. There are places a person can go . . ." He closed his eyes and gave his head a brief shake. "Jesus, I can't believe I'm telling you this."

Melody hadn't breathed in a full minute. "It's okay."

When he looked at her again, his gaze was a combination of heated and apologetic. "There are places a person can go, Mel. Clubs, sometimes private residences. I find women willing to be discreet and . . ." He raised an eyebrow, as if to say, *You get the picture.* "It's a transaction, not a relationship, and that clear line is comfortable to me."

"Oh," she whispered, regrouping her thoughts.

Beat interrupted the process when he pressed their foreheads together again. "Look at me."

"I'm looking."

"I haven't been to any of those places since I saw you again. I haven't wanted to."

Boneless, she nodded. Beat liked to be brought to the edge without being allowed to finish. Maybe she should have been shocked, but her brain only seemed capable of projecting images of Beat in the highest highs of hunger, his body keyed up and straining, teeth bared, eyes glassy. Who wouldn't want to be with him, feeding him what he wanted, in those moments?

"So . . . you like to be edged. Orgasm denial."

He huffed a pained laugh. "You use more technical terms than I do."

"I restored a copy of a classic sex help book once. I might have picked up a few things."

"Mel, you don't seem scandalized by this at all."

"Are you disappointed?"

"No. But knowing you're comfortable with this . . ." His lips trailed slowly across her cheek toward her mouth and settled there, breathing heavily enough to leave hot condensation. "I'm worried what I'll want to do."

"Why are you worried?"

He winced, almost like he was in pain. "Because this is my way of getting what I want without having to be vulnerable. It's satisfaction with none of the . . . emotion. None of the bond." His mouth was flush with hers when he spoke, muffling his words slightly. "I like fucking until I'm ready to explode, Mel. Then I stop. I can't . . . I don't know how to let anyone in at the end. I leave." He shifted his hips beneath her and made a low, tight-lipped sound. "I'd hurt your feelings, like I did last night. I don't think you realize how much that gutted me."

"My feelings were hurt, because I didn't understand. Now I do." She rushed to wet her dry lips. "And I think . . . if anything, your need for . . . hardship is proof that you have a soul. You recognize your good fortune. So many people in your position don't."

"Hmm." Her hand lifted on its own, her fingers spearing slowly into his hair, his eyelids falling more the farther they went. His hand on her thigh tightened and she couldn't stop, couldn't keep herself from sipping a kiss from his lips. "I just had a thought."

"Okay," he said, not moving. Holding his breath? "I'd really like to know what it is."

Instinct had her twisting her hips, rolling her spine, and adding pressure to the paperwork still lodged between them until he sucked in a breath. "Maybe we can try again. Now that I know what's coming—or in this case, *not* coming—" Briefly, she touched her tongue to the seam of his lips. "Maybe I would enjoy . . . *not* letting you."

A shudder ran through him. "*Mel.*"

It surprised her, the little surge of power that sparked in her fingertips. But the glimmer of something new and unique didn't scare her. No, it beckoned her closer. Using Beat's shoulder for leverage, she lifted her weight off his lap, closed her hand around the stack of papers, and moved them to the adjacent seat, before settling back down, inhaling roughly over the thick protrusion that greeted her.

"You knew what you were doing to my cock," he whispered harshly against her ear. "Didn't you, Peach?"

"Yes."

His rocky exhale blew the hair off her neck. "Imagine fucking each other." His hand fisted in her hair and pulled, his lips pushing flush to her exposed neck, making her gasp. "God, *imagine* it."

Oh, she was. In bright technicolor. There was a wealth of hesitation in his voice, though.

"But? I hear a but."

"I don't know how to do this without holding myself back. Keeping sex impersonal." Beat shook his head. "I could ruin this. I could hurt you—and that's unacceptable."

"Do you really think we can keep ourselves from trying?"

"It's getting harder to answer questions when you're sitting on my lap."

Maybe it was her elevated position that boosted her confidence or perhaps it was the intuition she possessed when it came to Beat, but she gripped his hair and twisted slightly, murmuring against his panting lips. "Starting now, you aren't allowed to finish." She kissed him sweetly, in direct contrast to her words. "Not until I say you can."

His eyes grew unfocused, his fingers digging roughly into her thigh. "Jesus, the irony. I could finish just hearing you say that to me." Conflict and lust warred in his expression. "I don't know if I'm good for you, Mel."

"Maybe. Maybe not." Melody shifted her hips, slowly turning in his lap until she was facing the front of the plane. She looked back at him over her shoulder and gave a slow roll of her lower body, memorizing the way his eyes darkened. "Are you going to let us find out?"

They remained there for several moments, Melody rocking in his lap, his chest rising and falling with more and more urgency. That battle between yes and no still waging itself on his handsome face. Until finally his right arm shot out, banding around her collarbone and drawing her back firmly to his chest. "Do you think I have a choice when I grow more obsessed with you by the fucking minute?" He sunk his teeth into her ear, reached for the coat draped on the seat beside him and covered them with it hastily, hiding their actions from view. "You made it hard, now grind on it. Tease me. Give me that good pain." Beneath the coat, his big hands palmed her breasts, teasing the buds in the center with his thumbs. "I want to be the one hurting, Mel. But God, I don't want to hurt *you* . . ."

Him stroking her nipples was making her anxious, desperate for friction. The importance of his words sunk into her subconscious to be unearthed and studied later, but just then, all she could do was embrace the new, exciting power tripping through her bloodstream. All she could do was give their needs a dose of oxygen and she did that by sinking down low against the V of his thighs, then riding back up, roughly, his strangled groan raising goose bumps on her skin. "Is that what you like?"

"From you? It's what I love," he said, struggling to breathe against her neck. "Keep going. Good girl. Fuck me through my pants. I'll tell you when I'm getting close."

"So I can s-stop?"

"That's right. So you can stop and leave me pussy-starved." He licked her, neck to cheek. "Only for yours."

That intense quickening she recalled from last night started in her midsection, sinking lower and lower until the pulse between her legs became impossible to ignore. She could have an orgasm like this. Denying him. Being praised for it. His hands were beneath her shirt now, thumbing aside the cups of her bra, making sweeping arcs against her bare nipples, but that wasn't supposed to be enough to give her an orgasm, was it?

Didn't matter. That's what was happening.

Just like last night, she was going to hit her peak hard and early—

"Five minutes until we land," called someone from the front of the plane.

Melody blinked her surroundings into focus, peeking up and over the seat in front of them. Danielle stood at the front of the aisle, speaking with the copilot, laughing at something he said. And indeed, Melody could feel the plane beginning to descend gradually, that telltale weightlessness making her stomach hover in the air. But their progress toward land wasn't the only thing filling her with that ticklish rush. It had a lot more to do with the man.

Without turning around, she could sense Beat attempting to gather himself. He palmed her breasts a final time, cursed, tugging her bra back into place. His sex was full and long beneath her bottom, his hips still tilting up, up, up slightly as if he couldn't help it.

"I should . . ." Leave this incredible warmth? Cut herself off from these singular sensations that only he could coax to life inside of her? Not high on her list. But what choice did she have? "I should go back to my seat. Before we land and he starts filming."

"Yeah," Beat said thickly, pulling her shirt down, before reaching up to smooth her hair. One stroke, two, then a light gripping of her strands. "Peach?" His teeth grazed the nape of her neck. "No one sees you turned on but me."

Melody was surprised how much that possessiveness gratified her. She leaned back and whispered in his ear, "You stay like this," riding the hard ridge of him one final time, listening to him swallow a moan, before standing up on shaky legs and returning to her seat for landing, filled with a lot more anticipation than she had been during takeoff.

## Chapter Seventeen

*A*n hour later, when they reached the compound, they did not find a cult worshipping a statue of Chester Cheeto. Arguably, the sight that greeted them was worse.

The SUV that had met them at the small airfield pulled up to a three-story house that stood in a cluster of trees at the edge of an expansive field, the ground of which was frozen and stark looking beneath a gray sky. None of them made any move to leave the warmth of the still-running vehicle. Instead, they all leaned to the left in unison to stare up at the haunted-looking Victorian, searching for indications of life on the inside.

There were none. There was, however, a painted, wooden sign over the door that read THE FREE LOVING ADVENTURE CLUB.

And Beat already wanted to take Melody back to New York.

This morning, when Melody voiced her fears of finding a cult, instead of the innocent-sounding Free Loving Adventure Club, he'd thought she was exaggerating. Now he wasn't so sure. He could easily see the Manson family dropping acid on the porch of this place.

Beside him, Melody fell back against the seat, chewing her lip. That soft, beautiful lip. Beat had to curl his fingers into his palm to prevent himself from reaching over and saving it from getting teeth marks. Damn. He'd barely kissed her on the plane. That had to be why he was now starved for the taste of her. That—and the ungodly blue balls she'd left him with.

A lot of men would be miserable in his current state of suffering. Not him. His blood pumped, heavy and hot. He could feel every breath that entered and exited his lungs. Everything was heightened. His hearing was sharper, the textures encountered by his fingertips became more interesting. Sensual. Running them over the slight perforations of the leather seat made his muscles contract, because it reminded Beat of her nipples. Her goose bumps.

Man, he was in deep lust with Melody. Really, extra deep.

*You stay like that.*

Every time he remembered her whispering that breathy command back at him, he stiffened up all over again. The only thing that could put a damper on his hunger was Melody's obvious anxiety about seeing her mother, and now that the moment had arrived, she was sinking down farther and farther into the seat. Beat took a deep breath and let the desire ebb from his body, his focus narrowing down to her in a different way.

"Hey. It's going to be fine." He raised a hand to brush back her hair, but he realized the camera was trained on them and let it drop. According to Danielle, the public were already pushing for them to be a couple. But something stopped him from touching her on camera. Maybe he wanted to keep the most intimate parts of Melody all to himself. Or maybe because he knew he should fight the physical pull between them. Because if he hurt this perfect person, he would never, ever forgive himself.

"Should we get out and knock?" Danielle asked.

No one moved.

"No one seems to be home. No cars in the surrounding area," Beat pointed out. "Unless . . . do they drive?"

"They bike everywhere. I remember my mother telling me that."

"Okay." Beat squeezed her hand on the seat. "I'll get out and check for bikes."

"*No.*" She grabbed his wrist to prevent him from opening the door. "Can you ask the driver to please honk the horn or something?"

*Beep beep.*

Silence.

The driver, a man in his sixties with a low-brimmed ball cap, took his time turning around in his seat. "Far be it from me to alarm you city folks, but I thought you should know. We get a lot of police activity up here."

Melody's back straightened. "What kind of police activity?"

"The sirens and flashing lights kind," the man drawled.

"Yes, but *why* are the cops called, sir?"

The driver gave a head tilt. "Do you know who you're up here visiting, girl?"

"My mother."

"Oh." He winced. "Is she the old rocker gal always walking around town in angel wings and combat boots?"

Melody covered her face with her hands. "Undoubtedly. Unless there are two people who fit that description."

"The locals don't like her much. None of her friends, neither." He gave Beat a pointed look. "They don't place much importance on hygiene."

Beat opened his mouth to ask the driver to please stop upsetting Melody, but he never got the chance to say anything. Because the peal of a police siren rent the air.

"That'd be them, now, probably," sniffed the driver, turning back around.

Joseph started to laugh.

"Shut up," Danielle whispered at him. Then to Melody, "I'm

sure that's just a coincidence. Let's just get out and have a look around, shall we?"

As soon as the producer opened the rear passenger door, the sound of beating drums could be heard in the distance. Danielle turned, looking back at everyone with a raised eyebrow, then climbed out, followed closely by the cameraman. "Hey," Joseph grumbled at her. "Stay close."

"Oh stop."

"I mean it, woman."

Danielle looked ready to reprimand him. Unfortunately, another siren joined the first and cut her right off. Beat resisted the urge to slam the door closed and ask the driver to return them to the airfield, but he got out of the SUV instead, turning to help Melody. She settled her hands on his shoulders and he tugged her out into his arms, allowing himself an extra second of holding her before letting her feet touch the ground. Taking her hand, they walked around the side of the house— and that's when the bonfire came into view.

About a quarter of a mile into the field, flames rose a story high, whipping and licking against the dull winter sky. Several figures surrounded the fire and appeared to be moving in a measured circle, some of them beating on drums. Although the police vehicles arriving one by one were definitely putting a damper on the proceedings.

"Enough with the drums," came a stern voice through a loudspeaker. "Put them down in front of you and keep your hands where we can see them."

The drumbeats grew louder. A familiar, defiant shout went up.

"Oh boy," Melody said, gulping. "That's Trina."

"Are you getting this?" Danielle asked Joseph. "How close can you zoom in?"

"It's like I'm there," answered the cameraman. "There are seven of them playing drums. Bongos. One of them is Trina. It's thirty-five degrees and not one of them is wearing a goddamn jacket."

"By all means, tell us the important parts," Danielle deadpanned.

Joseph cleared his throat. "Do you want me to tell you about the three men dressed like Santa Claus that just arrived?"

"*What?*" Beat, Melody, and Danielle shouted simultaneously.

"You heard me."

"We need to get closer." Danielle was already jogging for the SUV. "Let's go."

When Melody started to take off after the producer, Beat caught her around the waist with his forearm, drawing her to a quick stop. "I'd rather keep Melody *away* from the police activity than go toward it."

"For better or worse, she's my mother." Melody squirmed against him. "What if I can help?"

"Sounds like if she wanted help, she'd stop playing the drum."

"*Beat.*"

Against his will, he released Melody, stalking in her wake toward the SUV. Once they were all piled in and the driver was cutting across the field, Beat cupped Melody's chin and lifted it until they locked eyes. "Stay with me, okay? Please?"

"Okay."

"Notice the way he says *please*," Danielle said, poking Joseph in the shoulder.

A snort was all he offered in reply.

At any other time, Beat might have speculated more on the relationship between Danielle and Joseph, but he couldn't concentrate on anything but the scene that greeted them when they pulled up at the drum circle.

Because it was a *sight* to behold.

Trina Gallard stood in front of the bonfire wearing angel wings, but they weren't the pink, sparkly kind that came with a child's Halloween costume, like he'd wrongly pictured. No, they were black and purple, spanning at least six feet. Doc Martens were laced up to her knees. She wore spandex shorts and something he thought might be called a bustier. Or a corset, maybe?

"Miss Gallard . . ." The cop's exasperation came through the speaker. "I'm not going to ask you again to put down the drum."

"This is the great outdoors, Officer! Man has no jurisdiction here."

"Except you're on my land once again, Trina!" shouted one of the Santa Clauses, stabbing the air with his finger. "I've got the right to hold a peaceful gathering at my home without you hippies worshipping the sky or whatever weird shit you're up to this week."

"You heard him, Miss Gallard," the officer said. "You're trespassing. Again."

The former rock star blew a raspberry. "We're not bothering anyone."

"You're bothering me! You've gone too far this time, making a bonfire on my side of the property line. Officer, I want them arrested."

"Oh no," Melody said, groaning. "There has to be a way to mediate this."

"Melody, stay in the car, please," Beat said. "I'll handle it—"

She was already sliding out of the backseat and taking off after Danielle into the field. "So much for *please* making a difference." Joseph sighed, following the women. Beat exited into the icy air right behind him, striding after Melody.

Stress level: high.

The scene was already dissolving into chaos, but at the appearance of Melody, Danielle, Beat, and the man carrying a camera, everything only got worse. "Who the hell is this now?" a second

Santa wanted to know, visibly incited by their arrival. "Not only did you neglect to ask permission to be on our land and start a fire, now you're filming?"

"They're not with us!" snarled a man with a purple bandanna tied around his head.

Trina's hands dropped away from her bongos, surprise transforming her features. She took a step away from the bonfire and stopped, shielding her eyes. "Actually, that's . . . my daughter. That's my kid."

Purple Bandanna wheeled around. "You have a kid?"

Melody came to a jarring stop, as if she'd run into an invisible barrier. Beat couldn't see her face, but he knew exactly how it would look. Blank everywhere but her eyes. They'd be turbulent. Knowing that, anger flooded Beat at such a wild pace, it was a wonder he was able to keep walking, but somehow he did until he reached Melody, letting her feel his heat against her back. He slipped their fingers together and held tight.

Trina's eyes narrowed, ticking from her daughter to Beat, some of the color leaving her face. "That better not be who I think it is," she said, audibly short of breath.

Now the Santas were getting impatient. "Officer, when can we expect these hippies off our property? We're having our annual Christmas party and I know they timed this damn drum circle so it would interfere. I *know* they did."

Santa #2 stepped forward. "Is this because we didn't invite you?"

"We hate you! That's why!" This, from Santa #3.

Trina ignored them. "Answer me, Melody. Is that *her* son?"

"Yes, Mother. This is Beat Dawkins."

A sound of outrage slowly rose in volume until it was a full-on screech. "You would bring him here? To my *home?*"

"Technically, you're in our home," barked Santa #1.

Trina hauled back and *threw her bongo* at Santa #1—and it was a direct hit. The drum caught him in the dead center of his forehead and he staggered back, clutching the impact point, his bearded chin quivering in shock.

That's when all three Santas charged the bonfire.

The police officers, who were clearly not expecting a physical altercation, were slow to act, fumbling their radios and bumping into the open doors of their patrol cars, before running toward the bonfire in an effort to intercept the fight. Beat watched in disbelief as Trina's posse threw their drums in solidarity with their apparent leader and clashed head-on with the trio of Santa Clauses. He didn't know what he'd been expecting—but it wasn't this.

And he especially didn't expect Melody to run straight into the fray.

"Mom!"

His legs went so numb, it took Beat a second to take off after her. "*Mel!*" Pulse jackhammering in his temples, he watched Santa #3 snatch up a stick from the ground on his way to Trina. A long, gnarled one that maybe they'd been using to poke the bonfire. He thrust that thing up over his head like a spear, his mouth open on a high-pitched yell. Beat was still a good ten yards from reaching Melody when, to his utter horror, she stepped between Trina and Santa #3, balling her fists and preparing to defend her mother.

He'd never been so awed by anyone or so fucking panicked in his life.

Trina had just been outed as someone who never even *spoke* about Melody. To people she apparently *lived* with. She had this incredible daughter and didn't bother to claim her? She didn't deserve this type of loyalty, but Melody was giving it to her anyway. There wasn't a chance in hell, however, any of it was going to happen while Beat had breath in his lungs.

He made it to Melody's side, just in time for the stick to come down, his fist closing around it in midair. Two inches from the crown of Melody's head.

Teeth clenched so hard that his head ached, Beat looked Santa #3 in the eye and snapped the stick over his knee. "Back away from her or I swear to God, the next siren you hear will be your ambulance."

"Beat," Melody gasped behind him, distress in her voice, and he quickly saw why.

Santa #1 had reached Trina and a shoving match had ensued.

Once again, despite Beat's effort to reach the argument in time, Melody found her way in between them, pushing the man back. Santa #1 reached over Melody's head and jabbed Trina in the forehead with his index finger, prompting Melody to knee him hard between the legs.

The Santa doubled over and howled.

And finally, far too late, the cops reached the fray. "All right, you're both under arrest." One of the officers wrestled Trina to the ground. Beat assumed the second one would wrangle Santa #1, but to his horror, the officer jerked Melody's wrists behind her back instead, snapping a set of handcuffs closed with a metallic zip.

"What the hell are you doing?" Beat demanded, pulling a bound Melody up against him. "Why are you arresting her?"

"She just assaulted the man on his own property."

"He was attacking her mother!"

"He has a reasonable right to defend his own property and *her mother* started the damn thing by clocking him with the drum, in case you missed it."

"I'm bleeding!" Santa #1 added.

This wasn't happening. No way. Melody couldn't be arrested.

It vaguely occurred to Beat that all this was being fed out into a live stream, but honestly, that was the last goddamn thing on his mind. "Can you take me instead of her?"

"Ain't that sweet," crooned the officer, his lips flattening. "No."

Beat dropped the broken stick in his hand and plowed five fingers through his hair. The thought of Melody being taken into jail alone was causing an acid storm in his gut. "Should I get arrested, too?"

The police officer looked at Beat over the top of his aviators. "I wouldn't do anything stupid if I were you, son."

"Beat. Do not get arrested." Melody went up on her toes and pressed their cheeks together, making him feel like he'd swallowed a starfish. "We're going to need you to get us out."

With those words ringing in his head, Beat watched helplessly as the officers loaded his Melody—and her spitting mad mother—into the back of a patrol car. "Please," he rasped to no one in particular. "Please."

Danielle and Joseph flanked him, Joseph filming, Danielle punching madly at the screen of her phone. "I'm already searching for the closest bail bondsman." She squeezed Beat's shoulder. "We'll get her out. As soon as I get some release forms signed."

The hippie in the purple bandanna blocked his view of Melody, his teeth exposed in a broad grin. "Welcome to a typical afternoon with the Free Loving Adventure Club, man."

# Chapter Eighteen

*A*pparently, no warnings are given before the police snap one's mug shot.

There was barely time to register that she was standing in front of the height chart, when a camera flash blinded Melody. With the starburst still blooming in her eyes, a female officer shuffled Melody along a few feet to the right where they flipped open an inkpad and asked for her full name. This was really happening. She'd been arrested for kicking someone in the junk. "Is this something I will have to report to potential future employers?"

"That's a question for the judge." The officer waited for Melody's escort to uncuff her. "Thumb, please."

Melody barely had time to hold out the requested digit when Trina was ushered into the processing room behind her daughter, with the air of a middle schooler who had been sent to the principal's office. Again. "Well, I'm back, Officers! How many of you are secretly going to ask for an autograph this time?" Trina singsonged to the room, in general, her bare feet slapping on the floor with every step. "Guess I can't really fault you for taking Santa's side this close to Christmas. If you piss him off, he might not bring you a life—and you all desperately need one. Something to occupy your time besides arresting the local legend."

"You were a legend when you moved here. Now you're just annoying," drawled the officer holding her cuffed wrists behind her back. "Look straight at the camera."

She batted her eyelashes as the flash went off. "Pretend all you want. I see your Steel Birds tattoo peeking out."

The officer cleared his throat hard and yanked on the sleeve of his uniform, covering up a few ink spikes. "Team Octavia," he muttered.

"Yeah, that tracks." Trina rolled her eyes. "A couple of serial killers of joy. She'd probably love you."

"Really?"

Trina's head fell back on a groan. "For the love of God, put me in a cell. I'd rather be locked up than have this conversation."

"Mom," Melody ventured. "Let's just get through this without them adding any charges, okay? I'm sure Beat is already working on having us released."

"Oh. Yeah. *Speaking* of Octavia fangirls." Uncuffed now, Trina averted her gaze and slapped her thumb down into the inkpad, but not before Melody saw a trace of hurt. "My own kid. Unbelievable."

"I'm not a fangirl." Melody would have failed a lie detector test on that one, but Trina didn't need to know that. "I've only met her once."

"Is she still a petty bitch?"

"*Mom.*"

The officer stepped into Melody's line of vision. "I watched the whole meeting live, if you don't mind me saying so. My wife and I agreed that you really impressed her. And I can't imagine that's an easy thing to do. I mean, she really seemed just *taken* with you, Mel."

"*Mel?*" Trina kicked—kicked—the officer in the back of the leg. "You are not on a shortened-name basis with my daughter."

Instead of outraged, the man merely seemed smug. "That's what everyone's calling her, Trina. Magnificent Mel."

*What?*

Trina sputtered. "Who the hell is everyone?"

"It's a long story," Melody interjected quickly. Although . . . Magnificent Mel? Was it a nickname born of sarcasm or were viewers truly calling her that? "I'll probably have time to explain everything while we're waiting to get out."

"Oh, there's no *probably* about it," the officer said cheerfully. "Our bail bondsman is closed today. His daughter is getting married."

"Fuck." This, from Trina.

Melody refused to panic. Beyond the typical dread that came with being arrested and having to explain to her mother they were in the middle of a reality show, that was. "Beat will figure it out. I know he will."

Trina studied her long and hard. "If you tell me you're dating Octavia's son, I'm going to wish I'd actually been attacked with a stick by that rabid Santa Claus."

"We're not . . . dating."

The officer made a choked sound. Walked in a circle with hands on his head, like he was struggling to hang on to a whopper of a secret. "Beg pardon, Magnificent Mel, but I've got eyes in my head. That man is wild about you."

The pulse in her neck started to speed. "No, he's just—"

"I already know what you're going to say. That's just his nature. He makes every person feel like they're special. Yada yada yada. Well, I think—and my wife agrees—that you only say that to manage your expectations, because you have inadequacy issues."

Melody smiled. "We'd like to be put in that cell now."

The female officer who'd brought Melody into the processing

area sidled over. "You're going to scare her with all your babbling, Melvin. Jesus. Talking like you *know* someone."

"Don't pretend like you aren't dissecting every second of the live stream, Deena. I saw your post in the fan forum, too. TripleDCop45 is you, isn't it?" Melvin looked pleased with himself. "Your theory about the Steel Birds reunion only being a red herring is decent, I guess. The show might actually be about Beat and Melody at its core. But—"

"*Reunion?*" Trina screeched.

Melvin's mouth snapped shut. "Oh, she doesn't know yet?"

"Cell," Melody whispered.

With a glare at Melvin, TripleDCop45 tugged Melody down the long corridor leading to what looked like four holding cells. All were empty, except for one in which a man was passed out on a bench, snoring with his mouth hanging open. Melody could feel Trina's eyes drilling into the back of her neck. There would be no heartwarming mother-daughter chitchat today. They were heading straight into the fire, weren't they?

Yup.

As soon as they were led into the cell and the door was locked behind them, Trina slumped heavily against the far wall of the cell, scrubbing at her face with her hands. "What in the sweet burning hell is going on here, Melody Anne?"

An excited whisper carried down the corridor. "She called her Melody Anne!"

"I'm putting this on the message boards. People are going to shit."

"Guys, can we have a little privacy, please?" Melody called through the bars.

A squabbling discussion ensued. "Sure," TripleDCop45 called back, finally. "We need to watch Beat on the live stream, anyway."

Melvin hooted. "The poor man is fit to be tied. He wants you out of here. *Now*."

"His words, not ours." Some chairs scraped back. "Let's go watch in the break room."

A few moments later, a door opened and closed, leaving Melody and Trina in silence, save the buzzing of the overhead fluorescent light. Trina dropped her hands away from her face, letting out a gusty sigh. "Live stream. Message boards. Octavia's son. Reunion. These are the words giving me an ulcer—and I'm way too young to have ulcers."

Ulcers were more than possible at fifty-three, but now was not the time to mention it. "I agreed to be part of a reality show." Melody took a deep breath and straightened her spine. "Beat and I are attempting to reunite Steel Birds."

Long seconds ticked by, her mother's expression inscrutable.

Then a laugh started to unfurl from her mouth, building slowly into a jumble of loud, hysterical notes echoing off the walls of the jail cell. "I wouldn't appear onstage with that judgmental cow if she was the last person on earth."

Melody already had one foot in the grave, might as well lie down in it and roll around.

"She already agreed to the reunion."

That marked the first time she'd ever truly shocked her mother—and Melody would be lying if she said that reaction didn't enliven her. Challenging the status quo of their relationship was one of the reasons she'd agreed to participate in *Wreck the Halls*, wasn't it?

Trina pushed off the wall. "You're telling me that old hag wants to reunite?"

"That's what I'm telling you," Melody deadpanned. "Christmas Eve. Are you in?"

"Absolutely not."

While Melody had been expecting that response, she'd gotten a lot more invested in the outcome of this mission—perhaps unwisely so—and Trina's definitive answer hit her in the middle of the chest like a hurled dagger. The blade might have lodged in deeper, but then Melody saw something beyond shock on her mother's face. Something like . . . hope.

She could do this.

She'd found the edge of the tape, now she simply had to pry it up with her fingernail.

"The world is watching, Mom. As if people weren't already clamoring for this reunion, now 'Rattle the Cage' has gone viral after three decades. If Melvin and TripleDCop are an accurate sampling, the viewership is hyped. Think of the fans."

Trina laughed, but the mirth never reached her eyes. "The fans hate me. And they fucking love her. That's how it has always been."

"I . . ." Melody shook herself out of a daze. "I never knew you felt that way."

"Don't get me wrong," Trina rushed to add, jabbing the air with her finger. "I don't give a shit. I'm just stating the facts."

"Right."

Trina definitely gave a shit.

"I don't care if they all condemn me for what they think happened. I'm *happy*. I'm up here living free in the giddy mountain air while she's down in New York, in her gilded cage, rolling around in phony frippery."

Melody started to respond but found herself momentarily overcome.

"What?" Trina spat, folding her arms over her chest.

"Nothing," Melody managed, after a few moments. "It's just that sometimes I forget you were the lyricist. That you're incredible with words."

Trina turned away. To hide the softening of her eyes? "There's nothing you'll say to make me agree to reunite Steel Birds, Melody

Anne. Octavia is the one who asked for the breakup in the first place."

A sharp pang hit Melody just above the collarbone. "She is? I never knew. No one really knows what happened. I mean, speculation about a love triangle has always been there, but I've always wondered if the press was sensationalizing."

"If only." Trina didn't say anything for long moments. "Oh, kid. It's such a cliché. That's what ticks me off the most, you know?" Trina faced her again, disgust evident in the brackets around her mouth. "We swore from day one, we'll never be normal. We'll *never* be normal. But look what happened. A penis came between us. A human man. Not even a half-decent one." She appeared lost in thought for a beat. "Maybe I am the villain of her story, but I'm the hero of my own. I'm going to keep on being that for myself, if it's all right with the world."

This woman, her mother, had no idea that every sentence out of her mouth was a hit song. God. *God*, it was so intimidating. Standing in that jail cell, Melody felt like a lackluster teenage girl again, without a single merit that could bring her worldwide fame. The talent hadn't been passed to the next generation. It ended with Trina. Melody was just a quiet echo of something extraordinary.

Melody reached down deep, trying to tap into all the lessons she'd soaked up over the last decade and a half of therapy, but all she found was a dull, monotone baseline. A dead radio station.

What had she told Beat on the plane? They get to *just* be people? Maybe it would be easier to remember that later, when she wasn't staring greatness in the face.

"What's going on with you and the son?"

She was too winded to lie. "I don't know."

Trina shivered. "He is her clone. I can see it. Be wise and be careful."

"Careful of what?"

"That feeling. The one that says someone is always going to be there. In this life, Melody Anne, you can't depend on anyone but yourself. Haven't I told you that before?"

"No. You've shown me."

Trina reared back a touch, expression turning guarded. "I've what?"

"Nothing."

"No. Say it."

It was getting harder to draw a breath. She'd never, *ever* been critical of her mother out loud. Who was she to nitpick a lyrical genius? Who was she to try and analyze, pin down, pigeonhole a famously free spirit? Not her. Not the sweaty girl with braces.

Melody wasn't sure where she got the bravery now. Was it the fact that she'd taken a sword to her comfort zone and slashed it to ribbons by participating in the live stream? Was it . . . the spike of confidence she'd taken for herself on the plane by embodying a seductress? She wasn't sure. She only knew that her voice worked fine when she said, "You've shown me that I can only depend on myself. I *taught* myself how to be okay. Being okay is goals. But I don't think being okay means avoiding anyone who might test your version of okay. Sometimes the okay boundary changes. You have to fucking step into it. You have to find your okay again. And again and again. Until we die. Welcome to being human."

"Wait, I thought I was the lyricist."

A laugh puffed out of Melody. A rewarding one.

Trina half smiled, sadness dancing fleetingly through her eyes. "I'm sorry, Melody Anne. I'm done being everyone's bad girl." She looked around. "If I want to be bad now, it's on my terms, you know? The crowd sang along with me for years, worshipping me with their very souls. We abandoned ourselves to the universe together. And then they turned on me. They reached in and made mulch of my guts. And *she* led the mob. My best goddamn friend."

Heat pressed against the backs of Melody's eyes. "I'm sorry. I didn't know you'd been keeping all this locked inside."

"It's easier to let everyone think nothing touches me."

Melody wanted to let her get away with that. She really did. Her mother's explanation was genuine. Every word. And Melody didn't want to penalize Trina for being open with her when it was so rare. But she felt stronger today than she had in the past and didn't want to lose that. Didn't want to have regrets later. "I get that it's easier to let people believe you're untouchable, but I'm not everyone, Mom. I'm your daughter."

"I guess it's a good thing I only make you put up with me once a year, huh?" Trina laughed, pacing barefoot to the other side of the cell, signaling an end to their heart-to-heart. "Don't say I never did anything for you."

If the jail cell floor wasn't stained with God knew what, Melody might have lain down on it, knees to her chest. But if those splotches had managed to stain concrete, they had to be something serious, so she remained standing. Swaying a little in the wake of her mother's hurtful statement. Trina thought she was doing Melody a favor by being absent? How was she supposed to respond to that?

Thankfully, she never had to find out.

Beat's voice cut through the stale air like a violin string through cake. "I've spoken to the bondsman—he allowed me to do a wire transfer. You should have an email from him. Melody no longer has to go before a judge, because charges have not been pressed. I spoke to psychotic Santa myself." His tone invited zero nonsense. "Let her out, immediately."

"You mean them, Beat," Melody called into the hallway. "Let *them* out."

"*Mel*," he shouted back, "are you okay?"

At this rate, she was going to turn to a fine mist of relief and drift out through the metal bars. "I'm completely fine."

Physically.

"She better be fine," Beat informed Melvin as they came into view.

Oh . . . my.

Her blood thickened to hot syrup at the way Beat strode toward the jail cell, hair in disarray, the sleeves of his dress shirt shoved hastily to his elbows, those forearms in a full-on irritable flex, along with his jawline. He was in shambles, and yet he looked completely in command of the situation. Melody seriously hoped her weak-kneed, total body reaction to Beat's arrival wasn't showing on her face. One small mercy was that the camera wasn't there, likely forced to wait outside.

Melvin unlocked the jail cell door and Beat pulled her out by the wrist, stooping down slightly to wrap her in his arms, then lifting her clear off the floor.

"I got you out as quickly as I could." His voice was gruff paradise in her neck. "You're sure you're okay?"

"Yes."

He settled Melody onto her feet, but kept her close, that line of concern remaining deep in between his brows. "Let me see your wrists."

"Why?" she asked, confused but presenting them anyway.

Beat took her hands, holding them up to the light, turning them right and left. "If those cuffs left a mark on you, I'm going to fucking lose it."

"They didn't."

Melvin patted Beat on the shoulder. "Relax, man, she's been in the hands of a Melody-head. She's been treated like family!"

"Would someone mind letting *me* out of jail, too?" Trina shrieked.

"Guys, my mom!" Melody wiggled out of Beat's hold and reached for Trina's hand through the open door, pulling her out into the open. "Sorry."

"Don't you want to check my wrists, too?" Trina said tauntingly, wiggling her fingers at Beat.

"Nah," he drawled without missing a beat. "Sounds like your wrists are used to being cuffed. Hers aren't."

"Beat," Melody breathed, frowning up at him. Why did he look and sound so angry?

Trina cracked a knuckle. "I see your mother has properly poisoned you against me."

"She didn't, actually. That's not her style. I can make my own judgments."

Melody grabbed his hand and squeezed, imploring him without words to look down at her. In the great scheme of things, it didn't really matter if Beat and Trina liked each other. In fact, there was an extremely high probability that they wouldn't. The past was already working against them. For some reason, though, every dart they threw at each other was striking Melody in the process. "Please. Please stop."

His gaze veered toward Mel, running a lap around her face. "Yeah. Okay. I just don't like this place." A line moved in his cheek. "I don't like that Melody Gallard showed up and the so-called Free Loving Adventure Club didn't appreciate it enough."

"I haven't exactly had the chance, have I, golden boy? Or did you miss me getting rolled the minute she arrived?" Trina snapped, before she slowly settled into a cajoling smile, which she sent in Melody's direction. "There's always a little celebration back at the house when I get out of the slammer. Who's ready to party?"

Melvin cleared his throat. "I, for one, wouldn't mind unwinding—"

"Oh, fuck off, Melvin," Trina scoffed, sailing down the hallway toward the exit. "You're not invited. This one's for my kid." Just before she walked out of the jail, she turned. "It goes without saying that you're welcome to stay the night. We've got an extra room."

Melody followed her mother, Beat's hand warming the small of her back. "Only one?"

"Unfortunately, yes. It's a packed house."

She could feel Beat's gaze on the crown of her head and slowly raised her eyes to meet it. Were his pupils larger than usual or was it a trick of lighting? Melody wasn't sure. Nor was she sure what kind of night lay ahead of them.

But odds were, it was going to be interesting.

# Chapter Nineteen

$B$eat and Melody stood side by side, staring down at the twin-sized bed.

Correction: mattress. It was a mattress. On the floor in the corner of a room at the highest point of the house. The attic, if you will. There was no other furniture, except for a row of potted house plants lined up in front of a giant, circular window. The sun had set while Melody and Trina were in jail, leaving the sky a pitch-black canvas full of stars that seemed so close Beat felt he could reach out and rearrange them.

The celebratory music downstairs played loud enough to shake the floorboards beneath their feet. Madonna followed by Skynyrd followed by Bing Crosby singing "White Christmas." They'd been welcomed back to the house by a boisterous round of applause, and the alcohol had started flowing. Danielle ran around getting release forms signed while whiskey was poured into Solo cups with beer chasers and limes were sliced in the kitchen in anticipation of tequila shots.

There wasn't a chance in hell Beat was drinking tonight. Too many variables. Their main mission was to reunite Steel Birds, but his side mission was to get Melody back to New York without any further mishaps or harm.

And he was growing extremely skeptical of his odds of success. Mainly because of the bed. Mattress.

The *twin* mattress they were expected to share.

Hyperaware of the camera filming behind them, Beat forced a laugh. "Bet you wish you'd stayed in jail."

Her sides shook with mirth. "It *was* quieter."

"Less of a seventies cultlike atmosphere?"

"You don't think my mother's living situation holds a certain . . . charm?"

"No."

"Correct." She glanced at the door. "I guess we better show our faces downstairs. After all, they're holding the party in honor of the outlaws. Of which I am now one."

"Yeah."

Neither Beat or Melody made a move for the door.

More than life itself, he wanted the camera to leave so he could put his arms around Melody and run his palms over her hair, her face, her back. Put his mouth on her skin and inhale her, just to get her into his lungs. They hadn't been alone since he'd bailed her out, and he had no idea what took place inside the jail. He only knew a little bit of the sparkle was gone from her eyes and he wanted it back ASAP.

He also knew if he touched her, there was a very good chance they'd end up on that mattress. And the outcome of them getting physical could mean robbing even more of that twinkling life force from Melody's eyes. That left Beat trapped between a rock and a hard place. His need to touch Melody was a yawning physical ache and yet, if he gave in, she could end up hurt.

In other words, this was about to be the longest night of his life.

"Listen, I'll sleep against the wall. I'm tired enough to knock out in any position."

Melody's face became a mask of horror. "What? No." She wet

her lips and made a fluttery-fingered gesture at the mattress. "We'll go back-to-back. Or I'll face south and you face north?"

Beat raised an eyebrow. "Feet to face?"

"Why yes," she purred theatrically. "That's how I seduce all my men."

He laughed, even though it hurt. To be seduced by Melody. Christ, he wouldn't withstand five seconds before he started begging. No persuasion required. Watching her get arrested had been the cure for the hunger she'd incited on the plane, but hell if it wasn't back now, bigger and badder than ever. How was he supposed to combat it when the universe was throwing twin mattresses into his path?

"We'll figure it out," Melody said with a quick glance at the camera. "Just a friendly sleepover. Nothing to see here."

*Nothing but my multiplying obsession with you.*

"Nothing at all."

She rolled her lips inward and nodded. "Should we join the debauchery for a bit?"

Beat shoved his hands into the pockets of his dress pants to prevent himself from reaching for her. "What's the holiday season without a little debauchery?"

When she walked by him, his lungs filled themselves with air made so much sweeter with the scent of her, and he followed, Joseph taking up the rear. Danielle, who was waiting in the hallway furiously tapping away on her phone, smiled when they emerged and joined their slow-moving procession toward the earsplitting music, descending three staircases to the main level of the house. All four of them stopped at the bottom, surveying the scene in front of them. They'd only been in the attic for ten minutes and already, shit was getting wild.

Based on the number of occupied rooms in the house, at least a dozen people lived here with Trina. More than that if those individuals were sharing rooms. Based on the make-out session taking place in the shadowed nook beneath the staircase, at least two of Trina's guests were . . . roommates. It appeared every member of the household was in attendance at the celebration, and none of them seemed fazed by the camera or the quartet of strangers in their midst. Some of them even waved, Purple Bandanna man flashing a peace sign.

A Christmas tree decorated with big, vintage bulbs sat in one corner. Beyond that, there were only two lamps providing light to the downstairs space and their shades had been draped with colorful scarves, casting the room in a festive red and green glow. The pungent scent of marijuana hung in the atmosphere, but the house was so big and airy that it wasn't cloying. Beat was relieved to find that, in keeping with the bizarre throwback hippie compound vibe, everyone seemed relaxed and welcoming. Not quite relieved enough to let Melody out of his sight, though. Not after how quickly things had shifted that afternoon.

Melody tapped his elbow and pointed across the living room to where Trina stood on an old trunk, a bottle of Southern Comfort in one hand, a lit joint in the other, dancing to Wilson Phillips. The four of them took a collective step in Trina's direction when a man in ripped white jeans jumped up onto the trunk beside Melody's mother, grabbed the back of her neck, and planted a kiss on her mouth.

Melody skidded to a halt, blinking several times. "That's one way to meet my new dad."

Trina noticed them out of the corner of her eye and broke the kiss with a laugh that momentarily drowned out the music. Then she hopped down from the trunk and signaled for White Jeans to do the same. Once he'd done so, Trina clasped his hand and guided him through a group of dancing housemates toward Beat, Melody, Danielle, and Joseph.

"Hey you!" Trina shouted to Melody over the music. "This is Buck. Buck, this is my daughter, Melody Anne."

"So nice to meet you." Melody held out her hand for a shake, but Buck released Trina's hand and pulled Melody in for a shirtless hug instead, tensing every muscle in Beat's body.

Trina watched Beat's face the entire time, slowly sipping from the bottle in her hand.

Finally, Melody wiggled out of the young man's embrace, giving Buck an awkward pat on the shoulder. "Buck, you seem to be about my age, so I'm not sure about fatherly hugs from you, okay?"

"God, I fucking love her," Danielle growled, behind Beat.

Yeah. Beat was beginning to grow very familiar with the feeling.

"Have you been seeing my mother very long, Buck?" Melody asked.

Trina and Buck traded an amused glance. "In a manner of speaking," replied Melody's mother. "We don't necessarily confine ourselves to relationships in this house."

Melody was already nodding her understanding. "You know, halfway through my question, I got there. I put it together."

Buck leaned in. "If it makes you feel better, Melody Anne, your mother is my favorite."

"Oh, it does, Buck." Another series of shoulder pats. "Thank you."

Melody elbowed Beat in the ribs. "We should get a drink," Beat suggested, recognizing her cry for help. "Trina? Buck? Would you like anything from the kitchen?"

"We're good, thanks," Trina said, tone overly sweet. "Do you know how to prepare your own drink, Beat Dawkins? Doesn't the butler normally do that for you?"

It was a cheap jab, but it caught Beat in his sore spot, stiffening his shoulders.

"Mom, please," Melody sighed.

"I make my own drinks, thank you."

Trina snorted. "Maybe *your* mother wanted to raise a pampered child, but that's not how I chose to raise mine." She sent her daughter a pointed look. "You're letting him make you soft, Melody Anne."

An eruption was forming in the center of Beat's chest. Trina was telling the truth about one thing—she definitely hadn't raised a pampered child. She didn't do any raising *at all*, because she was never there, leaving Melody to live through the torture inflicted on her by the press. Beat opened his mouth to tell Trina exactly what he thought of her parenting style, but he should have known that Melody didn't need his help.

"Soft?" Melody breathed, her shoulders dipping and rising on a breath. "I stayed. I stayed in New York with all the cameras and scrutiny. You. Ran. *You* ran away because everyone was mean to you. Not me." Beat had never been prouder of anything or anyone in his life than when Melody stepped into her mother's personal space and lifted her chin. "If you ask me, you're the soft one, up here hiding behind some juvenile blame game. Why don't you write a song about that? Unless maybe you're too afraid to get onstage and sing it."

"Oh shit," muttered Joseph.

"Oh shit is right," Danielle said, reverently. "Did she throw down the reunion gauntlet by accident or is she an actual mastermind?"

Beat shook his head. He couldn't take his eyes off Melody. Her display of courage was prying his ribs apart. "She's not thinking about the reunion right now."

Silence had encompassed the living room, the music having been lowered in deference to the obvious argument taking place between Trina and Melody. Beat breathed through the urge to carry Melody out of the house and take her somewhere far, far away. He quelled the impulse, stood at her back, and waited for the smallest sign that she needed him.

Buck, of all people, broke the uneasy silence. "Hell, Trina definitely isn't afraid of being onstage. She sings for us all the time."

"Wow." Melody looked around. "Might as well be Madison Square Garden."

Trina's eye started to twitch.

Again, Buck attempted to lighten the mood. "Why don't you sing something for us right now, Trina?" He signaled someone across the room with a wave, as frantic as possible for someone with a peace sign tattoo. "What about 'Celebrity Skin' by Hole? You love that one."

A woman handed Buck a guitar and he strummed a few notes.

"Why don't you sing something by Steel Birds?" Melody suggested.

Audible gasps went up around the room. The music cut out completely.

Melody scanned the crowd that had formed around them. "What?"

Buck coughed into his fist. "We don't . . . we don't play them here. Don't talk about the band, either." He rubbed his jaw. "It's sort of a requirement to stay."

"Ah." Melody pursed her lips. "So it's all free love and living wild on the surface. But what you've *actually* got here is a strict set of rules designed to make yourself comfortable." Melody appeared amused by her revelation. Her chest started to rise faster, a sheen forming in her eyes. "Well, I don't live here. These people didn't even know I existed until today and I don't have to follow the rules."

Melody took the guitar from Buck and abruptly left the circle that had formed.

She stomped over to the trunk where Trina had been standing and made an attempt to climb on—and failed. She was too short. Beat was already on the move. He reached her within five seconds, prepared to boost her up onto the piece of furniture. Before he could reach her, however, she shocked the hell out of him by executing a flawless box jump.

"Oh!" She spun around, mouth open. "I did it!"

His chest felt fuzzy. "Next stop: two-year gym membership."

"They'll have to kill me first."

Beat's laugh cut off when she strummed a few notes. "Hold up. You play the guitar?" he asked, his eyes level with her stomach.

"I took reverse lessons," she whispered, voice shaking.

He repeated that explanation out loud. "What does that mean?"

"It means that, unlike box jumping, I got *worse* the more guitar lessons I took."

"I see."

"I was remembering what your mother said about sucker-punching the spotlight back next time. But with everyone looking at me, I'm suddenly regretting getting up here."

"No regrets." He squeezed her waist. "You're going to absolutely slay."

Her fingers strummed a couple of the strings, the notes perfectly familiar to him. "You're just saying that because you're my best friend."

*Was this what it was like to be 100 percent willing to die for someone?*

Out of the corner of his eye, Beat could see the camera's blinking red light and, honestly, it just didn't mean a goddamn thing in that moment. "You're my best friend, too, Peach."

"Best enough to sing with me?"

Was he supposed to be breathing right now? "Best enough for anything."

Melody shifted side to side, released a long, shuddering exhale.

"Okay, here goes." And to Beat's utter shock, her upper lip tugged into a snarl, the opening line of "Rattle the Cage" bursting out of her in a sold-out stadium-worthy growl. "Well, you can't get to heaven raising *this much hell*!"

He only had a split second to overcome his shock before she widened her eyes at him, begging him to join in. *Don't leave me hanging.*

Beat climbed up onto the trunk beside her, angling himself so he wouldn't disrupt her guitar playing. "Fingers wrapped tight around the bars of your cell," he shouted. Terribly. He couldn't sing for shit. "Now shake those motherfuckers, show them how they offend!"

They both held up a middle finger, as was tradition at this stage of the song.

"Rattle the cage," they sang together. "They won't keep *us* penned."

Danielle was the only one in the room cheering them on—and she did so with enthusiasm. Joseph stood in front of them filming, a grin splitting his face beneath the viewfinder. The inhabitants of the Free Loving Adventure Club looked distinctly uncomfortable, although a couple of them sang along under their breath. None of them existed, though, after the first verse. There was only Beat and Melody, trapped in this moment of time that felt fated. Someone had written it into their story a long time ago and they'd finally found their place on the correct page, so they could follow along.

She was glorious. Brave and uninhibited and a little sad. A lot wise.

Even as he sang, Beat's throat burned with the need to reach back into the past and rearrange every hour of his life, so it could have been spent with her. Knowing her.

He wished for it so vividly that he didn't even realize the song ended until the guitar dropped to Melody's side, remaining there until White Jeans collected it without a word. She was staring back at Beat in a way his body understood. Responded to.

Voraciously.

It was pure lust. It was *I need you now*. With them on the same page, he could do nothing but keep reading. Unable to stop himself, too hungry for his counterpart to second-guess his actions and their consequences, Beat jumped down off the trunk, helping Melody down and leading her behind him toward the staircase by the wrist.

Melody tugged him to a stop in front of Trina who was looking at her daughter with an impassive expression. "We're leaving in the morning," Melody said quietly. "And I'd rather you didn't come visit me in February."

"Done," Trina drawled into a sip of whiskey.

But Melody was already walking away, Beat at her side.

Wisely, Joseph didn't follow with the camera.

# Chapter Twenty

*T*hey crashed into the tiny attic room like tangled wrecking balls.

Melody's blood had never been so hot that she could feel it, the elevated temperature of it, flowing through her veins. Her throat hurt from singing at the top of her lungs, something she'd never attempted in her life, but Beat's mouth on hers was the perfect cure. She had no idea where these stolen moments in the starlight would lead, but just then, she didn't care.

She was cocky.

If she could imply her mother was a coward—to her face—and belt out a Steel Birds song in a room full of people, she could handle a potential broken heart. In fact, bring it on. Bring it all on. She was immortal tonight and she scorned the concept of regret or pain.

How could a single negative thing exist on this earth at the same time as his mouth? It was the perfect combination of reverent and aggressive, his adventurous tongue banishing any possibility of stopping. Or thinking. Or breathing. She opened her lips wide for him, their heads canting to their respective rights in tandem, like they were built for each other. To kiss this wildly in this house in the middle of nowhere, to taste each other without a hint of reservation or insecurity. The only thing present between them was feverish want and deep recognition of two souls that had been separated too long. Maybe not good for each other, but created as a pair for better or worse.

Melody's fingers plowed through Beat's hair, scrubbed down his flexing back, and came around the front to his belt, unbuckling it, using her thumb to free the top button.

Her hand hovered an inch from the thick jut of his erection, but didn't touch.

Two seconds passed. Three.

His breath coasted over her damp lips. "Kept it hard, like you asked me to."

A moan broke from deep in her throat. Those whispered words twisted hot in her center, liquid warmth making itself known between her thighs. She could feel it happening. The arousal of her body, her flesh going pliant everywhere. *Everywhere.* Intimacy with Beat was her only aphrodisiac and he was radiating the need for it, too. They were in too deep, but they were in it together so stopping was impossible. Togetherness was too good and right.

"What am I going to do with it?" she said, rubbing their wet lips together.

"Anything you goddamn want, Peach."

Was it normal to feel one's pupils expand? "Mmm." She traced the thick line of him with her index finger and watched his eyes go blind, a notch catching and locking in his throat. He needed to be touched, but he needed to *not* be touched even more, at least right now. Somehow, she knew. And she gave by withholding friction, leaving him panting while she went to unbutton his dress shirt instead, undoing the buttons from throat to belly. Their mouths devoured, his exploring hers desperately from above, never stopping, not even when she pushed the garment from his shoulders and let it fall to the ground, followed by his battery pack and microphone. Thank God they'd turned off the mics before coming up the stairs or America would be listening to groans and sighs and shifting clothing that only meant one thing.

Melody's shirt came off next, their hands colliding to unfasten the front snap of her bra, dislodging the mic while yanking the lingerie down her arms, leaving her breasts free. "I've wanted to get you out of these fucking jeans since you walked out of my guest room this morning," he rasped, attacking the side of her neck with kisses, rough licks of his tongue. "I can still feel the seam of them on my dick from the lap dance you gave me earlier. Can feel you riding me, working me until I'm stiff." He nipped at her mouth. "You've been arrested in those jeans. You sang 'Rattle the Cage' in them like you'd been saving it up your whole life. I don't think I'll ever be able to see you in these jeans again without feeling like I'm dying. Or living for the first time. I can't tell." His hands smoothed up the valleys of her sides and closed over her breasts, kneading, thumbing her nipples with the pads of his thumbs. "But right now, I want those jeans off." Slowly, he backed her toward the wall, just to the right of the giant, circular window, and dropped to his knees, his tongue leaving a shiny path from throat to belly button. "I want them off so I can give you some good fucking head."

He wasn't gentle about unfastening her jeans. The button was barely free when he wrestled with the zipper and began dragging the denim down her thighs, past her knees, to her ankles. When she kicked them off, he caught her right leg in midair and held her open, his breath hot against the front of her panties.

"Mel." He grazed her belly button with his teeth, then took a soft, full bite of her hip, shooting torpedoes of sensation all the way to her toes. Pulses she couldn't name started to pound. His tongue rode along the skin just above her waistband, hip to hip, his eyes heavy with lust and trained on her. And slowly, slowly, he peeled her panties down to her feet, a ripple passing through his shoulders when he bared her sex. "You should know that I want to get my cock so deep between your legs, it becomes your entire world while it's there." In keeping with Beat's words—his warning?—something animalistic flickered in the depths of his blue eyes that caused a flutter in Melody's throat, a long, anticipatory tightening in her core. "And I might stop right at my edge, but I don't hold back getting there."

"I'm ready for anything with you."

Her trust relaxed the line between his brows, his lips kissing a path from her belly button to the top of her slit. His breath heated her there for long seconds, moistening her flesh, his demeanor reminiscent of someone in prayer. And then he transformed right into a sinner, forming a V with his middle and index fingers to gently push apart her flesh. His tongue lapped once at her exposed center, and then brought it back into his mouth to savor her flavor with a groan, before he leaned in again with triple the eagerness. He made sounds in his throat while he delved his tongue into the valley of her sex again, again, again, his tongue meeting her clit with more firmness with every journey until it simply stayed there and rubbed, rubbed, rubbed. His blue eyes were trained on her face, glittering, as his thumbs dug into her hip abductors. And her thighs were a blur of trembling already, from the view, from the experience, yes, but the *friction*. It was raw and personal and he was visibly enjoying it. So much that he looked intoxicated, his shaft bulging through the opening of his dress pants, stretching his briefs, the proof of his own hunger drawing her deeper, deeper into her own enjoyment.

He delivered her oral pleasure like it was an honor, like he wouldn't survive without the next twist of his tongue against her entrance, the firm circling of her swelling nub.

*I'm so wet.*

Which he apparently loved, because he seemed to want that offering all over his chin, his mouth. He buried his face against her and turned it side to side, collecting her, pushing his tongue upward once again into the separation of her sex. Fucking her with his tongue, pressing it into her body while the V of his fingers spread her, giving him more access. And once he got it, those fingers took turns with his tongue, pumping inside of her, which was when it all came crashing down. She'd been so distracted by the overtly carnal side of Beat, so determined to memorize it, that she didn't acknowledge the gathering of her own release until it was on the verge of liberating her. It blew through her now with a vengeance, her right leg shooting up to wrap around the back of his head, her hips tilting, babble bubbling from her lips while those intimate muscles flexed and throbbed and set her free of tension.

Some of it.

Even with the exhilarating rush of her climax still cutting through her middle, holding her shaking legs captive, she felt her own hunger crest again, because Beat swiped a forearm across his shining mouth and then looked right at her while licking it off again. And her head swam, her nipples beading, the lowest part of her belly growing heavy with desire once more. With responsibility and anticipation and something more magical . . .

An electrical connection to this man that moved their bodies in unrehearsed choreography. Beat lunged to his feet, as if he sensed that she needed kissing, grounding, and he gave it to her, urging her lips open with his tongue and sharing the taste of her in a way that was unabashed, almost prideful. But she didn't require any reminder of the pleasure he'd just given her, because she could think of nothing else. Her right hand moved without a command from her brain, sliding beneath the waistband of his briefs, wanting, needing, to reciprocate.

"Ahhh, that's good, Peach. Grip it as hard as you can." His breath pelted her mouth, his thickly muscled chest lifting and falling. "I like when it hurts."

Melody followed her instinct, stroking him lightly, slowly, once, twice, three times, watching his teeth sink into his bottom lip, eyes squeezed shut, holding his breath. Then she tightened her hold and listened to his guttural grunt, looking down and watching him try to thrust into her hand, hips pumping upward. And she used that hard clutch of his shaft to turn their bodies and firmly press him up against the wall, watching in awe as his Adam's apple got stuck beneath his chin. His hands lifted, fisted his own hair, like he couldn't withstand the torture of being stroked by her. Combined with the immortality she'd earned downstairs, she'd never felt more formidable in her life. It *inebriated* her.

"I want you inside me." She elevated onto her toes and kissed his panting mouth, riding her palm up and down his inches at the same meandering pace, over and over until she felt a touch of sticky moisture on her knuckles, a gruff rendition of her name punctuating the air. "Make it happen."

Melody's command was still on her lips when Beat's back slid down the wall.

Never breaking eye contact with her—he wasn't even sure it was physically possible—he drew the elastic of his briefs down, leaving it beneath his balls. He offered her his lap, because she'd requested it. Even though being inside of Melody terrified him as much as it felt like an inevitability he couldn't live without. Couldn't fucking *breathe* without.

*Jesus Christ.*

It was dark in the room, except for the starlight casting her naked body in an ethereal glow, her pussy damp from his tongue, her gaze determined, but glazed. She was an angel drunk on the effect she had on him. An effect that was almost too pure and poignant to withstand as she got down on her knees in front of him—so beautiful that he held his breath—and climbed onto his lap, their foreheads meeting, eyes locking.

"Tell me when you're close and I'll stop," she whispered.

Gratitude swam in his chest. Lower, there was nothing but the thick bite of lust. "Tell me when you're close and I'll go harder."

She moaned right into his mouth and he swallowed the sound, sipping kisses from her lips while reaching down, bringing his cock between her thighs. He rubbed it up and back through the ample moisture, swelling more, more, until he worried he could come from that preliminary torture alone.

"You ready for it?"

"Yes."

"Lift up. Good girl. Now come back down—" His breath hissed out as she accepted the tip of him, her hips shifting side to side until she took more. "Oh shit. Oh God."

"*Beat.*"

His balls drew up painfully. "Don't whine like that. I'm going to come."

"*Beat.*"

"Don't move. Please, please, baby, stay still while I wrap my head around you. *Jesus.*" Fully inside of her now and reeling over her snug, wet warmth, he gathered her close, burying his face into her neck, seeing nothing in the room, oblivious to anything but his sense of touch. Feel. *Melody.* "Were you made for me? Is that what this is?"

Her hips undulated slowly. "You feel perfect for me, too."

He moaned, sparks blinking in front of his eyes. "Baby, don't start yet."

"I can't help it."

"*Fuck.*"

His hands raked down her back, caught her ass in his hands and ordered his body to remain just like this. Hard. Primed for her, ready for her use, but refusing to accept his own relief. He loved this, loved being the key to pleasure. Loved her getting the prize, while he was denied. Denial was the only thing that could fulfill him sexually, as far back as he could remember, but there would be no comparison to *this*. Sacrificing his own release for Melody. He'd only been inside of her a matter of seconds and the sex was fucking unparalleled, because he could feel it in his being. His heart, his bones, his blood. Christ, *everywhere*.

Was Melody the ultimate high he'd been chasing without realizing it?

His body told him yes, as she started to move. Or was he moving her? It was impossible to know who started the motion, whether it was the rock of her hips or the urgency of his hands on her ass cheeks. But once they were moving, the pace was immediately frantic. Her teeth sank into the side of his neck, deep enough to draw blood, and need became a welcome plague in his gut, the sound of her damp pussy accepting him again, again, again making him too horny to sit still, so he slid backward to plant his elbows on the ground, giving himself the leverage required to fuck her from below.

"Tell me how it feels," he growled.

"It's too good," she cried out into his neck. "It's too perfect. I can't stand it."

"I know. Jesus, Mel. Jesus."

He didn't know everything about Melody's sexual likes and dislikes yet. He would, though. For now, he just wanted to thank God. He wasn't a religious man, but he'd been a good enough person to earn this privilege. She'd confided in him about holding herself back from other partners in the past, but not with him. No. She trusted him enough to let go. He could practically *feel* her bestowing that honor on him, his body responding in kind.

"You let go with *me*," he breathed, letting go of her backside to cup the back of her neck, his hips lifting into her with vigorous slaps, her thighs trembling more with every upward punch. "Let *go* with me."

She made this whimpering sound that almost caused him to spill and tightened her thighs around his hips, her pace increasing to a gallop. Every time she took him balls deep, Beat swore he felt it in an undiscovered region of his stomach.

"I'm close," she said hoarsely.

His eyes rolled back into his head, his fingers curling into fists. "Go get it, Melody. Fuck me. Make me hurt. Then take it all away, before I get there, baby, please." His nails dug into his palms until they broke the skin. "Goddamn, you've got me so stiff."

Melody's tongue was hot and magical on his neck and he allowed himself to pretend that she required his taste in order to orgasm. It burned him alive with hunger, his hands molding to her ass again and yanking her up and back, his cock growing harder, reaching for that free fall of relief he wouldn't let himself take. And suddenly, her thighs jerked and she screamed into his shoulder, moisture pooling where their bodies joined and he couldn't help it. His heart demanded he delve his fingers into her hair and lift her head, so he could watch her eyes while she plummeted to earth.

He would well and truly never be the same again.

The axis of his world tilted, changed directions, desperation clawing even deeper into his being. This wasn't sex for the sake of lust, but a requirement to get as close to this woman as humanly possible. Before he could register his own actions, he was coming to his feet with Melody still impaled on his shaft and throwing her down onto the mattress, coming down on top of her and fucking her for broke.

"I was right. Pulling out of you is going to be pure hell. *God*, it's so wet."

Panic set in as the hedonism inside of him, inside of them both, ran wild. *Oh God.* He wasn't going to stop. He couldn't stop. Not with her so smooth beneath him, their eyes fastened together, flesh slapping sharply with every thrust. But he should have known to trust Melody to give him exactly what he was craving. She waited until his teeth were drawing blood from his bottom lip, his abdomen hollowing in warning and she leaned up, whispering, "Stop," against his mouth, her nails raking down his back, burying in the flesh of his ass. "Don't. Move."

Beat dropped his open mouth into the curve of her neck just in time to catch his hoarse groan. He shook so hard with the need to come that he had to clench his teeth to keep them from chattering. His toes twisted in the mattress, his balls in his fucking stomach. He wasn't going to make it out of this alive and while it was torture, it was also paradise. "*Yes. Please,*" he grunted, mentally commanding himself not to grind, not to pump. "Make me work for it. Make me work for you."

"Wouldn't it feel so good to keep going?" she whispered in his ear.

"*Yes,*" he growled through his teeth.

She constricted around him. "Too bad."

Pain was beginning to wrap around the base of his spine. "Please. Oh *fuck*, you're so *tight. Squeezing* me."

"You can ride me a little longer, but don't come."

The words were barely out of her mouth and Beat was bearing down on her, gripping her knees and pinning them up near her shoulders, his hips pistoning, sweat pouring down his spine, the sides of his face. He only managed about ten seconds before he felt the climax zippering his balls together, tightening, tightening. *You have to stop.*

"Jesus Christ, I'm so ruined for this pussy."

"Keep going."

"No. No, it's going to be over. You fuck so hot."

"Don't stop," she whispered, almost to herself.

"Mel. *Mel.*"

*No. Your life has enough rewards. You don't get this, too.*

He barely managed to pull out of her in time. The orgasm was like a bomb going off, pulling every tendon and muscle in his body into a taut, vibrating line. He rolled off Melody onto the mattress and buried his face in the crook of his elbow, muffling his roar, his opposite hand reaching down to help finish himself off, which was completely unnecessary as wave after wave after wave of bliss whipped through him, visions of her continuing to play in his head. Her tits bouncing, her mouth parting on whimpers, her knees in his hands. *Ohhh God*, it went on forever, his loins locking and releasing until his entire body went slack, heart continuing to sprint in his chest.

Bar none, the most incredible sex of his life. Nothing had ever and would ever compare. Not only was he relieved physically, but mentally. Soulfully. He'd lost consciousness and woken up in a land where nothing bad happened.

That's how he felt at first, anyway. In those initial moments of afterglow, he marveled over the way they'd fulfilled each other perfectly on the first try.

Until that glow started to fade and he realized . . . he wished, for once, that he was capable of sharing even more. Everything, including that final moment he'd never shared with anyone else. "Hey." With an oddly panicked feeling swamping his sternum, he turned on his side and reached for her. "Come here." Beat wrapped his arms around Melody, drew her up against his chest, and encompassed her in a bear hug, planting kisses all over her face, neck, and shoulders. "My peach."

With a hesitant smile, she allowed Beat to arrange her arms

around his torso, her head tucked beneath his chin, his embrace a crushing death grip.

"I've got you, I've got you, I've got you," he chanted, even though it wasn't enough.

But the next morning, he realized he didn't have her.

Not at all.

# Chapter Twenty-One

*December 17*

**M**elody wanted her bed.

She wanted her flannel pajamas and her loofah and her secret fruit snacks drawer.

She wanted to go home.

When she'd agreed to *Wreck the Halls*, she'd decided to take the adventure as it came. Not to worry about the outcome or ruminate over every little decision until she was blue in the face. She'd intended to shatter the walls of her comfort zone. Stir everything up so it would land differently. She'd wanted a new okay.

And she was feeling the consequences of being reckless now.

Emotional whiplash was her unofficial diagnosis and the symptoms were sitting in the back seat of the SUV that would transport them to the airport, staring straight ahead. Too dumbfounded by the last twenty-four hours to do anything but replay her uncharacteristically hasty decisions over and over again.

Not the least of which was having sex with Beat.

Although could one actually refer to what they'd done as sex?

It had been more like . . . mating?

There was none of the awkward pawing and requesting of

boundaries and laboring to find the correct rhythm. She'd had an animal mindset. Give, receive, don't think, get pleasure, give it back. Give, receive, give until the very sky was coming down. She'd expected sex with Beat to be amazing, unforgettable, orgasmic. And she'd severely underestimated it.

Shouldn't she be glowing and blushing and preening this morning?

She'd woken up wrapped in Beat's arms and something inside of her had been off. And being off with Beat around? That was new. It was usually the opposite.

Danielle turned in the front seat of the SUV, giving Melody a speculative once-over. "Are you sure you're okay?"

"Yes."

Several seconds passed.

Danielle checked her watch. "The plane should be ready and waiting. You said Beat is still upstairs sleeping?"

"Yeah." Melody shook herself out of her stupor. Somewhat. "Yeah, we went back down to the party for a while after you left for the motel last night." Lie. "Too much tequila."

"You mean, after you belted 'Rattle the Cage' and brought the house down?"

Melody forced a laugh. "Yes. After that."

Danielle studied her. "Are you sure that's all that happened?"

Before Melody could locate an answer, the front door of the house opened and Beat blew out into the early morning light, his hair in ninety directions, shirt still unbuttoned. His turbulent gaze searched the immediate area and homed right in on Melody where she sat in the back row of the SUV. They stared at each other through the glass for a handful of heavy seconds until she swallowed and looked away, her chest twisting like a pretzel.

Should she have stayed in bed? Been there when he woke up?

They might have made love again. God knew she would have enjoyed it.

So what was wrong with her?

*Please just get me home.*

A moment later, the back door of the SUV opened, shooting Melody's heart into her mouth. Beat climbed in beside her, his inviting smoky fireplace scent filling the vehicle's interior. If she glanced over, she would find him staring at her with that singular intensity. The warmth on her cheek and some unnamed intuition told her so.

Joseph settled in the middle row, hefting the camera up onto his shoulder. "Starting the live stream in three—"

"Wait," Beat clipped, tipping up Melody's chin. "Hey. Look at me."

She steeled herself before doing as he asked.

Whatever Beat saw caused some of the color to leave his face. "What's wrong, Peach?"

"I don't know," she said, honestly.

"Okay." He lowered his voice another octave, so it would only reach Melody's ears, a flicker of dread in his gaze. "Did I hurt you last night?"

"*No.* God, no. Nothing like that."

Air escaped him in a gust.

All right, she was worrying him. Being vague and evasive, which wasn't fair when he was clearly worried. What was wrong? She needed to figure out a way to say it out loud, put it on the table. "I guess . . . I loved what we did last night. Every second. It was perfect. But . . ." Hyperaware of the other two people in the SUV, she leaned over to speak near Beat's ear. "You told me on the plane that you don't want to let anyone in . . . at the end. And that's your right. That's totally okay, but I didn't expect it to make me feel so . . . lonely."

Devastation rolled off him in such thick waves, she almost

wanted to take back her explanation. "I made you feel lonely?" he asked, sounding hollow.

"Maybe it's me."

"No. Never."

"I mean, maybe I *need* to be let in. Maybe I need that trust. From you. With you. Or . . . nothing at all." She swallowed a rock. "There's nothing for either of us to be sorry about. There's no blame to cast. We decided to try—and we did."

Beat said nothing, continuing to stare out the car window on the other side of Melody.

A full minute of silence ticked by in the car before Danielle gently broke it. "Did you want to say goodbye to your mother, Mel?"

"No. I did that last night," she said, lips feeling stiff. "All set."

"Should I start the stream now?" asked Joseph.

Beat and Melody took a deep breath in tandem and nodded.

She watched the red light jump to life in the rearview mirror, watching the numbers multiply on Danielle's phone, though she was too far away to read them clearly. How many people had witnessed their impromptu show last night? How many people were wondering what happened after they left the room, obviously heading upstairs?

Melody almost laughed. Even the best guesses would be wrong.

"So I am going to go out on a limb here . . ." Melody started. "And say that we have a better chance of John Cena performing on Christmas Eve than Trina Gallard. Unless I misread her, there's no way she's going to do it."

"Where does that leave us?" Beat asked Danielle, while still looking at Melody.

The producer hummed. "Don't worry, I have a trick up my sleeve." She shimmied her shoulders. "Something to keep the conversation on the table . . ."

"Ooh." Melody produced a smile. "Does it involve me getting arrested again?"

"It better not," Beat said.

"No, it doesn't. But I need a couple of days to pull everything together." Danielle steepled her fingers as she spoke. "In light of Trina's refusal yesterday, I spent some time last night outlining our next approach. For now, we're going to split up for the next two days. With all the attention we're getting, the network approved a second cameraman."

"They won't be as good as me," Joseph rumbled.

Danielle's mouth twisted. "Do you want me to hold your camera so you can stroke your ego with both hands?"

Joseph glared at the producer. "Been doing more than enough stroking since I took this job."

If looks could kill, he would have been dead. "Of all people, you know we're live."

"You brought it up."

Danielle tipped her face up toward the ceiling. "I love my new plan. I can't *wait* to split up."

"If you think I'm letting you film with another cameraman, baby, you're sorely mistaken."

The producer was on the verge of arguing, but visibly swallowed her rejoinder. "As I was saying," she said, with a pointed look at the camera. "We're going to split up for two days. Beat will be with *one* of the cameramen and an associate producer. I'll stay with Mel and the other cameraman. If all goes according to plan, we'll reconvene on Tuesday morning . . ." She executed a mini drumroll on the back of the seat. "On the *Today* show. Bright and early."

"The *Today* show?" Melody exclaimed. "They want to bring us on?"

Danielle scoffed. "Melody, everyone wants to bring you two on. And I mean *everyone*." She left that grand statement dangling in the air. "Over the next two days, while I pull my plan together, just try and go about your normal lives. While being filmed, of course."

"Of course." Beat sounded dry, casual, but every muscle in his body was visibly unsettled. "How are we going to split up if Melody is staying at my place?"

"I'm not. I really need to go home."

He tensed further. "I thought we decided it wasn't safe."

"Then I'll collect some things and go to a hotel. I just . . ." Emotional exhaustion was beginning to creep up on her, making her eyes feel hot and gritty. "I just think a couple of days to regroup is a good idea." As lopsided as things were between herself and Beat at the moment, she didn't want to add to his stockpile of guilt, so she tacked on, "I have a bocce game tomorrow night, anyway. I should . . . mentally prepare."

"Ooh!" Danielle produced her clipboard seemingly from thin air. "I'll contact them today about filming and release forms."

Melody sputtered. "You're going to film my bocce game?"

"Yes, of course." Danielle's pen scratched on the clipboard. "Viewers will love it."

Beat leaned forward. "Is that going to be safe for her?"

Frustration welled in Melody's chest. "I can take care of myself. Stop worrying about me."

His voice rose. "Do you think I can just turn this off? Carve you out of my chest? I can't."

Melody remained unmoving in the wake of that statement, but her pulse rollicked at the pace of a racehorse rounding the bend. Danielle's gaze cut to Joseph, then away—because, oh God, they were streaming. The silence that followed was deafening. And Melody didn't know how to feel, either. Elated to be so important to Beat. Curious enough to read further into what he'd said. Or just plain sad because she couldn't simply enjoy mind-blowing sex without yearning for *more*. Most frustrating of all was the wretched ache inside of her, demanding she unfasten her seat belt, crawl into Beat's lap, and remain there forever.

Finally, Beat broke the uncomfortable silence he'd created. "Please just make sure she has the security team with her, all right?" he said, gruffly.

"Of course," Danielle murmured.

Nobody spoke for the remainder of the drive to the airport.

After an eerily silent flight, the foursome was woefully unprepared for the mayhem that greeted them back in New York. They deplaned and got into another waiting SUV, everything seemingly normal. But when they pulled through the exit gates of the tarmac, thousands of people were waiting.

At their appearance, a roar moved like a waking beast through the crowd, erupting in a deafening wail of cheers. Melody sat straight up in the rear seat, Beat sliding close and wrapping his arms around her shoulders, tugging her protectively to his chest. "How did they know where we were landing?"

"Either it was a lucky guess or the flight crew leaked it," Danielle responded, staring out the front windshield at the sea of bodies, their gloved hands holding up signs, their excited breaths vaporizing in the air. They beat the windows of the SUV with their fists, cupping their hands in an attempt to see inside, screaming Melody's and Beat's names.

Totally dumbstruck by the sight, Melody labored to fill her lungs.

"This is crazy. I don't understand it."

Danielle made a wishy-washy sound. "You asked me to keep the viewer count to myself, but, uh . . . you sort of broke the internet last night singing 'Rattle the Cage' in front of the woman who wrote it. And now refuses to perform it. And her much younger boyfriend. Basically, what I'm trying to say is—"

"It was good TV," Melody breathed.

The producer sighed. "That would be an understatement."

They passed a sign that read: MELODY GALLARD IS MY LOVE LANGUAGE.

Another one read: THEY'RE TOTALLY FUCKING.

Last: THE "ONLY ONE BED" TROPE IRL! MY LIFE IS COMPLETE.

Huh?

Police sirens cut through the quiet midmorning air, officers wading through the crowd to push the mass of bodies to one side or the other, allowing the SUV to drive through the exit. Several members of the crowd chased after the SUV, one of them holding out an open ring box, though Melody wasn't sure if they were proposing to her or Beat.

Danielle clapped her hands together. "Now that we've escaped Belody Mania—"

"What was that?" Beat interrupted.

"Belody is your ship name. It's what they're calling you."

He fell back against the seat, taking Melody with him. They were still being filmed.

What had her life become?

"Beat, do you have any plans over the next couple of days? I just want to make sure we get the itinerary straight before communicating it to the associate producer."

"Plans." He raked a hand through his hair, looking over Melody, as if to determine whether or not she'd escaped the mob without a scratch, even though they were *inside* the vehicle. "I . . . yes. Based on the number of missed calls on my phone, I'm guessing my mother either caught some of the live stream last night or heard about it. I should probably do some damage control there. Other than that, I have a Christmas party tomorrow night at seven. Small one at my friend Vance's place."

"Ahh, I see. Two events at once." Danielle chewed her lip and made another notation. "Maybe we can do a split screen, Mel at bocce, Beat at the party—"

"Ma'am, we're here," said the driver.

"Thank you." Danielle started to gather her things, gesturing for Melody to do the same. She'd been so caught off guard by the crowd she'd been slow to recognize her surroundings, but realized now that they'd stopped at the rental car section of the airport. "Melody, our driver and the new cameraperson are meeting us here."

Beat sat forward. "She's leaving *now?*"

"I'm leaving now?" she said at the same time, stopping just shy of reaching for Beat's hand. Which was ridiculous. She needed time and space to get her infatuation under control. Not to mention, come to terms with everything that had happened last night with her mother, like finding out Trina never even spoke about her. Maybe her mother loved her in some backward way, but Melody mostly felt like a bill that needed to be paid while Trina played make-believe with the adventure club—and that wasn't what Melody wanted. Or needed. Whether or not Melody earned the million-dollar payout from *Wreck the Halls*, she didn't want to be supported by her mother any longer. It didn't mean she wouldn't mourn the loss. For that, she needed time.

This break from Beat was good. This was healthy.

She turned to Beat and kissed his cheek. "See you in two days."

His voice was like gravel when he responded, his big chest lifting and falling. "Yeah."

If she left things unsettled between them, she'd regret it for the next forty-eight hours. Melody turned to look at the camera, then back at Beat, leaning close to whisper in his ear. "I think you hold yourself back, because you were taught—*we* were taught—that the truth is ugly and should always be private. Suppressed. I think you hold yourself back because you were outcasted by those kids after you opened up to them," she whispered, wetting her lips. "What you enjoy is beautiful if it's for the right reasons. But if it's for the wrong reasons, I'm just not sure *I* can . . . do what happened last night . . . again. No matter what, though, Beat, we're best friends. I think maybe we have been this whole time without even seeing each other. If we can still be best friends after one crazy night, I think that means we're in it for the long haul." She searched for the right words. "Maybe we just needed to get it out of our systems?"

He huffed a sound. "You'll never leave my system, Mel. You're one-half of it."

Again, she had to resist crawling into his lap and wrapping herself around him like a bow, but she remembered the jarring loneliness of last night too well. Not being trusted with all of him was worse than having none of him, wasn't it? Yes, it was. Especially when she wanted to give him everything. All she had. "It's not possible to get you out of mine, either. But maybe if we pretend long enough, we'll start to believe it." She savored the graze of his lips on her cheek. Accidental? "I don't want to go back to never seeing you."

Joseph cleared his throat.

They both reared back slightly, Beat visibly resentful of the interruption.

She slipped out of the SUV, feeling his gaze on her back while they met up with the new driver and drove away, knowing he watched until she disappeared.

But she didn't allow herself to look back once.

# Chapter Twenty-Two

**W**hen Beat walked into his mother's dining room later that afternoon—the new cameraman plodding in behind him—he could have heard a pin drop.

Octavia picked up her tall, slim glass of seltzer garnished with cranberries and sipped daintily, watching Beat over the rim through narrowed eyes. He sat down across from her with a sigh, setting his iPad and paper files down in front of him. He folded his hands and waited for her to start making sounds again. It might be time to face the music about his trip to Trina's New Hampshire compound, but he'd also be getting some work done.

Work. That was all he'd done after being dropped off. He treasured his position at Ovations and took it seriously. But today? He was just thankful for the distraction. Without decisions to be made regarding the scholarship, he would be climbing the walls.

Even now, it was a feat of inhuman proportions not to punch a few buttons on the iPad and watch Melody's live stream. He'd watched long enough this morning to make sure she arrived at a hotel and made it to her room safe and sound, before forcing himself to turn it off. Obviously, she'd wanted time alone and he should respect that. Millions of people were watching her every move. Then again, the person she'd needed space from was him.

Beat rubbed at the strained muscles of his throat and reached for his own drink, a tumbler of scotch, that had already been waiting for him upon arrival. He started to sip, but the burn was too welcome and he downed the whole goddamn thing.

"My goodness," Octavia murmured, leaning back in her chair. "Trying to banish the memory of my ex-bandmate? Can't say I blame you."

"Remember you're being recorded."

"What, me? Forget about the cameraman? He doesn't exactly blend in, dear."

Beat's eyes ticked up to the oversized mirror hanging on the wall, catching the reflection of the new guy. Ernest. Octavia's entire dining room was decorated in a pristine white. A crystal candelabra and chandelier sparkled, along with the white garland and twinkling lights she'd added for the holidays. Ernest, who said to call him Ernie, was in black-and-gray flannel, his beard red and bushy, looking about as comfortable as a wrestler at a dance recital.

"It sounds like you watched the live stream," Beat said, dryly, nodding his thanks to the housekeeper who breezed in and refilled his glass of scotch. "Thoughts?"

"I don't even know where to start."

"That makes two of us."

When he fully expected his mother to express her anger over the fact that Trina very obviously *hadn't* requested the reunion, as they'd led her to believe, she surprised him by leaning across the table and stabbing a finger into the gleaming surface. "I demand to know what happened in that attic last night."

Beat's hand froze in the act of reaching for his glass, then dropped. "*What?*"

"Oh, don't you dare feign shock with me. The entire world is speculating. You should see the message boards—they've lit up like a Christmas tree." She sniffed. "The way I see it, I should be privy to the truth as compensation for being totally betrayed."

"You're being a little dramatic, Mom."

"Me? A woman carried in on the backs of swan-men, dramatic? You don't say."

Beat bared his teeth in a smile. "There isn't a chance in hell I'm telling you what happened in the attic."

Octavia stuck out her bottom lip. "Magnificent Mel didn't seem herself afterward."

Beat's insides did their best to cram their way into his mouth. *Didn't seem herself afterward.* He'd done that. He'd driven her away. "You met Melody for all of ten minutes," he rasped, his hand unsteady as it closed around his tumbler, dragging the drink in front of him, but suddenly lacking the strength to pick it up.

"Yes," his mother said slowly. "Although isn't it odd? I feel as if I've known her much longer." If she only knew how much Beat could relate. "And if you must know, I've become something of a Melody-head since the gala, even though she told me a minor fib." She frowned over that statement while throwing herself back into her chair. "Liking her so much is very disconcerting, considering she sprung forth from the womb of a trifling banshee." She gestured to the camera with her drink. "Trina, if you're watching, where *did* you find your housemates, darling? Backstage at an Everclear concert?" Octavia's laughter was smug. "She'll know what that means."

"Maybe we should change the subject," Beat muttered, opening the file folder in front of him. "I've narrowed the field down to five applicants—"

"No, no. You're not getting off the hook that easy." She pursed her lips, obviously trying to appear casual. "When might you be bringing Melody over for dinner? I'm told she likes beignets. If

French cuisine is her thing, I'm going to hire out the chef from La Bernadin."

Beat's chest was currently held together by a zipper and with each mention of Melody, it was lowered a little more, everything on the verge of spilling out. "Is there any way we could avoid talking about this in front of millions of people?"

"Are you serious?" Octavia seemed genuinely perplexed. "Are you aware of how much you've been saying on camera, whether or not you actually *say* a single word?"

His pulse picked up. "What do you mean?"

"I *mean*"—she wiggled her fingers at the camera—"you haven't exactly been . . . subtle about your feelings. Or don't you remember threatening to drive a tractor into the side of that Podunk jail to get Melody out? And honestly, no one blames you. What man *could* be subtle with Magnificent Melody on the line?"

Beat had no earthly idea how to answer that. So many times over the last week, he'd tried to pump the brakes around Melody, make his infatuation less obvious. Apparently he hadn't been remotely successful. Why was he bothering to try and deny it now? At this stage, he was probably only making himself look like a fool. "You've been watching the live stream all day?" Beat asked, gruffly, waiting for his mother's nod. "How is she? Is she okay?"

"She's restoring an old copy of *Animal Farm*. Lord help me, it shouldn't be so riveting, but she keeps up this delightful commentary. I simply *couldn't* turn it off."

He would have sold his soul in that moment to see Melody, head bent over a book in her magnifying glass hat, explaining the restoration procedure in her unique tone of voice, so full of humor and grace.

Octavia's expression turned triumphant. "See? Look at you. One mention of her and your eyes melt like candle wax. You look

like Woody from *Toy Story* when Andy didn't take him to college."
Octavia gestured impatiently at the cameraman. "Are you getting
this?"

Beat pinched the bridge of his nose and held on to his patience
while Ernie circled to the other side of the table to get a better
angle of his face. "What do you want from me, Mom? You want me
to admit I have feelings for Melody?"

"At this stage, it's merely a formality. But yes." She waved at the
cameraman. "Get me in the background. They're sure to use this
clip as promo and I look fucking hot."

A smile couldn't help but tug at Beat's lips. "I have every single
feeling for her."

His mother yelped at that statement. "Then where is she?"

"Getting a well-deserved break from me." He tried to swallow
and couldn't. "I'm sorry, but I don't think she'll be coming over
for dinner anytime soon. Not as my date, anyway. As my friend?
Maybe." His mouth tasted bitter. "If I have to accept that, so do
you."

Octavia thought about it. "No. And you can't make me."

The housekeeper rushed into the room and whispered something in Octavia's ear, making her eyes widen with interest. "Wait
until you hear this. Melody is ordering room service." She listened to the housekeeper some more. "Spaghetti and a Diet Coke?
Damn. Now I don't know if I should hire a French or Italian chef
for our dinner."

Beat wanted to roll his eyes, except he'd been holding his breath
to find out her order, too. "I came here thinking you were going
to read me the riot act over Melody's claim that Trina wanted the
reunion. Instead, you're starting a Melody fan club."

She raised an eyebrow. "Wouldn't you be a member?"

He looked down at the paperwork without really seeing it. "I'd
be the president."

When he thought Octavia might say *I told you so*, she tilted her head at him instead. "What's the problem, Beat?"

"That's between me and her."

"And the attic." She hesitated. "Just blink twice if there was nudity."

"Really, Mom."

"I'm a rock star! Nothing shocks me!"

If he didn't turn the tables, this conversation was going to venture further into the place he didn't want it to go—definitely not publicly. "Are you still in for the reunion?"

Octavia's smile froze over. She reached for her glass. "Moot point, isn't it? Trina said no, didn't she?" Adding in a mutter, "Petty old witch."

Beat couldn't help but remember the look on Trina's face last night when Melody was singing. Even before that, when Melody stood up to her, she'd been almost . . . transfixed. Thoughtful. Like she'd been trapped in a time capsule and someone had finally opened the hatch. "I don't know. Danielle has us booked on the *Today* show Tuesday morning and apparently has a 'trick up her sleeve.' Although something tells me Trina is still considering the reunion, despite her unequivocal no."

"The way Melody took her to task . . ." Octavia stared off into the distance, a bemused smile on her face. "That was something to see, wasn't it? You were both off-key in the second verse of 'Rattle the Cage,' but nobody noticed. And I didn't post about it on the message boards." She scratched her eyebrow. "That definitely wasn't me."

"Right."

"It was me."

"Yes, I know." He tapped a finger against the open file. "Can we discuss these applicants now?"

"One more thing. I gathered during my many hours of Melody

viewing today that she's very nervous about this bocce match tomorrow night." She gave Beat a pointed look. "Perhaps she could use some moral support."

The very idea of Melody nervous about *anything* made Beat want to sink down onto the floor and never come up. Still . . . "She doesn't want that from me right now."

"Oh, darling." Sympathy shone in his mother's eyes. "Didn't I mention? She's not being subtle about her feelings, either. Friends shmends."

"It's complicated," he said, hoarsely.

"Are you in love with her?"

His heart answered for him, pounding behind his jugular. "Yes."

Tempered joy flooded Octavia's expression. "Then perhaps you should uncomplicate it."

*December 18*

The following night, Beat walked into his friend's party, handing over the bottle of champagne he'd brought—and he tried valiantly to pretend like the entire proceeding didn't screech to a standstill at his appearance.

"Beat . . ." Vance greeted him at the door looking like he'd seen a ghost. "We . . . I . . . you're *here*? I didn't expect you to come."

"Really?" He leaned in for a backslapping hug. "I RSVP'd in November."

"That was before you were a worldwide sensation."

Vance's eyes widened as the associate producer, Steve, ducked into the apartment, further drawing the attention of every guest in the room. "Sorry to interrupt, folks, but I'm going to need everyone to sign a waiver. If you choose not to be on camera . . . what's wrong with you? But okay. I'll need your name and the official diagnosis.

Just kidding. But seriously. I'm sure everyone here is excited to be on the live stream. Please step this way and sign the waiver, one by one. As quickly as possible, please, so we can get filming."

Beat's top layer of skin was on fire, head to toe. This shit was manageable when Melody was around. They were in it together. But doing it alone made him feel like a clown. "I'm sorry about this," he said to Vance. "I tried calling you to explain . . ."

"Shit. I've been running around for the last few hours. My place was an actual pigsty until about ten minutes ago. No bullshit." Vance gaped as the line of guests formed, his gaze swinging back to Beat. "I have ten thousand questions. And I'm not going to ask you any of them."

Beat's breath escaped like helium from a balloon. "Thank you."

"But someday you're going to get drunk and tell me everything."

"Sure. I'm going to sing like a canary."

Vance laughed, studying his face closely. "No, you're not." He opened his mouth, closed it, and started again. "I always had this weird intuition that I didn't know the real Beat Dawkins, you know? Now I know it wasn't just a feeling. It's true. After seeing you with Melody . . ." Someone across the room called both their names and Vance turned to wave, Beat following suit even though his arm suddenly weighed a hundred pounds. "You've kept a lot of yourself hidden, haven't you?"

Any other night, Beat would have pretended not to see the hurt and confusion in his friend's eyes, made a joke, and veered the conversation into a different lane. But Vance was the second person to call him on his behavior in the space of thirty-six hours . . . and Beat couldn't run from the accusation anymore. Had he taken his quest for privacy way too far? Was he now driving people away by keeping his hopes and fears and secrets buried under the surface?

It seemed so. His friend was looking at him like he barely knew him.

Melody wasn't standing at his side where she belonged. And yet she guided him now, her voice in his head, always revealing herself with such bald honesty. No pretense. No fear. God, he wanted to be more like her and holy shit, he missed her so much his bones ached.

"It's habit, you know?" Beat coughed into his fist. "I had to keep things to myself growing up to maintain Octavia's privacy. Later on, I sort of realized that when I spoke about my life to other people . . . my advantages became very obvious. I guess I just started keeping things to myself out of habit. I didn't mean to be . . . hidden."

Vance nodded slowly. "And with Mel . . ."

"With Mel, it's like we're both . . . in the same hiding spot. Together."

His friend visibly suppressed a laugh. "I have terrible news, man, you've been doing the opposite of hiding." He squinted an eye. "How drunk do I have to get you to find out—"

"The attic? There isn't enough alcohol in New York City."

"Had to shoot my shot."

"But did you?"

That was their last private moment before friends and acquaintances joined them, having finished signing the waivers. Ernie fired up the camera, the red light blinking, lens trained on Beat as he made forced small talk with friends of friends who obviously wanted to ask him about *Wreck the Halls* and the status of the reunion . . . and Melody.

What was she doing right at that moment? If she were here, he would trade a knowing look with her, because she would understand how everyone he spoke with wanted to pry and was valiantly holding themselves back. How he felt like not enough on his own, not enough without the juicy information about his famous family. How they were hoping Beat would offer a tidbit without them having to ask. He and Melody had performed these steps since they were children and in a short space of time, he'd gotten used to dancing with her, not without.

Half an hour into the party and Beat was no longer hearing the conversation around him. His gaze continually strayed to the window facing east—toward Brooklyn. Melody's bocce match would be starting right now. He'd called Danielle this afternoon to ask about the security they planned on providing and she'd been cagey, mumbling under her breath that the network was working with the NYPD to control the expected crowd.

Thinking about tiny Melody in the middle of all that mayhem caused a bead of sweat to roll down his back. She was dealing with Magnificent Melody Mania while he was in this private apartment without any need for security. She'd asked for space, but this was just wrong. Even if they'd hired enough security to protect the pope, no one could care for her like Beat.

"Excuse me," Beat murmured to the couple telling him about their first concert in a crystal-clear effort to broach the subject of Steel Birds. "I have to make a call."

That wasn't true. He'd just reached his breaking point. He'd made it thirty-six hours without watching Melody's live stream and that was all he could handle.

Beat closed himself in the bathroom and sat down on the edge of the bathtub, phone already in hand. He tapped the network app and opened the split screen, laughing without humor over the surreal quality of watching himself in conversation with party guests on one side, while Melody rode in the back of a dark SUV on the other.

In seconds, his palms were clammy, his pulse struggling to remain even. His breathing became ragged at the sight of her. God almighty, she looked beautiful. No, she *was* beautiful. Her Melodyness didn't require any effort—she simply embodied it. Breathless vulnerability meets poise. Charm and bravery. Kindness with the right amount of skepticism. There was nobody like her in the entire world. And he wanted her sitting in his lap so he could tell her.

But he'd lost that privilege. She'd been clear.

Friends. They were going to be the best of friends.

If only his heart could get on board with that reality.

Beat watched Melody on the screen of his phone, watched her eyes widen in alarm as she turned the corner onto the block of her bocce bar venue. Red and blue lights reflected in the inside windows of the SUV and Mel shrunk down into the seat, the bodyguard sitting beside her shifting, preparing. Jesus, what was she walking into?

Whatever it was, he needed to be there.

Yeah, she'd asked for space. But she'd also called Beat her best friend. She *wanted* that, right? If he couldn't be more to her than a friend, he would ignore the catastrophic yearning in his chest and he would be the best goddamn friend she could ask for.

Maybe . . . he'd even find the courage tonight to give Melody the remaining portions of his trust, which he'd been guarding so long he probably wouldn't know where to begin.

*She'll help. She makes everything easier.*

"I have to go," Beat said to the empty bathroom. Then to the phone, "Mel, I'm coming."

Beat lunged off the toilet and threw open the bathroom door, dodging the line of people waiting to use the toilet. Urgency throbbed in his temples. He really didn't have time to stop and say goodbye, but after his earlier exchange with Vance, he owed it to his friend not to bail without a word.

It took Beat a moment to locate Vance and when he did, what he saw in the living room took a moment to register. Everyone at the party was gathered around a laptop watching Mel on one side of the screen, him on the other. They all turned slowly. Guiltily.

Vance winced. "Sorry, it's just . . . the bocce match is starting."

A young woman gestured to the laptop, champagne sloshing over the side of her flute. "It's basically the World Cup final of reality shows. Or whatever this is."

"You're going, aren't you?" Vance asked.

On the screen, Melody was helped from the vehicle by a security guard to the epic roar of a police-barricaded crowd and Beat's legs turned to rubber. "If she's there . . ." His exhale stung his lungs. "I should already be there, too."

Someone on the fringe of the group burst into tears. "He loves her so much. Why can't I have what they have?"

*Sorry*, mouthed Vance, before his expression turned thoughtful. Out loud he said, "You want us to come along as backup? We could make one hell of a cheering section."

*No.*

That was his gut reaction. To go it alone. To keep his friends boxed off so they wouldn't see the more authentic sides of him. But they'd been watching him in his rawest form on the live stream for days, hadn't they? There was no use hiding now. And didn't Melody deserve the biggest cheering section he could offer her?

"Yeah." He nodded. "Come with me."

A loud chorus of hoots and hollers went up, everyone rushing to collect their coats and down the remaining champagne in their glasses.

"Hey, Vance. You wouldn't happen to have any pink paint lying around, would you?"

# Chapter Twenty-Three

**M**elody stood in a room full of people chanting her name.

Had it really only been a week since the last time she stood in this spot, preparing to take her turn on the bocce lane? Then, she'd been timid. Terrified of disappointing her coworkers and all the people watching.

Now?

Still terrified. Still timid.

*But* as she stood at the top of the lane, wooden bocce ball in hand, she knew she had the right to be standing there, taking up a little patch of space. To be on a team. Maybe imposter syndrome was a pitfall some people lived with their whole lives and maybe she would be no different, but breathing was easier now. Being there was easier.

She hadn't transformed. But over the past week—with Beat, with *Wreck the Halls*, with an absurd number of people cheering her on—she'd climbed a rung on some invisible ladder toward self-acceptance. Years of therapy might have prepared her for climbing higher, but it couldn't take that step *for* her. She'd had to do it herself.

Was this what a breakthrough felt like?

Maybe. Yes.

But in a room full of people shouting her name, she was lonely. What sense did that make? They called at her wherever she went. They asked, "Where is Beat?" They said things like, "You have the exact same chin as Keanu," and "Beat is in love with you." What was true and what was fabrication anymore? Were these things just being said to get a reaction?

Melody looked around at the oil painting of smiling faces, outlined in white Christmas lights that ran the gamut of the bar, not one of them giving her a sense of comfort or recognition. Not even Savelina or her coworkers who should have been familiar by now. Something—someone—was missing and there was no use pretending not to know who that someone was. Nearly two nights without him. She hadn't even turned on the live stream, worried she'd do something impulsive, like take a train to Manhattan and show up at his door.

The cheers around Melody were beginning to die down, because she was taking so long to make her shot. *Just throw it.* Tension pinched the back of her neck. She shifted, looked down at her toes to make sure they weren't creeping over the penalty line. Took a deep breath, closed her eyes. And Beat's image danced its way onto the backs of her lids, blue eyes attentive, inquisitive, confident, stormy. A cooling balm spreading in the center of her chest just thinking about him, simultaneously making her heart race.

As requested, she'd gotten two days of distance and holy Hannah, she missed him. She'd been reunited with a missing rib, only to have it cut back out. Two days of solitude hadn't changed her mind about being friends. If anything, the need to have Beat in her life in a close capacity had only cemented itself. Unfortunately, that mature decision, made in the name of self-preservation, didn't save her from the pitiful ache inside her.

Maybe her feelings for Beat would always be there, like imposter syndrome, bouts of loneliness, and the fear of disappointing others, but if she'd learned anything in the short time she'd been filming *Wreck the Halls*, it was that . . . she was stronger than she'd given herself credit for. Strong enough to stand up to Trina, kick a Santa in the balls, execute a successful box jump, sing in front of a room full of people, dance in public, and deny an orgasm to one of *People* magazine's sexiest men alive.

In other words, she could throw this mothereffing ball, right?

Just as Melody was preparing to take the shot, for better or worse, the cheering around her grew deafening. *The ground shook.* Fists bashed off the bar and Melody's team jumped up from their stools, visibly excited. And somehow, without even turning around, she knew.

Beat Dawkins had entered the building.

Relief flooded her insides with such intensity that her eyes watered. It was possible that some intuitive part of her knew he was coming and so she waited to take her first turn. Because she had more confidence in this man than anyone else in the world. He returned that confidence—and it was exactly what she needed right now.

Bracing herself for the rush that came from seeing Beat live and in person, Melody turned and looked over her shoulder. The crowd parted—

And she dropped the wooden ball.

Beat was shirtless.

A giant, pink "M" had been written on his chest. Two men followed behind him, sporting the "E" and the "L." *MEL.* A few young women hoisted bottles of champagne and danced through the bar behind the bare-chested trio. Melody only vaguely registered them, however, because she only had eyes for Beat. Her surroundings had resembled a blurry oil painting only moments earlier, but they came into sharp focus now, the bar noise going from muffled to clear, the air becoming more breathable. The loneliness inside of her burst like a bubble.

Beat stopped a few yards away, seemingly oblivious to the jam-packed bar going bananas behind him or the camera in his face. He simply looked at her, that jaw muscle bunching, and held open his arms. Without a single hesitation, she walked straight into them.

With a cutoff sound, he lifted her into a bear hug until her toes were barely scraping the ground and the bar went nuclear. "I'm getting paint all over you, Peach," he shouted over the pandemonium.

"I don't care." Melody barely resisted the urge to press her face into the side of his neck. "I'm just glad you're here."

His arms tightened. "I'll always show up for you, Mel."

"I know."

"I didn't give you the full two days . . ."

"Thank God."

Ever so briefly, he opened his mouth and breathed against her temple, before setting her down with visible reluctance. They stood way too close for a touch too long, Beat's eyes locked on her mouth, then they each shuffled back, turning to smile and wave their appreciation at the bar.

Before she could say another word to Beat, the "E" of their trio came from behind him, hand outstretched. "I know this fucker isn't going to introduce me, so I'll do it myself. I'm Vance. I've known Beat since college, but I use the term 'known' loosely. If my parents had locked up their liquor cabinet as tight as Beat locks up his secrets, I'd probably be a neurosurgeon by now." He let his tongue loll out of the side of his mouth. "I don't mean to overshare, I've been champagning all night."

Melody liked this guy immediately. "Look. When you paint a letter of my name on your chest and risk hypothermia to cheer me on, you get a lifetime oversharing pass."

"I would marry you," Vance said, without irony. "I'm not just saying that—"

"Yeah," Beat grunted, inserting himself in between Vance and Melody. "I think that's enough. Go be an 'E' somewhere else."

"We have to stand together or it won't make sense!"

"Where is the 'L'?" Melody asked, searching around, puzzled. After a few seconds, she found him and gaped at where he'd landed. "Oh. The 'L' is making out with my boss."

Vance rolled his shoulders back with a sigh. "I love the holidays."

The crowd started to chant her name again. "Oh God." She hurried to pick up the ball that she'd dropped. "They're not letting me off the hook."

Beat rubbed his hands together, scrutinizing the bocce pit with a groove between his brows. "Okay, I googled the rules of bocce on the ride over and I'm going to try to help you. Just give me a few seconds to calm down after Vance said he would marry you." He closed his eyes and let out a slow breath. "A few more seconds. Christ."

Melody's heart flopped around like a fish in the bottom of a boat. "He's been champagning, Beat."

"No," he said, drawing out the word. "He's been falling in love with you like the rest of the world." The corner of his lips tugged into a smile that he couldn't quite hold on to—and it dropped. "But no one is good enough for my . . . best friend."

"Beat . . ." Heat pricked the backs of her eyelids, a lump rising in her throat. "You picked a really interesting time to say all these sweet things to me." Numbly, she held up the bocce ball between them. "I can't feel my hands anymore."

"Sorry." His fingertips touched her elbow, stroking slowly upward where he massaged her wrist with magical circles of his thumb. "Is that better?"

"Friends, Beat," she whispered, trying to keep herself from slipping into a stupor. "Friends."

With a swallow, he relinquished her wrist. "Believe me, Mel, I know." Once again, he put some distance between them, but not much. He couldn't, really, if they wanted to continue communicating against the backdrop of noise. "Okay, what's your feeling here? What shot were you thinking of playing?"

"Before you arrived half naked?"

One end of his mouth jumped. "Noticed that, did you?"

"Ham. I was thinking there is no way I'm going to get my ball as close to the pallino as my opponent's ball, so I better try and knock his out. 'Try' being the operative word."

Beat stroked his chin. "I think you're right. Just knock it out."

"*Just?* I've got *maybe* a ten percent chance."

"That's a higher percentage chance than we had trying to reunite Steel Birds and you jumped feetfirst into that enterprise." He tucked a loose strand of hair behind her ear. "Mel. At the risk of adding even more pressure, you have millions of people believing you can do *anything*. And I don't think that many people can be wrong."

"What about you? Do you believe I can do anything?"

He huffed a laugh. "Do you even have to ask me that?"

She shook her head. "No."

After a prolonged moment of not-so-friendly staring, he dipped his chin and stepped away. "Knock it out."

Mel nodded and turned on a heel to face the bocce pit once again. Had her surroundings even been in color before? They were now. The neon flamingo mounted on the wall buzzed, pink and vibrant. The ball in her hands was a verdant green. The one she aimed to knock out was red. No, she *would* knock it out. She allowed herself to feel the energy of the people standing at her back. Their belief in her. Beat's. And she bowled her shot.

Halfway down the lane, she knew it was going to hit.

She heard Beat's hissing intake of breath, followed by the crack of the balls connecting and she watched in disbelief as her opponent's ball went rolling toward the back wall, a good two feet from the pallino. Hers remained in place, nearly kissing it.

An unbeatable shot.

The crowd erupted, along with her heart.

"Oh my God," she said breathlessly, turning and leaping into Beat's arms. He held her tight, spinning her in a circle as she clung, his heart pumping like an engine against hers.

"I'm so proud of you."

"Thank you."

She didn't realize her legs had naturally wrapped around his hips until they pulled away slightly, their mouths close enough to kiss. *So. Close.* His breath was warm and tasted like peppermint, throwing her senses into a tailspin. Dear Lord, how was she going to restrain herself from kissing him? Maybe she could keep it friendly?

A platonic, little kiss with minimal tongue never hurt anybody.

"Mel," Beat groaned, his chest shuddering. "That *skirt* you're wearing. With black tights?" He zeroed in on her mouth. "God help me, I'm not having friendly thoughts."

"Oh. Hmm." Her toes flexed with traitorous anticipation in her ankle boots. "They're not tights, though. They're stockings."

He squinted. "What's the difference?"

"These ones stop. At the tops of my thighs."

Beat let out a strangled cough.

"I should probably unwind m-my legs from your person."

"Hard, isn't it? When they feel like that's exactly where they belong?" With a curse, he made a visible effort to get himself under control, tilting his hips away as he slid her down the front of his body to her feet. Not quite enough for her to avoid his stiffness, though, the bulk of it dragging up the hemline of her skirt as she descended. "Maybe tonight isn't the best time to talk." He shook his head. "I don't trust myself."

Speaking openly about their attraction made that fiery funnel of need inside her spin faster, but Melody kept her features schooled. "M-maybe you're right. We should wait until—"

"Are you two ready to hear the idea of the century?" Vance stepped in between them while posing that question. "Besides me and Mel getting engaged and languishing in bed while naming our future babies, I mean."

"I don't want to have to kill you, man," Beat said with mock cheerfulness. "But I will."

Vance chuckled. "Relax. Anyone witnessing the last ten minutes of Belody knows I don't have a snowball's chance in hell. But. *Speaking* of snow." Vance elbowed each of them in the ribs, in turn. "While you two were mooning at each other over here like star-crossed lovers, we made friends with Melody's coworker nerds and decided that we weren't done quite yet with friendly, low-stakes competition for the evening." He paused for dramatic effect. "That's right, my friends. We're having a snowball fight in Prospect Park. Right now. It's on. Because we're drunk adults and that's the only excuse we need."

# Chapter Twenty-Four

*A*nother hour passed before they managed to extricate themselves from the bar, which they accomplished by Vance creating a diversion—aka juggling shot glasses—while Beat and Melody snuck out the rear entrance. By then, Melody's coworkers and Beat's friends were the kind of drunk where numbers were being exchanged and joint vacations were being planned. It was the good kind of drunk. The holiday drunk where the snowfall outside and the glow of lights on stoops and inside of shop windows makes everything surreal and trimmed with magic.

Beat walked beside Melody on the sidewalk, his hands shoved into the pockets of his overcoat so he wouldn't reach for her hand, the voices of their friends carrying back through the winter wind like a memory in the making.

Park Slope was winding down for the night, but revelers still reveled in the bistros and taverns they passed on the way to the park. Ubers idled at curbs, impatiently waiting for their fares to exit the establishments. A snowplow roared past, spitting out salt onto the streets to keep the snow from making the asphalt slick. Josh Groban's voice drifted out of an apartment window, serenading the street—and Melody . . .

Her cheeks and the tip of her nose, red from the cold, her bangs peeking out from beneath the edge of her multicolored beanie, smiling at the antics of their combined friend groups . . . well, she was the most beautiful moment of Beat's life. Perfect was just out of reach for myriad reasons, but he would savor this—savor her—because tonight was the closest he'd ever come. Escorting his best friend to a snowball fight, falling in love with her more with every step they took toward the park.

"If it's your friends versus mine," Melody mused aloud, "I guess that puts us on opposite teams. We're enemies this night, Dawkins. We shouldn't even be speaking right now."

He laughed. "I've had enough of that over the last two days."

The color of her cheeks deepened—not from the cold, this time. He really needed to stop voicing every goddamn sentiment that came to mind, but he was taking an odd kind of pleasure from her stunned reactions. *That's right. This is how I feel about you.* Restraining himself from having physical contact with her was hard enough, he couldn't seem to quell the honesty, too.

"What did you do during our break?" she asked, after a moment, voice softer than before.

"Worked. A lot. Went to the gym. Stopped by to see my mother. She's building you a shrine—it should be finished by Valentine's Day."

Melody stopped walking. "What?"

He halted, too. Faced her. "My mother. She adores you."

A knowing eyebrow raised. "Because I told Trina to go suck an egg?"

"I'm sure that didn't hurt, but it's more just . . . you. It's you. For everyone." *For the love of God, pull yourself together.* "She's debating between hiring an Italian or French chef when you come over for dinner. Do you prefer spaghetti or beignets?"

"That's like asking me to choose a favorite child. I simply cannot."

"You're a good mother."

"Thank you," she breathed, sweeping a dramatic hand to her chest.

They started walking again, each of them fighting a smile.

"Speaking of motherhood, do you *want* children someday?" Beat asked, despite telling himself that he shouldn't. Her answer could very well torture him for the rest of his life. Unfortunately, he really wanted to know. He wanted to know every damn thing about her. More than anyone ever had. Or ever would.

"It might be selfish not to bear at least one child," she said, a teasing half smile playing on her lips. "What if my mother's musical talent skipped a generation, like the red hair gene, and I'm destined to raise the next Adele?" Melody elbowed him in the side. "Same goes for you."

"You think I could have a mini Mick Jagger on deck?"

"That's the thing. It's a crapshoot." She shivered. "You might accidentally end up with a scientist or something."

"The horror."

She went on, "I used to be positive that I didn't want kids. I was dead set against it. What if I was having a baby just so I could be a better parent than Trina? That doesn't seem like a good enough reason to bring an entire human into the world." She exhaled, causing white vapor to dance in front of her mouth. "But I think it's good to be open to all possibilities, no matter how daunting. Sort of like this live stream." They both looked over their shoulders at the camera trailing them for an extended beat. "Maybe I'll never have children and that's okay. There are enough of them in Park Slope alone to keep the human race going. But I don't want to be closed off to the idea. What feels wrong one day might feel right the next."

Beat absorbed every word of that—and he couldn't help applying it to himself. The pattern of behavior he'd adopted at sixteen was no longer right for him, was it? No. Refusing to let anyone in was hurting his relationships now, including the most important one. His relationship with Melody. Could he stop feeling guilty for having so many advantages? That change seemed huge and impossible, but for the first time, he allowed himself to imagine what it would be like to stop punishing himself, to let himself open up and trust those closest to him—especially Melody—and he was surprised to find that his step felt momentarily lighter.

Had he reached a turning point?

Melody coming into his life was causing him to question everything. As her presence would probably do for any man worth a damn. But she deserved so much more than *any man*. She deserved the best. And he was nowhere near the best. Could he get there, though?

"What about you?" Melody asked, reaching for his hand to step over a patch of ice. He took it, helped her over the frozen puddle, and kept it securely in his, because holding her hand made breathing easier. "I think you'd be a really good dad."

"Do you?"

Melody nodded. "Kids just want to feel safe and . . ." She shrugged. "When you're around, it feels like nothing can go wrong. Or if something does go wrong, you'll be the one to help fix it." He desperately wanted her to look at him after she gave him that incredible compliment, but she didn't. "You have serious dad energy."

"And here I thought I was exuding serious daddy energy."

"Oh, don't worry, you've got that, too." They stopped at the edge of the park, watching their friends rush to the denser banks of white to begin shaping snowballs. "The question is, will it prevent you from getting crushed in this snowball fight?" Melody snorted. "Doubt it."

That startled a cough out of Beat. "Are you trash-talking me, Gallard?"

"It's your fault for coaching me to my first bocce victory," she said, squeezing his hand. "Now I've got an ugly competitive streak."

"Serious jock energy?"

Her laugh sounded incredible, like a warm bite of sound absorbed by the falling snow. "As soon as spring hits, I'll be challenging little kids to races in this park. Tripping them before the finish line. I'm going to be out of control."

"I'll stage the intervention."

"See?" Slowly, she let their fingers disconnect, walking backward into the park. "You're such a Fixer Daddy." To his amusement, she shot at him with finger guns. "And you're going down, baby."

Beat followed Melody, trying not to let it show how much he enjoyed her calling him baby. "What are the stakes of this snowball fight? Is there a prize?"

"Yes. If you win, I'll have a T-shirt made that says SERIOUS JOCK ENERGY and wear it to dinner at your mother's house. And if I win—"

"Let me guess. I wear a SERIOUS DADDY ENERGY shirt to dinner?"

Her smile spread in response. She knelt down and started crafting snow into balls.

Beat was pretty sure he was smiling, too—like a lovestruck teenager. There was nothing he could do to wipe the expression off his face, though. He was enjoying himself too much. A snowball fight with Melody? He didn't care who won. The fact that they were together was enough. Together with plans to see each other again in the future at his mother's house for Italian. Or French. What the hell else could he ask for?

All of her, that's what.

That meant being honest, though. That would mean total trust.

"Okay!" Vance piped up, trudging through the ankle-deep snow to a space in between the two groups. "We need an impartial judge to declare the winner. And as I was on the debate team in high school, I think that qualifies me to sit back and determine the champion."

"Are you serious?" Beat shouted. "You organize this snowball fight and then *sit out*? No way. Not happening. Melody should be the judge."

"You just don't want her getting hit with snowballs," Vance accused.

"Correct."

There was a loud chorus of sighs from all the women present.

A snowball unexpectedly clocked Beat in the side of the head.

To his utter disbelief, it was Melody who'd thrown it.

"What's wrong, Dawkins?" She pursed her lips. "You scared of me?"

It was an image Beat would remember vividly decades from now. Melody with snow melting in her hair, cheeks rosy from the cold, the streetlamp making her eyes luminous, expression taunting and tipsy and playful. He hated spending money on frivolous luxuries, but he would be commissioning a painting of Melody in that moment. Needing to capture it somehow in the meantime, he took out his phone and snapped a quick picture.

"I'll be the judge!" someone volunteered behind him, their steps crunching in the snow as they got out of harm's way.

"Great." Vance clapped his hands, made eye contact with everyone. "We now commence the first annual Prospect Park Rumble: Nerds versus Preppies. A few rules before we begin—"

Beat caught Vance in the neck with a line drive. "No rules," Beat called, shooting Melody a wink. "No mercy."

Melody threw up her fists. "To the death!"

Utter chaos ensued.

Everyone scrambled at once, some of them too drunk to remember where they'd put their premade snowballs. Participants were falling without even being hit, getting stuck in the deeper drifts of snow. Others treated it like a proper war, mainly Melody's co-workers. They formed a V, spearheaded by Savelina, squatting to collect snow in their palms and hurling the balls like major-league pitchers.

"No fair," Vance screeched, after taking a snowball to the throat and staggering backward. "They have home field advantage."

Behind Vance, someone pinwheeled and ass-planted after getting hit in the knee.

Beat shook his head. "You guys are embarrassing me."

"Fan out!" Melody's boss shouted. "Their defenses are weakening. It's time to press our advantage."

Melody jogged out from behind Savelina with—no joke—an armful of snowballs. One by one, she launched them at Beat, striking him repeatedly in the chest. Meanwhile, he had one single snowball in his hand. Up until now, Melody had been in the rear of the V formation, so Beat's targets had mainly been her coworkers. Now that she was out in the open—and apparently trying to kill him—he couldn't bring himself to throw an object at her. Even if that object was soft and slushy.

"Stop taking it easy on me!" she yelled, laughing and pelting him harder than before.

"I'm not!" he fibbed smoothly. "I can't get a clear shot."

Melody gasped. "You *liar*."

Having no choice, Beat lobbed the snowball at Melody. Underhand. She watched it arc upward and soar gently downward where it landed softly on her shoulder.

She leveled him with a look of disgust. "Really?"

He cleared his throat hard. "That was a valid shot."

Melody pointed to the girl standing twenty yards away. "Judge?"

The girl presented a definitive and dramatic thumbs-down.

"I will not stand for this insult," Melody said, staggering back when Vance hit her in the stomach with a brutal throw.

"*Hey!*" Beat growled at his friend. "Watch it."

Vance gulped.

Beat strongly considered turning on his friend, but Melody demanded his attention when she shouted, "I'm coming for you, Dawkins." Once again, she produced an artillery of snowballs seemingly out of thin air, cradling them in her arm as she ran toward him, firing as she came closer. They'd already established that Beat couldn't bring himself to throw anything at Melody, giving him no choice but to jog backward, deflecting the balls being launched at him. One by one, white burst in the air as the snowballs connected with his palms. When there was finally a cease-fire and Beat realized she'd run out of ammunition, he watched in disbelief as she barreled toward him, launched herself through the air, and tackled him backward into a snowdrift.

Melody, who just about reached his shoulder, had brought him down. And pure joy almost fractured his chest muscles. Tendons stretched to allow the feeling to expand and it didn't merely spread, it ran wild, rocketing a laugh upward from the deepest recesses of his stomach, busting down a sky-high barrier—a barrier against feeling this much happiness all at once—he'd put in place without even realizing it. There was no keeping her out, though. She kicked it down and hurled herself over the debris and he could barely breathe over the rush of . . . everything. All at once.

Relief. Shock. Gratitude.

Love.

The avalanche of emotion was so overwhelming that it took Beat a moment to realize Melody had lifted her head to watch him in awe. "Ohhh . . ." she breathed.

"What?"

"You're letting me see it, Beat," she whispered.

He started to breathe hard, more tendons snapping in his chest.

"You're so beautiful like this. Not hiding anything from me. From yourself."

Despite being lodged in a snowbank, he was hot. Everywhere. His skin prickled and heated more and more. What the hell was happening inside of him? He didn't know. But he couldn't look away from her unblinking eyes. She was the anchor holding him in place. Hiding wasn't an option. Not from Melody.

"Mel, I want to tell you everything tonight," he said gruffly. "Why I need the network's money. Why I needed to do this god-awful live stream. All of it. Okay?" He wet his lips, desperate to get the rest out. "Maybe I needed two days away from you to realize . . . you're this gift I've been given and I'm squandering you by keeping things to myself. You're the one person who will get it. Get me. Every time."

"Beat," she murmured, a sheen forming in her eyes, her mouth lowering to his—

"Hey, guys. I hate to interrupt." Beat jolted, wrapping his arms around Melody on instinct, tucking her face into his neck. Jesus Christ. There was the camera, pointing straight at them from ten yards away. Vance stepped into the shot, possibly on purpose, with Savelina at his side. "There are people coming. Like, a lot of people."

Savelina shot a look toward the edge of the park. "They must have figured out your location pretty quickly, thanks to the live stream."

"But fear not." Vance waggled his eyebrows. "We have an idea."

Beat watched as both groups of friends, nerds and preppies alike, moved in a big herd and blocked them from view of the camera. Meanwhile, Vance and Savelina hurriedly removed their outerwear. "Quick," said Melody's boss. "Swap jackets and hats with us. We'll lead them one direction, you guys run in the other."

Melody pushed up into a sitting position but remained on Beat's lap. "Really?"

"Hurry," Vance prompted. "I have to pee."

Savelina giggled, throwing her orange beanie at Melody, shouldering off her black parka. "We *have* to hang out again," she said to Vance.

"What are you doing tomorrow?"

"What else? Watching these two pretend they wouldn't die for each other."

"Oooh. Viewing party?"

"I'll bring sangria."

"We can hear you guys," Melody murmured, casting Beat a fleeting sidelong glance.

He took her chin before she could look away, holding her stare, smoothing his thumb across her plush bottom lip. "I'm not pretending," he said firmly. "You know that, right?"

A shudder coursed through Melody. She nodded.

"Good," Beat said, releasing her chin to unzip his coat.

The clothing trade took under a minute. Beat put on Vance's jacket, though it was a tight fit, and donned his flannel ski cap. Melody pulled Savelina's orange beanie down low over her ears and buttoned up the black parka. It was going to be a tough sell that Vance and Savelina were Melody and Beat, but maybe from a distance?

Didn't matter. He would have taken any odds in the hopes of being alone with Melody right now. Tonight. Something inside of him had changed and he didn't know what it meant for him. For them. He only knew Melody would be there while he figured it out—and that made everything okay.

# Chapter Twenty-Five

Melody took Beat's borrowed jacket and hung it on her coatrack, studying his face as he saw her apartment for the first time. Having him there didn't feel real. Especially after running six blocks in disguise to ditch two pissed-off producers *and* avoid a mob of people who knew way too much about them. The direction in which Melody's life was headed remained unclear, but she was allowing herself to settle into this state of limbo. The unknown.

It wasn't scary when her best friend was beside her.

Right. Best friend.

She could still feel his fingers clasping her chin. *I'm not pretending. You know that, right?*

He'd been referring to the implication that they would die for each other.

These were big feelings, big declarations. Big things happening under the title of friendship that she wasn't sure belonged there. Or maybe she and Beat had their own category of relationship that wasn't discovered yet. Was that arrogant? Maybe. She was really leaning into the whole jock vibe, apparently.

"It's exactly what I pictured," Beat said. Was his voice deeper than usual?

"Which is to say . . ."

He hummed while choosing how to respond, his steps carrying him into the living area. "Everywhere I look, there's something that feels like you. That string of yellow yarn holding back the curtain. Colorful ceramics, but simple white flowers. The fuzzy sock sticking out from between those couch cushions, your nightshirt on the coffee table." He ran his index finger along the back of the piece of furniture in question and cast her a sidelong look. "You fall asleep on this couch a lot, Mel?"

She was still watching that sensual finger where it dragged side to side on the leather. Her leather. Up and back on the seam. "Every night, actually. I finally gave in and bought a huge couch. It takes up too much space, but it doubles as a bed."

"I fall asleep on the couch every night, too."

"Really?"

"Yeah." He was using his thumb on the cushion seam now, raking it up. Down. "The attic at Trina's house was the first time I've fallen asleep in a bed in years."

Words spoken so casually about the night they'd had sex were like a velvet punch to the belly, followed by a long, slow twist. "Imagine that."

Beat's thumb dug into the cushion hard. "I do, Peach. All the time."

The air was growing thicker by the second, Melody's pulse traveling lower, lower, to a dangerous region of her body. It would be so easy to pretend she hadn't set a boundary between them in New Hampshire. But she had and she would be doing herself a disservice by ignoring it. "Beat . . ."

"Something feels different tonight, Mel. Different from in the attic or any time before." A line ticked in his cheek, his gaze more intense than she'd ever seen it. "I have no right to ask. You can tell me to fuck off right now, but . . . I want a lot more than friendship with you."

Was the ground moving or was that her imagination? "What changed between now and then?" she managed, barely able to hear over the pounding of her heart.

"I don't know exactly." Beat swallowed. "I can't stop thinking of the way you looked at me, back in the park. When you tackled me," he added wryly, before sliding toward serious again. "Maybe I'll never be unguarded like that with my friends. With anyone. But I loved being that way with you. Just . . . open. Exposed. There's no judgment. No guilt. And I think that's because you're the good part of me I've been missing. You're the one who gets me. I just want you to have all of me." His chest lifted, plummeted, lifted again. "God knows I want all of you."

Heat seared the backs of Melody's eyelids. There was a monotone ring in her ears, the kind she imagined would hit her during a flight-or-fight ultimatum. This man standing in front of her held half her heart in his hands. She'd given it over the first time they met—and he was completely and utterly worthy of it. He was. But she had to protect the half still in her possession. The one she'd healed through years of therapy and self-acceptance.

"We'll take it slow," she whispered.

He made a gruff sound, his grip tightening on the back of the couch. "Thank you."

Oh God, she needed to do something with her hands. She was going to stretch and twist the hem of her turtleneck to the point of no return. They wanted very much to reach for Beat, stroke the whisker growth on his cheeks, warm the wind-reddened skin of his neck, reacquaint themselves with the dips and swells of his pecs and abdomen. But they would move too fast if she did that. The next time she touched him, she didn't want to feel rushed. She needed to know it was right.

"Are you hungry?"

"Famished."

"I can make us sandwiches." Melody waited a moment, then brought up the subject that had been riding on her shoulders since the snowball fight. "We can eat while you tell me why you need the Applause Network's money."

Beat was already nodding, as if he'd expected her to go there. Yet she couldn't help but notice the way his expression became momentarily hollow. "Yes."

She took a step in his direction. "Whatever it is, we can handle it."

Those nods turned into headshakes. "There's nothing for you to handle, Mel."

"Let me be the judge of that?"

Beat wanted to argue, that much was plain, but he followed Melody in silence to the kitchen instead. He pulled out a chair at the breakfast bar and watched as she removed fixings from the fridge—ham, cheese, mayo—and whole grain bread from the pantry. Having this man watch her make sandwiches was a new experience, to say the least. The butter knife felt awkward in her hands. Her fingers tingled, along with the backs of her thighs. She could feel him wondering where the tops of her stockings ended and that intuition caused her to drop the knife twice before successfully cutting the sandwiches in half.

After plating the snack, she settled it on the counter in between them.

"I love watching you do . . . Jesus, everything," he said, his teeth sinking into the bread. Chewing. "I want to hate every single person watching your daily life on the live stream, but I understand the obsession. You move like everything you're doing is new. Like you're experiencing it for the first time and want to get it right."

Her sandwich was paused halfway to her mouth. "Example?"

"Like settling into a seat on the plane. Studying the survival manual, figuring out what each button does, testing out five sitting positions until you find a comfortable one."

"You've been watching me closely."

A small, humorless laugh escaped him. "Some might say too closely."

"Not me," she whispered. "I like knowing you do."

Beat's hand fisted on the breakfast bar. "Come here, Peach," he ordered gruffly. "Come sit on my lap."

"Talk first," she forced out. "I'm not going to be distracted."

His gaze traveled down the front of her body. "Your nipples say otherwise."

"Beat."

"Okay." He raked a hand down his face, appearing to gather himself. Gather courage? When he let the hand drop, several seconds passed without him saying anything. "Mel, I need the network money because I'm being blackmailed."

That last word clattered into the kitchen like a falling drawer full of silverware. It was the last thing in the world she expected him to say. Maybe because this man was the most wonderful being alive, in her eyes, and she couldn't imagine anyone wanting to cause him harm, whether physical, emotional, or financial. "*Blackmailed?*" She braced her head in her hands, trying to keep her racing thoughts from melting out of her ears. "By who?"

A snowplow rumbled by on the street, the room taking its time descending back into silence. "My biological father." He blew out a sharp breath. "Oh shit. That's the first time I've said it out loud. My dad . . . Rudy. He isn't really my dad. And he has no idea."

Weight pressed down on her sternum. "Yes, he is. He *is* your dad," she said firmly, somehow knowing that sentiment was important for him to hear, but there was so much more to unpack. "Help me understand. Your biological father is blackmailing you," she said slowly. "If you don't give him money, he'll inform the public?"

"Yeah," Beat said, voice rusted through. "Mel . . ."

"Yes?"

"It's been going on for five years," he rasped. "The amount of money he wants gets bigger every time he resurfaces."

"Five *years*?" Moisture flooded her eyes, her legs beginning to tremble. "Oh my God. How are you living with the . . . the *stress* of this?"

"I live with it, so they don't have to."

"Meaning Octavia and Rudy have no idea? You've just been shouldering this all alone?"

He just barely inclined his head.

She felt dizzy. "Where has the money been coming from until now?"

"My own. The money I earn working for the foundation. Cashing in savings bonds, selling stocks. I won't touch Ovations money, Mel. I won't fucking touch it."

"I know you won't. Of course, you wouldn't."

He slowly let out a breath, as if relieved by her belief in him. "Until this year, my own funds were enough, but like I said, the amount escalates."

"Beat. You have to tell your mother."

"No," he said emphatically. "After this life she's given me, I can handle this one goddamn thing for her. I can stop her being dragged by the press, like they did to you. Being adored is her lifeblood. And my dad . . ." He closed his eyes. "Imagine finding out the wife you've been worshipping for over three decades cheated and your son isn't really your son? I can protect them from that pain."

"It's not your job, Beat," she said in a shaky voice. "You won't be able to sustain the increasing demand for money forever. Or the stress is going to kill you. *Please.*"

His eyes remained closed for a breath. "For now, can telling you about this be enough?"

*No*, she wanted to scream out of fear and frustration. "It can be a good first step," she said, overruling the urge. "I'm glad you told me."

A touch of tension left his bunched shoulders. "I'm glad, too."

She curled her fingers into the hem of her skirt and squeezed. "Who is he?"

"No one of consequence to you, Mel." His tone held a note of warning. "If you think I'm being unreasonable by protecting my parents from this, you don't want to see how I'd react if this bullshit came anywhere near *you*."

The flash of malice in his gaze gave Melody some idea. She had no choice but to refrain from pressing the issue. For now. She needed him to continue to confide in her. Needed him to be comfortable opening up to her so she could help him. Patience was key. If he'd told no one, not a single person in five years of suffering through the constant blackmail, tonight's progress was big enough already. "Do you want a drink?"

"Oh yeah."

"Go sit on the couch. I'll bring it in."

With a weary nod, Beat stood, braced his hands on the breakfast bar for a moment, and watched her beneath drawn-together brows. Then he pushed off and went toward the living room, sinking down onto the couch. Melody retrieved a bottle of whiskey from her cabinet, which she'd actually bought for a cupcake recipe, eons ago, and poured him a glass. After some thought, she poured herself one, too, and carried both into the living area.

Her stocking-clad feet didn't make a sound. That was probably why he didn't hear her coming. Probably why he crushed her nightshirt to his nose and inhaled roughly, making a low sound, before doing it again. Desperately taking in the scent of her, no idea she watched from the space in between the kitchen and the living area, her pulse accelerating, a sandbag dropping low, low, low in her belly.

Knowing she had to make her presence known soon, Melody took a step—and the floorboard beneath her foot creaked. Beat dropped the nightshirt guiltily, raking a hand through his hair. He closed his eyes, as if knowing he'd been caught.

Melody set the drinks down on her coffee table and sat down beside him.

She only survived five seconds without looking sideways at him, cherishing the way the lamplight highlighted and shadowed his cheekbones, rejoicing in the way he looked in her apartment, among her things. And then she urged him down onto the couch so he was lying on his side. After a few moments of studying him— savoring his quickened breathing, the expansion of his pupils— she followed suit, lying on her side in front of him, her back to his chest.

When his forearm wrapped around her hips and drew her closer, slowly, and she felt his physical reaction to holding her so intimately, she admitted to herself that going slow might have been ambitious. With Beat finding the courage to confide in her, the night had become them against the world. She'd never felt more connected to another person in her life . . . and she couldn't help wanting to get even closer.

# Chapter Twenty-Six

*I*t was by the grace of God that Beat didn't roll Melody onto her back and devour her.

This woman was his refuge, the fulfillment of his lust, his heart. So important. And his body just wanted to show her that. His mouth wanted to communicate it to her in ways he couldn't. Christ, not yet. He'd just dropped a ton of bricks onto her head by coming clean about the blackmail and he'd done it right on the heels of her asking to go slow.

Slowly into . . . what?

A relationship? What a hilarious word for this bond between them.

Melody Gallard knew the floor plan of his soul. This transcended a mere relationship.

Still, going slowly made a hell of a lot of sense. They'd taken a tandem dive into the deep end without learning how to swim together first. She had enough grace to allow him a second chance and he didn't want to squander it. Keeping his hands to himself, however, was like asking him to stop his heart from beating.

Impossible.

He buried his mouth in her snow-dampened hair, pressing his chest to her spine so she could feel the way his heart pounded, heavy and fast. In response, she took his hand from where it was molding her hip, guiding it between her tits and flattening his palm there, because this generous, perfect person wanted him to know her heart raced just as fast. And fuck, she rolled her ass in his lap at the same time, making him see double.

"You make me feel so good to be hard," he groaned into the back of her neck. "That's how I know . . . I wasn't doing this right until you. I wasn't just enjoying it, I was giving myself an excuse not to trust anybody. But I can't hold back my enjoyment of you, Mel . . . because it's impossible. I don't want to keep anything from you ever again, inside of bed or out."

"Good," she whispered unsteadily. "I need all of you."

Those words washed over him like a baptism. God, he'd never felt more grateful and alive and *hungry*. So hungry for this woman that his palm skated downward from between her tits, traveling over her stomach, stopping just beneath her belly button. "Tell me what you mean when you say all of me, Mel."

"I want you to confide in me. Be honest with me, no exceptions."

"I can. I will," he breathed against the nape of her neck. "What about with my body? Can I touch you everywhere?"

"Yes."

He flipped up the hem of her skirt and slowly, roughly gripped her pussy. "You want me to fuck you until I come inside of this?"

She moaned, her legs squeezing around his clutching hand. "*Please.*"

"I need to hear the words." His middle and ring finger massaged her through the dampening cotton of her panties. "I need to know I've got permission for what I'm going to do between your thighs tonight."

"You have permission."

"Mel."

"Fuck me until you come," she whispered. "Inside of me."

It almost ended then and there, his vision expanding in a rush, his balls quickening until they felt like fucking concrete. "Damn," he grated. "I'm going to have to keep your mouth occupied before it finishes me. We're only getting started."

She looked back at him over her shoulder, face flushing to a deeper shade of rose every time he stroked her, her panties growing more sodden by the second. "What did you have in mind?"

"Give me that mouth," he growled, snaring her lips in a kiss. They lingered in the hot suction for long moments, his fingers sneaking underneath the waistband of her panties, so he could slick his middle finger down the center of her smooth, sexy flesh, finding that pearl and teasing it swollen. Their tongues wound together, again and again, until he was on the verge of unzipping his pants, pulling down her panties, and taking them off.

*Too fast. Slow down.*

Melody was the only woman on the planet who could overwhelm him, but tonight was important. He'd been given a second chance and needed to do this right. That meant slow, diligent care of her body.

Melody had other ideas.

They were breaking for oxygen when she sat up on the edge of the couch, stripping her turtleneck off—without warning, but much to his delight—followed by her bra. And suddenly, Melody was left in nothing but a short skirt and stockings. That was enough to stop the breath in his lungs, because Jesus, there wasn't a more beautiful sight on the planet. But when she reached for the button of his pants while scooting down the couch to kneel between the V of his thighs, Beat learned what it was *really* like to forget to breathe.

"What are you doing?"

"Is this bad?"

"God no, it's not bad. You just don't have to."

She unzipped his pants, leaned forward, and nuzzled his cock with her nose, her mouth, and his heels pressed violently into the couch cushions. "Don't. Please don't. I'm going to come as soon as you breathe on it."

Carefully, she tugged down the waistband of his briefs, her lips parting on a rattling inhale when he sprung free, the aching length of him straining against his belly. "You're beautiful. Everywhere," she whispered, licking his stomach. Long, unabashed laps. Then that tongue dragged up the side of his swollen sex, running circles around the tip. "You can still enjoy this."

"Of course I'm enjoying it," he gritted out. "I'm enjoying it too much."

"No, I mean . . . the waiting. The edging." She kissed the head of his cock. "You're still allowed to enjoy it, even if this ends with you still inside of me."

Blood rushed north, creating a whooshing sound in his ears, before journeying back south with a vengeance and stiffening him to the point of pain. Melody was kneeling between his thighs, sucking him into her mouth, her fist circling him in a way that wasn't necessarily firm enough to get him off. Just enough to keep him balanced on the edge. Her lips remained loose, her tongue teasing him with light strokes, but every so often she clamped her lips tight and sucked hard enough to make his hips jerk on the couch, his very life flashing in front of his eyes.

When he reached the point of no return, she seemed to know it, halting her torture and reverting back to light touches of her tongue, slow, lazy strokes, until he was panting.

"*Mel*," he growled between his teeth. "Fuck. Fuck. *Fuck.*"

"Uh-uh." She kissed his crown again, her lips plumping against his hardness, then lapped at the bead of moisture that formed. "Not yet."

His body was on fire in the best way, sweat slicking his skin, the anticipation of pleasure racking his muscles. Was Melody right? Could he still enjoy being denied . . . in a healthy way? It had never felt like this before. *Healthy.* Solely in the name of pleasure, because of the person he was sharing it with. There was no heaviness in his chest or guilt or shame. Only decadence.

Only love and connection and Melody. Always Melody.

"Come on, baby, give me one of those hard sucks."

She dragged the tip of her tongue up the side of his distended shaft, slow enough that he was groaning by the time she reached the top. "How bad do you want it?"

Christ, he was literally shaking, one hand gripped the back of the couch, the other one clamped onto the edge. "Really fucking bad."

"I'm going to give it to you . . ." she whispered, her lips poised at his tip. "Because you're incredible. And I love the taste of you."

The fact that he didn't explode from the sheer pressure in his chest was an inhuman feat. He barely made it through the next part. The part where she gave him what he asked for, but not for the reason he'd always needed it. No. She turned his guilt inside out, turned his kink into something exciting instead of a punishment and all the while, she praised him with her eyes, the intense suction of her perfect fucking mouth and he knew. He knew life would be better from now on. Because she existed and knew him better than he knew himself and he'd somehow taken a right turn and ended up in heaven with an angel.

"I'm so fucking close," he hissed, his stomach flexed so tightly to stop himself from ejaculating that he'd be sore for a week. Worth it. Worth every second. "I'm a wreck without your mouth on mine, baby. Come kiss me. Come fuck me."

His entire world was narrowed down to his soulmate straddling his hips, still in that dick tease skirt and stockings, her tits pouting at him in the lamplight. Their hands collided while reaching between her thighs and they ripped her panties off in a joint effort, Beat dragging his cock to her entrance and groaning deep in his throat. Melody correctly interpreted that as his wordless plea to lower down, and she did, her knees trembling against his rib cage, her eyes losing focus with every new inch she took inside of her.

"*Oh my God.*" He flexed his ass and lifted, grinding up into her, transfixed by her teeth sinking into her lip, the palms that slid through the sweat on his chest to clutch his shoulders, her hips beginning to punch and roll. Punch and roll. The sight of her enjoying herself on his cock, no reservation, no pretense, was so erotic and awe inspiring, Beat felt almost greedy gripping her ass cheeks and riding her harder. But he was too lost, his body moving of its own volition in a perfectly synced dance with Melody's, as if they'd been born to fuck each other. "*Mouth*, Mel. I don't think you understand, I'll fucking die without it."

She muffled that last word with her lips and color went off like a firework in his head, his lungs replenished with oxygen, heart booming out of control. His right hand left her backside to bury in her hair and if he died in that moment, he would have died happy, because Melody's tongue was in his mouth and she was . . . *Christ* . . . she was edging him again. She'd slid her knees back and was now rubbing her clit on him slowly, but no longer plunging him in and out of her body. Just leaving him fully buried, her walls throbbing around him, her mouth devastating him with every stroke of her tongue. But no movement. She left him on the verge of an orgasm without enough friction to get there.

"Good girl," he said, not recognizing his own voice, his chest heaving between them. "Get your own. Take your own. Use me to come. Please. That's all I want in my fucking life is to be the man who gets you off, Peach." He pulled her forehead down to his. "Tell me I fill it up tight. Tell me it's yours."

"It's mine," she gasped, her trembles turning more severe.

He couldn't help it. He started upthrusting, his flesh smacking in quick succession off hers. Making rough love to her from below. "Tell me *you* are mine."

"I'm yours. I've always been yours."

"I'm yours, too, Mel. All of me. Take it."

"D-don't stop. Keep doing that."

"Don't stop what?" He pressed their cheeks together, so he could speak against her ear. "Plowing your little wet cunt? Couldn't if I tried."

She made a strangled sound, her intimate muscles constricting around him.

*Almost there.*

The hand still clutching her ass applied more pressure, shoving her hips down to meet his upward drives. "I know it's a long fall, but I'm going to catch you. Every time," he said through his teeth. "Let go."

That reminder of their unique trust turned out to be the push she needed and the results would be seared on his brain for the rest of his life. The way she bore down with her lower body and let out a muffled scream into his neck, her pussy shrinking up tight around his shaft and throbbing through an orgasm, her back, thighs, and belly shaking, every inch of their sweating bodies fused together. Colors that hadn't been invented splashed on the backs of his eyelids, his mind in a state of total and complete nirvana over giving Melody pleasure.

But more. He needed more. He needed to consume her, so he wouldn't have to live a minute of his life without feeling her presence in his fucking bones. *Get deeper.* Taking her mouth in a rough kiss, he flipped them over on the couch, using his shoulder to press her knees high, all the way to her shoulders and he lost it. He completely lost his mind.

*I don't have to pull out.*

*I don't have to stop.*

More than that, though, he couldn't fathom doing either of those things. Who would want to leave the cradle of this perfect human's body until they were forced to?

Not him. Never again.

Her bent legs were preventing him from kissing her, so he threw them over his shoulders, the cushion of her calves meeting the breadth of his back. He slung one arm beneath her hips to hold her steady and gripped the arm of the couch with the other, riding her in an aggressive way, encouraged by her kisses and moans, that he'd never associated with love, not until now. But then again, he'd never expected to be this deeply devoted to anyone. Never expected to find out what romantic devotion even meant.

For Beat and Melody, it meant trying to exchange souls through every eager kiss, every rough slam of his hips. For them it was a battle they both could win.

"I've never come inside of anyone," he panted in between plunders of her mouth. "And I'll never come inside of anyone else." His lips raked over to her ear, his teeth closing around her lobe in a light snap. "I know that's part of what's making you so wet."

"Fair is fair," she hiccuped, reaching overhead to cling to the arm of the couch. Looking him in the eye. "You're my only one, too."

"Mel," he choked out, his abdominals reaching peak strain. "Melody, I'm there."

"I know, baby. You're so big now."

"*Jesus Christ,*" he groaned, pinpricks of light appearing in his vision. Melody calling him "baby" drop-kicked him right over the edge. And he didn't have a single second thought about pulling out. There was no option but joining himself completely with this woman.

His woman.

"Stay inside me," she whispered, planting kisses on his jaw.

"I am. I will. No choice," he said hoarsely, seeing nothing now. Only feeling. "A matter of survival. That's what you are. Goddammit, it's . . . oh fuck, it feels so good. Wrap your ankles around my neck. Oh shit, I'm coming inside of you." The muscles of his back, neck, chest, and stomach pulled taut to the point he was positive they would snap until some kind of otherworldly bliss cut through him like a buzz saw, elevating his stomach to his mouth, his eyes lost in the back of his head. "Oh my God, Melody. *Melody. It's so fucking good.*"

His body screamed at him with urgency after that first wave of undiluted pleasure and he drove into her frantically, trying to eradicate the rest, shouting her name as he fought through the raw ecstasy of release. Beat became someone else in those frenzied moments, someone with no filter or self-control, his teeth razing her neck, his hips bucking roughly, filth spewing from his mouth into her perfect, delicate ear.

"I will worship you every day," he growled. "I will wreck you every chance I get. I want to *live* between these legs." Then the filth turned into sap and he couldn't control that, either. "You're so beautiful, Peach. It hurts to look at you, but I can't look anywhere else. I just want you naked and *looking* at me all the fucking time." His lower body bore down. "Moan for me until the last drop. Do it. Please."

"Beat . . . Beat . . ."

Some small part of him might have worried that he was going too far with those feverish words, but the nails digging into his buttocks, helping him rock and grind out that final wave, the kisses she continued to leave on his throat, his face, they told him she was matching him beat for beat. A perfect harmony. They were the greatest song ever written. And when he collapsed beside her and they locked together like two pieces from the same puzzle, one heart thundering against another, he planned on singing their song for the rest of his life.

# Chapter Twenty-Seven

*December 19*

*T*hey woke up to the sound of the intercom buzzer going off.

Melody's brain commanded her to open her eyes, but only one of them cooperated, revealing a blurry, off-balance world. Better to skip life today and resume tomorrow. Sleeping longer was the only option. This wasn't normal sleeping, though. She didn't usually wake up plastered to another human body, not a stitch of clothing between them.

She was spooning. With Beat. In her bedroom.

Her rear end was in his lap, her feet sandwiched between his calves, her head resting near his shoulder. His heart thunked steadily against her spine, his breathing even and beloved. His body was warm and welcoming, his angles corresponding perfectly to her curves. The fingers of their left hands were entwined in front of her on the mattress, his thick, lightly tanned digits braided together with her shorter, paler ones.

An enormous sense of rightness expanded in her rib cage until moisture pooled in Melody's eyes. *I'm in love. I am most definitely in love.*

Last night felt like a dream.

After they'd been together on the couch, they'd hydrated, showered as a pair—laughing as pink paint circled the drain—and ended up stumbling wet from the bathroom onto her bed where they'd engaged in a very slippery, very soapy round two. Doggy style! She'd never imagined herself a down-on-all-fours kind of girl, but behold, Melody hath seen the light. She flushed to the roots of her hair now remembering the slap of Beat's lap against her bottom, his fingers digging into her hips, fondling her breasts, his wild breath in her ear.

*Now that I've come inside of you once, I'm addicted*, he'd panted. *I can't stop.*

Fine by her.

They would just stay in this bedroom forever. Watch nostalgic movies and order takeout and do it until the end of time. Nobody could stop them.

The buzzer went off again, longer and louder this time.

With a growing sense of trepidation, Melody unlaced her fingers from Beat's and reached out to grab her phone off the side table—

"No," Beat growled into her neck, seizing her hand and pinning it to the mattress.

She giggled breathlessly, happiness popping like a champagne bottle in her chest. Beat was awake. They were awake *together*. "Someone is at the front door."

"I don't care. They can wait."

"It's probably Danielle." Her eyelashes fluttered involuntarily as Beat's tongue licked up the side of her neck, the landscape of his lap changing in a very rapid way. "I don't know what time it is, but I'm pretty sure we should be streaming by now."

"That's their problem, Melody. *I* need to fuck you again." He rolled Melody on to her back and she was wet in a matter of seconds, because Lord have mercy, this man was gorgeous on a regular basis, but in the morning? He was plucked straight from the pages of Greek mythology. If he'd woken up in a crown of olive branches, she wouldn't even have questioned it. He was bare chested and scruffy and his hair was a disaster, his lips and eyes softened from sleep. A God woken from slumber. With needs.

Yet he chose to satisfy hers instead.

She twisted the fitted sheet in her hands while he used his tongue between her legs, his thumbs massaging her inner thighs, his breath hot, his lips suctioning, his tongue debauched. Worrying her clit with the tip of his tongue, his right hand rode up her torso to knead her breasts, right, then left, and all the while a quickening grew more intense below her belly button. He wasn't going to stop. Oh God, he wasn't going to stop.

"*Beat.*"

His tongue kept going. Faster. *Faster.*

He looked directly at her and pushed two fingers inside of her body, rotating them, rubbing an undiscovered spot that made colors bleed together in her line of vision, then pumping them in and out. Hard. Fast. Mimicking what he'd done to her with his body last night and her back arched off the bed, her cry of his name singeing her throat.

No sooner did the spasms ebb than Beat was guiding himself between her legs, thrusting home with a strangled curse. Taking a moment to look into her eyes, to revel with her in the wonder of them being joined so perfectly. Just as suddenly, her back left the mattress, Beat lifting her upright with her legs locked around his waist. He walked on his knees until he could press her back up against the solid wood headboard—and then he fucked her against it in a way that could only be described as brutally beautiful.

"Before millions of eyes are on you today." He drove deep and held, held, held until she started to whimper, squirming between his strong body and the unmovable barrier. "I just want to remind you that I'm the only one who gets you like this."

"Yes, yes, yes, *please. Please.* Don't stop."

"There's no Beat without a Melody."

Her heart grew almost unbearably tight.

"I dreamed about you," he breathed in her ear, beginning a slow bump and grind that made her neck lose power, falling back against the headboard. "You were right beside me and I was still searching for you." His swallow was audible. "I hope it's not going to be a problem that I'm obsessed with you, Peach."

Time seemed to suspend itself. "Is it going to be a problem that I'm obsessed with you, too?"

Intense eyes zeroed in on hers, his jaw flexing as he started driving harder again, in that no-mercy fashion, banging the headboard off the wall. *Boom. Boom. Boom.* "Look at me. I can't keep my cock out of you. Two days without you and I felt like I was losing my mind. Do you think it's going to be a problem?"

"No," she breathed.

"Correct," he grated, right on top of her mouth. "Come on it, baby. Feed me."

Melody's body must have sworn its allegiance to Beat without consulting her, because she didn't have a say in the matter. Everything inside of her simply obeyed, her belly getting that achingly light flutter, her thighs ticklish on the insides, the effect of overstimulation coming to a head at once and coursing through her like a current of hot water, jolting her knees and robbing her of sight. "*Beat*," she wailed—pinned to the headboard roughly as he climaxed with her, his groans of satisfaction loud in her ear, his hips jerking out of rhythm, holding, holding as the pleasure washed away in degrees.

With Melody still in his arms, Beat toppled backward on the

bed, her laughter sounding foreign in a room where she'd never laughed with anyone. He pushed her hair back and she stared down into his beautiful face, leaving her heart hovering somewhere in the clouds.

"I can't wait until Christmas is over and the cameras are gone." He leaned up to kiss her softly. "I would love to take you somewhere for a month until all the mania dies down."

"*Wreck the Halls* is streaming in forty countries," she reminded him gently.

"We'll go to the moon."

"I'm in."

The buzzer stayed buzzing for a good thirty seconds this time. There was no more avoiding reality—or the reality *show*, to be exact—and they gave in with twin groans of frustration, reluctantly climbing out of bed. Melody put on her robe while Beat traipsed into the living room to find his pants. They met, haphazardly dressed, in front of the door a moment later. "Brace yourself for the wrath of Danielle," Melody yawned.

She opened the door.

Approximately nine thousand camera flashes went off.

Capturing her in a robe, hair mussed from three rounds of sex, Beat standing beside her shirtless with a bite mark on his shoulder.

Danielle stood still as a statue, observing them in a wide-eyed sweep.

Joseph stood behind her, camera on his shoulder, red light flashing. Filming.

The cheers could probably be heard in Berlin.

"Serves you right," the producer sniffed, pushing her way into the apartment. "I've been calling you for an hour trying to warn you."

Beat finally snapped out of his shock, wrapped an arm around Melody, and drew her against his chest, hiding her with his body as he slammed the door. For a count of five, he stood there holding her until a laugh rumbled in his chest, steadily growing louder.

Melody looked up at him. "What are you laughing at?"

He laid a firm kiss on her forehead, appearing thoughtful. "Well, I started to get upset—and I am, in a way. I don't want these people standing outside of your apartment. I want you safe and we'll have to work harder to make that happen. On the other hand . . ." He ducked down to whisper for her ears alone. "I'm kind of . . . glad that we're going to be all over the internet looking like we just spent the night in bed together. Why wouldn't I want everyone to know I'm sleeping with you? Actually, I'm fucking thrilled about it."

Joy was like fizz tickling the insides of her throat. "I can't say I mind it, either."

"Good." Beat nodded once. And all Melody could do was stand there with her jaw on the floor as he threw open the front door. "That's right. I spent the night," he shouted. "And it's *exactly* what you're thinking." Utterly, intoxicatingly hot in nothing but an unbuttoned pair of pants, Beat propped a hand high on the doorjamb, his toned muscles shifting in the morning light. "Our apologies to the neighbors." He closed the door again to the roar of cheering and whistles from the crowd, engaging the lock while looking inordinately pleased with himself. "Now. Who wants breakfast?"

"We don't have time for breakfast," Danielle screeched. "It's ten o'clock in the morning. In case you forgot, I have you scheduled for the final slot on the *Today* show. Even if we leave now, I'm not sure we're going to make it! And you both look like you just crossed the finish line of a sex marathon."

"I did cross it," Melody said brightly, looking at the camera. "Several times."

Beat's rich laughter flooded the apartment.

Danielle shook her head in bemusement. "Just when I thought

we'd peaked at snowball fight, you two go and prove me wrong."
She waved her hands around in a flurry. "Just . . . get dressed in
something. Anything. I am not going to disappoint Hoda Kotb."

Melody didn't want that, either, because who didn't adore
Hoda? She jogged into the bedroom and threw open her closet,
her eyes landing on the brightest, most fashion forward dress in
her closet because she felt daring and alive and bursting at the
seams in that moment. She reached for the red chiffon cloud with
billowed sleeves that only reached the upper middle of her thighs,
removed her robe and threw on the dress, along with a pair of
sparkly, vintage heels. Next, she dashed to the bathroom where
she brushed her teeth, splashed cold water on her face, applied
deodorant, snatched up her makeup kit—which she planned to
make use of on the ride to Manhattan—and skidded back into the
living room.

Danielle looked impressed. "Go off."

Beat turned to witness her entrance and fell back a step, whistling. "*Damn.*"

"I was hoping you'd say that."

Never taking his eyes off her, Beat lifted her borrowed coat
from the peg and closed the distance between them, holding it
open behind her so she could slip in her arms. Beat took another
minute to button and tuck in his own shirt then put on his jacket,
before wrapping an arm around Melody's shoulder. He relaxed
when he saw the security team was now waiting outside of the
apartment door to escort them to the SUV.

Still, he leaned down and kissed her temple, saying, "Stay close
to me."

She leaned into his warmth. "Always."

# Chapter Twenty-Eight

*T*hey arrived with four minutes to spare.

Beat stood backstage with Melody watching Hoda tease the upcoming segment, their sides heaving from the mad dash into 30 Rockefeller Center, then down a maze of hallways to the *Today* show soundstage. He dodged the makeup sponge that a young woman in a headset attempted to dab on his face, thanking her with a polite smile. And basically, just went back to staring at Melody—a habit he would never, ever be kicking.

His shoulders were lighter today, along with his head. He'd been living with misplaced guilt for so long, he'd grown used to it. Learned to carry it while acting normal. But Melody . . . she'd come along and helped him peel it off. Maybe he would never be a man who took his advantages for granted, but that was a good thing. As long as he could look into this woman's eyes and hold nothing back, he was free.

This incredible lightness, the exhilaration of being in love, made Beat want to do something impulsive. Like propose to Melody on the *Today* show.

Was it too soon?

On paper, yes. Way too soon.

But they would know better. They would know they'd always

been soulmates, they'd just been living separate lives. This reality show was the last resort that turned out to be the best decision he'd ever made. It brought them together and he'd be forever
grateful for that.

*What if I just do it?*

*What if I just ask her to marry me?*

She would say yes. He'd move to Brooklyn or she'd join him
across the river. They would get married with no cameras around,
just the two of them. He would lay a map out in front of her and ask
her where she wanted to go until this pandemonium died down.
Budapest, Bruges, Bali. Anywhere. As long as they were together.

Someone shouted a one-minute warning and Melody squeezed
his hand.

She gave him the most trusting look while Danielle ran a brush
through Melody's hair and everything was right in the world. They
might not reunite Steel Birds, but as soon as Christmas Eve came
and went and the live stream went dark, he would come up with
the money to pay off the blackmailer, whether the money came via
a loan or the network's coffers—and he'd be over that final hurdle.

Nothing but time to spend on Melody.

God, his chest was going to split wide open from carrying this
much optimism. When was the last time he'd felt any at all? It was
her. It was this miracle standing beside him.

*That does it. I'm proposing.*

Hoda's voice rose once again from the soundstage and a stoic
man stood in front of them counting down their entrance on his
fingers without a word. The host turned her smiling face toward
the backstage exit and they were directed to a row of chairs.

Three chairs.

That didn't necessarily strike Beat as odd. Maybe the next segment had three guests?

"And now! They are the worldwide phenomenon that has shaken

the internet this week, making them household names overnight. The *Today* show gives a warm welcome to Beat Dawkins and Melody Gallard!"

Beat helped Melody on to the high seat, blocking her lower body from view while she crossed her legs and arranged the dress, because that sucker was hot as hell, but it was *short*. If they'd arrived in time to spend a single second alone in the green room, Beat was positive his hands would have been beneath that thing, exploring every sweet inch of her. God, he'd never been hornier in his life and his thirst for Melody was unquenchable.

Finished arranging herself, Melody gave him a grateful smile and he leaned down to kiss her mouth, before taking his own seat, squinting into the powerful lighting.

"Well, consider me flustered!" Hoda enthused, fanning herself with the cards in her hand. "In fact, consider the entire world flustered. I can't even begin to imagine what a wild ride *Wreck the Halls* has been for you both—but that's the thing! I don't have to imagine it, because I can watch every single second of the journey. Did you expect your lives to be turned completely upside down?"

Beat squeezed Melody's knee, keeping his hand there. *Go ahead,* he mouthed.

"No, I don't think we anticipated having to don disguises to escape Prospect Park," she answered Hoda with a small smile, but she stopped herself and thought for a moment. "Maybe we didn't expect *this* degree of interest, but I think we knew we had to be ready for everything. The Steel Birds have always been a fascination and we wanted to reunite them. Naturally people would be interested."

Hoda nodded eagerly. "Yes, but somewhere along the line, the show became more about you two than the band! Did your romance begin to take shape during that famous—and mysterious— night in the attic? Or was it before that?"

"Before," Beat said, leaving it at that.

"Before," Melody echoed, her cheeks flushing slightly.

Hoda tilted her head. "Are you going to give us any clue about what happened in the attic? You know I have to ask!"

Melody gave him a serious look. "I think it's time."

His brows drew together. "Are you sure?"

"Yes." Melody took a deep breath, blew it out, and looked at Hoda. "We played Uno."

"She won the first game. I took the second. I think we passed out during the third?"

"Yes. You woke up with a Reverse card stuck to your forehead."

Beat sighed. "It's all true."

Hoda was laughing. "Oh, you two. We're going to get it out of you someday!" She scrunched up her nose. "Can you at least confirm you're officially girlfriend and boyfriend?"

"Yes," Melody said, no hesitation and Beat's heart tripled in size. "We are."

This was it. No better moment to make her his fiancée.

Beat started to rise from the chair, but Hoda pressed on in a different voice than before. As if what she was preparing to say held a lot of gravity.

He hesitated—and it cost him.

"Now. While the show might have become a Beat and Melody lovefest, of course everyone still wants to see Steel Birds grace the stage again." Hoda paused, her attention darting briefly toward the crew. "And in that vein, we have a little surprise for you! We have called in reinforcements to help make this reunion happen. *Today* show, please welcome the *original* drummer of the legendary Steel Birds, Fletcher Carr."

Beat's heart dropped into his stomach. In an instant, his skin turned hot and clammy.

Hoda's voice became distorted as his biological father walked out from behind a black curtain and sat down in the chair beside him. Beat couldn't feel his fingertips, nor could he hear what was being said. Not over the riotous pounding of his pulse.

This couldn't be happening. This wasn't happening.

*God oh God.* His first instinct was to get Melody far away from this man. Carry her out of there in his arms. Put as much distance between them as possible so Carr's filth wouldn't touch her. But Beat couldn't do that without giving himself away, could he? Without making it obvious that he had an existing relationship with the drummer? At the very least, questions would abound and he wasn't ready or prepared to answer them.

What if Carr had come onto the show specifically to out Octavia?

With the current interest surrounding Steel Birds, not to mention the explosion of *Wreck the Halls,* maybe he was offered more money for his story than he'd demanded from Beat. He couldn't ask, because they were live on the air. And Melody was looking at him curiously, probably because sweat was forming on his hairline and his hand was attempting to squeeze the life out of her knee. *Calm down. Brazen it out. Don't let him rattle you.*

"Am I correct in saying you're meeting for the very first time?" Hoda asked, completely unaware of the five years of paranoia and panic this man had inflicted.

"Yes," Beat managed, clearing his throat. Though it made his skin crawl, he reached over and shook the hand of his biological father. When Melody did the same, Beat had to physically restrain himself from ripping their hands apart. "I do know from my mother that he didn't complete the final tour with the band."

"No, I did not," Fletcher confirmed with a toothy grin. "Considering your moms broke up before they could finish that last tour, maybe I was the secret ingredient all along."

Hoda laughed, but her indulgent smile had faded slightly. "Interesting theory—"

"I did run into Octavia after they kicked me out of the band, however," Fletcher interrupted, snapping his fingers and looking pointedly at Beat. "I can't speak for Trina, but Octavia definitely missed me. Despite what she might say."

Beat's pulse faltered, the studio lights looming like giant suns.

"And now for the even bigger surprise!" Hoda pressed the cue cards to her chest. "Fletcher is offering to be part of the Christmas Eve reunion!"

"That's right. I'd love to be a part of it." The drummer winked at the camera. "If they'll have me, of course. The original trio. Back together." Outside in the plaza, the crowd watching the broadcast live erupted in a deafening cacophony of cheers. The drummer chuckled and leaned back in his chair. "I guess the public has spoken."

Beat could barely remember the rest of the segment. It might have lasted a minute or an hour. Melody and Hoda carried the conversation, which was mostly about Trina and the odds of her changing her mind about reuniting. Beat could feel Fletcher's eyes on him the whole time and he endured it happily, because it was better than Fletcher looking at Melody.

When Hoda bid them good luck and went to commercial, Beat forced himself to stand and help Melody from the chair, keeping himself as a barrier between his real father and the girl he wanted to marry. Melody and Hoda fell into a lively conversation about her dress, leading to Melody complimenting Hoda's wardrobe.

"I'm done for the day, Melody," Hoda said, unclipping her microphone. "Can you sneak back to my dressing room for a moment? That's where my phone is charging and I'd love a selfie."

"I'd love one, too!" Melody glanced back at Beat, beautiful in her excitement. "I'll be right back."

He nodded jerkily, once again quelling the urge to hustle her out of there.

"Great," said Fletcher behind him. "That'll give us a chance to talk. Man to man."

They were within earshot of several crew members and since Beat wouldn't put it past the bastard to air his family's dirty laundry in front of everyone, he strode past the drummer into the backstage area, which was now beginning to empty of crew members, the show having wrapped for the day. "There doesn't need to be a conversation," Beat said, turning to face his father. "Nothing has changed since the last time we talked."

Fletcher took his time responding. "Hasn't it?"

The nape of Beat's neck turned like a crank. "What is that supposed to mean?"

"Cute little girlfriend you've got there."

It took every ounce of his self-control not to punch the motherfucker in the face. *Don't you dare talk about her.* That's what he wanted to say, but the vise around his neck was closing. This man had brought up Melody for a reason and Beat's blood turned icy with dread.

"Congratulations. She's head over heels for you, man. I bet she'd do just about anything for you," Fletcher said, removing a pack of cigarettes from the inside pocket of his suit jacket, smacking it against the heel of his hand. "For instance, pay me to keep your big secret."

A warning screeched in Beat's head, the veins in his temples pounding painfully.

No, this had to be a nightmare. His mouth was too dry to speak, shock immobilizing him.

"Yeah, that lovestruck way she looks at you? I guarantee she'd protect you at all costs." He winked at Beat. "Could mean double the payday for me."

The rage finally exploded within Beat. "Leave her out of this. Or I will kill you."

Fletcher made a tsking sound. "Your own *father*?"

Beat had informed this man he wasn't his father a hundred times, so he didn't bother wasting his breath now. His only focus in that moment was to protect Melody any way he could. Christ, he'd brought this man into her life. He'd been swallowing Fletcher's poison for five years and by asking Melody to be part of the show, he'd served her the same toxic brew.

No. This couldn't go a single step further.

"It's all for the cameras," Beat said, desperate. Fucking desperate to keep her out of this maniac's line of fire. "Haven't you heard of a scripted reality show? As soon as it's over, I'll probably never see her again."

The lie set his throat on fire, made his stomach pitch with nausea.

Fletcher studied him through narrowed eyes, as if trying to decipher the truth.

Despite the turmoil wreaking havoc on his insides, Beat stared back unblinkingly.

"Sorry if you thought this was some magical love story, but it's not. You're welcome to try and pump her for cash, but she'll tell you to go to hell," Beat bluffed. "And then *she'll* be able to leverage that secret. It'll lose its power and become her bargaining chip if she wants to sell the story. And you know tell-all offers are going to roll in for her. This thing is huge."

Beat took no satisfaction in the smugness leaking from his father's expression.

"I know what I saw. You two are the real deal," said the drummer, but it was easy to see he wasn't as positive as before. No, he was second-guessing the whole angle.

*Good.*

*Leave her alone.*

*Don't you dare go near my girl.*

Melody walked backstage with Joseph trailing behind her, filming, but one of the *Today* show producers beckoned to him. Joseph looked conflicted for a moment, as if deciding whether to speak to a colleague or continue filming. In the end, he switched off the camera and approached the other crew member with a handshake. Beat dug his fingernails into his palms, drawing blood to keep from reaching for Melody. Wrapping her in a bear hug, guarding her against this man's evil. She held up the screen of her phone so Beat could see the selfie she'd taken with Hoda and he nodded stiffly.

"She wants me to teach her how to play bocce, too! We're going to have a lady date after the holidays." Melody reached for Beat's hand with her free one, natural as breathing, and he forced himself to cross his arms, avoiding it, in what might have been the single worst moment of his life. Melody blinked at him, then at Fletcher, color appearing on her cheekbones.

He'd embarrassed her.

This was a living nightmare.

"Sorry," she muttered. "Did I interrupt?"

"Nah, honey. We're just shooting the shit," Fletcher said, observing them in an almost reptilian manner. "You must have another big day of filming ahead. Where are you two jetting off to next?"

Melody lifted a shoulder. "We don't really have any plans—"

"I need to work," Beat cut in, the backstage area closing in around him. He had to numb himself. That was the only way he would get through this. Obviously Fletcher had been watching the live stream. The more time he spent observing Beat and Melody, the more positive he was going to be that they were really in love.

And he would go after Melody. Being in a relationship with Beat was a liability to her. "Actually, I'm going to be working right up until Christmas Eve."

"Oh," Melody said after a few seconds. "Are we . . . giving up on Steel Birds?" She nodded at the drummer. "What if Fletcher's offer changes something?"

Beat couldn't even look at her. "Danielle will let me know if Trina comes around." He gave her a flat smile. "If by some miracle, she agrees to the reunion, I'll see you on Christmas Eve."

He could feel the hurt he was exacting on Melody and his insides were deteriorating the longer he stood there. He had to get out of there now, before he caused any more damage. Without a word, he strode for the exit that let out into the hallway.

"Beat, wait," Melody called after him, catching up with him right before he could walk out the door. Still within spitting distance of his blackmailer. *Her* potential blackmailer, too, now. Because of him. "Is . . . is something wrong? You're acting weird."

"It's just my turn for a break, Melody. All right?"

She jerked back like he'd slapped her. "Is this because I said we were official on the air?" she asked. "You told the crowd outside of my apartment that we'd spent the night together and I think I just . . . assumed we were . . . you were my boyfriend. Should I have spoken to you about that first?"

"Yeah," he rasped, hammering the final nail into his coffin. "Maybe you should have."

It was for her own good.

This was to keep her safe.

Repeating those assurances to himself, over and over, was the only thing that kept him walking upright until the elevator doors closed behind him and he slid down the wall to the floor, head buried in his hands. "*Melody.*"

# Chapter Twenty-Nine

December 22

*M*elody never expected to be grateful for the camera trailing five feet behind her on the sidewalk, but here she was. Without its presence, she probably would have stayed in bed for the entirety of the three days that followed Beat breaking up with her. Although he hadn't technically *broken up* with her, because they'd never really been together in the first place, had they? Reconciling that fact with the aftermath of destruction in her chest wasn't easy—they'd *felt* like boyfriend and girlfriend—but she didn't really have a choice, did she?

A strong wind carried down the block lined with brownstones, whipping the ends of her white woolen scarf and tickling the newer, shorter fringe of her bangs. She'd cut them herself last night after watching two measly TikToks on the subject. They didn't turn out terrible, but she wasn't winning any prizes for precision, either. They only reached the center of her forehead, instead of her eyebrows, where she'd been aiming. There she was—a walking cliché. Break her heart and watch her desperately find a way to make matters worse.

Oh well.

They would grow back. Her heart probably wouldn't. Or if it did grow back, it would be some awkwardly stitched-up Franken-stein version of it.

"Miss Gallard, the crowd is assembling quickly," said a member of the security team. One of six who was flanking her on the way down the sidewalk after a trip to the bookstore to pick up her lat-est project. An old copy of *The Giver* that desperately needed to be restored to its former glory. "Do you mind walking a little faster?"

"Sure," she said, looking down at her feet and ordering them to comply. They could barely manage a slow slog, let alone a brisk pace, but she did her best, everything hurting. *Everything.* The sockets of her eyeballs pounded, her ribs were sore, fingers stiff, skin cold. The world around her looked like fake plastic movie sets. What happened?

What *happened?*

Melody realized she'd stopped walking completely when Dani-elle left Joseph's side and rested a palm in the center of her back. "Mel, are you okay?"

*No. I can't even feel the package in my hand.*

Up ahead, a group of onlookers were taking pictures of her with their camera phones. On the way to the bookstore, she'd seen her-self on television through the window of a pub under the head-line, "What Caused the Split?" For the last three days, every time she ventured outside, people asked, "Where is Beat? Why did you break up?" It was *constant.* On the internet, theories were flying. They ranged from an unwanted pregnancy to another woman to a difference of opinion on pizza toppings.

"Mel," Danielle prompted, softly. "Do you want me to call an Uber?"

Before Melody could answer, Danielle's phone started to ring. Again. It had been ringing nonstop for the last three days, probably the network wondering why she wasn't doing anything to bolster ratings. Apparently cutting her bangs didn't count.

Danielle sighed and answered the phone. She shot Melody a glance and then turned away. "She's surrounded by security," Melody thought she overheard. Followed by, "Turn on the live stream and see for yourself . . . well, if you never turn it off, then why do you keep calling to check in? You can see everything that's happening. You can *see* she's safe . . ."

Security started ushering her forward then, obviously having given up on her actual feet. Come on, she could do this. *Walk.* Her apartment was only two more blocks, long though they were. Bracing her shoulders, Melody reached down deep for some strength and worked up a brisk pace, setting one foot in front of the other. Security moved with her, Joseph taking up the rear of their posse. People ran alongside them in the street or stopped their cars in the middle of the road to watch her pass, their curiosity about the breakup coming across loud and clear, even when they didn't ask.

Join the club.

She had no idea what happened.

One minute, she'd been on cloud nine, in love with the most magical human ever to be created and lucky enough to have her affections returned. The next, the lights had gone out and she'd been surrounded by impenetrable darkness.

When they passed the community garden on her right, Melody knew they were only half a block away from her destination and she glanced up, hoping that seeing her door might give her the final impetus she needed to get inside, away from the cloying curiosity. But instead of seeing her door, she saw a person instead. A woman.

A manacle closed around her throat and locked tight when she realized it was Trina.

Trina stood outside of her door.

Her mother was here.

Her guitar case was propped up against the metal gate—and if that pungent scent in the air was any indication, Trina had recently partaken in a midafternoon joint.

"Mom?" Melody called, as they drew closer.

"Oh my God," Danielle whispered behind her, apparently having finished her phone call.

The people who had been following Melody on her errand took a collective gasp—and all hell broke loose. Camera phones changed their target, flashes went off, voices rose in volume. Trina didn't even bat an eyelash. Didn't pay them the least bit of attention, really. Her focus was trained on her daughter.

"I know. You told me not to come. Either way, I'm not due a visit for another five or six weeks, but . . ." she started, jerking a thumb over her shoulder, "mind if I crash for a few nights anyway?"

Trina's unexpected appearance was Melody's tipping point.

For the last three days, she'd been too numb, in too much shock, to cry. Trina showing up on her doorstep in the middle of her anguish proved to be the kick she needed to burst the dam. Scalding tears pressed to the backs of her eyelids and overflowed, a sob bursting from her mouth. She cried like a toddler, right there in front of everyone in the middle of the sidewalk. Vaguely, Melody was aware of Danielle's phone starting to ring again, but the sound faded behind her as she jogged through the gate to Trina and threw herself into her mother's arms. Halfway there, it occurred to her Trina might not hug her back after the scene in New Hampshire, but her heart couldn't be broken any worse than it already was, could it?

Might as well be reckless.

Thankfully, after a surprised jolt, Trina did wrap her arms around Melody.

Chaos was breaking loose in the street, more and more people arriving, probably having watched the rock star's arrival on the live stream.

"We should get inside," Melody muttered thickly, fumbling for her keys in the small cross-body pouch she was wearing.

"Sounds good." Trina coughed, her own eyes holding a suspicious sheen as she surveyed the street, her attention drawn by the shouts of her name. "Damn. How long has it been like this?"

"Since the stream started, pretty much. It has died down in the last three days because I've done nothing but work and watch Bob Ross reruns." Melody unlocked the door and stepped aside to allow Trina, Danielle, and Joseph to follow them in. "There was a spike in viewership when I cut my own bangs. I think we broke the record for most crying emojis sent at one time on the internet. So that's nice."

Trina brushed Melody's bangs with her index finger. "Very punk rock."

"A bad demo tape, maybe." Melody unbuttoned her jacket and hung it on the peg, her mind automatically flashing back to Beat hanging up her coat on Monday night, his scent and size and safety making her apartment feel like a little bubble of heaven. "What are you doing here?"

Trina eyed the camera. "Is that thing going to keep rolling the whole time?"

"It's here until Christmas Eve. Part of the contract I signed with the devil." She winced. "No offense, Danielle."

"None taken." The producer was half hidden behind Joseph. "I'm not here."

Melody hummed. "Do you want something to drink, Mom?"

"Something stiff, if you please." Trina skirted around the couch and sat down, in the way only a rock star could. She sprawled, her limbs taking up as much space as possible. "Why am I here, you asked. Well. I guess I'm still piecing that together." Trina gave one final, wary look at the camera and sighed. "I hated the way we left things, Melody Anne. A phone call didn't seem like it was going to be enough."

Melody processed that while pouring a glass of whiskey for her mother, carrying it into the living room and finding what little couch room was left for herself. "You didn't come here because you changed your mind about the Steel Birds reunion?"

"I'd still rather die."

"Womp *womp*," Melody said, looking straight into the camera lens.

A corner of Trina's lips jumped, but her amusement ebbed just as quickly. "You don't usually cry when you see me. Is there something wrong?"

"You really make zero use of the internet, huh?"

"Hell no. It's a man-made plague." Trina shifted her position, crossing her arms over her middle in a way that was almost . . . self-conscious? "But if I did hate my sanity enough to look at the internet, I would find out what's wrong with you on there?"

"You would find a lot of theories."

"What's the truth?"

Melody's throat ached harder and harder until she sucked in a breath. "Figures that the first time we ever have a heart-to-heart conversation, millions of people are watching."

Trina scoffed. "We've had heart-to-heart conversations before." Her confidence in that statement faded almost immediately. "Haven't we?"

Melody attempted a smile, but her mouth wouldn't cooperate today.

"It's that man, isn't it?" Trina said quietly. "I warned you about him. He comes from spiteful stock."

Those words struck Melody like stones. Even now, her heart denied them. Beat wasn't spiteful. He was wonderful. She was missing something. She wasn't seeing the full picture. That's all. Or was she pathetic to be thinking like that? "Mom, I should warn you that Octavia Dawkins apparently watches this live stream."

"Does she?" Trina turned slowly to face the camera, smiled, and lifted a middle finger. "Sit and spin on it, you pretentious hag."

"That's nice," Melody murmured.

"Uh-oh," Danielle said from the other side of the room. "Hold that thought. The server crashed. The viewer count started shooting up when Trina arrived and it just kept going . . ."

"Looks like I've still got it," Trina said, openly preening.

"Yes," Danielle confirmed. "Well, I've got to work on this. Don't say anything important until we get the feed up and running again."

The producer and the cameraman left through the front door, a cacophony of excited shouts filling the apartment, before they were once again muffled. Some of the tension released from Melody's shoulders at the reality of being off camera, even temporarily. God, she wanted it to be over. It was bearable before because she'd had a teammate, but the weight of expectations and pressure was too hard to carry alone.

For good measure, she reached back and turned off her microphone.

After a full ten seconds of heavy silence, Trina cleared her throat. "Melody Anne . . ." She put down her drink. "I don't know where to begin."

"Begin with what?"

Her mother laughed without humor. "Everything." She paused. "First of all, you made the devil dance with your performance of 'Rattle the Cage.' Did me proud, even though I was pissed as hell." She frowned. "When did you learn how to play the guitar?"

Being given a compliment by her mother made speaking difficult. "Years ago. In my early twenties."

"That long?" Trina blinked. "You didn't think I'd care to know? I'm a musician."

"You just answered your own question. I wouldn't have been . . ." She shrugged jerkily. "It's just that you've had this grand success and it's hard not to measure myself, and everything I do, against that. It's hard not to assume *you're* measuring everything against it."

"Oh. Damn." Trina seemed to take that in. "I'm sorry, I didn't know you felt that way."

Melody nodded. "Well, I'm sorry I called you out in front of your friends."

Her mother's eyebrow rose. "Are you? Seemed to me, you were enjoying it."

"I didn't say I didn't enjoy it. I just said I was sorry."

Trina laughed, good and long. "That's fair enough. I suppose I had it coming." After a moment, she grew serious. "It's a little ironic that you didn't tell me about learning to play the guitar because you didn't think you'd measure up. Because . . . I don't talk to my housemates about you because I know I haven't been a very good mother. They'd probably ask me questions about you and I wouldn't know the answers."

"You could." Melody sat very still, afraid to rupture the moment. "You could ask me."

"I'm going to start, if that's okay." Trina coughed to cover her voice cracking. "Every time I leave my comfort zone and come down to New York, I feel like I'm reliving the past and I'm just so exposed and regretful, I can't think of anything else. I should have been focusing on you. I should have been doing that for a long time."

Acknowledgment. Apparently that was all it took to want to forgive someone. Just to have them acknowledge that you were hurt, out loud. "We can start now, Mom."

"Thank you." Trina slapped some moisture from under her

eyes, visibly trying to regroup. "Seems like a good chance to tell me what happened," Trina said, trying to sound casual despite the emotion still threading her tone. "With the enemy spawn, that is."

A chuckle snuck out of Melody, but it transformed into a shaky sigh. "That's the thing, I don't really know what happened. We spent the night together, things were . . . I thought they were great. Me and Beat, Mom . . . when we're together, I feel like I've known him my whole life. I can almost read his thoughts. And I swore it was the same for him. No . . ." She shook her head adamantly. "I *know* it's the same for him. That's why I'm so confused. He would never hurt me . . . but he has. I don't get it."

"What did he say?"

"We went on the *Today* show and I sort of confirmed we were together. But we hadn't officially *decided* to be together. It just seemed like a given."

Trina leaned back against the couch cushion, considering that with pursed lips. "You're right. That doesn't make any sense."

Being validated by her mother was like taking a deep breath for the first time in days. "Really?"

"Really." Trina frowned. "The man might have been carried in the womb of a demoness, but, uh . . ." She rolled her eyes. "I mean, you were in the county jail for an hour and he acted like you'd served a ten-year sentence of hard labor. It was obvious that his sun rose and set on your happiness, Melody Anne. When you were singing 'Rattle the Cage,' he looked at you like his heart was dangling from your pinkie finger."

That was painful to hear. All of it. "Maybe he changed his mind." Melody swiped quickly at the tears that escaped her eyes. "I'm trying to remember everything we said while we were live on the air, but it's a blur. I think we were both caught off guard by them bringing out Fletcher as a surprise guest—"

"Who?" Trina's back went ramrod straight. "They brought out who?"

"Fletcher Carr," Melody repeated. "You remember, the original Steel Birds drummer."

"*Remember* him? He's the reason the band broke up."

That confession knocked the wind out of Melody. "He is?"

"My God." The color had leached from her mother's face. What was going on here? "Why the hell would he resurface after all this time?"

"This is why you need the internet, Mom. Or at least an email address." Melody wet her lips, wary of how Trina would receive this next piece of information if the man's reappearance had *already* triggered her so hard. "He offered to be part of the reunion. Live on the air."

Trina shot to her feet and stomped to the other side of the living room. "Oh, the unmitigated *nerve* of that bastard." Were her mother's hands shaking? "Does Octavia know about this?"

"I assume she does."

"And?"

"And . . . I don't know. I haven't spoken to Beat in three days."

Her voice cracked on that last word, drawing her mother's attention. "I'm sorry if it seems like I'm ignoring your pain. I just . . . I can't believe Fletcher would pop up like this out of nowhere. I'll be honest, I was hoping he'd died in a freak accident or something. But isn't it just like him to sit around, waiting in the shadows for his chance to terrorize us again."

The truth hit Melody like a thunderbolt to the stomach.

*Waiting in the shadows.*

*Terrorize us.*

Beat's odd reaction to Fletcher walking onto the soundstage. How he'd hardly spoken after the drummer's appearance. And afterward, when they were off the air, he'd been an entirely different person. Not the man she loved. Not Beat.

"Oh shit," Melody breathed, nearly doubling over. "Oh my God, Mom."

Trina stopped pacing. "What?"

Telling Beat's secret was wrong, but Melody did it anyway, because the truth was going to tear her in half if she didn't let it out. "Beat has been getting blackmailed for five years. By his biological father. He wouldn't tell me the man's identity, but that's him. It's Fletcher Carr." Her entire body was starting to shake—for so many reason. Chiefly among them was denial that Beat had been confronted with his emotional captor live on the air and he'd been reeling from that blow all by himself. Without her. Ridiculous that she should leap to worry for him while in the midst of her own torturous pain, but that was love, apparently. Putting someone's well-being in front of your own. He would have done it for her . . .

He would have done it for her.

Melody lunged into a standing position, then had to use the arm of the couch for support so she wouldn't topple over on her shaky legs. "That man. He must have said something to Beat. He must have . . . something to do with me, maybe? I don't know."

She was so lost in the shock of her realization that she didn't notice her mother had gone white as a sheet. "Melody Anne . . ." Trina closed her eyes, swiping a wrist across her brow. "I can't believe I'm going to say this, but take me to Octavia, please."

# Chapter Thirty

*I*f Beat didn't get out of his apartment, he was going to tear the walls down with his bare hands. The live stream had gone black half an hour ago and Danielle was no longer answering her phone. He'd been calling the producer nonstop for the last three days to assure himself of Melody's safety, living in frozen fear that Fletcher Carr would show up on her doorstep looking for money, despite Beat's efforts to throw the drummer off the trail—and the fact that staying away from her was eating him alive, bite by bite.

Now, his last image of Melody was of her sitting on her couch with Trina, shadows under her eyes. So delicate and strong and perfectly Melody, refusing to talk about him on camera.

Checking the live stream was slowly torturing him to death, but he couldn't stop himself from sneaking into the bathroom to watch it where Ernie couldn't film him. At this point, the cameraman thought Beat was a compulsive showerer, but Beat couldn't sever his last remaining connection to Melody. In between distracted bouts of working, he hunkered down on the tile floor of his bathroom and watched her walk around Brooklyn surrounded by teeming throngs of people, seemingly oblivious to their fervor and sending his blood pressure shooting through the roof every single time.

What if they'd gotten past security and into her apartment and that was why the live stream had gone dark? With the arrival of Trina, it wasn't that far-fetched. He couldn't simply take the train or hop in an Uber and go to her apartment, though, could he? No. No, because he would kneel at her feet and beg for redemption. Fletcher would see it happen live and Beat's actions would once again throw her right back into the line of fire. The last three days and all the endless days ahead would be for nothing.

He would have hurt her for *nothing*.

Beat shoved his feet into a pair of loafers, yanked on his coat, and blew out the door of his apartment, dialing Danielle again as soon as he got in the elevator. Just before the metal doors could smack shut, a foot inserted itself into the elevator and they reopened, allowing Ernie to follow him with the camera. When a man forgets he's actively filming a reality show, things have officially taken a turn for the worse.

"Sorry," he muttered, squeezing his gritty eyes closed. "Pick up the phone, Danielle. Pick up—"

"She's fine," Danielle chirped in his ear. "The stream crashed. But I can't talk, we're on the move."

Relief clattered in his chest. "On the move to where?"

"Talk later, Beat."

The line went dead.

He stashed the phone into his pocket and fell back against the elevator wall. Okay. Melody was fine. And he . . . was most definitely not. He needed to get a grip on himself. For better or worse, Christmas Eve was two days away. Without a reunion—or the million dollars—in sight, he'd instructed his accountant to secure the loan. Come hell or high water, by Christmas morning, the terrible pressure would be off his back and that should have afforded him a small sense of comfort.

But it didn't.

In fact, he only felt worse.

Keeping his mother's reputation intact and his father's heart from breaking had always been enough to keep him motivated to appease the blackmailer. Now? Those things were still more than worthy of protecting, but he needed to start acknowledging the cycle.

This was never going to stop. It would continue forever.

He was guarding a secret that took shape before he was even born. Over thirty years ago, when his parents were in their twenties. Octavia had been a rock star, constantly on the road—who was to say that sleeping with the drummer while in a relationship with his father was the *only* mistake she'd made? Maybe there was more and Rudy was aware of it all. Loved her despite everything?

Beat couldn't know because he'd never asked.

He didn't know how his parents would react, because he'd locked up the truth and decided to manage the blackmail situation all by himself, when it could have been over years ago. If he'd just trusted the people he loved enough to be honest with them . . .

Trust.

That was what it came down to, didn't it? That was what Melody had taught him.

He needed to come clean to Octavia. Now. Today. His silence had cost him Melody, and the loss of his mental well-being was nipping at his heels. Octavia wouldn't want that, especially over a secret that involved her. And he couldn't carry the burden alone anymore. Another piece of straw added to the weight would break his back.

Or maybe it already had.

He was walking down the sidewalk to his parents' building in a T-shirt and slippers in twenty-two-degree weather—and feeling none of the cold. None whatsoever. There was only the yawning canyon in the middle of his chest. Cars honked on the avenues as they passed, people changed directions to follow him on the sidewalk. By the time Beat reached Octavia's high-rise, he was flanked by dozens of pedestrians, all of them wanting to know one thing.

Where is Melody?

Why weren't they together?

Why was he doing this to them?

Every time someone asked one of those questions, a steel-toed boot stomped on his heart. Why weren't they together? Because in his brief time with the most stunningly incredible woman in the world, he'd learned nothing from her. It was time to fix that.

Beat stared at his reflection in the elevator mirror on the ride up to his mother's penthouse, finding himself unrecognizable. He'd be lucky if Octavia didn't call security.

The doors opened and he entered the foyer, stopping short at the wall of silence, Ernie nearly mowing him down from behind. "Octavia?" There was no one in the opulent living space or the home gym, so he took the staircase to her office.

The moment he stepped through the entry, he knew something was wrong.

Octavia sat at her desk staring straight ahead, her face white as a sheet.

Instinctively, Beat fumbled for his microphone's battery pack and turned it off, apologizing to Ernie as he locked him out of the office.

"Mom." Frowning, Beat strode over and placed a hand on her shoulder, drawing back when she flinched. "What's wrong?"

She shook herself, tried to speak, but nothing came out. Not right away.

After a bracing breath, she pointed at the screen of her laptop. "The *Today* show . . ." She wet her lips and started again. "Obviously I was pissed when Fletcher Carr ambushed you and Melody live on the air. I don't want that man anywhere near the two of you, not that the *Today* show is required to consult me. Still, I called a producer friend because I felt like complaining. And she sent me . . . she just sent me this . . . recording."

The hair on the back of Beat's neck stood straight up. "What recording?"

Finally, Octavia looked up at him. "After the live segment, you had a conversation with Fletcher." His mother looked at him like she'd never seen him before in her life. "Your microphone was still hot."

Beat's temples pounded, his mind sluggish while processing that information. He couldn't remember the conversation word for word. He could only remember the parts about Melody. He could only remember the horrible things he'd said to her afterward. "Mom . . ."

"How long have you known he's your father?"

His lungs emptied like he'd been socked in the stomach. Holy shit. He'd dreaded this moment so long, he couldn't believe it was happening. Finding his voice was next to impossible, but he finally managed it. "Five years."

Octavia closed her eyes. "Oh my God."

Beat's first instinct was to comfort her. He started to kneel beside her chair, so they could talk through the situation together and God, he *hated* upsetting his mother, but the relief of having this secret exposed was like emerging from a locked room after being imprisoned for half a decade. His blood rushed in a new direction, legs rubbery.

Before he could say a word, his mother's housekeeper walked into the room. "Mrs. Dawkins, I—" She spied Beat standing beside the desk and sniffed. "I'm sorry, I was having a necessary moment in the bathroom or I would have informed you of your son's arrival."

"It's fine," Octavia said dully, dropping her head into her hands. "But I'm afraid more guests have just arrived, Mrs. Dawkins."

His mother's eyebrows knit together. "Who?"

"It's me, you old bitch," Trina Gallard said, sailing into the office. "Before you ask, no, you're not dreaming. I actually still have the body of a twenty-two-year-old."

"*Trina?*" Slowly, Octavia rose to her feet, her eyes round in shock, fingers trembling where she planted them on the desk's surface. "You . . . what are you doing here?"

"Livening up the place." She sauntered around the office, leaving boot impressions on the white rug. "Jesus, Octavia, your home is the official Museum of Boring."

Octavia raised an eyebrow. "You wouldn't know taste if it bit you on the ass."

"Taste *did* bite me on the ass once. Wasn't he the bass player from Infinite Jesters?"

"My goodness, you haven't changed at all."

"My *goodness*," mocked Trina, pretending to clutch at some invisible pearls. "Does the mistress of the house require her smelling salts?"

"*You* require some manners. This is my home you've invaded. Uninvited!"

"I'd have turned to dust waiting for that invitation!"

"Why don't you bite the dust instead, you vulgar, backstabbing hippie wannabe?"

"Oh, that's rich coming from—"

Melody walked into the room behind Trina.

The air around Beat's head turned to glass and shattered, his heart breaking into a sprint. Oh . . . *God.* She was the most beautiful thing he'd ever seen in his life. "Mel," he said hoarsely, his feet carrying across the room before he could think better of his actions. Or before he could analyze the consequences. He went because he was compelled. Because he had no choice but to get her into his arms, by any means necessary.

She made a shaky sound as he swept her up off the ground in a bear hug, burying his face in her hair, inhaling her scent like it would revive him, a dead man—and she did. Life rushed back into his limbs, his fingertips, his chest, the simultaneous effect nearly sending him to his knees. "Beat," she whispered into his neck.

"Mel," he said again, more adamantly.

She'd know what it meant. She would understand.

He was convinced they would continue in this embrace for the rest of time, because he felt like their organs would tumble out without it, but Melody wedged a hand between them and broke their contact. She pushed until there was distance between them. But it was too much. Inches felt like miles and his hands were in fists to keep from drawing her back in, harder, permanently. She wanted to be held by him—her desperate gaze on his throat told him that loud and clear—but she was fighting the need.

"For God's sake," Trina muttered unevenly, behind Beat. "A song about them would write itself. I'd just be holding the pencil."

"The camera doesn't really do them justice, does it?" Octavia asked quietly. Then she snapped her fingers at the cameramen—Joseph *and* Ernie—hovering just inside the door beside a rapt Danielle. "All right. You've got your reunion, now we require some privacy."

Danielle's shoulders slumped. "Fine. The live stream crashed again, anyway." Her phone started ringing and she gestured both cameramen out of the office. "Keep in mind that we should have it back up and running in ten."

"Ten minutes is all I'll be able to stand," Trina said, circling one of the chairs facing Octavia's desk and dropping into it unceremoniously. "Your son is being blackmailed, Oc."

Beat had gone back to staring into Melody's eyes when that pronouncement was made and he watched them go from yearning, but guarded . . . to apologetic. "I'm sorry. I didn't plan on telling her, telling anyone, but she was there when I figured out who it was. Your father."

He lifted his hands to grasp her shoulders, but she stepped out of his reach, sending Beat's stomach plummeting to the ground. "You have *nothing* to be sorry about," he managed. "I came here to tell Octavia everything."

"You did?" Melody's tone held a note of wistfulness. "That's good, Beat. That's *great.*"

"I'd already found out on my own, however," Octavia said, followed by the sound of her sitting down again behind her desk. Beat closed his eyes when he heard the tapping of keys, knowing what would follow. Unsure if he should dread the recording being played out loud or if he welcomed having his actions out in the open.

*Congratulations. She's head over heels for you, man. I bet she'd do just about anything for you. For instance, pay me to keep your big secret. Yeah, that lovestruck way she looks at you? I guarantee she'd protect you at all costs. Could mean double the payday for me.*

*Leave her out of this,* Beat's voice returned. *Or I will kill you.*

Right there in front of him, Melody's eyes developed a sheen.

*Your own father?*

*It's all for the cameras. Haven't you heard of a scripted reality show? As soon as it's over, I'll probably never see her again.*

"I was lying, Mel," he said through his teeth.

"I know," she whispered, nodding. "I know."

Thank God. Thank God she knew. Why wasn't she back in his arms yet?

*Sorry if you thought this was some magical love story, but it's not. You're welcome to try and pump her for cash, but she'll tell you to go to hell. And then she'll be able to leverage that secret. It'll lose its power and become her bargaining chip if she wants to sell the story. And you know offers are going to roll in. This thing is huge.*

"He's really selling that lie," Trina remarked. "Like son, like mother, I guess."

"Zip it, you smelly old relic," Octavia fired back.

"That's right, I have sweat glands, like a normal human. Did your Botox guy remove those for you, along with your sense of humor?"

*I know what I saw. You two are the real deal,* interrupted Fletcher's voice on the recording, followed by footsteps in the background. Melody's. Beat's gut seized up. He couldn't bear to look at her for this part, so he moved to the window and braced his hands on either side of the sill, staring out at the avenue but seeing nothing.

*She wants me to teach her how to play bocce, too! We're going to have a lady date after the holidays.* That was where he'd refused the hand she'd offered. The memory was like a torpedo to the center of his stomach. *Sorry. Did I interrupt?*

*Nah, honey. We're just shooting the shit. You must have another big day of filming ahead. Where are you two jetting off to next?*

*We don't really have any plans—*

"Turn it off," Beat demanded, pushing away from the window. "You've heard the part you needed to hear. Please, God, turn it off."

Octavia tapped a key and the office went silent, except for Melody's long, winded intake of breath. She wouldn't look at him, though. What was she thinking?

Finally, Trina broke the silence. "I'm no mathematician, but what it sounds like, old pal, is you had yourself a little indiscretion in between tours."

Not a single muscle shifted in the lead singer's face. "Was there a paternity test, Beat?"

"Yes." His voice was like gravel. "I wouldn't give him a dime until I knew for sure. He's my father. My biological one, anyway."

Octavia's head fell forward.

"Just to recap." Trina raised a handful of fingers and started ticking them off. "He dated you. Lied to me, saying you were the one who broke it off with *him*. I started dating him—a move that, let's face it, was the beginning of the end. The end of Steel Birds. Our *creation*. And then, after we booted him for another drummer, he still managed to wiggle back in and sleep with you one more time. Even after everything."

"I was just . . . it was vanity and jealousy and . . . being twenty-three, goddammit. I wanted to hurt you back. We were already fighting constantly, ditching recording sessions, and blowing off label meetings. What would it matter if I screwed everything up a little more? And damn, I wanted to prove he still wanted me the most. It was stupid and it didn't fix *anything*. If you want to hate me for it, fine, but I'm pretty sure I'm paying a steep enough price without adding your ridicule, Trina." Octavia slammed a closed fist down on the desk. The only one who didn't flinch was Trina. "He's been blackmailing my son for five years!"

Trina reached out and knocked over a porcelain glass full of white pens. "There you are! I thought the woman who sang 'Bitch on Wheels' at the top of her lungs was dead and gone."

"I want to fillet this motherfucker's balls, grill them until they're well-done, and dine on them with a bottle of wine," Octavia growled.

Beat's jaw dropped.

He'd seen countless hours of Steel Birds concert footage. He'd seen his mother unleash hell into a microphone. But in *real* life, she was his polished, routine-oriented mother. That was still true, but apparently the take-no-prisoners rock vocalist had been lurking inside of her this whole time.

He traded a look of bemused disbelief with Melody.

She was almost smiling at Beat when she caught herself and broke eye contact.

Trina stabbed the desk with her index finger. "Here is what I have to say. If you disagree with me, Oc, I'll leave, and another thirty years might go by until we cross paths again." She paused, shifting in her seat. "But the way I see it, Fletcher has had too much business in my life. He's had too much of an effect for such a worthless piece of garbage—and I just can't stand to see him have any more."

"He came for our kids," Octavia breathed.

Trina nodded. "Came *between* our kids."

"He's breaking up the band. Twice."

"Only if we let him."

Octavia's eyes took on sharp focus, catching Trina's gaze and holding—and it was an incredible thing to witness. Beat would tell the story a thousand times over the course of his life and never be able to do justice to the magic that wove the two women back together right there in front of their very eyes. It was almost a visible stitching of the disrupted air between them, a magnetic force that lifted them out of their chairs at the very same time, like two monoliths rising from the earth.

Trina raised an eyebrow. "Is this gig happening, or what?"

"Oh, it's happening. Right after we tell Fletcher Carr to keep his poison away from our families."

"I've got a better idea." Trina smiled and scooped up Octavia's phone from its resting position on the desk, handing it to her former—er, current?—bandmate. "Accept his offer to join the reunion."

# Chapter Thirty-One

**M**elody watched, incredulous, as the former enemies huddled together to discuss their plan, leaning into each other's sides, uproarious laughter erupting between them, as if thirty years of vitriol and anger had never happened.

She and Beat had done the impossible.

They'd reunited Steel Birds.

They'd gained everything in the process—friendship and love and personal growth. But they'd lost it all, too. For one brief, shining moment as she watched the two legends re-form their once-in-a-lifetime bond, she wondered if her pain might have been worth the outcome. Maybe. Yes? But when Beat moved to stand in front of her, her confidence in that answer slipped and scattered.

Nothing was worth this.

Loving him so deeply and having to live without him.

"Melody, can we talk?"

There was nothing more enticing than the idea of being alone with Beat somewhere. Retreating to their own little world where they were the only inhabitants and the rest of the planet was inconsequential. But pretending the hurt he'd caused wasn't a sharp, lingering thing would only make it worse. He'd promised her that night in her apartment to be truthful with her, always, no exceptions. They'd come so far where his trust was concerned. But at the first opportunity, he'd gone back on his word. He might have done it for noble reasons, to protect her, but she didn't want to be protected when they could be a team, instead. She was stronger than that now. "I think it might be better if I go."

Panic flared in his features. "Please. Don't leave."

"Mom," Melody called, desperation rising inside of her to get out of there. Before she gave in and let Beat's presence sink too deep where she'd never get him out. Maybe that was already the case and she was delusional to think she could save herself now. But she had to try. She'd fought so hard to create standards for herself and others. No way she was going to compromise them now. "Mom, when you're done here, take an Uber back to my place, all right? Stay as long as you want."

Both women regarded Melody and Beat with troubled eyes.

"Okay, Melody Anne," Trina said finally.

"Are you sure you can't stay for dinner?" Octavia asked hopefully. "Surely I can track down some beignets."

"Another time," Melody said, throat stiff.

Beat cleared his throat hard. "I'll walk you out."

Refusing the offer would have been childish, so she nodded once and moved toward the doors. As soon as she laid her hand on the knob, a wave of reluctance washed over her. She could hear Danielle on the other side, arguing with the network. The cameramen were talking about the best route to take back to Brooklyn. *I just want to be alone.* At the very least, she didn't want to be filmed for a while.

Learning the real reason behind Beat's sudden distance, followed by the emotional curveball of reuniting Steel Birds—actually *managing* the lofty goal they'd set out to accomplish—Melody was restless and keyed up and needed some time to decompress. The cameras made that impossible.

"What is it?" Beat asked, close to her ear.

Her body warmed, her nipples slowly hardening into peaks. "I just don't want to be filmed for a while. I want to get away from the cameras."

Beat hummed in his throat. "There's a service elevator my mother takes sometimes if she doesn't want to run into any fans outside. It lets her out in the boiler room and she takes a set of stairs up to the street. You can exit on the opposite side." He placed a hand on the small of her back and something dangerous inside of her outright purred. "I'll take you."

She tipped her chin toward the door. "How are we going to get past them?"

"Us?" He scoffed, turning the knob. "We can do anything."

Three heads came up when they left the office, though Danielle continued to spit technical jargon at whoever was on the other end of her call.

"Just showing her the bathroom," Beat said casually, ushering Melody through the doorway.

Melody didn't miss the suspicious look in Joseph's eyes, but he let them pass.

Beat's hand remained at the base of her spine, just above the battery pack, as they walked through the all-white living room and dining room. When Melody guessed they would have hooked a right for the bathroom, Beat surreptitiously glanced behind them and hustled her to the front door instead. Being in cahoots with Beat reminded Melody of the night of the snowball fight when they fooled the cameramen by dressing like Vance and Savelina, and now the center of her chest ached.

Closing the door of the penthouse behind them with only the barest click, Beat took her hand and they jogged side by side past the public elevator, through another metal door, into an industrial concrete room with a different elevator.

Beat pressed the call button and it started to whir, approaching the top floor.

That hand was still on her back, but his thumb stroked sideways over her spine now, making her nipples tingle, her thighs loose. And when he very purposefully turned off her microphone, a wild whirlwind of sound started in her ears.

"I can figure it out from here," she said, voice thready.

"Mel, please," he said gruffly. "Just talk to me for five minutes."

"Eventually I will, okay? But I can't right now."

"Why?"

"I don't know. I miss you too much to think clearly."

He made a harsh sound. "You're going to wait until you stop missing me to talk? If you miss me a fraction of how much I miss you, that won't happen. Not in a million years."

The door trundled open. They didn't move for a full three seconds, then stepped in at the same time, facing forward. The door closed, the elevator beginning to descend. Before Beat even slapped the emergency stop button, she knew what was coming. She sensed he was going to do it—but she still gasped when the metal conveyance ground to a halt.

"Melody, I'm in love with you." Beat took her by the shoulders, turning her to face him and tipping up her chin, giving her no choice but to stare straight into the storm taking place in his eyes. "I will love you for eternity."

A sob tried to rip her throat open. "Beat—"

"I hope you know I was lying." His fingertips left her chin, delved into her hair. "Did you really think I would be upset that you made us official on national television? I would have *proposed* to you if they hadn't brought out my father."

Every word out of his mouth set off reverberations in her breast, like a gong being banged repeatedly. "I knew I was missing something. I knew you wouldn't hurt me like that."

"*Good.*"

"I understand why you cut me off in front of him. You wanted him to leave me alone. But I want you to imagine if I'd done that to you, instead of treating you as my teammate. We could have faced him together, instead of letting him break us apart. You put your walls up and shut me out. It's the *trust*, Beat. I need to know you're not going to . . . to *hurt* me. That I'm not going to get blindsided every time you want to protect me. Odds are, with all this attention we're getting, something like this could happen again and I don't feel . . . secure anymore."

"What would you have done? If he showed up at your door and pumped you for money to keep my family's secret?" He paused, intently searching her face. "You'd have paid it and the cycle would start all over again. All I could think about was protecting you."

"I don't know what I would have done. But I *do* know that I would have talked to you about it." Her voice started to break. "You have no excuse for leaving me dangling for three days. All it would have taken was a phone call. A text. You could have come to see me when the cameras shut down for the day. You didn't do *any* of those things."

"He's the worst part of my life, Mel," he said through his teeth. "Now I was bringing it down on your head, too? I fed you to the lion. Being with me was *hurting* you."

"No. Being apart is worse. You know it is."

"You're right. I do. God, do I fucking know." He dropped his mouth to her neck, rubbed his open lips up the soft slope of tendons to her ear, kissing the lobe, the space beneath. His big hands lifted to grip her hips, guiding her backward toward the elevator wall. "I haven't slept in three days. I lock myself in the bathroom and watch you on my screen like an obsessed fan. Maybe that's what I am."

Melody's nerve endings were beginning to shoot sparks, her

lungs laboring to draw breath. As soon as Beat's hips pinned her to the wall, she knew. Resistance was futile. Even her frustration with him, with the whole situation, was making her more desperate for that wild and enduring connection they shared. To feel it everywhere. Bathe in it. She'd gone three days thinking she might never feel it again, starved of it, and now her body wanted to gorge.

"I hear what you're telling me," Beat said, grazing their lips together, his eyes zeroed in on her mouth. Tortured. "You need complete trust or nothing at all. A partnership. Full disclosure always. I'll give that to you. I *need* to give you that."

"I want to believe that."

"Please." He captured her mouth and her neck went limp, requiring his hand to cup the back of her head. He held her up, while his lips opened over hers, slanted, then took her with long, devastating strokes of his tongue. "Believe in me again, Mel. I'm so fucking sorry."

"I know," she whispered, kissing him back hungrily. "I know you are."

"I'm your boyfriend. Fiancé. Soulmate. Call me all of them. Or just one. I'll take *one*."

The ache that had burdened her for the last three days swelled up like a life raft, pushing her ribs out from the inside. All the time she'd spent doubting herself, staring at her phone and hoping it would ring, the emptiness. If he'd trusted her the way she trusted him, they would have avoided it all. "I can't right now."

He growled brokenly against her mouth. "Maybe I'll make you say it."

Her intimate muscles contracted, leaving wetness behind. They were a mile into dangerous territory now. Past the point of no return. His erection was thick and ready between their bodies and her stomach cradled it, rubbing side to side. Unconscious, desperate moves of a woman in love, even when she'd been wronged. "Maybe I . . . want you to try."

Beat moaned above her head, his hands raking down her breasts, squeezing them roughly in his hands. "You're not taking me back," he rasped, dipping his head to lick her hard nipples through her thin sweater. "But you're going to let me fuck you?"

"Yes."

"Are you trying to hurt me back?" he demanded against her mouth.

"No. *No.*"

"Of course, you wouldn't. Not my perfect Melody." His kiss was filled with longing, his hands trailing down the front of her body, fingertips tucking beneath the hem of her skirt to raise it up, up and over her hips. "Although I would let you, wouldn't I? I would beg for whatever you'd give me. Love, pain, forgiveness."

"I don't know when I'll be able to offer those things. And this isn't going to solve anything," she whispered, her fingers wrestling with his belt. She unfastened the buckle, sliding free the button of his pants and dragging down the zipper over the bulging crotch of his briefs. "But I can't help wanting to feel close to you."

"I'm going to get so close." His mouth was back on hers, kissing her feverishly, his fingertips diving past the waistband of her panties, parting her flesh with his middle finger, finding her clit in one stroke. "There'll be nothing but us."

He would get close. He would, but it would be a temporary fix. And she was starved for that fix.

"Now," she gasped against his mouth. "Now, now, now."

"God yes. But only because you're wet enough." He boosted her up against the wall with nothing but a roll of his hips, hooking his index finger in the material of her panties and dragging them to one side. "I take care of you. That's what I do."

"No, Beat. That's not how it works." She wrapped her thighs tightly around his waist, her body shaking with the anticipation of being filled. Feeling that hardness invade her, give her pleasure, use her. *Fuck* her. "We take care of *each other.*"

She could see the moment it all clicked for him, a line forming between his brows, his hands pausing in the act of guiding his shaft between her thighs. At the outset of their relationship, he'd kept the blackmail a secret, then the identity of his father. He'd locked her out. The night of the snowball fight, he'd promised to change. He'd *felt* changed. But he'd fallen back into his old pattern. Refusing the trust, to burden anyone with his problems. After all the progress they'd made, of course this would be a blow to Melody.

Beat's breath raced in and out as he pressed himself inside of Melody and bucked home—*hard*—snapping his teeth against the curve of her neck. "I love you so much, Mel. I'll never lock you out again."

Her back slid up and down the wall with every thrust, her fingers digging into his shoulders to balance the quickening deep in her sex. "Beat. Beat. *Beat.*"

"That's the name of your soulmate." His mouth found hers and shredded her final thread of rational thought, kissing her like it was the first time. Or last time. She couldn't be sure; all she knew was that her heart climbed high in her throat and she clung, thighs scrambling higher around his waist. Her tongue tangled with his greedily, her body an inferno for this man she'd become addicted to and robbed of in such a short span of time. "You hear my name in your sleep, Peach, the same way I hear yours."

"Yes," she whispered, opening her knees and leaning back slightly, craving the sight of him entering her, thickness into slick, hard into soft, best friend into lover, soulmates blurring into one. "I always will."

Beat's eyes flashed. "You always will, because I'll be in bed beside you, whispering it in your ear, Melody." He bared his teeth against her mouth. "I'll be moaning it while I lick between your legs. I'll call it out loud when I walk through the front door every night."

Images were bombarding her, reviving the hope that had withered during their separation. She wasn't quite ready to embrace it, to trust the happiness that came along with it, so she focused on the raw throb that increased with intensity every time his hips punched upward, slamming her buttocks into the wall of the elevator, his beloved fingers leaving bruises where they gripped her thighs and hips.

The words "I love you" were razing the inside of her throat. They wanted to be set loose so badly. She couldn't yet, though. She couldn't speak that truth until she could commit to him, to trying again, completely. To do otherwise would be cruel.

*Distract yourself.*

"Deeper," she whispered. "Get it deeper."

He let out a muffled roar into her shoulder, hooked his elbows beneath her knees to draw them higher and dialed the rhythm up to eleven. Based on the way she elevated even farther against the wall, she guessed he was going up on his toes to grind into her. The image of that made her clench uncontrollably, his name turning into a hoarse chant coming from deep, deep in her throat, her thighs starting to quake.

"God, I would love to get you pregnant someday, you know that?" His voice was rich and guttural in her hair, his mouth planting kisses on her hairline, her cheeks. "I haven't stopped thinking about it since we talked about having kids. I want to be the man who makes it feel right for you. I want to take the good inside of you and double it."

"Beat. *Please.*"

"Am I going too far? *Good.* Soak me into your bones the way you're in mine."

That was it. She lost her footing on the balance beam and went crashing down to the ground without a harness. "I need you so much. I need you so much."

His sturdy frame started to shake, a choked sound leaving him. "*Melody.*"

They climaxed like two asteroids colliding in the sky, sending rubble and debris in a hundred directions. She whimpered and tightened her thighs, twisting her fingers in his hair and bearing down, accepting the pleasure for all it was worth, glorying in the flooding sensation he let loose inside of her. She felt the slick wetness that pooled with her own while her soulmate's body jerked violently against her, moaning brokenly into her neck as if he hadn't released in a hundred years. It felt the same way for her. Urgent and consuming and mind-blowing.

The orgasm took so much out of her that she collapsed as soon as it ended, her limbs turning to dead weight. But Beat, even in his own state of depletion, compensated to hold her upright, his arms going around her like twin vises. "Shhhh, Melody," he whispered against her temple, kissed it reverently. "Everything is going to be better now."

The organ in her chest squeezed painfully.

It would be so simple to stay in those arms forever. To forget the zombielike state he'd left her in after the *Today* show. She'd been a soaring bird one moment and roadkill the next, and the wound was still too fresh. She hoped she wouldn't need to nurse it forever, but if that was the case, so be it. Her responsibility was to herself first and she couldn't let her relationship with Beat heal around her broken bone. She needed to set it first or nothing would ever feel right.

"You're still leaving, aren't you?" he said, sounding almost dazed.

After a second, she nodded, holding him tighter. "Christmas Eve is only two days away. I'll see you then."

He didn't seem capable of responding, though it took her several tries to extricate herself from the death grip his arms had around her. Once she accomplished that feat, she pulled her skirt back down. Leaving after what they'd just shared felt extremely wrong, so wrong that she could barely lift her finger to press the button that brought the elevator back to life.

It moved downward sluggishly while her pulse beat seven thousand miles an hour in her chest, her head demanding she do the right thing and go home, get some perspective, while her heart screamed at her to turn and run back into his perfect arms.

In the end, her mind won.

"The crazy thing is . . ." he said behind her, almost to himself. "In the end, it was fine, wasn't it? I guarded this secret like it would set the world on fire. I don't know what's going to happen with my father—maybe it *will* burn his world down. I don't know. But . . . it's out there now. The truth. And everything is still standing. The show goes on. Everything just carries on. She didn't even look at me any differently than she always has."

"Love doesn't come and go that easily, Beat. You need to believe you can lean on it, even when you have to lean really hard." Melody swallowed the lump in her throat. "I think maybe the people who love us want to be tested and leaned on sometimes, so they can show us how much we mean. Expressing love and trust is a gift to the person who receives it."

His chest dipped and expanded. "I'll give those things to you, Melody Gallard. Every day. If you let me back in."

"When," she whispered. "When. You'll have to trust me on that."

Beat sucked in a breath and nodded, falling back against the elevator wall to watch her leave through bloodshot eyes.

# Chapter Thirty-Two

December 24

$\mathcal{B}$eat watched his parents embrace from the opposite end of the limousine and felt a multitude of knots loosen in his chest. He hadn't been privy to their conversation, but their body language throughout the ride to Rockefeller Center told him exactly what they were discussing. Octavia was making her confession. His mother shook as she spoke, his father reaching out in concern. Offering forgiveness and comforting Octavia.

Just like that.

A thirty-year-old secret, shame, and regret abolished by love.

Even as the relief swept Beat, he couldn't appreciate it to the fullest. Not without his heart. That thing that used to beat inside of his rib cage was walking around outside of his body, probably in her kelly green coat. Maybe she'd already made it to Rockefeller Center with Trina, where they would meet with the production team and Steel Birds would take the stage.

The city passed in a blur outside, snow beginning to wander down lazily from the sky. New Yorkers were doing last-minute shopping, tourists posed for pictures in front of Radio City Music Hall, Santa rang a bell for the Salvation Army on the corner, sirens blipped every so often, and steam rose from the edges of a manhole cover. Was Melody seeing all this? What did she think about the city this time of night? Was she smiling at that very moment?

Beat's fingers dug into his bent knees and tried to slow down his pulse. Not easy, knowing he'd be seeing her in a few minutes. Although, honestly, he'd been seeing her everywhere he looked for the last forty-eight hours. It didn't matter that they'd ceased the live stream, due to a lack of bandwidth to support the viewership, and he could no longer watch Melody on his phone. She was tattooed on the back of his eyelids.

The determined curl of her upper lip as she sang "Rattle the Cage" at the compound.

That giggle she let loose sometimes when she wasn't prepared to laugh.

Her beautiful eyes full of tears, happy and sad and angry ones.

Her flushed face as he fucked her two days ago.

Everywhere. She was everywhere. And that was where he wanted her. He didn't want a single ounce of her to slip free, so he endured the ice pick that buried in his chest every time another memory presented itself and made him miss her even more.

More and more and more.

Bring it on.

The limousine came to a stop outside of the Applause Network building on Forty-Ninth Street, located a half block from the Rockefeller Center stage where the reunion would take place. Beat could hear the crowd from there—and obviously, so could Octavia. She pressed a hand to the center of her chest and sucked in a long breath through her nose.

"Wow," she said, laughing. "I'd forgotten what this feels like."

"You're going to knock them dead, darling," Rudy said, his voice laden with more emotion than usual. "Just like you always did."

"Thank you," she whispered, kissing her husband. "Beat, you're still okay with introducing us?"

He cleared the rust from his throat. "Are you kidding? It's an honor."

The limousine door opened, the driver's hand appearing inside to help Octavia step out of the vehicle, but she didn't take it right away. Instead, she tilted her head at Beat, her expression brimming with sympathy. "I have a good feeling about tonight," she said. "No one can stay mad at anyone for long on a snowy Christmas Eve."

"She isn't mad at me," he rasped, losing his breath just by talking about her.

She simply couldn't be with him.

He'd been careless with the world's most priceless treasure. Melody's heart. And she didn't trust him with it anymore.

Beat's eye sockets burned like they'd been freshly branded onto his face. He dug his thumbs into them to counteract the sting, but it only got worse. His reflection in the window of the limousine was haggard and drawn. Sunken, lifeless eyes and a bristled jaw. Rudy called his name and he realized it was their turn to exit the limousine. A crowd had assembled on the curb and they screamed, some of them being physically restrained by security as Octavia passed through the parted sea of people and disappeared into the building.

"Beat," his father said again.

"Yes?"

Rudy tapped an unlit cigar on his thigh, turning it over end by end. "I just wanted to say . . . you're my boy, you know. I was there the day you were born." He ceased his nervous movements. "You're still my son. Right?"

Physically, Beat could not handle this moment, but he tried; he dug deep and found the strength because he sensed how important the answer was to his father. "I'm your son," he said firmly. "You're the only father I need or want. In this case, a bond is stronger than blood."

Rudy ducked his head swiftly. "Thank you."

"I should be thanking you for being so understanding about this. I'm sorry I kept the truth from you. From Octavia. I didn't give either of you enough credit."

"You were protecting your mother. I'll never find any fault in that."

Beat took a deep breath to compose himself and let it out fast, his father mirroring the move in the exact same manner, at the exact same time. And they laughed.

"Into the fray once more, young man," said his father, lighting his cigar and heaving himself out of the limousine. Beat listened to shouts of his father's name, the increasing demands for Beat to make an appearance. Through the window, he read the signs being held aloft and his stomach flipped over.

BEAT + MELODY = COUPLE GOALS

PUT A RING ON IT, BEAT

If they only knew he was burning alive with the need to propose. Christ, at this point, he would be happy with a text message from her. A smile. Anything.

A security guard stuck his head in through the open door of the limousine. "Mr. Dawkins, we can't control the crowd indefinitely. You're needed inside."

"Right. Sorry." He crouch-walked to the other side of the vehicle and forced himself out into the cold, buttoning his suit jacket as he straightened, the blast of cheers nearly knocking him back a step. The metal barriers holding the crowd at bay scraped forward on the concrete, more signs popping up, pictures of him and Melody taped to them. One had Melody lying on top of him in the snowbank and he slowed his step to look at it, his lungs burning on a harsh intake of breath. Take him back to that night. God, he would give *anything*.

"Mr. Dawkins," said the security guard, more impatiently this time, and they moved in tandem through the open side door of the building. They traveled through an ornate lobby, to an elevator that took him to the second floor. "We're using the atrium as the backstage area. It exits into the plaza where the band will be performing."

"I see."

The elevator doors opened, the guard gesturing for Beat to precede him down another hallway, until finally he was ushered into the atrium, a large, enclosed dome of glass that was lit up like the inside of a snow globe. In the near distance, he could see the row of international flags that lined Rockefeller Center. They were steps away. As one of the opening bands was finishing, the crowd was already demanding the Steel Birds make their appearance next, but he could barely register his surroundings, because he was looking for Melody—

And there she was.

Looking at him across the atrium with her fucking heart in her eyes.

God, kill him now.

Men weren't built to withstand this kind of pain. She needed him, he was in love with her to the point of madness, yet she didn't run into his arms. She couldn't, because of the ditch he'd dug in between them. Despite the searing pain in his chest, Beat strode forward to join the group, nodding at Danielle and Joseph—who for once was without his camera—in greeting. Beat exchanged a measuring glance with Trina. Then he went right back to staring at the love of his life, while she stared back, utterly gorgeous in her white turtleneck dress and kelly green coat. Black boots that circled her ankles, the way his hands were dying to do.

"All right, folks. We're just waiting on one more and then I'll go over—"

"I'm here," called a familiar voice.

They all turned at once to watch the original Steel Birds drummer saunter into the atrium in ripped jeans and a Steel Birds 1991 tour shirt. Trina's quiet intake of breath was the only reaction among the group to the man's arrival. Octavia's smile was bland. Melody's was bright and welcoming, as if she knew nothing, although Beat knew her well enough to tell it was costing her serious effort to smile. Rudy pretended to take a call and moseyed over to the other side of the space.

"They say a man's wardrobe pauses on the best years of his life and never changes," Trina said, crossing her arms. "Guess we know when you peaked, huh, Fletcher?"

Octavia hummed. "While riding our coattails."

"Lovely to see you again, too, ladies. I'd love to make a joke about riding a lot more than your coattails, but I have more class than that."

Red filtered into Beat's vision and he bristled, ready to bury his fist in the center of the drummer's face, but Melody subtly shook her head at him, anchoring him with her eyes. He could practically read her mind and it was saying *You've been fighting the battle long enough, it's their turn.* And she was right. Tonight was for the band.

"Do you hear that, Oc?" Trina mused. "The guy who once left a puke trail from the tour bus to the stage has suddenly decided he's classy."

"Imagine that. People really do change."

"Okay," Danielle said, waving to get everyone's attention. "As much as I would love to prolong this part of the reunion, we have a very large, very demanding crowd waiting to see the greatest female rock duo in history live onstage."

"Notice she said 'duo,'" Trina remarked, winking at Fletcher.

"Beat," Danielle continued with determination. "You will go on first and introduce the band—"

"Shouldn't Mel be with me?" he interrupted, unplanned.

That brought the producer up short. All five sets of gazes swung to him, then to Melody.

Meanwhile Melody's heart was back to being in her perfect goddamn eyes again, her affection for him so pure and clear, it was carving him wide open. Who could survive this?

Danielle coughed. "I . . . just assumed, since Melody isn't all that comfortable with the spotlight that she might want to stay backstage, but if I'm wrong, Melody you are more than welcome to join Beat for the introduction."

His jaw ached from grinding his teeth. "You're too beautiful to hide backstage."

"Beat," she whispered, flattening a hand over her middle. "Please."

"Seems like a real relationship to me," singsonged his biological father near his ear.

"That's because it is." He looked the man in the eye. "Always has been."

Danielle made an uncomfortable sound. "Sorry, guys. There will be more time for conversation after the show, but right now, I'm going to need Beat to begin the introduction. And Melody, too, if she so chooses."

Melody nodded, still staring at him. What was she thinking? He'd have crawled over ten miles of broken glass to find out.

"Beat and Melody, exit the left side of the stage. Trina, Octavia, and Fletcher, you will enter stage right and take a bow while the crowd gives you some much deserved accolades. I assume you've discussed the set list?"

"We have," Octavia confirmed, trading a smirk with Trina.

"No one discussed it with me," scoffed the drummer.

"Just try and keep up, you fool," Trina responded without missing a beat.

"It's time," someone called from the tunnel at the end of the atrium.

Beat held out his hand to Melody and she took it, nearly felling him with gratitude. He savored the natural glide of her slim fingers twining between his bigger ones, barely banking the impulse to bring them to his mouth and kiss them. They walked side by side through the tunnel, flanked by security, bright lights beckoning to them from the other end. The cheering, chanting, stomping, and whistling grew louder, until they couldn't have traded words even if they tried. So they simply stood at the bottom of the stairs leading up to the stage breathing in each other's air. Melody allowed Beat to rest his lips against her forehead, their fingers tightening in each other's grips.

"We're back from commercial," called a young woman in a headset. "In ten . . . nine . . ."

"Are we just winging it?" Melody shouted up at him while quickly handing her coat to someone in a headset. "Or do you have lines prepared?"

"We're winging it."

Her eyes sparkled. "Sort of like we've been doing this whole time?"

He laughed and it hurt.

*We better go*, she mouthed, as if she knew.

Reluctantly, he nodded and they walked out onto the stage to the roar of a seemingly endless crowd. It extended beyond the barriers of Rockefeller Center, spilling out into the avenue and side streets. People hung out of office building windows, lining rooftops, and standing on top of cars.

Someone in front of the stage signaled him, circling their finger rapidly.

In other words, *hurry the hell up.*

"Ladies and gentlemen . . ." Beat started.

He angled the microphone downward so Melody could reach it. "We are ever so proud to *reintroduce* . . ."

"The Terror Twins."

"The Dirty Duo."

"Our mothers."

"*Steel Birds,*" they shouted into the same microphone, their lips brushing together due to the proximity and Beat's body quite simply took over, demanding to kiss the mouth that would torment him for the rest of his life. He planted one on her, oblivious to the crowd—at least until their approval turned deafening. To the point that security had to surround them behind the microphone and ferry them toward stage left.

Beat's whole body throbbed to continue that kiss, but he couldn't physically touch her another second without having *everything.* Being with her. Knowing they would be together every single morning, every single night. Anything less was painful, so as soon as they came off the stage and she disconnected their fingers, he kept walking.

And he didn't stop.

## Chapter Thirty-Three

Melody pressed her fingers to her lips as Beat walked away.

The crowd continued to go wild and her heart did the same. It vacillated between hurt and elation and conflict, going haywire.

She should go after him.

She *had* to go after him.

She'd needed time to regain her trust in him, but she'd never wanted a breach between them and it seemed to be widening by the second.

"Beat!"

The volume of the cheers was too loud—he couldn't hear her. She could barely hear herself. Although her legs were still wobbly from the kiss, she turned to follow him, but Steel Birds took the stage at that moment—and the ground started to pulse. Fletcher emerged first and took a quick seat at the drums, picking up his sticks, followed by Trina and Octavia walking out into the open side by side, continuing until they were at the very edge of the raised platform. They basked in the white spotlights for a full minute while the audience screamed. Octavia flipped her hair and Trina flexed her biceps, ratcheting up the noise another degree.

And then they joined hands, raising their tightly clasped fists to the sky and the spotlight turned an electric shade of blue. The crowd's enthusiastic response had Melody slapping her hands over her ears to muffle the noise. She could almost see the high decibels rippling the air around her, the hair raising on her arms.

They were riveting.

Melody couldn't take her eyes off them. Especially when Trina picked up her guitar, strummed a single note, and shot Melody a wink. As badly as she needed to go after Beat, she couldn't miss this moment for her mother. For them. She'd accomplished what she'd set out to do and her relationship with Trina would never be the same. It would be better.

Melody's eyes watered, blurring the last remaining sight of Beat's back. He'd been swallowed up by the chaotic backstage crowd. She could almost feel it in her stomach the moment he left the building. Where was he going?

Melody was distracted when Octavia picked up her guitar, lifted it over her head, and approached the microphone. "It might be Christmas Eve, but that's not going to stop us from causing some trouble, is it, Trina?"

"Nothing has ever stopped us before," purred Trina.

Fletcher laughed into his microphone, as if he was in on the joke, slowly turning the heads of both women. They looked at Fletcher, before returning their attention to each other. Nodding. "For thirty years, people have been asking us the question, 'What broke up the band?'" Octavia tipped her head toward the drummer. "Well, you're looking at him."

Some of the smugness fled from Fletcher's face.

He leaned forward to speak into the microphone, but he only got out one word before the sound miraculously cut off. The cheers died down, the crowd sensing the gravity of what was taking place.

"When Trina and I started Steel Birds, we vowed we'd never fall victim to the jealousy and inflated egos that break up nearly every great band, but that promise got lost somewhere along the way. I guess we got a little lost ourselves."

"It took our kids to come along and pull our heads out of our asses." Trina punctuated that statement with a low chord on her guitar, the audience whistling and clapping at the mention of Melody and Beat. "Can I say ass on television?"

"We're fifty-three. We can say whatever the hell we want."

Trina smiled. "I like that."

Octavia hummed into the mic while the laughter rose and faded. "Bottom line is . . . we let a man come between us. And we're never going to do that again."

"Especially not this one," Trina added, calling, "Security?"

Melody watched with her jaw on the floor as two security guards wrestled Fletcher backward out of his seat, whisking him off the stage in Melody's direction while he sputtered. Before he could disappear into the backstage area entirely, Octavia stepped into his path, her expression a combination of cold and righteous.

"My family knows the secret of Beat's paternity now. And I'll quite happily tell the whole world before you see another dime that you didn't earn. Your power is *gone*, do you hear me?" She flicked him a disgusted look, as if he was nothing more than a piece of lint. "Now go fade into obscurity where you belong."

A sound that could only be described as a victory screech rent the air and Melody realized it had come from her own mouth. She'd also thrown her arms up like a referee announcing a touchdown. The only thing missing was Beat. And the lack of him was like a giant hole in the atmosphere.

Swiping at her dampening eyes, Melody took out her phone and started tapping out a text to him, but she couldn't see the screen. Too blurry.

"Ladies and gentleman, please welcome Hank Turin to the

stage," Trina said into the microphone, gesturing to a small man with a ponytail who was making his way to the drum kit, the spotlight following his progress.

"He was with us on that final, disastrous tour and he was a gentleman the entire time," said Octavia. "Even when we were fighting like a couple of alley cats."

"Well." Trina winked at the new drummer. "He wasn't a gentleman the *entire* time."

Octavia belted a laugh. "You could never leave those drummers alone."

Trina gave the lead singer a pointed look. "Neither could you."

The women were sharing a laugh with the audience when Danielle came up beside Melody. "They are absolutely killing and they haven't even played a song yet."

"They're really special, aren't they?"

"Yes, they are," Danielle agreed, putting an arm around Melody's shoulders. "Look what you pulled off."

"I didn't do it alone."

Before Danielle could respond, Octavia spoke again, her voice carrying through the plaza, backstage and beyond. "We'd like to open the show with a tribute to Beat and Melody." Once again, the cheers rose to a deafening level. "Somehow, we don't think you'll mind."

The stage went dark.

Danielle squeezed Melody's shoulder, then stepped away, leaving her standing alone to watch the screen behind the stage light up. A movie began to play. No . . . not a movie. It was Melody and Beat. They were sitting at a table. Was it the day of the initial meeting with Danielle? Yes. There were beignets between them. Coffee.

But they weren't supposed to be filmed. The conversation had been private.

Or so they'd thought.

Obviously Danielle had pulled a fast one.

My God, the way they looked at each other. The way he stared at her, not breathing, like she was operating on his heart. The way she gazed back at him, like she couldn't believe the honor. Witnessing that visible connection from this point of view, from the outside, was like jumper cables clamping around her heart, electrifying it in her chest.

"Do you need me to do this show with you, Beat?" murmured on-screen Melody.

Beat shook his head. "I don't want to put that kind of pressure on you."

"Do you need me?" she asked again.

He hesitated. "There isn't a single other person in the world I would ask."

Color bloomed madly in her cheeks. "Then, okay."

Scenes played one after the other, their initial on-screen interview about Steel Birds, dancing at the Christmas party, Melody falling on her butt, Beat all but carrying Melody out of jail, him arriving shirtless at bocce with a giant "M" on his chest, the snowball fight, the morning after. She blinked back tears, trying desperately to take in every second, all the ways they quietly communicated with each other. Through touches and looks, a language only they recognized.

The final clip that played on the screen made the world spin slower, Melody's mind struggling to play catch-up with what she was seeing.

It was them—at age sixteen.

There was footage of them meeting at the *Behind the Music* interview, Beat's hands closed around her arms, his expression earnest, hers magnetized. Totally dumbstruck. Even though there was no sound to accompany the video, she could still remember what he'd said to her, word for word. That conversation, those fleeting moments, were etched on her soul.

On the screen, they were hustled in different directions. And then she was watching Beat walk into his interview room, the assistant clipping a microphone to his collar while he sat there looking dazed. A sixteen-year-old boy staring off into the distance.

"Is everything okay?" asked the interviewer, getting no response. "Mr. Dawkins?"

"Sorry, I . . ." He looked back at the door through which he'd entered. "I finally got to meet Melody Gallard."

"Was she everything you expected?"

"No." His chest rose and fell. "She was better."

The screen faded to black, spotlights blasting the stage.

Melody shook all the way down to her toes, her heart detonating like a bomb inside of her chest. She couldn't swallow, could barely see through the wall of moisture in her eyes.

She knew she had to run . . . to find him.

She'd put distance in between her and Beat, because he'd hurt her, not trusting her enough to be honest about Fletcher's threat against her. But while he might have made a mistake in an effort to protect her, the trust had been there since the beginning.

*Do you need me?*

*There isn't a single other person in this world I would ask.*

After everything she'd learned about Beat during this process, she couldn't even fathom how difficult it had been for him to ask the favor. To trust her with it. To admit his vulnerability in front of her. And he'd done it on day one. He'd had faith in her at the start. He still did. She'd just been too hurt to recognize it.

"Danielle," Melody called, turning in a frantic circle, locking eyes with several people in headsets, but no producer. "Did you see where Danielle went?"

A young man pointed backstage and Melody jogged in that direction, calling the producer's name. Danielle would know where Beat had gone. Maybe a camera had followed him? Was that too much to hope for? Unfortunately, Danielle was nowhere to be found. Melody was beginning to give up hope when she heard a thump and turned around to find a supply closet door shaking on its hinges.

Melody opened the door to find Danielle and Joseph locked in a passionate embrace on the other side, his mouth moving over hers from above. "Oh! My God." Melody covered her eyes. "I'm sorry. I knew it. But I'm sorry."

"Can I . . ." Breathless, Danielle hurriedly smoothed her hair, obviously unaware of the lipstick smeared down her chin. "What's wrong? Do you need something?"

"I need something," the cameraman muttered, eyeing the producer's neck.

"I'll leave you alone to get that . . . something . . . but I'm wondering if you know where Beat went?" Urgency rose like a bubble in Melody's throat. "Please, I need to find him."

Danielle's shoulders slumped. "He asked us not to follow him, Mel. And I didn't think it was necessary, considering, well . . . mission accomplished."

"Right." Oh God, her entire chest was caving in. "I'll find him."

The producer laid a consoling hand on Melody's arm, but she ignored it. And she ran.

She wove through the crew in the atrium and out the side door of the network building—straight into a throng of waiting fans. The ones closest to her did a double take, before starting to scream.

"It's her! It's Magnificent Melody!"

Her eardrums protested the blast of noise, throbbing. But the cheers cut out immediately when she held up a peace sign, something her third-grade teacher used to do. And miracle of miracles, it worked. Everyone else held up a peace sign, too, mouths snapping shut.

"I need you guys to help me find him."

They knew exactly who she meant without having to say his name.

The peace signs dropped and everyone sprang into action at once. In other words, they started swiping on their phones. "Someone on the message board said he walked past them on the east side," shouted a man.

"He went east!" another girl shrieked from the back.

"Okay, thank you!" East didn't begin to narrow down Beat's location. East constituted an entire half of the island of Manhattan, but at least she had a starting point. She jogged for a block before realizing two things. One, it was snowing and she'd forgotten her coat and two, the crowd was following her. Like, an entire mob of people were moving as one giant unit less than ten yards behind her, their footsteps shuffling on the snowy sidewalk.

"We've got another sighting," yelled the same man as before. "Fifty-First Street. Just crossed Park Avenue, moving at a fast clip. Some witnesses are claiming he appears deep in thought. Others say he is morose and taciturn."

"Is that Mad4Mel99? She is a total wordsmith."

"Too flowery! I hate her."

"I love her. I trust her updates more than anyone."

Melody was marveling over the fact that an entire community had created itself around *Wreck the Halls* while she'd been busy falling in love, but a woman approached from the opposite direction and blocked her progress on the sidewalk. "I'm Mad4Mel99," said an expressionless woman wearing a shirt with Melody's face on it. "Follow me if you want to live."

"Oh. Uh . . ."

"Just kidding. He's this way." Mad4Mel99 changed directions and maybe she wasn't operating with an eye toward safety, but Melody trusted her gut and went. And so did everyone else. As they jogged east, people recognized her and joined the group until they were spilling out into intersections and blocking the progress of traffic, much to the delight of Yellow Cab drivers who were already being hindered by the falling snow. There had to be over a hundred people. More. And Melody couldn't help but be comforted by the support—with her heart bleeding in her chest, she needed as much as she could get.

"This is where I saw him last," shouted Mad4Mel99. "He was crossing Park and going east. He couldn't have gotten far."

Melody kept going, only vaguely aware of her shivers, because they were nothing compared to the ache everywhere else. She'd be fine once she was in his arms. She'd be able to breathe normally again and the world wouldn't feel upside down. *Beat, please. Let me find you. I'm ready.* They blew past Lexington, then Third, her hope starting to dwindle.

"Maybe he went into a bar? Or a coffee shop?" Melody chattered.

"Fan out!" Mad4Mel99 shouted, like a drill sergeant. "No one goes home until they're back together where they belong."

"We do belong together," Melody sniffed, beginning to feel delirious.

The crowd behind her *ahhhh*'d.

A little farther. She could go a little farther. Maybe it was the sixth sense she had when it came to Beat? Something told her she was almost there. Almost with him.

The white cloud of breath in front of her face almost obscured the park on her right. It was small, just a little sliver of concrete, snow-covered tables and trees.

A figure sat at the far end of the park, hands clasped between his knees. Head bowed.

"Beat," she whispered. Then louder, "*Beat!*"

The man shot to his feet so quickly, he upset the chair, sending it crashing up against the brick wall. He took a step in Melody's direction, the moonlight bathing his handsome, yet haggard, face. "Mel?" His brows slashed together as he ripped off his coat, marching toward her at a brisk pace and wrapping it around her. His arms turned to steel bands next, surrounding her in warmth, as his lips dropped hard kisses on her hairline. "Oh God, Peach, you're *freezing.*"

She'd been right. As soon as his arms were around her, everything was better. "I had to come find you."

"Without your coat?" he asked, sounding tortured.

"It was urgent." When the warmth finally allowed her teeth to unclench, she looked up at him. "You're so much better than I was expecting, too."

His features softened, his eyes exploring hers intently. "What?"

"That's what you said. When we were sixteen, right after we met. You said I was better than you expected."

"You were, Melody," he said gruffly. "You are."

"We become better when we're together. Every second, every minute, makes both of us better. You feel that, too, don't you?"

"Do I feel it?" He choked out a sound. "How could I feel anything else when I've got *you* believing in me?"

"And you believe in me, too," she said, going up on her toes to brush their lips together. "You believed in me enough to bring me on this journey with you. Brought me along to fight the monsters. You might have made choices to keep me out of the battles. And I understand why. I understand that protecting me is how you show your love, but we fought the war together. We won, because we get to love each other. We won because there is no one you trust more than me and no one I trust more than you. I believe in that. You showed me that by finding me again in the first place." She kissed him, long and sweet, his forearm lifting her off the ground, up against his chest as the kiss accelerated. "We get to be together, Beat. It's such a gift."

He opened his mouth and closed it, seemingly at a loss for words, a sheen forming in his eyes. "You're forgiving me, Mel?"

"I'm understanding you. That's what we do."

She could sense the relief crashing through him, knocking him back a step. "We understand each other. Better than anyone," he rasped. Their lips stroked, slicked sideways and back, reveling in the friction. "We love each other."

"Like nobody else," she whispered.

His uneven exhale bathed her face. "Forever, Mel? Are you going to give me forever?"

She looked into the eyes that could see clear through to her soul. "I'd give us ten forevers if I could."

Relief rolled off him in palpable waves. "I wouldn't bet against us. We're pretty good at accomplishing the impossible."

"You're right. We better get on the case."

"I've got your first forever right here," Beat said, setting her down and taking a ring box out of his pocket. Getting down on one knee, right there in the falling snow. "Please take it?"

Melody laughed through her tears. "Consider it taken."

"I'm going to love you every day for the rest of our lives like I'm making up for fourteen years away from you."

Her heart rejoiced in colliding with his, two becoming one. "I'll love you back the same way."

Beat slipped on the diamond ring with unsteady hands, lunged to his feet, and folded Melody in his arms, their laughter ringing up to the sky as he turned her in circles to the tune of applause and whistles. People cheered from the windows of apartment buildings above. Christmas magic spun around the pair and would continue to weave miracles and happiness throughout the decades that were yet to unfold.

Keep an eye out for the first book in
Tessa's next series . . .

# Fangirl Down

A new sports rom-com duology,
starting spring 2024!

## About the Author

#1 *New York Times* bestselling author Tessa Bailey can solve all problems except for her own, so she focuses those efforts on stubborn, fictional blue-collar men and loyal, lovable heroines. She lives on Long Island, avoiding the sun and social interactions, then wonders why no one has called. Dubbed the "Michelangelo of dirty talk" by *Entertainment Weekly*, Tessa writes with spice, spirit, swoon, and a guaranteed happily ever after. Catch her on TikTok @authortessabailey or check out tessabailey.com for a complete list of her books.

MORE ROM-COMS FROM #1 *NEW YORK TIMES*
BESTSELLING AUTHOR
# TESSA BAILEY

## SECRETLY YOURS
The first in a steamy new duology about a starchy professor and the
bubbly neighbor he clashes with at every turn...

## UNFORTUNATELY YOURS
The hilarious follow-up to *Secretly Yours*, in which a down-on-her-luck
Napa heiress suggests a mutually beneficial marriage of convenience
to a man she can't stand... only to discover there's a fine line
between love and hate.

## IT HAPPENED ONE SUMMER
The *Schitt's Creek*–inspired TikTok sensation about a Hollywood
"It Girl" who's cut off from her wealthy family and exiled to a small
Pacific Northwest beach town... where she butts heads with a
surly, sexy local who thinks she doesn't belong.

## HOOK, LINE, AND SINKER
A former player accidentally falls for his best friend while
trying to help her land a different man...

## FIX HER UP
A bad-boy professional baseball player falls for the girl next
door... who also happens to be his best friend's little sister.

## LOVE HER OR LOSE HER
A young married couple signs up for relationship boot camp
in order to rehab their rocky romance and finds a
second chance at love!

## TOOLS OF ENGAGEMENT
Two enemies team up to flip a house... and the sparks between
them might burn the place down or ignite a passion that neither
can ignore!

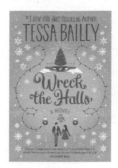

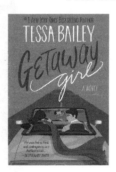
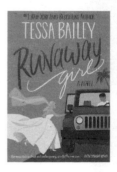
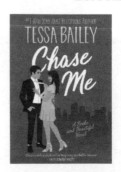